SUPER
ADJACENT

SUPER ADJACENT

CRYSTAL CESTARI

HYPERION
LOS ANGELES   NEW YORK

First Edition, March 2020
1 3 5 7 9 10 8 6 4 2
FAC-020093-20031
Printed in the United States of America

This book is set in Bradley Hand ITC Std,
Dante MT Pro, Dinn Next LT Pro/Monotype;
Ernest and Emily/Fontspring
Designed by Jamie Alloy

Library of Congress Control Number: 2019954326

ISBN 978-1-368-0-2398-6

Reinforced binding
Visit www.hyperionteens.com

SUSTAINABLE FORESTRY INITIATIVE

Certified Sourcing
www.sfiprogram.org
SFI-00993

Logo Applies to Text Stock Only

TO MY MOM, MY HERO

JUST SOLD OUT!
WARRIOR NATION FAN EVENT

Saturday, September 1
McCormick Center, 12:00–4:00 p.m.

Meet the heroes who keep our city safe! Get to know the individuals behind the masks and learn about what it's like to put your life on the line, day in and day out. Become an honorary Warrior through an interactive training program, complete with mind-bending puzzles and physically challenging obstacle courses.

All four Chicago Warriors scheduled to appear, including Blue Streak, Vaporizer, Earthquake, and Aqua Maiden.

Events include:
- Photo and signing booth with the Warriors
- Merchandise
- Cosplay contest
- Panel led by chapter president Roy Masterson, aka Mr. Know-It-All

Workshops in self-defense, anti-bullying, and team building offered at an additional cost.

All proceeds go to benefit Chicago Children's Hospital.

Visit our website for more details.

CLAIRE

I DON'T KNOW HOW THE WARRIORS DO IT. After walking three miles on the Lakefront Trail on the hottest day on earth, I'm sweating like a pig, even with the cooling assist from Lake Michigan. Every inch of my body is a moist, stinky mess, and I *hate* even thinking the word "moist." What is the point of wearing moisture-wicking workout gear if you still end up looking like you just crawled out of the world's most polluted ocean? Heroes don't have this problem. They could emerge from a burning building, carrying multiple victims on their backs, and barely drip a drop, able to save lives and be camera-ready seconds later. It's so freaking amazing. I love them so much.

"Claire, are we almost done here?" my best friend, Demi, asks, wrestling a tangled web of dog leashes attached to a pack of five panting pooches. I told her I'd help with her dog-walking business today but didn't exactly mention how far I planned to go. "I don't think the dogs can make it much farther in this heat. And honestly my shorts are beyond wedged up my butt."

"I know, I'm sorry," I say, watching an English bulldog drool all over the Lakefront Trail and melt under the blazing sun. It's only the first day of summer break, but Chicago weather can never just ease into a new season. It's either freezing cold or unbearably hot, with little to no in between. "Just . . . five more minutes? Please? I really need to make this happen today, or else they might not pick me. And then my life would be over. You don't want to end my existence, do you?" I bat my lashes, giving an innocent smile.

Demi groans, sitting down as she pulls out yet another water bottle from her custom-designed dog-walking vest to quench the pups' thirst. She's a one-stop shop for doggy needs, with treats, poop bags, tennis balls, and more tucked into those meticulously planned pockets. "Ask me again when I'm not responsible for the well-being of all these rich people's dogs." From another pocket she grabs cooling towelettes, which she rubs on the dogs' bellies, much to their delight. I kind of wish she would offer one to me, but I already know I'm pushing my luck. "Why couldn't you just get a normal internship that doesn't make you jump through all these hoops? I would've hired you full-time this summer."

"Because normal is boring," I say, wiping my face with my shirt. "Heroes are never boring, and neither are we."

She sticks her tongue out at me, and I teasingly mirror the expression. In a world full of superpowers, us nobodies must work extra hard to stay in the game. Not that I'd consider myself a nobody, but I certainly can't crush concrete with my bare hands or jump ten city blocks in seconds flat. I used to dream

I'd wake up one day and suddenly be able to scale walls with suction-cup fingertips or zap opponents with a literally withering stare, but my origin story is sadly void of any supernatural plot twists. The average hero's powers develop during childhood, and since I'm seventeen, I guess that ship has sailed. I could cry about it (and, okay, I definitely have), but eventually, you have to make the best of the hand you've been dealt. It doesn't mean I'm a nobody. It just means I have to go the extra mile to be somebody.

Which is why I'm out here today, dripping sweat in humid air that's so thick, it feels like breathing in clam chowder, all to make a lifelong dream come true. Last week I found out I was in the FINALS for a Warrior Nation summer internship, and the interview process has been grueling. Not only did I have to submit a background check and application (complete with six letters of recommendation and three essays on what heroism, service, and community mean to me), but I've also undergone countless aptitude tests in logic, problem solving, cognitive ability, and more. While each test has been thrilling, they've all been completed remotely, with no in-person assessments or interviews yet. Just seeing official Warrior Nation correspondence in my inbox has been enough to make my heart explode, but I'm ready to take it to the next level.

What at first seemed like an impossible goal is now so close I can taste it, and every bar I clear, every test I ace, brings me that much closer to connecting with the greatest, most amazing organization the world has ever known. I can't fail now, especially when I'm so close! I may not have super strength, X-ray vision, or any real tangible power like traditional heroes, but if they could just meet me, they'd see what a smart, strong, kick-ass contribution to the team I would be. They'd *have* to. I JUST KNOW IT.

Warrior Nation is rumored to have a giant headquarters hidden underneath the city, with entrances scattered throughout Chicago so heroes can safely escape into the underground lair that spans the Loop. The final internship round is to try and find one of the secret passageways. Which is no small feat! People have been looking for these entrances for years. In the past couple weeks, I have personally visited each and every theorized entrance, only to turn up empty-handed. And time is running out. But I won't give up. I won't!

I take a seat next to Demi, who has successfully managed to keep the pups comfortable. They crowd around her, happily slobbering on her bare chestnut legs like she's the best human to have ever lived. She definitely has the whole dog-whisperer thing down, which will come in handy, since she wants to be a vet someday. "So, where are you headed, anyway?" she asks, stroking an enthusiastic pug. "Since you hijacked our walk and all."

"Well, since you're wondering . . ." As a golden retriever tail fans my face, I pull out my Warrior Nation guidebook—or grail diary, as I like to call it—to check my notes. "North Avenue Beach."

My grail diary is absolutely bulging with Post-its and scraps

4

of paper; I can only close it with a leather cord I wrap around the outside. This isn't some cheap "ultimate fan" hero book written by a novice and sold at Walmart—no, it's a lifetime-in-the-making collection of Warrior Nation specs, lore, charts, and drawings. Every hero throughout the decades, every fan theory worth its salt, is cataloged in these pages, and I'm going to use them to my benefit. Last night I read on WarriorHunt.usa— one of my favorite WarNat fansites—that there's a hidden HQ entrance somewhere near the North Avenue boathouse, which is where I'm headed today. I doubt Warrior Nation would place an escape route in such a visible, touristy area, but I have to check it out, just to cross it off my list. I couldn't live with myself if this DID turn out to be the one rumor that was true.

Demi shakes her head, pulling her locs up into a ponytail. "Nope, too far. I'm almost out of water, and I need to take these dogs home, anyway, since my next walk is starting in forty minutes."

"How many walks are you doing today?" I ask.

She looks up, mentally reviewing her schedule. "Ten. Fifty dogs total."

"Fifty?!"

"Yeah. Veterinary school isn't going to pay for itself."

I laugh, though I shouldn't be surprised she's tripled her dog-walking business now that school's out. Demi is the most ambitious person I know, myself not included. We've been battling it out for valedictorian ever since freshman year, trying to one-up each other by adding on new clubs and academic organizations to lead. It wasn't until sophomore year, when we were running against each other as president for National Honor Society, that we decided to ditch the rivalry because we'd be more powerful as allies. It was like two supervillains teaming up for ultimate domination, and I loved it. She's been my best friend ever since, even if she is currently in the lead for valedictorian by one-tenth of a point. Don't worry, there's still all of senior year for me to beat her.

"Okay, well, thanks for totally abandoning me in my moment of need," I joke, petting the bulldog's wrinkly head.

"Oh, please." She rolls her eyes. "If Warrior Nation doesn't pick you for this internship, I'm sure you'll pester them to death with an angry letter campaign, just like you did when the academic decathlon timed out your final math equation."

"They were in the wrong and they knew it!" I shout while Demi rounds up her canine friends.

"Text me if you find anything!" she calls as the dogs pull her back up the trail. I wave, happy that she came with me this far. Demi may not be a WarNat, but she gets prestige when she sees it. We've both been working on our college application essays since eighth grade, and landing this internship would put me over the top at any university. But that's not why I'm doing it. In fact, even though I've toured schools with Demi and have stacks of university brochures on my desk, I have no intention of going to college. Working for Warrior Nation—being one of them—is my true purpose, the only thing I want to devote real energy toward.

Tucking my grail diary back in my bag, I stop at a fountain, splashing water all over my face and hair, thankful that I recently shaved down the undercut on the right side of my head, leaving me with less weight in the tangled bun hanging limp on my neck. I originally got an undercut because Demi dared me to, saying I needed to upgrade my "basic brown-noser" look, and while it definitely did accomplish that, I now have no idea how to ever grow it out, so I guess this is my look for life. The other half of my long wavy locks are dyed dark purple; I would've done blue to match the Warrior Nation logo, but worried it'd give off a hypothermia vibe. Ahead on the trail I spot a massive boat-shaped building hugging the shoreline, which puts some extra pep in my step. I pick up the pace, letting the red-white-and-blue vessel act as my finish line.

It is so hot, but the scenery can't be beat with the mix of high-rises glittering on my right to the lapping waves of Lake Michigan on my left. Once I reach North Avenue Beach, I start canvassing the perimeter of the boathouse, which was designed to look like an ocean liner washed ashore. Out on the sand, scantily clad bodies play beach volleyball, splash in the waves, and drink brightly colored beverages with little umbrellas poking out. B96 blares from a random speaker, prompting people to sway to the pop beats. But now is not the time to soak up the sun: I need to focus.

Taking on the role of a hero anthropologist, I get to work, carefully observing the double-decker boat, weaving in and out of the people buying overpriced chicken fingers and sunscreen.

I run my hands over the concrete walls, looking for cracks in the foundation or levers hidden in plain sight. Heroes are all about hiding in plain sight: secret identities and whatnot. They spend their whole lives living a double existence, both proudly in the public eye and quietly amongst the rest of us. I mean, there could be a hero standing around us *right now*, fully concealed in their civilian persona, pretending to be in awe of this wannabe *Titanic*. I'd like to think I could spot a hero even when they are Clark Kent–ing it, though. I certainly spend enough time scrolling through forums and fansites to have every available scrap of Warrior Nation info implanted in my brain.

Of course, out of all the heroes in all the world, the one I'd want to find most is Blue Streak. The legend. The *inspiration*. The man who started it all for me. *Blue Streak!* God, I love him. All the heroes give me life, but he's the beating heart, pulsing in my veins every day. No other hero in any chapter can even aspire to the bravery and selflessness he's exhibited over the past several decades. He's the oldest, most decorated Warrior ever to have lived, and if you ask me (which you should because I'm the expert), he's the greatest American hero of all time.

Just thinking of bumping into him now—his strong, commanding frame draped in iconic red-white-and-blue spandex and cape—gives me goose bumps, and the reality of meeting a real-life hero sets in. If I stumble upon an HQ entrance today like I desperately need to do, I could be face-to-face with one of my idols. Ahh! Excitement and nerves tangle together in my chest: Even though I have several drafts of my "What to Say to a Hero" speech in my grail diary, each composed for different kinds of encounters (being rescued, being recognized as the official WarNat Club president, etc.), I suddenly can't remember any of the words and my heart races at the thought of being caught off guard. If unprepared, I'll revert to a fangirl freakout, and I have to show them I am different than the average squealing WarNat.

I take a beat, sitting against the cool concrete while flipping to my written speech. Taking deep breaths, I review my carefully composed "Meeting a Hero as Equals" speech:

Hello, my name is Claire Rice, and I am so honored to meet you. Your service and heroism has inspired me to commit my life to community, and I hope to one day join your ranks. . . .

I run the words over and over in my head, their clarity resetting the hysteria in my head and helping me resume my mission. But after thirty more minutes of exploring, my search comes up fruitless. Fake fish in decorative nets laugh at me as my thoughts return to their usual question: *Where are you, Warrior Nation? Please reveal yourself to me! I'm worthy, I swear!*

My phone buzzes with a text:

Hi hon! How's it going? Any luck yet?

Oh, Mom. She's just as excited about this and almost called

off work today to help me. But we can't really afford a missed day of work, so I've been trying to live-text my progress.

Not yet, but I'm not giving up

Never cease, never cower!

Nice, the Warrior Nation creed. She's the best. I can't let her down.

I've poked my head through every porthole and looked for clues in every room, though . . . maybe there's a trapdoor on the top of the boat? Actually, that would make sense! An entrance only a hero could spot from the air! It's genius!

Two red ocean-liner funnels stare down at me, taunting me with possibility. A bold "DO NOT CLIMB" sign also stares me down, challenging my rule-following heart. Upholding a model-citizen status gives me another advantage for Warrior Nation recruitment, but even heroes have to break the rules sometimes in the pursuit of justice, right? I grab hold of a pole, sneakers screeching as I try to shinny up to the roof, which is more than challenging, seeing as how my physical abilities cannot compete with my academic prowess. My upper arms quiver in resistance, but after a couple pathetic attempts, I manage to pull myself onto the roof, only to find I'm not alone at the top.

"Hey!" a voice calls, and before I know it, an exceptionally strong girl is balling up the front of my sweaty tank in her fist, hoisting me an inch off the ground like it's nothing. Her nose hovers just above mine as I screech in fear, her bright blue eyes squinting in disapproval. "Who are you? Who sent you? Are you part of the siege?"

Still catching my breath from my awkward climb, I gasp, "Do I look like a person who's conducting a siege?" My toes dangle over the edge of the roof, and I grab her arms in desperation. I really don't have time to break a limb today. "Please put me down!"

Brows pinched, she sneers. "Hmm, lucky for you I'm not supposed to apprehend suspects just yet." Setting me down, she releases the death grip on my top and steps back to observe my trembling body with a smirk. "Besides, I don't think a real siege against the city would involve a shrimpy teen girl."

"Shrimpy?" I readjust my shirt over my admittedly lanky frame, pointing my chin up to give me some extra height. Who does this girl think she is? I mean, super-scary strength aside, she's wearing a freaking jean jacket on the hottest day on earth and doesn't even look like she's dripping a drop. I'll never understand people who don't dress seasonally appropriate and yet don't suffer the consequences, like Chicagoans who break out the flip-flops the second the snow melts. She stands there, extremely self-satisfied, with her non-sweaty long blond hair and smudge-free white shorts, and I immediately decide this girl embodies all the flawless, annoying popular people at school who float through life without ever having to face the problems we mortals do every day. Ugh. What is she even doing on top of this fake boat right now? Wait a minute. . . . "Why are you up here?"

Taken aback, she crosses her arms. "Why are you?"

Suddenly I freeze, the real stakes of this random encounter hitting me hard. There's only one reason this wannabe badass is climbing around the North Ave beach house on the hottest day imaginable: She must be out for the internship too! NO! I won't let her win.

"Something's off about you . . ." the girl says, head tilting to the side as a golden curl falls over her shoulder. Her tanned skin shimmers in the sun, free of the red heat splotches my peachy arms and legs are covered in. Annoying. "You know something, don't you?"

"I know lots of things, but I'm not telling you. Especially if you're my competition!"

She laughs, crossing her arms. "Competition? I don't think so. My spot is locked down."

"What?" I panic, feeling my future slip away. "How? They aren't supposed to finalize their decision until tomorrow!" This can't be happening. It's not fair! I've worked too hard for too long. . . . How do pretty girls just get everything handed to them?! How?!

"I'm not sure what you're talking about; I was recruited weeks ago," she says with a sassy grin.

That can't be right! I wrote down the final internship deadline in my calendar in Sharpie! No way I messed it up. Brain scrambling, I ask, "Are there multiple positions or something?"

Her smile widens, taking pleasure in my meltdown. "Not that I know of."

Argh! This reminds me of the time Heather Warren tried to psych me out of running for student council in sixth grade. She tricked me into thinking she was a shoo-in since her dad just donated a new candy vending machine to the school. But I didn't back down then, and I won't now. "You're just trying to mess with me, but guess what: My whole life has built up to this internship. It's my spot, I've earned it, and I don't care if you did get here first or if I am shrimpy—I will fight you for it!" Balling up my fists, I get into a boxer's stance, closing my eyes and praying that years of watching Warrior fight-scene footage has implanted some kind of phantom muscle memory into me.

But my attempt to look tough is met with pitying laughter as my opponent lowers my fists with her palms. "Slow down, killer. I'm not after your internship."

I open my eyes as relief waterfalls through me. "You're not?"

"No. But damn, you must want it really bad. That was both the bravest and most pathetic thing I've ever seen."

"Thanks?" I feel my chest starting to break into hives.

"You must be one of those crazy WarNats I've heard so much about," she says, looking down on me.

"Wait, aren't you?"

She considers this, tapping a pale pink nail against her chin. "Well, I guess I am, now that I think about it. . . ."

"Enough!" I stomp my foot, tired of this weird game she's playing. "Can you just stop speaking in circles?! The clock is ticking, and if I don't find an HQ entrance soon, then—"

Her blue eyes flash with mischief. "Oh, you mean like *this*?"

She taps a barely discernible button on the ground with her flip-flop, which sends up some kind of light-blocking force field all around us. She leans over a circular glass plate on the floor, which instantly scans her face for recognition. A faint *ping!* chimes as a latch springs open and the glass door lifts, revealing a blue tunnel slide that can only lead to one place. . . .

"OH MY GOD!" I scream in a pitch I'm sure only Demi's dogs can hear. "How did you . . . Who . . . Oh my god! I found it! An HQ entrance! I DID IT!" My extreme happiness takes the form of a single tear sliding down my cheek; it's like I'm dying and yet am now truly alive, experiencing a moment of euphoria so intense, it's as if I'm being engulfed by the sun.

"Hey, um, are you okay?" the girl asks, waving a hand in front of my face to make sure I'm not having a stroke.

I blink rapidly and try to regain motor function. "Yeah," I warble.

"Wow, you must really be into this hero stuff," she laughs, batting her lashes in disbelief.

I wipe my face clean. "You have no idea. This is . . ." I feel myself starting to cry again. ". . . everything. How did you . . . ?"

She shrugs casually, as if she didn't just change my life forever. "Eh, don't worry about it. It's what heroes do, or so I'm told." I stare at her blankly, completely fried from the emotional ride of almost losing everything only to have my ultimate dream come true. She continues, breaking into a playful smile. "I'm Joy, by the way."

"Claire," I say, but I can't let this whole "knowing how to

access an HQ entrance" thing drop. "But seriously, how did you do that?"

"Oh, that," she says, sliding her hands into her back pockets, puffing up her chest and shaking out her hair like she's in a damn shampoo commercial. "I mean, I probably shouldn't say this, but whatever: I'm the newest hero in the Chicago Warrior chapter."

It takes a second for her words to fully register. "WHAT?! Seriously? This is . . ." My insides erupt with an uncontainable explosion of questions. "Oh my god! What is your power? How long have you had it? When did you get approached? What is your hero name?" Her eyes grow wide at the sudden interrogation, but I keep going, breathless. "Most importantly, how did I not know about this?!" The introduction of a new hero is a big deal—press conferences, parades, social media campaigns—so when there's a new Warrior, the world is made aware. But even before that, WarNats usually sniff out recruits way ahead of time, thanks to our obsessive ways. There can only be four heroes per chapter, so if Joy is in, who is out? How did this happen, and how did I find myself standing next to the newest addition to my favorite lineup? I have to text Demi . . . and my mom! I CANNOT BELIEVE THIS!

But Joy is growing impatient with my rapid-fire questioning. "Um, we've got about five seconds until this door times out and snaps closed. Are you gonna stay here nerding out, or can you contain yourself so we can just go to HQ already?" She sits on the edge of the slide, gesturing to me like some wicked temptress tricking me into a perilous adventure. "C'mon, killer—time to woman up."

She disappears down the slide, and I take a seat on the blue plastic flume. What—or who—will I find when I get down there? Earthquake, Aqua Maiden, Vaporizer . . . BLUE STREAK? Oh my god . . . oh my god! Heart pounding, barely breathing, I push off, ready for anything and everything.

Top 5 Warrior Nation Looks
herobzzz.usa

We love heroes who look fly while they swoop in to save the day. Warrior Nation is known for serving justice, but who serves the best looks? From stunning spandex to eye-catching masks, here are our favorite hero styles across chapters.

#5—Blue Streak—Chicago Some may call him old, but we prefer "retro." Harking back to heroes from days gone by, Blue Streak's classic red-white-and-blue color palette summons an Americana vibe that has us at full salute. And have you seen those spandex briefs? The man is cheating Father Time.

#4—Boom Shakka Lakka—Boston This explosive hero from Beantown likes to shake things up wherever he goes, and his silver slim-fitting shorts and tank give us all front-row tickets to the gun show.

#3—Webby—NYC Like a black widow spider, this mysterious seductress lures bad guys and lookie-loos alike with her head-to-toe leather detailed with laser-cut web shapes.

#2—Kitty Vicious—Los Angeles Let's just say that no other hero is bringing animal print to the game like Kitty. Meow!

#1—Vaporizer—Chicago You knew this charming Casper would take the top spot, just like he's stolen our hearts. With that pearly white mask showing off his rascally smile, Vaporizer's formfitting alabaster suit accentuates his toned body in all the right places: How could anyone not drool? It's a shame when he goes invisible, because we just love to look at him.

BRIDGETTE

I AM GOING TO KILL VAPORIZER.

If he doesn't waft through that door in five minutes, that's it; I'm done. He knew tonight was important to me, and yet still he places strangers' needs above his own girlfriend's. Just once, I'd like him to say, "Hey, fellow Warriors, mind if I take the night off? My girl has a big event and I need to be there for her." They would cover for him; I know they would. It's Matt who never relents.

Breathe, I tell myself as I take a lap around the gallery, giving my eyes a break from the door. *This is about you, not your boyfriend.* The night is coming to an end, and I've been so busy running around, I haven't had a chance to take it all in. White walls come alive with a kaleidoscope of colors and mediums, with everything from overexposed black-and-white Polaroids to dreamy sunset watercolors. Even though I've already spent hours analyzing each and every entry here, admiring all the talent and beauty around me now resets my heart, calming me down in a way that only the creative world can.

I stop at my own piece, an abstract paper sculpture meant to symbolize desperation. I worked so hard on this installation, there may actually be flecks of blood dotting the handmade parchment. Creating this piece, I felt so in the zone, cutting hundreds of tiny, precise slashes with my X-Acto knife. From far away, the details are hard to decipher, but when you hold the poster-board-size piece up to a bulb, light peers through the slits, frantically trying to break free. It's one of my largest works yet and definitely the most intricate. My fingers ache to graze the paper, to feel the fibers against my skin, but I resist, knowing touching art is a major faux pas, even if it's mine.

Mine. I made this—this entire night—and I'm proud. Everything looks amazing, from the art on the walls to my tasteful black dress. And why shouldn't it? This show has been my baby for months now and is one of the reasons why the Chicago Arts Academy is tentatively holding a spot for me in next year's prestigious Spring Student Showcase. They usually don't allow transfer students to present until after a year of studio time, and since I'm not starting classes there until the fall, I missed the deadline by a long shot. But that didn't work for me. My parents' divorce and subsequent financial problems forced me into two years at community college, so when my transfer to CAC was official, I couldn't wait any longer to delve into the art education I've always wanted. After much persuasion, Dean Hucksley said if I could demonstrate significant skill and dedication toward the arts, he might—MIGHT—consider finding a loophole for me.

Tonight is phase one of that loophole. Phase two? To assemble the greatest college junior portfolio the world has ever seen by the end of the summer.

My mom's best friend, Terese, owns a gallery in the River North neighborhood, and she kindly agreed to let me organize a showcase for all my fellow Daley community college students. The only catch was I had to do everything myself. The guest list, the marketing, the curating—all of it. Which I didn't mind, because if you want to do something right, you have to do it yourself. I spent two months putting together this show, spending hours evaluating my classmates' submissions. I wanted the perfect blend of styles and mediums, from photography to sculpture, classical to abstract. My submission process was probably stricter than our school's. And for good reason: If this fell below Terese's standards, there was no way she'd let me work here part-time this summer, meaning tonight is a double test. I had to impress both Terese *and* Dean Hucksley. That was why I'd locked myself in my room to work every day for the last few weeks, shielding myself from all fun and distraction, just to make sure it was perfect.

And what has Matt been doing? Snapchatting Vaporizer fans and working on a new line of action figures. Insert eye roll here.

Stop it. Focus on the positive, I repeat to myself. It's so easy for me to get swept up in hero drama, I have to make a conscious effort to step back and be present. The gallery is filled with patrons, and they aren't only Daley students and parents. I invited many of the regular artists who show here, and they were generous enough to stop by and offer advice and critique. Getting feedback from professional artists is worth more than money can buy, so I'm hoping my peers use this time to their advantage.

"Bridgette!" calls out a friendly voice, and I turn to see Jilly, a girl from my school. Red hair pulled up in a messy bun, she's got a bit of bruschetta topping on her cardigan, but it falls off before I can tell her. "I can't believe you did all this!"

"Oh, thanks!" I say, looking around at all the happy faces. "Are you having fun?"

"Yes! Oh my god, yes. It is so cool that you chose my painting!" She whips around to take a peek at her canvas hanging on the wall, instantly blushing. "I never thought I would get to do anything like this. I feel so professional."

To be honest, Jilly's work isn't exactly something I'd normally choose. She's a self-admitted novice, but makes up for it in enthusiasm. Her art is just for fun, and that's okay.

"You should be proud!" I say, and she touches her freckled face in embarrassment.

"You should too! Wow, you're going to do so great at CAC next year." When my transfer first got accepted, it didn't take long for people to start whispering. About how I only got in to such a prestigious program because of my ties to Warrior Nation. About how I probably just get whatever I want thanks to Matt. The usual garbage. But Jilly was nothing but supportive. We're not that close, but her friendliness was appreciated, and I wanted to return the favor tonight.

21

"Thanks. We'll keep in touch!"

As I weave through the crowd, a couple pairs of curious eyes find mine. Girls, young ones, hoping that my hunky hero boyfriend will show. Lovesick fans who spend time tracking not only the Warriors they love but their significant others, memorizing my life details even though all I did was fall in love with a guy who turned out to have superpowers. I guess that's enough to pique people's interest, though sometimes I feel these WarNats are a breed all their own.

One of them breaks away from her pack, the rest watching and giggling from a safe distance. "Are you Bridgette Rey?" she asks with mock excitement.

"Yes . . ." I hold my chin high, knowing exactly what's coming next.

The girl looks me up and down, sizing me up with a cynical sneer. "Matt could do, like, so much better," she taunts, clearly proud of herself. As if she's the first to have thought this, let alone said it to my face. The names they've called me, the threats I've received: I'll never understand what would motivate a person to tear down a total stranger.

"Maybe," I say, doing my best to kill her with kindness, which is never the response they want or expect. "But he chose me, so . . ." I turn on my heel, leaving it at that. It would be easier (and way more fun) to go full attack mode, to scream insults and pull hair. But that's what they want. Proof that I'm a monster, hope that maybe Matt will dump me for one of them. And I'm not having it, especially not tonight. I'm unwilling to let their infatuation with my boyfriend ruin my hard work.

"Ignore those dumb WarNats," says my friend Houston, meeting me with a heaping plate of caramelized onion tarts. Houston, who is dating Aqua Maiden, never falls victim to online trolling, skating by on forgettable late-twenties attractiveness and the fact that he's a man.

"That's easy for you to say," I reply. "When was the last time you were verbally attacked in public?"

"Yeah, when?" chimes in Anna, girlfriend of Earthquake and master of awkwardly inserting herself into conversations. "You, like, don't even know what Bridgette and I go through. People can be so mean! It's so hard for girls—I hate it. And it's not the same for guys! It never is." Chest puffed up in feminist solidarity, she gives Houston some major side-eye from behind her glasses, even though we both know she also doesn't receive the same onslaught of hate that's part of my daily existence.

"Okay, geez, sorry." Houston shakes his head, shoving down a few more tarts. Like myself, he's been sidelined during enough interviews and red carpets to know when his opinion isn't wanted, and can quickly slip into bland, Ken-doll mode on command. "Ashleigh sends her love, by the way. She's on duty tonight."

"Oh! And Ryan too!" Anna pipes up, curls bouncing against her overblushed cheeks. "He wanted to be here, you know, supporting the extended Warrior family and all, but he's out there, patrolling those city streets—"

"Wait, *both* of them are active tonight?" I ask to their

confused nods. The Warriors operate on a partner system, fighting in pairs so they can watch each other's backs. If Aqua Maiden and Earthquake are on duty, then where. The hell. Is Matt? "Sorry, um, I gotta keep this party going. But it really means a lot to me that you're both here." Anna and Houston, while not my closest personal friends, are some of the only people on the planet who understand what it's like to date a hero. To have your life constantly turned upside down due to your partner's line of work, to have danger woven into every fiber of your relationship.

To have the person you love most miss out on your most important events.

I do another lap of the space, cleaning up discarded wine glasses and appetizer napkins as I go. Light, happy chatter surrounds me, and I feel like maybe I really did pull this off. The gallery is packed, everyone is smiling, and even Dean Hucksley, who is known for being a pretentious snob, is chatting with guests as he swirls his sauvignon blanc. He spots me looking at him, and before I turn away in embarrassment over being a creeper, he raises his glass in my direction and gives me a nod of approval.

Yes! I celebrate silently, biting my bottom lip so I don't shout a cheer into the room. *I did it!* All that work seems to be paying off. Phase one complete!

Someone taps my shoulder from behind. "Excuse me, miss," says a strange voice. My heart leaps, thinking maybe it's Matt putting on a disguised inflection, but when I spin around, it's my older sister, Becca, doing her best "fancy-pants rich lady" impression. "You're out of champagne and the goat cheese spread is running dangerously low." She points at the appetizer table with a raised pinkie, which looks both uncomfortable and ridiculous.

I smack her arm with a napkin, smiling. "Stop eating all the food!"

"Uh, no way. You promised me all-I-can-eat cheese, and trust me, I can eat a *lot* more." She rubs her belly for emphasis.

I roll my eyes as I stifle a laugh. "You're gross, and I'm trying to host a sophisticated event here." I turn but bump directly into Sam, Becca's boyfriend, who is pantomiming smoking a pipe.

"Hear, hear! 'Tis the event of the century!" he cheers in an over-the-top British accent, raising a monocle that he is definitely not wearing. Becca laughs, and I feel my face turning red.

"Did you guys just get out of improv class or something?" I whisper. Becca and Sam are both actors, a profession I generally respect but am currently finding annoying. "I mean, can you be more embarrassing right now?"

They look at each other, like I just gave them a challenge. "Yeah, we can totally take it up a notch."

I groan and try to walk away, but Becca hooks my arm. "Sorry, sorry, we'll tone it down. We're leaving soon anyway, for said improv class. But I wanted to tell you, all joking aside, that tonight was really great. You know this isn't one hundred percent my scene, but it was actually really cool." She pulls me in for a hug, her long brunette hair covering my face. "I'm proud of you, even if that jerk you're dating isn't here to say it," she whispers in my ear. My heart aches at her words as she lets go, reaching out to ruffle my hair like I'm a child, but I weave out of arm's reach before she can catch me. She and Sam both blow me kisses goodbye, and I check the clock: five minutes until the event ends.

Still no Matt.

I step into the back office to make sure all the caprese skewers went out, doing a quick mirror check. Luckily, the glittering shadow I chose to complement the green flecks in my eyes has stayed mostly in place despite my running around, with only a few golden specks resting on my ivory cheeks. But, ugh, my shorter-than-short brown hair is curling up weirdly on the right side. I can't wait for this horrendously choppy disaster to grow out. I comb through my micro bangs and adjust my nose ring, ready to give a final thank-you to everyone for attending.

The second I turn around and lift a champagne flute to start a toast, the front window shatters into a million pieces. I scream along with everyone else as a body comes flying into the center of the gallery.

What the—

I drop to my knees as my guests crouch down and cover their faces all around me. Heart racing, I look up and assess the destruction. Years of dating a superhero have taught me to be hyperalert in these situations, suppressing my panic so as not to do something stupid and get myself hurt. The stranger on the floor moves, groaning as he twists his body. Grabbing a nearby cheese knife, I tuck myself into a ball on my feet, glass crunching under my heels. Classmates quiver around me as I inch closer, only to discover the intruder isn't a suicide bomber or random victim: It's Matt, brushing broken glass off his tattered shirt and tie.

"Oh my god!" I kneel at his side, dropping my knife to check his body for signs of injury. "Are you hurt? Are you okay?"

He stands tall, instantly drawing sighs of relief and excitement from the gallery, and runs back to the broken window, peering up and down the street for signs of his attacker. When the coast is clear, he turns back to the room and asks, "Is everyone okay?" A few shocked faces nod as people's heart rates drop back to normal. "Apologies for the dramatic entrance, but it looks like I was able to ward off danger before it arrived at your door." Applause and thankful cheers begin to fill the space, which Matt receives with a dashing "oh, it was nothing" smile.

"Great party, babe," he whispers to me, shaking debris from his wild mocha hair. "Really . . . smashing." He raises his eyebrows, proud of himself.

Well, there's no way he's hurt, or else he wouldn't be resorting to dumb jokes. My girlfriend dial turns from concern to frustration. "What the hell, Matt?" I snap through my teeth. "How can you make wisecracks when you just went FLYING THROUGH A WINDOW?"

He waves my comment away, undisturbed. "C'mon, you know I've been working on my quips! All the greats make them!

I was flipping through some of the other Warriors' comic books last night, and dang, they have some classic puns. Like Storm Chaser! That guy—"

I exhale sharply. "This is not a comic book. This is real life! Where were you? What happened?"

"Well . . ." he starts, but suddenly he's not just talking to me, but the entire room, all back on their feet and eager to hear about his super adventures. After all, it's not every day you get to see a superhero in the flesh. Unless you're me, of course. Minutes ago everyone was reverently discussing art and culture, but now nearly the whole crowd has dissolved into a starstruck frenzy. Matt's out of his usual gleaming-white Vaporizer spandex, but it doesn't matter. He's the only Warrior who thinks secret identities are lame, meaning he gets recognized every single moment of every single day. Any fan across the country could describe his handsome, impish face, right down to the scar on his jawline. Those dark chocolate eyes and grinning caramel cheeks are pinned up on bedroom walls from coast to coast, my boyfriend desired by all. "I was almost here, when a guy grabbed me from behind and yelled, 'Get ready for the siege!' before throwing me through the window!" A few girls gasp, even though they saw it happen. "Total low blow, if you ask me. But don't worry. I'll get him next time! I always do." He winks, and I force my eyes not to roll.

The crowd continues their applause, and I get squeezed out of the way as Matt poses for selfies and autographs the evening's programs I designed, giving the crowd all the attention they crave. My classmates, their parents, even some of the professional artists can't get enough of him as he poses and shouts Warrior Nation catchphrases. *"Never cease, never cower!"* Sigh. More like "Never get enough of the spotlight."

I stand at the back of the cluster for a good ten minutes before he even notices I'm still there and finally moves through the throng to continue our conversation. With a kiss on my cheek, he says, "I'm sorry I'm late, I really am. I tried to get here."

I nod, tamping down the disappointment and heartbreak churning inside. I spent this entire day worrying, getting to the gallery at five a.m. to ensure the event went off without a single hitch. It would've been nice to have my boyfriend of four years by my side, squeezing my hand and telling me it would be okay. Just once, I wanted to be the one in the limelight, to grab a sliver of attention for a job well done. To feel that rush of success, like I had done some good in the world. But no. Even after all my hard work, Matt is still the star tonight, with everyone clamoring to be in his orbit. As if he doesn't get enough of that every single day.

But this is not the time nor the place to talk, because as I've painfully learned from experience, you never know who may be listening. Even though I'm more than ready to stake my claim to the world, I've had my face in enough tabloids to last a lifetime, and I already see people directing their phones our way, hoping to catch a private moment of a public figure. I'll have to keep my true feelings buried until we can be alone.

"Thank you for coming," I tell him, squeezing back a tear. "It means so much to me."

"Of course," he returns, tracing my face with his thumb. "I wouldn't have missed it." Even though he did. His entrance instantly brought an end to the event, the canvases and sculptures sitting forgotten behind us. Feeling eyes on him, Vaporizer turns around to face his admirers, physically unable to resist a chance to ham it up. "I must be the luckiest guy in the world," he declares, turning his back to me, "to be dating such a talented artist." The crowd applauds, and I muster up the most adoring glance I can, tortured at how a look of love is something I once never needed to fake.

Terese breaks through the cluster of admirers, waving her arms in frustration. Her blue eyes are magnified by overly bedazzled glasses as they take in the mess and wreckage of her beloved gallery, her thin lips tight with disappointment. "Excuse me! Attention—hello!" she shouts, followed by the deep hacking coughs of a lifetime smoker. "Thank you for coming tonight, but we're closed now. Good night." The crowd stays still, bewitched under Matt's spell. "GOOD NIGHT," Terese repeats, on the verge of yelling, but when nobody moves, I tug at Matt's jacket, giving him a look.

"Oh, right," he mumbles, slow to realize he's the problem. "Um, good night, friends! Stay safe out there!" Then he turns invisible, vanishing from my side like vapor escaping into the night. People are floored, clapping and chatting about how amazing he is and how they can't believe how lucky they are to have been here tonight. Not because of the art, but because of the spectacle. The drama. The excitement.

Houston and Anna shoot me pained looks as they walk out the door, sympathetic eyes wishing there was something they could do. But we all know there's not. This is the price we pay. I do appreciate, though, that at least someone here understands.

Once everyone has filtered out, I stare at the remains of months of work. Photos, paintings, and sculptures sit quietly under their spotlights, forgotten against the shimmer of celebrity and sea of broken glass. My heart sinks, crushed to realize that in the end, it didn't matter how hard I tried to make tonight a success. It didn't matter that I curated a three-hour playlist of orchestral music to highlight the themes of my classmates' work, or that each appetizer subtlety nodded to a different art movement. As long as Matt was in attendance, everything I'd done would be overshadowed.

I shouldn't have to be sad right now; I should be doing cartwheels and sipping the remaining champagne to celebrate. But the room's a mess and Terese looks like she's regretting ever giving me a chance.

"I'm so sorry, Terese," I say, rushing to the back to grab a broom. "I will take care of this."

Matt reappears, flesh and bone where there was nothing. "Don't worry about it, babe; I'll call the Warrior cleanup crew. They'll fix this up."

"No," Terese snaps, arms crossed. "I don't want any more so-called heroes in my gallery."

"'So-called'?" Matt scoffs, but I run interference.

"Warrior Nation has a repair team that handles any

31

property damage incurred during a battle," I tell her. "They're really fast; they once patched my parents' roof in like a day after Matt was in a brawl with the Dark Vulture."

"Oh yeah!" His face lights up. "I remember that fight! I kept disappearing and totally disorienting the guy. That's why he punched a hole in the ceiling!"

I shoot him a venomous "not right now" stare.

"That's not what I'm worried about," Terese says, giant sculptural earrings clinking as she huffs. "Bridgette, you did an amazing job tonight, and I know you want to work here this summer, but . . ." But? Buts are never good. I swallow hard as she gathers her thoughts. "I can't have things like this happening." She gestures to the gaping glass hole leading to a dark Chicago night. "I can't be worried about my patrons being in danger. If he shows up, someone could get hurt."

Matt tries to stay calm. "With all due respect, ma'am, it's my job to keep this community safe."

"Well, I certainly didn't feel safe seeing your body flying through my window! People were scared, and when they're scared, they're less inclined to spend money on beautiful things." She frowns, looking my way. "I told your mother I would give you a chance, and while I'm happy with what you did tonight, I need to think about this summer. I hope you'll understand."

I nod. I want to tell her this was a one-time occurrence, that nothing like this will ever happen again. But I know I can't guarantee it, nor fault her reasoning. This isn't the first time

Warrior Nation has made my life difficult, and I'm sure it won't be the last.

The moment the cleanup crew arrives, I take off, walking as fast as I can in my black heels. Matt trails behind me.

"Sheesh, what was all that about?" he asks, reaching my side. "She's not going to hire you now? After all you did for tonight?"

"You destroyed her gallery, Matt," I huff, my pace quickening my breath. "She has a right to be mad."

He snorts. "Well, that's ridiculous. If that's how she's going to react to one itty-bitty broken window, maybe you don't want to work there anyway."

I stop, stomping my heel into the sidewalk. I look up and down the street to make sure we're alone, because this volcano is about to erupt. "No, I *do* want to work there! Desperately! Why do you think I've been busting my ass the past couple weeks?"

Dark eyes go wide, nervous he's stepped into dangerous territory. "I thought you were trying to impress that dean guy. . . ."

"Yes, partially. And I'm sure he was really impressed to get glass shards in his chardonnay."

"He came up and shook my hand!" Matt exclaims, trying to defuse the situation. "Thanked me for everything I do."

"And *that's* what he'll remember! You, creating a spectacle!" I yell, inching closer. Even with my heels, I barely reach Matt's chin, but my anger fills me with a flame I can't contain. "When he thinks back on tonight, what do you think he'll recall? The casual yet sophisticated collection of art, or a superhero crashing through the window?" Matt's head hangs low. "This was big for me, and you couldn't even show up on time."

Matt reaches for me, but I push him away. "I didn't do this on purpose; flying through windows isn't exactly my idea of fun. I can't just tell villains to stop committing crimes. Evil doesn't care about special occasions."

"But you missed it. You missed everything. Again," I sniffle. I can feel tears welling up, but I stare up at the sky, forcing them back in. "Do you even care?"

He takes my hand. "Are you kidding? Of course I care. My whole life is devoted to caring."

"Right, caring for those in danger or who want to take your picture." I pull my palm away. "Everyone else always comes first—"

"Stop, just stop," Matt interjects. His boyish features twist, patience waning. "Do you even know where I was tonight, huh? Did you even ask what kept me from being here on time?" I remain quiet, staring off like I don't care. "I stopped a kidnapping from taking place; I kept a family intact. Without my help, some poor girl would be trapped in a stranger's van, probably destined to never see her home again."

I shake my head, almost laughing to myself. Because . . . what is there to say to that? What possible arguments can I return after hearing of the good Matt does? Whether he's saved a single family or the entire city, his reasons are always just, so

I'm the one who ends up looking like a villain. I'm the bad guy, because I want him with me. I'm always in the wrong, because he's always doing right.

"That's great, Matt," I say softly. "I'm happy that girl is safe."

Jaw unclenched, he manages to get close enough to touch my elbow, but that's all I'll allow. He's mistaken my sudden calm for acceptance, when really it's just exhaustion.

"I want to make this up to you. Do you want to stay at my place tonight?" he asks. "We can watch a movie—your pick—and have some pie or something? Apple? Key lime?"

"No, I . . . I'm really tired. I'd probably just fall asleep."

"That's okay too. I make a good pillow."

The thought of curling up in his arms right now makes me want to cry. "I'm just gonna walk to Becca's, clear my mind."

"Are you sure?" His breath is warm on my skin. "Do you want company?"

I shake my head, looking at the pavement.

"For what it's worth, I know you did a great job tonight, even if I didn't see it all. Everything you do is great." He kisses the top of my head as a tear sneaks down my cheek. "I'll text you later, okay? I love you," he says with a smile, evaporating before my eyes.

I stand for a minute, alone in the dark. But it doesn't take long before I'm full-on crying, shoulders shaking with the burden of what's been building in my heart.

I don't think I can do this anymore with Matt. The drama, the sacrifice. The longer I stay his girlfriend, the harder it will be for my life to ever take precedence. To matter more than the danger of the day. Holding his hand is holding me back, though I'm not sure how to let go.

How does one break up with a superhero?

Vaporizer sighting!!!

WarriorHunt.usa

My older brother dragged me to this SUPER-BORING art thing tonight, but GUESS WHO SHOWED UP—VAPORIZER!!! YES. PRAISE. Omg, he is everything. I even got a picture with him!!!!!!!!! His cheek grazed my cheek, you guys. SKIN ON SKIN! I AM DEAD!

I also snagged a pic of him with his train wreck of a girlfriend, Bridgette. God, seriously. Look at her, giving death eyes to our beautiful Vaporizer like a black widow getting ready to devour her mate. I will NEVER understand what he sees in that wench. He could do soooooo much better! Everything about that girl bothers me. Like why can't she just stop existing already. Would it be soooo bad if she got swept up in one of those recent attacks and couldn't be saved? Lolololol

@VaporLover29
omg u r so bad. But agreed!

@NeverCeaseNeverSour
Matt loses 3 hotness points for dating her. +10 if he dropped her off the Hancock

@invisiblegirlfriend
I bet she kicks puppies

@hot4heroes
Bridgette literally doesn't care about WarNats AT ALL! If she did, she'd join the community and share her precious insider details. Instead she hoards them all for herself. Bitch.

@SillyMouseTrap
maybe she has an incurable disease and he dates
her out of pity? Seems like something he'd do. Can't
think of any other logical explanation.

@futureWarriorQueen
her face burns a hole in my heart

@WNlyfer
HATE HER!

CLAIRE

WHEN I REACH THE BOTTOM OF THE SLIDE, I crumple into a giant blue floor pillow, the strap of my bag tangling around my neck. Joy leans over me, hands on her bare knees, head cocked to an annoyingly condescending degree. "You all right there, killer?"

"Fine. I'm fine," I groan, though it takes me a ridiculous amount of effort to pull myself up off the landing cushion. We're standing in a cramped underground room—no bigger than an elevator shaft—dimly lit by a single blue bulb above. A silver door with a screen and panel of buttons stands before us, just waiting to reveal my dream world behind it.

"We're still about a half mile from headquarters," Joy says. "This entrance is one of the farthest ones out from the loop, so we'll need to walk for a bit. Hopefully you'll have some time to compose yourself." She scans my trembling body judgmentally, and I clench every possible muscle to appear like I'm in control, though it's not easy, because my heart feels like it's full of rocket fuel. Joy places her palm on the screen, and after a red light reads her fingerprints, she taps in a key code on the buttons below. As the door slides open, she looks back at me and says, "Now, don't faint or anything, okay?"

I hold my breath, ready to take in everything before me. What do these underground tunnels actually look like? WarNats have theorized everything you could imagine, dreaming up moving walkways and integrated robot assistants and booby-trapped paths like something out of *Indiana Jones*. In reality, I'm greeted with a plain concrete hallway, but I still pull out my grail diary to write down every detail of what I'm witnessing, from the length of my slide down here (thirty-three seconds) to the paint color on the walls (baby blue). I mastered the art of writing while walking during a Girl Scout scavenger hunt in fourth grade, during which I found all twenty-six nature items in record time.

"What's that?" Joy asks, peering down at my furious scribbling as we make our way.

I clutch my diary to my chest, face burning up again. "Nothing."

"Oh, it's definitely something." With zero effort, she snatches it from my hands, flipping through years of handwritten notes, drawings, and diagrams. She chokes on a laugh, like she can't believe what she's seeing. "Holy . . ."

"Careful!" I plead, grasping for my most prized possession, but her super strength easily keeps me at bay.

"This is . . ."

"Amazing?" I suggest defiantly. "Incredibly comprehensive?"

"I was gonna say ridiculous, but you're not wrong about the comprehensive part."

Huh? What's ridiculous about writing down every single detail of something you love? Isn't that called having a hobby?

Joy lands on my section about Blue Streak, which is not hard to do since it's probably more than a third of the book. "Whoa," she breathes, her face dropping its mocking expression. She looks at me with a sudden sadness I can't quite place. "You're, like, really into this guy."

"Of course I am—he's the best," I insist, snagging back my diary. "Besides, everyone has a favorite."

"I don't." Joy shrugs without a care. "I didn't even really pay attention to Warrior Nation until like two months ago."

This throws a dagger in my heart, and I'm stopped in my tracks. "I'm sorry . . . what?"

She spins around, curvy hip cocked to one side. "Is there a problem?"

"Uh . . . yeah! You've been recruited into this chapter and you don't even know anything about them? Their history . . . their lore?"

She swings her arms out. "It's not a big deal, Claire. I'll figure it out. They gave me some sort of pamphlet to read—"

"A pamphlet?!" I screech, my frustration bouncing off the concrete walls. "You can't fit decades of heroism into a trifold. I mean, look at this!" I hold up my bulging diary for emphasis. "This is every scrap of info I've collected since I started following Warrior Nation, and that's only seven years' worth."

"Calm down," she commands, turning back on her heel. "I'm sure I'll be fine."

I laugh. "Doubtful." I run to catch up with her, staring down the false confidence in her stride. "How can you be so casual about this? Do you even know what you're getting into?"

"God! Enough!" she groans. "I thought you were cute up on the roof, what with your sad little fists ready to defend your birthright or however you built it up in your mind, but I never would've brought you down here if I'd known how annoying you really are."

"How did you even fall into this anyway?" I persist, ignoring her comment. "There are people way more obsessed than me who have literally killed themselves to become Warriors, pushing their powers to the limits to prove their worth as heroes. You've never heard of people accidentally drowning or electrocuting themselves for this? Jumping off buildings, throwing themselves into fights? The audition-fail videos are all over the internet." She keeps walking, eyes straight ahead, eyebrows furrowed. "But not you. You didn't have to do a thing! You're walking into one of the greatest organizations ever and you don't even care. What, did you just happen to chat up a Warrior recruiter one day and make them fall in love with your smile or something dumb like that?" I shake my head. "God, I hate pretty girls! Everything is just handed to you."

We're almost at the end of the hallway, bright blue doors painted with the Warrior Nation logo waiting for us. The swirling silver "W" and "N" curl around a navy-blue shield, an image that is practically tattooed on my brain. Seeing it here, in this context, helps shift my frustration slightly; I won't let some girl ruin this moment.

"Look," Joy says, standing between me and the door. "I didn't ask to be chosen for this. I had different ideas for my life, but I woke up one day to discover I could lift an SUV over my head. And now I'm here, and you can be sure that when I commit to something, I give it my all. So write that down in your damn diary." She spins around, blond hair flying, and pushes open the double doors.

Whatever, I think as the doors close behind her. If she thinks she can jump into this world blind, then best of luck. But I'm not relying on chance. I've spent every day since I was ten preparing for this, and I am ready.

I'm here. Warrior Nation headquarters.

I open the doors, revealing a spacious control room. I instantly have to catch my breath, senses on overload as I begin mentally cataloging every single microscopic detail of my surroundings. It's bright, despite there being no natural light, as everything is either painted white or made of glass. The styling is retro-futuristic, with furniture looking like it could have been modern in the 1960s paired with next-gen technology. Multiple movie-theater-size screens flash news reports and events taking place around Chicago, like the most wide-reaching security system ever. People hustle by, a straight-up army of support staff scurrying off to save the day in their own way.

It is the most beautiful thing I have ever seen.

I stand on the edge of it all, feet itching to take off and explore, and spot Joy talking to a familiar face, a tiny wisp of a woman with a severe gray bob and thick, giant glasses resting against her slightly wrinkled ivory face. She makes no effort to contain a sneer as she taps away on a tablet that's almost as big as her. OMG! I suppress a squeal upon realizing she's Millie Montouse, Chicago's Warrior Nation spokesperson.

"You're late for hand-to-hand combat training, Miss Goodwin," Millie says in disapproval.

"Sorry, ma'am," Joy answers.

"I am disappointed with your performance this week," Millie continues, not even looking up from her screen. "You are not where we expected you to be by now."

"Sorry," Joy repeats, hanging her head. For some reason, this puts a little pep in my step, seeing Miss Cockypants cower a bit. Joy spots me grinning out of the corner of her eye and sends me back a scowl. When Joy doesn't immediately take off for where she needs to be, Millie looks up, giving her a withering stare, but then she notices me.

"And who are you?" she asks, scurrying over my way like a curious squirrel. "How did you get in here?" Her finger hovers over a red button on her screen that reads "Security," so I quickly answer before anyone can drag me away.

"My name is Claire Rice, Ms. Montouse." I extend a hand she chooses not to shake. "I am a finalist for the summer internship program, and I completed the last task."

"Claire Rice," she repeats, tapping my name into her tablet, instantly bringing up my applicant files. Her mouth remains expressionless as she scans all my paperwork. "Well, Miss Rice, then I suppose congratulations are in order. You're the first to find the entrance, so that means the internship is yours."

The first! Which means I'm already in the running to be *the best*. Yes! My future Warrior career trajectory flashes before my eyes, starting as an intern and climbing my way all the way up to the executive team. I also envision myself receiving a medal, something future me will rub in Demi's face. "Thank you," I say, smiling like an idiot.

"How, may I ask, did you accomplish this task?"

I glance at Joy, who gives a subtle shake of her head. I'm guessing bringing a civilian down to HQ unannounced is not exactly protocol and won't reflect well on her. I probably shouldn't be making enemies on my first day, but the opportunity to put Joy in her place is too good to pass up. "I was exploring the North Ave boathouse and saw Joy on the roof. She helped me."

"Interesting," Millie says, noting something on her tablet. "How very clever of you, Miss Rice. Miss Goodwin, please wait for me in my office." Joy hunches like a puppy who's just been scolded, but not before giving me one last dirty look. I cheerfully wave her goodbye. "Now," Millie continues, "the internship doesn't officially begin until next week, but I suppose there's no harm in getting an early start. I'll have my assistant, Teddy, give you a tour and get you set up with security." She calls for him, and then takes off, surprisingly fast considering how short her legs are. The fabric of her bland pantsuit swishes with every step.

Millie Montouse is a Warrior Nation legend. She's been their public representative for as long as I can remember. I watch all her briefs: very tough, no nonsense. I don't think her face is capable of smiling. But she's amazing, always standing up for the truth and protecting the heroes. What a cool job! Still, I didn't know she was so short. They must have her stand on a platform when she speaks to the press.

I have a million questions to ask her, but I can't get a single one to pass my lips. My eyes are too busy scanning the unbelievable scenery. We pass by a hallway of rooms, each with walls of glass: There's a personal training room filled with weapons and workout equipment alike; a kitchen with chefs plucking fresh ingredients from an indoor greenhouse; a dry cleaner's with rows and rows of duplicate hero suits, some with blood, burn marks, or holes waiting to be repaired. I see several white Vaporizer getups, along with earth-toned jumpsuits belonging to Earthquake. I'm keeping my eyes extra peeled for a glimpse of one of the actual heroes in person, but nothing yet.

We meet up with a fancy-haired twentysomething guy in a perfectly pressed button-down and tie. I feel so underdressed in my tank top and shorts; I'll need to up my game on my first actual day of work. He holds a tablet just like Millie's and has a Bluetooth device curled around his ear. An official Warrior Nation badge reading "Teddy Sizemore" hangs around his neck, and it's so cool, I hope I get one just like it.

"So this is our intern?" Teddy says coolly, looking down at me.

"Yes, this is Miss Rice. Please get her set up. We'll need to make some space for her at your desk."

"My desk?" he asks, crestfallen.

"Is that a problem?"

"No, of course not." He does a funny little bow, though she doesn't notice, busy reading something on her screen. Then she heads off without saying goodbye, off to do something important, I'm sure. Once she's a safe distance away, Teddy exhales and introduces himself. "Hi, I'm Teddy."

"I'm Claire. Nice to meet you."

"Welcome to the madness." He gestures all around.

"It's incredible." I sigh as some assistants walk by with what look like new Aqua Maiden costume prototypes. She recently announced on her social media that she wanted to glam up her look and would be revealing a new hero suit soon, and based on the amount of sequins and shimmer passing me by, the woman is going for bling.

"Eh, you'll get used to it," Teddy says with a shrug. "I've been here two years now, and it's weird how all this becomes normal."

Impossible. I'll never stop thinking this is the most amazing place on earth.

"Well, c'mon, let's go. Millie is heading into a meeting now, but I'll need to be by her side when it lets out. You've gone through all the background checks, correct?"

"Oh, yeah, all five of them." I smile. My gleaming record got me through with ease.

"Perfect." We continue walking deeper into the facility, an endless stream of glass-encased rooms rushing past us. Teddy goes into full tour-guide mode, spouting off some facts I know and some I doubt any WarNat has ever heard.

"Our headquarters is a series of tunnels and offices buried under the Chicago Loop and surrounding neighborhoods, spanning almost four square miles. There are nineteen hidden entrances, each with multitiered security clearances. This facility houses all major internal teams, from training, weaponry, logistics, all the way to marketing, publicity, and philanthropy. We have about four hundred employees in total, each with varying levels of clearance."

I desperately want to reach for my grail diary to capture all this juicy intel, but based on how Joy reacted to it, I decide to keep it hidden for now. Oh, how I wish I had an audio recorder in my brain!

We stop at the security office so I can get the badge I will cherish forever, but before I can decide on whether I should smile or try to look more serious and intimidating for my photo, Teddy stops me, passing his tablet my way.

"What is this?" I ask, looking down at a bunch of words that I know are in English but look like a bunch of gibberish.

"Our nondisclosure agreement. Nothing you see or hear here can ever leave HQ."

"Nothing? You can't even talk to your friends and family about where you work?" I can't imagine not sharing everything I've witnessed here today with my mom, who's just as big a WarNat as me, or Demi, who will surely get super jealous over all this. Not to mention the WarNat forums!

Teddy shakes his head. His hair, basically a shiny black helmet thanks to really glossy gel, doesn't move. "My parents think I work for a law firm. It's just easier than having them ask questions all the time. Besides, once you're here, you won't really have time for relationships, romantic or otherwise. I haven't had a boyfriend in a year."

Well, that I can understand. You don't get to be secretary of both student council and Model UN by just hanging out after school or flirting with all the cute girls. There's no such thing as free time when you have a dream to fulfill. I scan the document, but it's all legalese that's impossible to understand. I stop on a section titled "Intellectual Property Protection" with a line that reads: *Hero safety above self.*

But when I point it out to Teddy, he just shrugs. "Don't worry about that. It's not like you'll ever be thrown into battle as an intern, unless you find getting the morning coffee orders particularly harrowing. This mostly means that you won't do anything to endanger the heroes, jeopardize their missions— stuff like that."

"I would sooner die!" I blurt out, and sign immediately,

knowing I could never do anything to hurt my beloved Warriors. And with that, I'm handed a beautiful new badge that I hang around my neck with pride. This is the best day of my life!

An alarm goes off on Teddy's tablet, and he immediately picks up his pace. "Millie's meeting is almost over; we need to go." Worried about getting there on time, he cuts his narration, leaving me to wonder about all the rooms we're whizzing past.

Down a darkened hallway, I hear loud, angry yelling and can't help but ask, "What's down there?" wondering if I would find Room E33, a hidden room invented by conspiracy-loving WarNats that is theorized to contain all of Warrior Nation's alleged secrets.

"Our holding cell," he answers, not slowing his pace. "It's been very full lately. We're trying to gain intel on a new criminal element—some kind of siege—and the heroes have been rounding up some of the city's most notorious villains for questioning."

So that's what Joy was asking about when we were up on the roof. *Are you part of the siege?*

"Don't get any ideas," Teddy adds. "You don't have enough clearance to go down there."

"Oh, no big. I was just curious."

He looks down at me with a kind smile. "Sure. Look, I'm on your side. I love heroes too, but this is not going to be some big adventure for you. I've seen a lot of young kids come in here thinking they're going to save the world. But it's not like that. Heroes don't pull people like us into their business. You'll probably just be getting Millie's dry cleaning." When I start to frown, he adds, "People have been fired—or worse—for sticking their nose where it didn't belong. If you want to survive, you need to stay focused."

I nod. He's right; I need to listen to him. While other kids at school may mouth off to teachers or think it's cool to rebel against authority, I learned a long time ago that shutting up and following the rules would serve me better. Call me a brown-noser or teacher's pet, but I don't care: My dreams are coming true, and that's all that matters. I'm not afraid to jump through hoops if they lead to my goals. I swallow down my fangirling and resolve to fill my summer with nothing but lunch orders and message taking, but that's when I see him.

In a glass conference room, straight ahead. Signing papers and talking to a group of executives, including Millie. Dressed in street wear, but I'd know that face anywhere.

Blue Streak. He's here. Right now. Just a few feet away, with only a pane of glass between us.

My knees go weak as I lose all rational thought, body dissolving into a puddle of emotion. A high-pitched gasp escapes my lips as I crumble, Teddy grabbing on to me before I completely fall to the ground.

"Claire!" he yelps, wrapping an arm around my waist. "Are you . . . ?" He sees where I'm looking, and is instantly disappointed. "Really? What did I just say? You can't geek out when you see them!"

"I'm sorry," I croak, heart beating in my ears. "It's just . . . Blue Streak saved my life."

"Whoa. For real?"

I go into a trance, almost hypnotized by my hero's presence. "I was ten," I start, the scene rushing back to me. "My mom and I decided to have a mother-daughter day in the city: shopping, a fancy lunch, all that. My mom made reservations for us to have high tea, and even though I've never been into that super-girly stuff, I was really excited.

"We had to take the Brown Line to our tea, but about half-way there, our train stopped. We waited forever, with no movement nor conductor announcement, when suddenly we heard shouting from an adjoining car. Screaming." I pause, remembering how loud it was, how the sounds of people in danger rattled me to the core. The memory shakes me, and Teddy looks at me with concern. "A gang burst into our train car, guns in the air, yelling at the people to hand over their wallets. Everyone had their hands up; everyone was crying. Mom was sobbing, clutching me like it might be the last thing she'd ever do.

"One of the gang members came our way. He pointed a gun at Mom's head when she didn't hand over her purse fast enough. She couldn't, because she was holding on to me." I swallow hard, her terrified face haunting me. I'd never seen her look like that, never witnessed anything but her being brave. "Just then, something flew past the window and the train doors were pried off by a man in a cape. Everything seemed to happen at once. My mom tackled me to the ground; there was shooting all around us. It was so loud, and she begged me not to look. But through my fingers, I caught glimpses of the action. This beast of a man deflected all their bullets, swiftly pulling the bad guys off the train like it was nothing. He took out the gang and returned all the valuables. I couldn't believe what I was seeing. It happened so fast—the man was a blur of red, white, and blue, like a magical comet of justice who had flown in from another planet to save the day. He wasn't scared like we were; he didn't even blink in the face of danger. It was the most amazing thing I'd ever seen."

I feel a tear run down my cheek as Teddy hangs on my every word. "Later, I learned his name was Blue Streak. I'd always known that Warrior Nation was a thing, but until that day, I never really paid attention. After that, after Blue Streak saved my life and Mom's, I had to know everything about the Warriors. Seeing him in action—watching him make the world a better, safer place—changed me. I knew right then and there that I wanted to be part of it."

"That's . . . Wow, Claire," Teddy gasps, blinking back his own tears. "How lucky, then, that you get to see him on his last day."

My insides turn to ice. "What?"

He nods, wiping the corner of his eye. "He's retiring. Thirty-four years of service, saving people just like you. It's truly incredible."

I hear the words, but they don't make sense. Retirement? No. It's not like heroes never willingly leave the line of duty, but Blue Streak always seemed like he was in it for life. In fact, I know it—my "Quotable Blue Streak" diary page has him stating his greatest honor would be giving his life for another. Why now? What changed? "I don't understand."

"He's old, Claire. I mean, don't get me wrong—he's awesome. Clearly. But he's also more than double the age of our latest recruit."

Oh my god . . . "Joy?" *She's* taking *his* place? Now, this is just ridiculous. Some hotshot pretty face filling the shoes of an absolute god? I feel my knees go weak again, only this time from rage.

"Yeah, have you met her?" Teddy asks. "I think she's going to be great. A lot of charisma with that one. She's a marketing team's dream."

I force a smile, even though my bones are turning into a liquefied paste.

But there isn't much time to dwell on the world's most unjust changing of the guard, because suddenly Blue Streak's meeting is over and he's heading this way. I watch in paralyzed awe as my hero holds the door for everyone, kindly shaking hands with and graciously smiling at everyone in the room. He's always been a man of few words in interviews, and even today, he only offers brief exchanges of gratitude. Teddy pinches my waist to keep me from passing out, and I hold my breath as Blue Streak strides by. Over six feet tall, shoulders broad as an ox, massive hands that have punched through buildings swaying at his sides. Only his graying hair and a few worry lines etched into his fair skin give away his age. Otherwise, he looks as strong and powerful as the day he saved my life.

He walks by with a gentle smile, giving me a wink with steel-gray eyes that peer into my soul, and I swear I have an out-of-body experience, a supernova of emotion launching me to a different plane.

It isn't until he's gone, possibly forever, that I finally resume normal motor functions. "Oh my god!" I cry, hands flying to my face. "Did that really just happen?"

Teddy sighs, smiling. "Just another day at Warrior Nation."

Is There a New Chicago Warrior?
WarriorHunt.usa

Guys, Roy Masterson was just doing a ribbon cutting at some random new bakery on the north side, and he let it slip that some "exciting chapter changes" will be announced soon! That's right, Mr. Know-It-All himself basically just spilled the beans that we're about to be blessed with a new hero! AHHHHHHHHH!

> **@TruWarriorGrrl**
> um no offense but that sounds like jumping to conclusions hon. Like his statement could mean literally anything

> **@invisiblegirlfriend**
> excuse you he's the Chicago chapter president so what else would he be talking about? It's not like we'd care if they get new business cards or something dumb.

> **@TruWarriorGrrl**
> you think I don't know who he is? rolls eyes

> **@NeverCeaseNeverSour**
> if there's a new Warrior, then who is out? Don't remember anyone dying recently

> **@VaporLover29**
> IF SOMETHING HAPPENED TO VAPORIZER I WILL LOSE MY SHIT

> **@WNlyfer**

if there is a new hero I hope it's a girl bc this chapter needs more womens

@invisiblegirlfriend
agreed!

BRIDGETTE

STRIPES OF PINK AND LAVENDER warm the morning sky as I lie motionless on the couch. Dawn is usually my most productive time of the day, but this morning I can't even get up to make coffee. Wrapped in a blanket, I watch the city wake up, sunlight streaming through windows and gently welcoming the world to the day. I don't have anything on my schedule today, so I could easily go back to sleep, but this is the time I should be doing my actual work. There's something about creating before the world is awake. To sketch, to explore, to turn paper into new and interesting shapes. In the quiet stillness of sunrise, I only have to answer to myself, and starting on an artistic note fills me and sets me up for success.

But even though my sketchbook is inches away on the floor, I don't reach over, paralyzed by my decision from last night.

I have to break up with Matt.

I pull the blanket tighter. Even having the words scroll through my head makes me shiver, not because it's the wrong choice, but because I know, deep down, I should've done it a long time ago. It's not like last night was the first time he let me down. I could've said *The End* after the Chicago police force charity ball, when he left me alone all night to schmooze with strangers while he worked the red carpet. Or two months ago, when Chomper and his goons threw me in the back of their beat-up van and drove around in circles until I puked. Matt wasn't even the one to save me that time; it was Earthquake who finally got behind the wheel and drove me to safety.

But honestly, none of this hits the root of the issue. He's a celebrity; it's been that way from almost the start, and dating a public figure comes with baggage. Add on the fact that his star shines with an extra helping of danger, and the chances of being a normal couple are pretty much nonexistent. That stuff I can deal with—and have—for years; it's when my trajectory gets thrown off by his plans that the knife cuts deep. We used to be able to balance the demands of his life with mine, and I was never an afterthought, even when he had to save the world or appear at cons. He used to know, just from a look, when I was feeling down or needed a shoulder. Now I can't even be sure he'll show up. We were partners in this crazy adventure, but somewhere along the way, we were thrown off course.

I look around Becca's apartment, sunlight warming the messy one-bedroom space. Since our parents are in the middle of the world's most epic divorce, Becca's been letting me crash on her couch. I don't want to live with either of my parents, and I can't stay in the dorms until the fall, so even though my sister's place is cramped, storing my stuff in Target bags is better than getting tossed around in a power struggle. Besides, Becca is an up-and-coming actress, tending bar when she isn't lighting up the stage, and I like the cozy, bohemian artist collective we've got going.

I hear a thump from outside the living room window, so I sit up to see if our unofficial pet squirrel, Nutty, has returned to our fire escape. Why a squirrel would climb three stories day after day for extremely inadequate shelter is a mystery to me. It's not like we feed him. But oh well. I don't see the furry little guy, or anything else for that matter, so I'm about to sink back down for ten more minutes of sulking meditation when a shape begins to materialize on top of the metal slats. Huddled tight in a ball, a human form fades in, and where once there was nothing, suddenly there's a man, wrapped mostly in white yet flecked with red.

Oh, Matt.

Part of me wants to close the curtain and pretend I never saw him, go on with my day and get things done. But that's just Bad Bridgette talking—the persona the fangirls and WarNats have put on me. In their eyes, I'm just a heartless, fame-chasing wench who only cares about myself and never prioritizes his needs. But I'd never actually leave him there. My heart hasn't hardened to the sight of seeing someone I care about hurt. Someone needs to tend to his battle scars, so I open the window and give him a gentle nudge on his thigh, unsure where his injury stems from.

"Hey," I call out, slightly above a whisper. "Matt." He doesn't move. I shake his leg. "Matt? Are you okay?" He releases something resembling a moan but remains motionless. "How long have you been out here?"

His face is half-covered by his white cape, his mask all crumpled up in his disheveled dark hair, yet I still hear him say, "All my life, waiting for you."

Sigh. He's always doing this: downplaying his suffering with a joke or cheesy line. Maybe this was comforting when he first became a Warrior, but sometimes I wish he would drop the act and just be real with me.

He props himself up on an elbow, falling once before sticking the landing. Once his eyes focus, they widen, jaw dropping in tandem. "Wow," he gasps. "You look . . . You look . . . Do you have a twin?"

"What?"

"I'm seeing double." He makes a pinching motion with his spare hand. "Just a little."

I close my eyes, worried. *Please don't have another head injury.* "Did you get hit in the head? Who did this to you?"

Matt doesn't respond, curling back into a ball.

"Who?"

"It doesn't matter," he mumbles, picking at a tear in his white spandex suit. "It's fine now."

"Actually it's not fine. You are bleeding and possibly concussed."

At this he chuckles, which transforms into a few violent coughs. He wipes his mouth on his sleeve, leaving another streak of red, and I swallow back the bile rising in my throat.

"Let's get you in here and cleaned up. We don't want the neighbors selling pictures of you like this. Again." Matt hates being photographed in a weakened state, so this gets him moving. "C'mon. Nice and slow." With effort, he makes his limbs cooperate, clambering through and hurling himself onto the couch, a pile of black-and-blue boyfriend.

I pull Becca's blankets away before he can soil them, going into autopilot with my caretaker duties. I untie his ivory boots and unclip his cape so he doesn't strangle himself. It's nearly impossible to wrangle him out of his spandex when he's injured. He turns into 160 pounds of man-baby, unable to participate in the clothes removal dance, so I let that be. I grab a first aid kit from the bathroom closet, popping off the lid and taking a seat on the hardwood floor next to the couch.

Matt's hand hangs lifelessly off the side. I hold it gently, inspecting the battered knuckles. For a guy in his early twenties, his hands look like he's been working the mines for fifty-plus years: they're scarred, callused, hard. I remember the first time we held hands, after I'd bombed my initial try at the SATs. He told me it would be fine, that I could take the test again, and as his fingers linked with mine, my whole body tingled, instantly forgetting all the word associations and quadratic equations I'd just messed up. He saved me that day, though he wasn't a hero yet, his hands pulling me out of my inner turmoil. But so much has happened in the past four years. His hands don't feel the same anymore.

I unscrew the hydrogen peroxide bottle and begin

cleaning the wounds around his knuckles. He flinches, gritting his teeth at the sting. His Vaporizer mask is dotted with red, so I slide it back off his forehead, inadvertently running my fingers through his damp mocha hair. He smiles, slowly shifting positions to wrap his battered arms around me. Before I can stop him, Matt's pulled me close, pressing his face into my chest while my legs hang awkwardly off the couch.

"I love you," he croaks, squeezing me with whatever strength he has left.

"I—" The words catch in my throat. I love him, of course I do, but this love has changed from something that used to lift me up into a burden that drags me down. It was a slow, subtle transformation, taking place over years of kidnappings and killings, hardships and hospital visits. Each of these incidents would have been manageable on their own, but piled up they're enough to squeeze the oxygen out of anyone's lungs. And I've made my final gasp for air.

"Matt." I try to squirm out of his grasp, but he's surprisingly strong post-battle. I never turn him away if he's in need, but being in his arms like this feels wrong. "Please let go. I'm trying to help you."

"You are helping me."

"You know what I mean. You have bloodstains all over you."

"Am I bleeding?"

"Stop trying to be cute."

"Can't stop that," he says with a wink, which instantly sets me off. The wink. That stupid trademarked wink. Something for the cameras, the posters: not me. I push him off and spring across the room.

"Sorry," he groans, running his hands over his face. "Force of habit."

I hurl a package of Band-Aids at the floor. "If you have energy to be Vaporizer right now, then you can clean your own damn wounds!"

He sits up, confused. "Geez, where is this coming from? I had a long night after I left you, and—"

"You are not the only one who had a bad night, Matt," I cry. "There are other people in this world who have things going on besides you."

He pushes his head back farther into the cushion. "God, *obviously*. I wasn't making some blanket statement that my night was somehow more important than yours. Saying that my night was long doesn't somehow negate the length of your evening. Do we have to do this right now?"

"Yes, yes we do!" I yell, though I instantly catch myself, not wanting to wake my sister, who usually rolls in after two a.m. I lower my voice. "Last night was devastating for me. I was counting on Terese to give me that job—it was *important*. But that never seems to matter, because Vaporizer always trumps me with heroic acts of bravery. I mean, god, you are lying there hurt—and here I am yelling at you like some heartless monster!" I shake my head, embarrassed to be acting this way, but there's never a good time for me to express myself. He's *always* hurt; he's *always* in need. But I can't go on feeling like this. "My life is just not as important as yours."

"What? And who decided that?" he asks incredulously.

"Certainly not me." Fat tears stream down my cheeks, and he pulls himself off the couch. "Listen," he says, reaching for me and trying to restore calm. "You shouldn't have to feel this way. We can work this out."

"How?" I sob. "Are you going to quit Warrior Nation?"

He freezes.

"No. You're not," I answer for him, my voice trembling. "And you shouldn't have to. But I shouldn't have to give up my dreams either."

"Bridge, what are you trying to say?" He runs his battered fingers through my short, choppy hair, pulling me close to him.

Am I really doing this? I lean back, staring up at his handsome face. Stubble lines his slightly crooked jaw, full lips pinched in worry. I have loved this face ever since high school. Yet I have to let him go. "I—"

But before I can get the words out, his Warrior Nation communicator goes off on his suit's belt, a buzzing vibration accompanied by a flashing yellow light.

"Shit," he groans, turning off the signal. Yellow means report to HQ immediately, a command he can't exactly ignore. His hands touch my face, chocolate eyes full of regret. "God, I'm so sorry, Bridge, but—"

"I know. You have to go." I wrap my arms around my chest

as he collects himself, sliding the Vaporizer mask over my boy-friend's face. Our time is over; the city needs its hero.

"I will call you the second whatever this is is done, okay?" he says with one foot out the window. I nod, watching as he disappears, running off toward whoever needs him most.

I'm the only one he runs away from.

Dear Diary,

I am in love. I know it. I've never felt this way about anyone or anything before. These past couple months have been a total whirlwind, but every second has built up to this, and being in love is unlike anything I've ever imagined. I'm a different person, but a better one, like the best possible version of myself. Every part of me feels electric, ignited, and I just cannot stop smiling.

Today I ditched the second half of studio hours. That's right—me—I bailed on my most favorite part of the week. But I couldn't help it. The studio was mostly empty (not all freshmen take advantage of this time), and I was playing around with some fan brushes when a pair of hands covered my eyes. It was Matt; he bailed on his American History class because he wanted to see me in action. It was so sweet and unexpected. What high school boy does that? He wrapped his arms around my waist and silently watched me work, occasionally sneaking some kisses on my neck or running his fingers through my hair. Eventually, I couldn't take it anymore; I spun around on my stool, wrapped my legs around him, and pulled him in for a real kiss. It was so unlike me! But it felt so good. We left shortly after that, my canvas mostly blank. But I definitely have inspiration for what to paint next. ☺

Love,
Bridgette

CLAIRE

STEPPING ONTO MICHIGAN AVE, I feel like I just woke up from a dream. A blue-lit, emotionally charged dreamscape where I not only walked through scenes from my imagination but saw my idol with my very own eyes. Was it real? Is it true? Did I actually just tour Warrior Nation HQ and see Blue Streak walk away, possibly forever? I reach into my pocket, where my plastic security badge remains as a touchstone of my new reality.

Holy shit. My whole world has changed.

I didn't say much as Teddy packed me into the elevator that took me up to Water Tower Place, an eight-story mall so packed with shoppers dazzled by designers, no one has time to notice what anyone else is doing. Back in cell range, my phone starts blowing up with a stream of texts from both Mom and Demi.

So did you find it or are you dead from heat stroke

I've been talking to dogs for the past several hours. Need human interaction.

HELLO?!?

How's it going sweetie?

I believe in you!

When you're done saving the world, can you please pick up a pizza or something for dinner? Love you!

My fingers fly, typing out long and detailed replies to them both, but before my thumb hits send, I pause, realizing that even though I just lived the most singularly perfect day of my life, I can't tell either of them what I saw. No names, no details—the only thing I can share is that I do have an internship at Warrior Nation, but nothing beyond that fact.

Crap. How am I going to live like this?

It's nearly five p.m., meaning Mom will be leaving work soon. I order some Lou Malnati's deep dish and hop on the Brown Line back up to our Lincoln Square neighborhood, savoring the day's events as the L car sways. I keep playing Blue Streak's wink over and over in my head, a slo-mo reel of the coolest thing that has ever happened to me. I wish I could have had the guts to say something—to thank him for my life— but hopefully he sensed my eternal gratitude through my head-to-toe quivering of glee. I pull out my grail diary, finally free to capture all the details. Even if I can't tell Mom and Demi, I can pour my guts out here. Maybe writing it all down first will keep me from saying something I shouldn't later. My pen can't write fast enough . . . until I turn to a fresh page for Joy.

Hmph.

Every hero in Warrior history has their own section in my diary, detailing their power, catchphrase, weaknesses, and most notable highlights. But it doesn't feel right to immortalize Joy's name in ink. Not yet, anyway. Untrained and inexperienced, she's not like any other hero I've known. I mean, does she even have a hero identity? Besides her super strength, I don't know anything about her, except that she has impossibly large shoes to fill. It's been several years since Chicago had a new hero, and now they're swapping out a seasoned fifty-five-year-old man for a hot teenage girl? I shake my head. The WarNats are going to eat her alive.

Off the train and walking up my street, I spot a herd of dogs ahead, tangling their leashes into a giant knot. Oh, poor Demi. She usually does her last walk of the day in our neighborhood so that she can flop on her couch as soon as she's done. Even from several houses away, I can tell the dogs are leading her, not the other way around. I sprint ahead to give her a hand, but the second I grab a leash, she spins around, full of fury.

"Hey! Hands off!" she yelps, karate-chopping my arm before realizing it's attached to me. "Oh, Claire! Jesus! I'm sorry, I thought you were a dognapper."

"Ow," I moan, rubbing my forearm. That self-defense class we took together really made an impact, literally. "Are there such things as dognappers?"

"I don't know. It's a sick world, so probably." Demi bends down to pacify a particularly feisty poodle. "So? Did you find it or what?"

71

I flash all my pearly whites. "I did it—I'm in!"

"No way!" she exclaims, her excitement riling up the dogs. "Where was the entrance?!"

"It was—" I stop myself, remembering the NDA I signed. I really want to tell this story, but how can I share without the actual details? "Not far from where you left me."

"Okay, but, like, where specifically?"

I cringe. "I . . . can't say."

"Are you serious?" Her face hardens. "I passed on two SAT study sessions last week to help you map out all your possible spots, and you can't even tell me which one was the winner?"

"I'm sorry! I really want to, but they swore me to secrecy."

She leans her head back, releasing an exasperated sigh to the sky. "Ugh! Fine. Well, at least tell me how you found it."

That seems within reason, as long as I stay vague. "I was exploring the . . . area . . . and there was this girl—"

"A girl?"

"—and she was poking around the same places as me. I thought she was after the internship, but as it turns out . . ." Uh-oh, I'm veering into dangerous territory. Demi opens her eyes wide, waiting. "She . . ."

"What? Spit it out before this dog humps my leg!"

Ah! Do I reveal there's a new hero? It's gotta be public news soon, right? Keeping a Warrior under wraps is an almost-impossible job. In fact, the last hero recruited to the Boston chapter, Bomb Diggity, was actually announced by suspicious

WarNats, not the Boston chapter's spokesperson. I lean into Demi, whispering, "She's . . . new to the chapter."

"As in . . . she's a new hero?"

I freeze, not confirming nor denying her guess, though she takes my silence as affirmation.

"Holy crap! You must've lost your mind!"

"I know!" I exhale, hoping my technicality of not actually saying anything counts.

"So what's her deal?"

Her deal? "She's kind of annoying, honestly. Listen to this— she doesn't even know anything about Warrior Nation. Nothing! She's one of those disgusting Miss Perfect types who gets away with murder just because she's blond and pretty."

Demi laughs to herself, brown eyes full of pity. "Oh, Claire. You are in trouble."

"What? Why?" She turns, dogs trailing in her wake. "What?" I insist.

"Just don't make out with her," she warns with extra sass.

"*What?*" I shout. "Are you even listening? Did you not hear me say how annoying she is?"

"Please." Demi waves my comment away. "A cute blonde swoops into your life *and* she's a *hero*? Give me a break. You worship heroes, and you're telling me you're not gonna fall for one?"

For a second, I'm speechless, choking on my own indignation. "But she's—" I stop myself just in time. Joy is taking Blue Streak's spot; I could never betray his legacy like that.

But I can't reveal that news to Demi, so I say, "She's not even my type."

"You have a type now?"

"Yeah!" I shout unconvincingly. "And it's . . . not her."

She rolls her eyes. "Sure. Suuuuuuuure."

"Besides, I have a job to do," I say, continuing my case. "This is my future—I wouldn't throw it away for some cute girl I don't even know or like."

Demi stops, a terrier crashing into her leg. "Two words: Jenny Bradley."

"Oh that is low, even for you," I fume. Jenny was on a rival debate team, and last year, right before we went onstage for the semifinals, she pulled me out of line and kissed me so spectacularly, I completely forgot my opening argument against capital punishment. We lost the debate, and Demi never let it go.

"Just saying." She smiles sweetly.

"That was a year ago. I've grown."

"Uh-huh. Don't forget to invite me to the wedding."

"*Bye!*" I break off, shutting out her nonsense, just as I see the pizza guy pulling up to my building. I run upstairs with my pie, tidying up our apartment before Mom gets home, while Demi's teasing loops around my head. God, I hate it when she gets like this. Even though we called a truce over our academic pursuits, whenever I achieve something cooler or better than her, she gets all jealous and mean, finding a way to belittle my success. It's not fair, especially since I don't do that to her.

Not to mention that she's lost her mind if she thinks I'm

crushing on a girl I just met . . . a girl who tried to drop me from a two-story boat! I'm pretty sure I was too busy realizing a lifelong dream to be distracted by a girl, no matter how cute. Ugh, Demi. She's too competitive for her own good; I can't help it if my summer is going to be epic while she's outside scooping dog poop.

I toss the pizza on the counter and throw the morning's coffee mugs in the sink, doing my best to straighten up our tiny apartment. I do what I can to help around here, since being a working single parent takes a toll on Mom. Managing a two-bedroom place on one salary isn't easy, but Mom uses her accountant skills to crunch the budget and make it work. Most of the time. Sometimes I contribute some grocery money when things get tight by walking some of Demi's dogs, but Mom always gets mad at me when I do, saying I need to focus on school. There's really no way she'll be able to swing college tuition, so she's banking on me raking in some serious scholarships. Of course, I'm counting on my time at Warrior Nation leading to a job after graduation, so we'll see. Either way, I have to make things happen. For the both of us.

When things look good, I head to my room, firing up my laptop to scroll through my Warrior Nation fansites to see what I missed during the past eight hours. Even if I'm not allowed to post anything, there's no way I'll ever give up this habit.

There's a story about Kitty Vicious, a Los Angeles Warrior, who saved a bus full of schoolkids from plummeting off a cliff in the Hollywood Hills. She's pictured showing off her razor-sharp claws in a leopard-print bodysuit, back arched in a semi-provocative feline pose. The LA heroes can be so over the top. One of them—Storm Chaser—even drops his catchphrase as a hashtag mid-rescue. As in, "Hashtag make it rain!" Stupid. It's one of the reasons I haven't taken to Vaporizer as much as the other Chicago heroes. Since he joined four years ago, he's probably posed for more fan photos than the rest of the chapter combined. Yeah, he's young and hot, but the dude spends so much time chasing fame, I don't know how he gets anything else done. Maybe I'm basic, but I like heroes who flex muscle over celebrity.

There's other posts about Earthquake's new line of "ground-shaking" sneakers, and how the NYC chapter participated in a firefighter charity event, but I zero in on the top story of the day everyone is flipping out over:

> *Blue Streak announces retirement!*
> *Press conference to live-stream at*
> *8:00 p.m. tonight!*

My heart tightens even though I already heard the news. I still can't believe this is happening. Maybe Teddy was right about my being lucky today—at least I found out in the way that I did, and I got to see my hero in the flesh.

I look up at my wall, where a vintage poster of Blue Streak smiles down at me. It's comforting, still, to see that strong jaw and kind eyes proudly posing in the sun. Surrounding him is a giant mural of all my most precious and important hero artwork, clippings, and ephemera: things that are too big or too precious to be taped into my grail diary. I started the collection when I was ten, and over the past seven years, it's grown to be the ultimate snapshot of a WarNat's heart.

In the center is my self-made "map of heroes," a USA-shape bulletin board where I've pinned pictures of every hero from every chapter: Chicago, New York City, Los Angeles, Boston, and Dallas, and the mini chapters in New Orleans, Phoenix, and Philadelphia. It's heartbreaking, really, how quickly the chapter rosters can change, but I keep all the heroes up there, even when they've retired or died, because they all deserve respect for their dedication and bravery. The rest of my mural is mainly devoted to Blue Streak, and includes magazine covers, souvenir photos, fan art, and a full-size replica of his suit that I found on Etsy. I also have an official Blue Streak winged eye mask that I sometimes wear when I'm feeling sad. Maybe I'll wear it tonight while watching his press conference.

"Helloooooo?" I hear my mom call from the door. "Anyone home?"

"Coming!" I race to the living room, and upon seeing my burst of excitement, she drops her purse, covering her mouth with her hands.

"Oh my god, you did it?" she cries. "You really did it?"

"Yes!" I launch myself into her. "Mom, I was at Warrior Nation today! I'm the first intern to ever find an entrance!"

"AHHHH!" We both start screaming, jumping up and down as if we just won the lottery. And as far as I'm concerned, we did! Mom dances around in her low-slung heels and blazer, dirty-blond bob bouncing in the air. We join hands and she swings me around, before pulling me in for a tight hug.

"I am so, so proud of you," she whispers into my purple hair. "I always knew you could do it."

"Thanks, Mom."

"Now, tell me every single detail!" she demands, grabbing us some plates. "Do not leave anything out or I will know—mothers always know."

NDA be damned—I tell her everything. I mean, this is my mom; I can't keep secrets from her. Over multiple slices of deep-dish pepperoni, I spill about secret slides, underground offices, Millie, Teddy, and Joy. I only wish I didn't have to end the story on a sad note.

"There is one more thing," I say, setting down my crust.

"Whamp?" she mumbles through a bite of cheese.

"So, you know Joy? The new girl? She's replacing Blue Streak. He's . . . gone."

Mom starts violently coughing, spitting out her last bite. "What happened to him? I've been buried in spreadsheets all day. Is he . . . ?"

"No! OMG, no, he's not dead. He's just retiring."

She presses a hand to her chest. "Claire! You nearly give me a damn heart attack!"

"Sorry. There's going to be a press conference tonight, in like ten minutes."

She nods sadly. "Okay. Let me go put on pj's and pour

some wine—I wasn't ready for this." Mom loves Blue Streak just as much as I do. How could she not? He saved both our lives.

We settle into the couch, each wearing our officially licensed Warrior Nation pajamas we gave each other for Christmas. The laptop sits between us, and before I know it, the heroes' blue-and-silver insignia lights up the screen as Millie Montouse and Roy Masterson, Chicago chapter president, take the stage. Millie walks right past Roy and steps up to the podium, giant glasses making her humorless eyes appear double in size. It's so weird to think that I was actually talking to her mere hours ago!

"Did you know she's like four ten?" I tell my mom.

"No way! She's always scared me a little."

"I know. She's even more intense in person."

"Thank you all for being here today on such short notice," Millie begins, her voice calm and clear, without a hint of emotion. "Today, Warrior Nation is saying goodbye to one of our most prolific heroes, a man who has guided this chapter with strength, wisdom, and dependability. While we are saddened to lose a true legend, we are honored that he dedicated his life to the city of Chicago, protecting its citizens as if they were his own family and bringing peace to the Windy City. Ladies and gentlemen, I give you Blue Streak."

The room breaks out into thunderous applause, as reporters jump to their feet, waving their notepads and recorders in the air. Blue Streak takes the stage, wearing his hero suit: red-white-and-blue spandex, with a long blue cape trailing him. Only today he's not covering his face with his mask, letting everyone see him for the man he truly is. Mom grabs my arm, snuggling her cheek into my shoulder. I realize I'm holding my breath, not wanting to miss a word.

The first reporter begins. "Blue Streak, let me be the first to say thank you for your service. You are the true embodiment of a hero."

Blue Streak nods. "Thank you."

"We were all shocked to learn of your retirement today. Was this something you've been planning for a while?"

Blue Streak rubs his chin, massive fingers grazing over stubble. "As a younger man, I couldn't imagine walking away from this life. But after thirty-four years of serving this great city, it is time to hang up my cape."

Another reporter jumps in. "What prompted your decision, then?"

"Sometimes life takes . . . unexpected turns." He looks off, wistful. "I'm fifty-five. There were days I wasn't sure I would even make it this far. And now the game has changed."

"I don't blame him," Mom interjects. "I wouldn't want to be out there in tights at his age. Although he's still pulling them off."

"Shhh!" I scold.

"The remaining Chicago heroes are less than half your age," starts another journalist.

Blue Streak waits, then asks, "Was that a question?" Everyone in the room laughs.

"Do you think Warrior Nation is trending toward younger members?"

He frowns. "Look, Warriors tend to start young. I was only twenty-one when I joined. It was a big adjustment even then, and that was before selfies and social media." The crowd laughs again. "There's a lot of pressure on these heroes today to not only save lives, but build personal brands. My focus has always been on one thing: public safety."

"Were you part of your replacement's selection?" someone asks.

"No."

"Any advice for the next generation?"

He considers this, scanning the room. I want him to spout off something inspirational, something to carry me for years to come, but instead, all he leaves us with is "Stay alert."

Millie rushes back up, telling the room there will be no further questions as the screen fades to the Warrior Nation logo. I stare at it, a symbol that usually fills me with hope, but tonight, there's a twinge of sadness.

"I just can't believe he's leaving," I say, my voice hollow.

"I'll miss him too, but he did great things with his time," Mom says, wrapping her arm around my shoulder. "Now it's time for you to do good."

I lean into her. "Thanks, Mom. I love you."

"I love you too."

We sit there for a while, lost in memories of the man who

saved our lives, when Mom says, "Do you need cookies? I think sugar will help us through this."

"Definitely. Do we have any of those double chocolate chip ones left?"

"I'll go check." She jumps up, "Never cease, never cower!" written across her butt in silver letters, and I stifle a laugh. Just then, my phone buzzes with a text from Demi.

hey sorry I was a jerk earlier. I just heard about Blue Streak. I know that dude is your jam. You okay?

No, but I will be, I write back.

Besides, new adventures await.

ABC 7 Chicago news brief

Earlier this evening, Warrior Nation held a press conference to announce the retirement of Blue Streak, the organization's longest-running hero. The news was met with shock and disappointment, with an entire city left wondering who could possibly take his place.

In a tearful salute, hundreds of fans have gathered in Daley Plaza to show their appreciation of their retired hero, waving blue flags, ribbons, and signs with messages such as "Don't leave us!" "The end of an era," and "Forever blue skies."

When asked to comment on the outpouring of emotion from Chicago fans, Blue Streak simply stated, "It has been my honor to serve."

BRIDGETTE

THE WHIPPED CREAM ON THESE FRAPPUCCINOS IS MELTING.

I'm sitting on the stoop of River North Arts, Terese's gallery, waiting for her to arrive. I don't even usually like fancy coffees, but figured I needed the one-two punch of caffeine and sugar to give me extra courage for this ambush. Terese has to give me that job. And I have to make her see that I'm more than a broken window.

I spot her coming up the street, a long, flowery caftan breezing behind her. She takes a long puff of her e-cig, happily letting the vapor cascade around her as she smiles up at the sun. But her leisurely morning walk is interrupted when she glimpses me. Visibly disappointed, she contorts in what could only be called a full-body eye roll, but still I hop up, giving her thick black sunglasses and asymmetrical haircut the biggest smile I can muster.

"Good morning!" I cheer, handing her a slightly melted coffee.

She looks at the overpriced drink as if I'm giving her a lab rat. "What am I supposed to do with this?"

"Drink it?"

She pushes it away, jingling her keys to open the door. Since she doesn't immediately lock it behind her, I take it as an invitation and suck down the rest of my caramel mocha before heading inside.

An art gallery is such a different place in the dark. Beauty shrouded in shadows, there's a haunted aura that forces you to whisper, lest the ghosts of artists past are listening. Lighting is so important with art; you want it to be bright enough to highlight the brushstrokes and brilliance, but not so glaring that it blows out the subtleties. It took me four days to properly hang, position, and illuminate the twenty-seven pieces my classmates submitted, and I felt really proud about how beautifully everything turned out. But here, in the dark, I don't recognize a thing—it's only been a few days, but Terese has already swapped them out for a new collection. Grim and gritty shots of the city loom over me, making me feel like I'm lost in a place I love.

"Bridgette," Terese says from the back of the room, flipping on a few of the lights. "What are you doing here?"

Her frustrated tone isn't enough to overpower the last shred of hope coursing through my system. "I just wanted to leave things on a more positive note, to discuss the highlights of the event, and not just—"

"The broken window?" she callously calls over her shoulder.

"Right." I look down at the floor, remembering what it looked like covered in glass, Matt's body crumpled in a pile.

"I told you I needed some time to think," Terese adds, lighting some aromatherapy wax melts. The scent of jasmine blossoms.

"Yes, and I understand that, but—"

"Did you know"—she strides toward me, arms folded, flower print flowing at her heels—"those Warrior repairmen may have replaced the glass, but they couldn't fix everything. When your boyfriend came flying through the window, broken shards slit holes in two of your classmates' paintings, damaging them beyond repair." Bejeweled glasses look down at me, as if I didn't already feel bad enough.

I rub my forehead with my palm, my heart starting to race. "I didn't know." I was so emotional that night, I left without grabbing my artwork. I worked on that piece for weeks; I'd be heartbroken if it got ruined. No wonder none of my classmates have reached out to me since. They probably all hate me now, just like those online WarNat trolls who love pointing out how I'm not worthy to date a hero. "I'm so sorry."

Terese frowns, uninterested in my apology. "I was surprised to discover this wasn't even the first time something like this has happened. Your mother told me all about your high school graduation."

Oh god. Graduation. Why did Mom have to bring that up?

Matt and I had been dating for two years at that point, but he'd been homeschooled for most of his senior year since being recruited for Warrior Nation. It was a chaotic time for both of us, trying to learn how to be in the public eye while finishing high school, but our principal agreed to let Matt walk as long as he didn't make a scene.

My art club friends and I had created this beautiful installation that our school used as a backdrop on the stage. Dozens and dozens of hand-painted tiles formed to make a golden eagle, our school mascot. The plan was to permanently install the tiles as a mural in our cafeteria, but unfortunately, that never happened. Matt used his invisibility to stay hidden for most of the ceremony, but when they called his name, he reappeared, and the crowd went nuts. Some WarNat forum had published the location of our graduation, and little did we know that fans had filled the football field, patiently waiting for the second they could get closer to him.

It was like nothing I'd ever seen. Girls rushed the stage, pushing and fighting to get a piece of my boyfriend. He disappeared behind the mural, but they wouldn't stop, ultimately tipping it over and smashing nearly all the tiles. I can still remember the sound of all that porcelain shattering as it hit the ground. So much time and talent, destroyed in an instant.

A girl I'd never met punched me right in the face, jealously screaming that I didn't deserve Matt, that *her* love for him was pure. At the time, I thought it was an unforseeable, freak disaster, fueled by fans with nothing else to do. I didn't care that I had a black eye or that a couple friends cut ties with me; I'd probably just lose touch with them after high school anyway. I was just grateful that in the end Matt and I were both okay. A little bruised, but okay.

I didn't know graduation would be the first in a long string of unpredictable catastrophes, an endless line of terrible surprises waiting to ruin our everyday moments. No one plans them; they're nobody's fault. But still, they happen, over and over again, wreaking havoc on the trajectory of my life.

There's nothing I can say. All the sugar in my veins has hardened into one solid lump in my stomach. I'm not getting this job. I'm not getting anywhere.

"Do you know what I think?" Terese says, more gently than before. "I think you've been carrying around a lot of deadweight for a long time. Drop the boy and move on."

I cover my face, embarrassed to feel a swell of emotions in front of someone I'm trying to impress. "It's not that easy."

"Why not?"

"Because . . ."

"Because you love him?" She clicks her tongue. "Trust me, hon, when you get to be my age, you learn that love isn't always enough."

I hate the way her words sound. So cold and brutal, so absolutely certain. But what I hate even more is that part of me agrees. I'm not an idiot—on paper, my relationship with Matt is a total train wreck. I've been kidnapped more times than I can count, held for ransom on more than one occasion, and made more trips to the emergency room than the average person does in their entire life. I know—logically—this pattern of drama and danger will go on until the end of time, yet a piece of my heart still hopes Matt and I can make it to a place where the world isn't always on fire. Where we can just be, together. It's a pointless dream that will never come true, but I'm still having trouble letting it flame out.

"At some point, Bridgette, you'll need to ask yourself what you want more."

Just then, the front door opens, and my classmate Jilly comes walking in, wearing a blazer and holding her portfolio. She gives me a wide grin, a bit of coral lipstick smudged on her teeth.

"Hi, Bridgette!" She beams. "Nice to see you!"

"Hey . . ." I return, wondering why she's here so early in the morning. And so professionally attired.

"Jilly, wonderful. Right on time." Terese nods, ushering her past me. "Let's head back to my office and we'll get you started." She gives me one last pitying look, then turns on her heel.

Jilly clasps my arm before following. "Wish me luck! It's my first day. I never would've gotten this job if it wasn't for your event! Thanks, girl!" She skips off, happily taking the role that should have been mine, leaving me with my mouth hanging open in shock.

Jilly got the job? Jilly, who up until very recently didn't know the difference between acrylic and watercolor paint? Art isn't even her major; she was only taking a few classes for fun. Why would Terese hire *her*? Why? Don't get me wrong, Jilly is a sweet girl, but she doesn't have the kind of drive or passion I do for this field. She doesn't spend all of her free time at the Museum of Contemporary Art or dream about owning an art gallery one day. She once told me she's not sure what she wants to be when she grows up, and she's twenty-one!

I storm out, sunshine smacking me in the face, though a rain cloud would be more appropriate. I speed-walk through the River North neighborhood, upscale bridal shops and trendy taco bars in my peripheral view. *It's not fair . . . it's not fair!* repeats the voice in my head, stuck on this true but pointless thought. The world doesn't care about fairness. Ask any innocent person who found themselves at the wrong place at the wrong time when a villain chose to attack. It's never fair that bystanders get caught in the cross fire, but it happens all the time. They are victims.

I am done with being a victim.

ATTENTION, CITIZENS!

Do you have superpowers?

Can you fly, fight, or fend off enemy advances?

Have you auditioned for Warrior Nation only to be rejected?

Do you want to do more with your gifts?

We want to talk to you.

CLAIRE

TEDDY'S INSTRUCTIONS DON'T MAKE ANY SENSE.

I'm standing in the alley behind the Chicago Theatre, looking for yet another HQ entrance. According to the secure email Teddy sent me at five a.m., I have to use a separate entrance every time I come to work, so as not to draw the attention of people in the area. But this plan has already epically failed, because a teenager on the verge of a panic attack searching for a hidden door screams SUSPICIOUS BEHAVIOR!

Gah, 8:55! I cannot be late on my first real day! I reread his email for the forty-seventh time:

Entrance 9: Chicago Theatre
Pass box office, turn into alley. Walk exactly 63 steps.
Press hand into door.

Either I take non-average-size steps, or his directions are wrong, because I'm currently standing between two different yet almost identical metal doors, and touching my hand to both of them has produced zero results. I've rubbed my fingerprints all over these rusty rectangles! Just open up already! Teddy didn't give me a number to call, and I'm sure Millie would look down on me for tardiness.

Well, not literally. But still! Not good!

I lean up against the second of the two, head banging on the metal surface. *What would Blue Streak do?* I think. He definitely wouldn't admit defeat, especially after spending an hour putting on makeup and getting all dressed up in a skirt and tights. No! I make a fist, punching the door behind me, and hear a faint *click*. Turning around, I notice a small crack in the entrance. Aha! Yes! Prying it open, I slide inside, finding myself in an incredibly small room, not unlike the one at the bottom of the slide. Only this one is much darker, and has what looks like an ancient, broken ATM machine sitting in the corner. What am I supposed to do with this? Teddy didn't tell me!

The only other piece of Warrior Nation intel on my person is my security badge, which I slide into the machine as a last resort. Miraculously, it works, triggering a release on a pocket door I didn't even see. Thank god! I race down several flights of blue-lit stairs, going as fast as my ballet flats will take me, until I make it to the bottom, where Teddy awaits.

"Eight fifty-nine," he says with a haughty smirk. "I was worried you might be late."

"You know, your instructions could've been just a bit clearer," I say, trying to catch my breath.

"Just keeping you sharp," he singsongs, then heads off, his

tailored suit and shiny shoes quickly leading us toward his desk. Free of any photos or personal knickknacks, it's the saddest workspace I've ever seen. Only a water bottle, Granny Smith apple, and tablet are there to greet us.

"I thought you said you've worked here two years."

"Yes. And?" His black eyebrows pinch in confusion.

"Well . . . this could be anyone's desk. You don't have any stuff here?"

He looks at his space as if noticing this for the first time. "I'm hardly ever at my desk. In fact, don't get comfortable. Millie and the exec team have a meeting at nine thirty and we need to get the conference room ready."

A Warrior Nation executive meeting? SO COOL. "Sure, of course! How can I help?"

"Refreshments. Go to the east wing cafeteria and get whatever looks good. Donuts, fruit, coffee. Lots of coffee. Millie takes hers black, but grab cream and sugar for the room."

I keep nodding, even though I'm starting to feel overwhelmed. "Got it. Except, where is the east wing?"

Teddy hands me the tablet from his desk, activating the screen. "This is for you. There's a map on there. Meet me back at conference room 1A in ten minutes." He looks off, and I realize someone must be talking into his earpiece. "Yes, I'm handling it now, Ms. Montouse," he says.

I start tapping on my fancy new technology, which is packed with countless internal Warrior Nation apps like human resources, payroll, and a company calendar. When I touch something called "Daily Briefing," a giant yellow pop-up reads "SECURITY CLEARANCE DENIED." But still! There's enough here to keep me happy for a long time.

Teddy, still on the phone, mouths a frustrated *Go!* my way, so I hurry off to find the east wing cafeteria. A little dot on the screen (which is actually a tiny Warrior Nation shield—so cool) guides the way.

Just before reaching the cafeteria, I feel a slight rumble under my feet. A subtle shaking that stops me in my tracks. Could it be the Red Line speeding by? We are underground, after all. But no, it's more random than train vibrations. More like footsteps. My heart skips a beat—could it be? I race around the corner to find Earthquake himself, blending a protein shake at the counter.

Oh my god! I feel my neck turn red as I watch him in his element, pouring egg whites and spinach into a blender. The man is absolutely gargantuan, with shoulders wider than my arm span and muscles upon muscles upon *even more* muscles. His bald head and ebony skin shine with sweat, and based on his moisture-wicking attire, he must've just finished a work-out. I can't believe I'm sharing the same space as Earthquake! He can literally make the earth and all its minerals bend to his command, and here he is, stirring stevia into a smoothie.

Stay cool, I tell myself, as I start looking through the cabinets for coffee mugs. Of course, I instantly drop the first cup I find, but Earthquake makes a smooth save, catching the mug in his mighty palm.

"Did you drop this?" he asks in a soft baritone.

"Oh, um . . ." I fumble, completely forgetting how to breathe. Is it *in-out in-out*, or *in-in-out*, or . . . ?

"It's okay," he says gently. "I'm Ryan. First day?"

"Yeah." My voice trembles.

"Well, don't worry. It won't be worse than my first day. I had to catch a criminal running through Grant Park, but I was sprinting so hard, I accidentally created a sinkhole." He laughs to himself. "It was so embarrassing."

I remember the headline: *Earthquake—A Man-Made Disaster.*

"If I can make it through that, you can make it through today."

"Thanks." I blush, trying not to vomit pure joy. *I just got a pep talk from a hero!* This is going in the grail diary for sure.

Earthquake wipes his brow, grabbing his protein drink. "Well, back to the gym. See ya." The ground quivers as he walks away.

Talking to him energizes me, and I quickly assemble a tray of breakfast items, piling on everything I can find—bagels, oranges, cereal, three kinds of milk (skim, chocolate, almond), granola, strawberries, and muffins. Plus the coffee! There's so much on my platter, it's like breakfast Jenga, and I can barely see over the top, where my tablet precariously sits. Following the wisdom of my map dot, I blindly walk through the halls, finding my way to conference room 1A, but not before bumping smack into someone at the door.

No! Everything goes slo-mo as I watch muffins and milk go sideways. Yet nothing hits the floor, thanks to two strong hands that grab my tray last minute.

"Whoa, killer. Got enough stuff here?"

"Joy?" I stumble back, my heart in my throat. She has a golden glow, even under the blue-tinted fluorescent lights, her blond waves cascading over her leather jacket. "What are you doing here?"

"Uh, I work here, remember?" She balances my whole tray on one finger, Harlem Globetrotter–style. "The idiot girl who knows nothing about Warrior Nation?"

I resist an eye roll, seeing as how she did just save my butt. "I meant in this room."

She shrugs, setting down the breakfast spread on the conference room table. "Millie calls a meeting; I show up. They don't like it when I'm late."

"Most people wouldn't." Who doesn't show up to things on time? I almost break into hives just thinking about it.

"Good. You're here," says a voice behind me, and Teddy stares down at my messy breakfast. "Um, can we make this more presentable? Did you get lost in the wind tunnel or something?"

"Wait, there's a wind tunnel?!" I cry, even though I know he's scolding me.

He sighs. "Yes, for flight training. Now clean this up!" As I busy myself straightening the fruit and wiping up spilled milk, Teddy begins fawning over Joy.

"It's so nice to see you, Miss Goodwin! Are you ready for today?"

"Oh, I'm more than ready. It's time to take this to the streets!" She punches a fist into her palm.

"What's today?" I ask, stacking the bagels in order from sweet to savory.

"They're revealing my superhero persona," Joy says. Plucking a strawberry from the spread, she takes a slow bite before adding, "Name, outfit, the whole thing. Finally!"

I stop my tablescaping. "Are you serious? Right now, today?" I get to witness the birth of a Warrior? I forget how to breathe again. "That is so freaking cool!"

She gives a half smile at my geek-out. "I hope so. And they better have done a good job. I don't want some lame-o hero branding. Two months of nonstop training and tests—this better be worth it."

I'm ready to respond with a "How could it not be?" but Millie Montouse and six other Warrior Nation executives enter the room, each expressionless and dressed in drab grays and khakis. At the end of the line is Roy Masterson, chapter president and former hero Mr. Know-It-All, the only man in the room wearing a bright, optimistic smile. Even though he holds the record for fewest days in active service, it's still thrilling to see another Warrior in the flesh.

Mr. Know-It-All's power was the ability to sense other people's superpowers, which seemed cool but proved to be kind of worthless in the heat of battle. Knowing someone could liquefy your bones or shrink you down and squash you like a bug is great, but since he didn't have any power to stop those attacks, he frequently found himself on the receiving end of serious injury.

Pulled from the chapter lineup after only two months, his ability eventually proved useful once he was transferred to the recruitment department. He personally brought Earthquake and Vaporizer to the team before being promoted to Chicago chapter president, choices that cemented him in the WarNats' good graces. A bit of a goof with severe substitute-teacher vibes, he must've played a part in recruiting Joy too.

"Can't wait to see what you've put together here, Millie!" Roy exclaims once everyone finds their seats around the table. I try envisioning him in his former super suit, a bumpy pink jumpsuit that I think was supposed to represent a brain or something, but really just looked like he had constant measles. His current bow tie and sweater-vest combo suits him much better, sandy-blond hair askew across his pasty forehead. "I'm sure you've done a real bang-up job!"

Millie quickly grumbles something under her breath, turning her back on Roy while firing up the projector screen in the front. No one even reaches for the coffee and treats I so painstakingly gathered, but once everyone is comfortable, Teddy dims the lights and the two of us stand in the shadows.

A slideshow begins as Millie goes into TED Talk mode. "Joy, on behalf of everyone at Warrior Nation, I want to say how thrilled we are to have you as part of this organization.

A strong, powerful female like you is exactly what this chapter needs to reach new levels of success. Our design and marketing departments have come up with a brand and hero look we think you'll really love." She pauses, letting the final slide take the full spotlight: a rendering of Joy, hands on hips, gazing into the theoretical sunset, fully decked out in an extremely low-cut hot-pink leotard, with sparkly letters reading "Girl Power" beside her.

. . . Girl . . . Power?

"Girl Power is epic, the ultimate personification of female empowerment," Millie dramatizes, with the most inflection I've ever heard come out of her tiny body. Her fists clench in excitement, and . . . is that a smile I see on her face?! "This woman is smart, fierce, not to mention kick-ass. Females across the world will look to her, as she fights their battles and wears their victories with pride."

Roy jumps out of his seat, fervently clapping with his string-bean arms, but once he realizes no one else in the room is sharing his enthusiasm, he awkwardly slides back into his seat.

There's a long pause as Joy takes in the concept art. "I'm . . . not wearing much at all," Joy croaks, her face suddenly drained of color. And she's not wrong: Her alter ego on the screen wears a spandex bodysuit cut high over her hips, with a deeply plunging neckline and over-the-knee high-heeled boots. Posed in several provocative stances that I've never once seen an actual hero strike out in the field, Girl Power winks at the camera, her look accessorized with bracelets that crisscross up her arms and an afterthought of an eye mask, but to be honest, with all that skin, who would be looking at her face? Joy, who minutes ago was arrogantly bragging about being ready for the superhero life, has suddenly turned sheet white, frozen in her chair. When she doesn't say anything else, a man who looks like the world's most boring accountant offers, "This tested very well with our focus groups."

I muffle a groan. It's disappointing but not surprising. Back in the day, hyper-sexualized superwomen were the name of the game. Even though all the early female Warriors had talent to spare, somehow their super suits were designed to stun opponents with their looks alone. This Girl Power concept is not the worst outfit I've seen: That crown goes to a 1970s-era hero named She Bangs who fought evil in a string bikini. But still, Warrior Nation doesn't have to go to this extreme.

Joy remains frozen, blue eyes wide with worry. Millie, sensing discomfort in the room, switches to the next slide, which features another rendering of Girl Power, but this time in an even more come-hither pose that sends a bead of sweat down my back. "Yes, particularly with males ages thirty-five and up—"

"Wait," Joy cries, breaking out of her stunned silence. "Wait. I . . . don't want to hear about what old dudes think of this. I want to know what someone *my* age thinks."

Millie flips through slides flashing pie charts and bar graphs, searching for statistics to support her cause. "No." Joy stops her. "Not data. Not some random opinions. From someone who gets it." Her eyes dart around the dark room, finding me in the back. "Claire," she cries out. "I want to hear what Claire thinks."

I almost drop my tablet as six suits swing their heads my way. "Me?" I choke. "Why me?"

Millie, frustrated that her presentation was not a slam dunk, tries to intervene. "Miss Goodwin, with all due respect, Miss Rice is an intern, and—"

"But this is her world!" Joy insists. "She is straight obsessed with heroes! She knows what works and what doesn't." She crosses her arms, eyebrows furrowed. "I am not moving forward without her opinion."

The executives murmur amongst themselves as I feel my chest burn with nerves. What is happening right now? Why is Joy asking me this? I mean, from the moment we met, it's been nothing but frustrating trying to talk to her, and now she wants my help?

Heads nod, and Millie relents, turning the lights back on. "Miss Rice, you have the floor," she grumbles.

I step to the front of the room, trembling. It's not like I've never given a speech, nor shared my opinion in a dramatic way. You don't lead the world to victory in Model UN by being a wallflower. But those situations are always fake, simulations with no real consequences. No debate has ever been as important as this.

"Well, um . . ." I gracefully start, looking to Joy for guidance. She nods at me, giving me a small smile of encouragement. My heart pinches with nerves as I dive right in. "My first thought is this outfit seems really impractical. Chicago winters don't lend themselves to wearing glorified swimsuits outdoors. Plus, it seems hard to fight in. I mean, over-the-knee high-heeled boots? Who can run in those?" Joy flashes an approving grin, so I continue. "I know you all sell a lot of licensed costumes; there will be little girls and boys who want to dress up as Girl Power, so maybe we can find a cut that is less sternum-driven? Also, pink is a little obvious, and sexist, honestly. What about blue? It would go with her eyes. Plus, it'd be a nice homage to whom she's replacing."

This generates a lot of chatter. "But what do you think about the name—Girl Power?" asks a man to my right.

"It's . . . a little cheesy," I admit, cringing. "But I can already see the headline: *Girl Power Saves the Day!*"

A man sitting next to Joy is not appreciative of my feedback. "Aqua Maiden generates tons of buzz on her social every time she posts a bathing suit photo," he observes. "That was the direction we were going with here."

"Yeah, but those are personal photos, not on-the-job action shots," I say without missing a beat, envisioning the images in question. "I mean, sure, her hot poolside pictures practically break the internet, and good for her, but that is not what she fights in. She still has a super suit that gives her the support she needs to kick ass."

There's more murmuring, but I've yet to sway everyone. "Listen, little lady, launching a female superhero is very complicated," my opponent sneers, folding his arms. "How a woman looks will affect the way she's ultimately received."

Oh, barf, because what this conversation really needs is some mansplaining about female image. Time for me to wrap this up, debate team–style. "Funny, though, how you don't ask Vaporizer or Earthquake to fight topless in the snow, or cut holes in their suits to show off their muscles. The public loves these heroes not because of what they're wearing, but because doing good deeds and saving the day is inherently attractive. They love them for who they are and what they do."

"Yes, but—"

"Look, heroes can dress however they want, because what's sexy is confidence. The Warriors need to feel good. Unstoppable. Their super suits are meant to enhance their power and protect them in battle. Would you want to do your job with half a butt cheek hanging out?"

His face reddens. "No, but I'm not a hero."

"Well, Joy is. And clearly she's uncomfortable with this direction. It has to be about what *she* wants, not what a focus group says. She'll be the one out there doing the work, so she needs a look that makes her feel strong. Fearless. Ready to demolish her enemies and exude Girl Power during every second of every battle."

Roy is back on his feet applauding, but this time the room joins him, smiling faces persuaded by my words. I did it! I can't believe it! Even Joy seems thrilled by what I said, and suddenly the executives are coming up to me one by one.

"Those were some very astute observations regarding the merchandising," one says. "Have you ever considered a career in marketing?"

"I—"

"Or design?" another chimes in. "You have a good eye for details."

"Thank you, I—"

"Claire, I really loved your speech. Congratulations!" Suddenly Mr. Know-It-All himself is shaking my hand, turning my arm to jelly. "How lucky we are to have such a brilliant new mind on the team!"

A former hero, congratulating me?! I'm now out of words until the end of time.

"Ladies and gentlemen," Millie calls out, silencing the clamor. "It appears we have a lot of work to do. Let's get to it." Before ushering the suits out, she stops at my side to say quietly, "Nice job, Miss Rice. Your observations were very . . . shrewd."

My heart explodes. Again. Millie thinks I'm smart! Ahhh! But before I can thank her, she's off, followed by Teddy, who makes a point of making eye contact with me just so he can shoot me a jealous stare. Geez. I don't let it faze me; I see it all the time when I beat people at school, even Demi. But I shouldn't have to feel bad for doing a good job.

Only Joy is left behind as I start cleaning up the breakfast no one touched.

"Thanks for that," she says, bending down to meet my eyes.

"Oh, no problem. It was nothing."

"Uh, no it wasn't. It was everything. I mean, did they really think I was going to wear a hot-pink bathing suit to fight crime?"

I laugh a little. "Well, some of those guys seemed to be thinking with their other brain." She rolls her eyes in agreement. "Of course, they weren't wrong in that you could totally pull that look off." My skin burns the second the words leave my lips. *What?! Claire!* Why did I just say that?!

"Oh . . ." She trails off, pulling at the ends of her golden hair. "Really?"

I wish at this very moment Earthquake could swallow me up in one of his classic sinkholes, but the ground stays sadly intact. "Yeah, well, it's still a weird choice, and you obviously don't need all that since you're . . . I mean . . . look at you, you're . . ." I gesture toward her beautiful sun-kissed face, the image of her curvaceous, flirtatious alter ego tickling my senses. *CLAIRE! Get yourself together!* Instantly sweating, I feel more exposed now than when the entire room was staring at me. "You know what? I'm just going to shut up forever."

A pretty pink blush spreads across Joy's cheeks as she says, "Well, I hope not forever."

"At least for the foreseeable future, because I am a hot mess right now." I stack up the rest of the unused coffee mugs, unwilling to meet her gaze while these thoughts are running through my head.

"Okay, killer, cut it out." Joy puts her hands on top of mine, soft skin pausing my frantic cleaning. "Let's be real: I need someone like you here. Someone who's not gonna bullshit me into a bad situation. Those guys back there? They just wanted to turn me into a hot piece of ass. And hey, I don't blame them—I would look damn fine in that suit." I swallow hard. "But not for fighting crime! God!" She presses a finger into my shoulder. "You had the guts to speak the truth.

"And honestly? You were right about what you said before: I don't know anything about this world. And I don't want to make a total fool of myself. Maybe you should be my personal assistant, help show me the ropes."

My heart leaps at the possibility. "Really?"

"Only . . . I'm too afraid of Millie to ask."

"That's fair; she's terrifying," I say, calming down a little now that my attraction to her is not the topic of discussion. "Did you know WarNats call her the Mousetrap? She may be small, but she can definitely take your head off."

Joy laughs, loud and throaty. It's kind of an ugly sound, but it's real. It's her. Not some twisted patriarchal fantasy of female beauty. Better, because it's true. I like it.

Uh-oh.

Chicago WTF?
WarriorHunt.usa

Have you all noticed that's something's off in Chicago lately? Besides Blue Streak randomly retiring, I've been tracking the city's recent crime stats, and they have almost doubled from this same time last year. Nothing crazy—some vandalism, minor assault, petty theft—but still. Weird? Or no? This new Girl Power chick is gonna have her hands full I guess.

> **@SillyMouseTrap**
> dunno. Feels like people always go nuts in the summer tbh

> **@hot4heroes**
> it's so humid maybe their brains are melting

> **@greatestheroesintheworld**
> that chapter is soft—come to NYC and we'll show you what's up

> **@SillyMouseTrap**
> not a comparison, man! God

> **@greatestheroesintheworld**
> well then calm down bro

BRIDGETTE

"THANKS, EVERYBODY, THAT'S OUR SHOW!"

My sister takes a bow alongside her comedy group as the audience breaks into applause. The intimate, fifty-seat theater is packed, except for the one next to me, where Matt was supposed to sit. He promised he wouldn't miss opening night of Becca's new show, *Watch Out, It's a Trap!*, but as always, something came up. I know there's been a rise in villainous activity these past couple weeks, but tonight was going to be it: our breakup, for real. Guess I'll have to rob a bank or set something on fire to get his attention.

Once the house has cleared, I scoot backstage, where Becca is enjoying a post-show drink with her rowdy castmates. Still wearing the eye patch from her last sketch, she screams, "Bridgette!" upon seeing me, and the rest of her cohorts echo my name with enthusiasm.

"You were so great!" I cheer, presenting her with a bouquet of chocolate-dipped pretzel rods instead of flowers, as is our tradition.

She grabs the salty-sweet treat, ripping off the cellophane and ribbons I so carefully tied together. "Yesssss, thank you!" she says through a giant bite. "Performing makes me so hungry."

"Well, you deserve it! The show was hilarious. I loved the bit about Jane Austen on Tinder."

"Really?" Becca beams, flipping up the eye patch. "Sam said it was dumb." She sticks her chocolaty tongue out at her boyfriend, who for some reason has begun putting more stage makeup on, even though the show is over. "See? Bridgette liked it."

"Bridgette is too well-read," Sam replies, smearing some gray cream through his closely cropped black curls to make them look like he's aged fifty years. "I prefer lowbrow comedy."

"Oh, shut up, you do not!" Becca teases, throwing an empty water bottle at his head. "And stop playing with the makeup! I don't want you looking like a cradle-robbing creeper when we're out tonight."

He laughs, brushing out the hair product. "B, where's that boy of yours?"

"Oh. You know." I don't bother coming up with an excuse. They've heard them all before.

Becca wraps an arm around me, pulling me in. "Come out with us tonight, little sis. We're thinking karaoke and chili fries," she says, quickly steering the conversation away from my invisible boyfriend.

She's a bit sweaty from the stage lights, but I stay close anyway. "Now that sounds like a winning combination."

"Right? The chili gives you a solid base layer of confidence to take the stage."

"I thought that's what beer does for you."

"Either way! You can't lose." She grins. I know what she's trying to do. Becca revoked her Matt Rodriguez Fan Club membership a while ago, though she hung on longer than both our parents. Since moving in with her, there's been no way to hide my romantic tailspin, and she's said more than once that she's tired of seeing me cry.

"I don't know. I don't really feel like going out."

"C'mooooooooooon," she begs, grabbing my hands and spinning me around the small backstage dressing room. I almost trip over some of the costume pieces strewn on the floor. "That's exactly why you go out. To change your mood! And even if you're sad, it will fuel your singing. Just ask Adele, or Kelly Clarkson! Both of whom are excellent karaoke choices, by the way."

"Yes, please come," Sam chimes in. "I'll be singing Journey, and you don't want to miss that."

I laugh, so thankful to have these two goofs in my life. "I love and appreciate you both, but I'm just gonna go home."

"You sure?" Becca gives me puppy dog eyes. I nod. "Okay, but if I find out you sat alone in the dark on a Friday night, eating the rest of my Ben and Jerry's because of . . . him, I'm going to be pissed."

"I won't. Cross my heart."

She kisses my forehead. "Okay. Thanks for coming tonight."

"I wouldn't miss it for the world." I call an Uber and leave the laughter-filled theater for the warm summer night. As I wait, I watch a couple stroll down the sidewalk, arm in arm, whispering something sweet to each other. I can't hear their words, yet I melt into their moment, desperately wishing I could feel the way they look. Light, easy. Happily sharing a beautiful Chicago evening with someone I love.

I check my phone for messages from Matt, but there are none. I do have a notification that Vaporizer recently started an Instagram Live, though, so I click, only to see him outside Wrigley Field, fully dressed in his white super suit, celebrating a Cubs win with a bunch of fans, holding some kind of radioactive-looking energy drink. Oh, great, a sponsored ad. Some emergency.

My Uber arrives, and I slide into the backseat, but out of nowhere, the front passenger door swings open and a masked man jumps in, pressing a gun to the driver's head.

"No!" I scream, as another man climbs into the backseat with me, pressing his hairy arm into my throat so I can barely breathe. I gasp, squirming against my seat and trying to reach for the door handle, but he has me pinned.

"You're not going anywhere," he says smugly, cigarette smoke on his breath.

I try fighting but quickly give up as the car pulls away. This is exactly what I didn't need right now. To be kidnapped. Again.

Is there a punch card for this kind of thing?

Kapow Ad Spot

Matt: There's nothing that gets me more fired up than a Cubs win—except a Kapow energy drink! Packed with a powerful punch of caffeine and super-natural ingredients, every can of Kapow brings out the Warrior in me! Yeah!

CLAIRE

THE BROWN LINE CAR SWAYS AS I SCRIBBLE down notes about my first week at Warrior Nation. I could probably write a novel at this point about all the things I've seen, especially since the only one I can confide in is my grail diary. But instead of writing about all the different training rooms (thirteen in total, including martial arts, aquatics, and ax throwing) or how many retired hero suits are hanging in the Hall of Honor (thirty-six), I focus on one hero aspect in particular: Joy. Now that her superhero branding is being reimagined in a more practical yet powerful direction, I'm finally ready for Girl Power to have her own page in my records.

Girl Power

Power: super strength
Weaknesses: no knowledge of Warrior Nation
Highlights: -when she took her first official hero headshot
            and I helped advise during the shoot

> -when she told Millie she wants all Girl Power
> branding to be approved by our unofficial
> teenage-culture correspondent (aka me!)
> -when we bumped into each other in the kitchen
> and ended up talking for an hour over ice cream
> sandwiches we found in the back of the freezer

I stop writing, unable to contain a grin. I should probably erase that last point, since it's not legitimate Warrior business, but it was definitely a high point in my week. Seeing her tough, determined face melt into something soft and sweet was like a sucker punch right in the feels, but it's been pinned to my heart ever since.

I wonder what she's going to do this weekend, or if heroes even get days off. What does she like to do when she's not flexing her super strength? Is she an outdoorsy kind of girl? An athlete? A gamer? Her husky laugh rings through my ears, cracking up at me for thinking of her outside of work, but thoughts of her bright blue eyes and pale pink lips are interrupted by another face, this one not in my head, staring back at me.

A man just a few rows away on the train has fixated on me. Hungry eyes rove my body, making all the hair on my arms stand at attention. Wearing a large woolen hat and a bulky turtleneck that is completely off-season, a subtle, thin-lipped smile creeps across his bearded face. I look away, my heart taking off like a machine gun. *Why is he looking at me like that?* I glance over my shoulder to see if there's anyone else in his line of sight, but no, there's no one behind me. I hear him crack his knuckles, sending a shiver down my spine, but my eyes are glued to my lap.

Stay calm, I tell myself, although my stomach has already tied itself in knots. *Think. What would Blue Streak do?* The train comes to a stop in Wrigleyville, and even though I still have four more stops to go, I jump off, unable to spend one more minute breathing the same air as that creep. Stepping onto the Addison platform, I exhale deeply as the train pulls away. But my relief is short-lived, because once I reach the sidewalk, I hear those knuckles crack again.

It's him! He followed me! Shit, shit, shit!

Adrenaline taking over, I pick up my pace, pulling out my phone. Mom doesn't pick up, texting back that she's in a meeting, but I'm walking too fast and my hands are shaking too violently to write back. I dial Demi, who lets it ring and ring and ring. PICK UP THE PHONE!

"Claire, why are you calling me?" she groans when she finally bothers to answer. "You know I have Latin lessons on Friday nights."

"DEMI!" I pant, tears streaming down my face. "Someone is following me!"

Her tone immediately shifts. "Holy shit, are you serious?"

"Yes! There was a guy on the train. . . . He followed me off. . . . He's right behind me!"

"Claire, run! Where are you? I'll call the police!" my friend yells.

"I'm—" But the man grabs my arm, callused hands pulling me into an alley. He throws my phone, smashing it on the sidewalk, pinning me to the wall. Foul breath wafts over me, and I scream, crying out for help. But no one comes.

"Shhh," he says, bringing a soaked rag to my lips. "Time to go to sleep, girlie." I struggle, fighting against his crushing grip, but I'm no match for his strength. I feel a scratchy burlap bag slide over my head as my eyes slide shut.

★

When I open my eyes, I'm staring down at my lap. Head hanging heavy, I'm sitting, but only because my hands and feet have been tied to a chair. Purple hair dangles in my peripheral vision as I cautiously survey the scene. Foggy from the ether-soaked rag, it takes a second for me to get my bearings. Gray concrete floors, a metal garage door, cardboard boxes stacked high: Am I in a warehouse? Where? And more importantly, why?

I swallow hard, throat screamed raw, like my fear tried to scratch itself out from the inside. How did I get here? What did they do to me in transit? My body aches, feeling like I just went through a rock tumbler; I picture myself in the back of a windowless van, banging around like a loose pinball. I must be covered in black-and-blue bruises. *Blue.* My favorite hero crosses my mind, the thought of him out of commission even more heartbreaking at this moment. A fat tear rolls down my cheek, salt coating my quivering bottom lip. This quickly evolves into a full-body convulsion, as deep, aching sobs rattle my core, shaking my shoulders and everything else.

"Don't cry," says a female voice behind me. Surprised to not be alone, I try wiggling free from my binds, but rope burns my wrists and every movement feels like torture.

"Who . . . who's there?" I ask, voice wobbling. I hate the sound of it—weak, afraid. Yet I couldn't make myself sound more confident right now if I tried.

"Relax, I'm not one of them."

"How do I know that?"

"Because I'm strapped to this chair too."

Oh. I move my fingers to feel a second pair bound to mine. Knowing I'm not on my own in this hostage situation makes me want to grab on to this stranger for dear life. But I don't. Mostly because I can't.

"I'm Bridgette," she reveals, and my heart leaps in recognition. I know that name! Bridgette Rey! Vaporizer's girlfriend, the envy of WarNats everywhere. I don't spend as much time following the comings and goings of hero significant others as some fans do, but I keep them on my radar because I'm nothing if not a completist.

"Really?" I gasp, too rattled to keep any residual fangirling at bay. I've seen her face in countless forum posts. Vaporizer always saves his girl (much to his fans' dismay), meaning that if she's here, help is definitely on the way!

"Yes, and I guess your reaction means you know who I am," Bridgette continues. "I'm sure we'll be out of here soon, wherever *here* is." She sounds tired, almost blasé, as if being tied to a chair in an abandoned warehouse is not a complete nightmare situation. Is this, like, just a regular Friday night for her?

"Do you think Vaporizer will come?" I ask.

She exhales sharply. "Yes, he'll be here. He always seems to make time for things like this." What does that mean? His girl-friend has to be at the top of his priority list, right? I can't even imagine a scenario where that wouldn't be true. "You must be dating Joy, right? The one who replaced Charles?"

"What?"

"Blue Streak?"

"Yeah, I know his real name—"

"So you must be with her, or else you wouldn't be here."

"I don't under—"

"They like to take the love interests," she sighs, as if it's the most obvious statement in history. "It adds that element of intrigue. Plus, it usually gets the Warriors to their trap faster."

It makes sense, of course. In every Warrior Nation news brief I've read, the hero and villain are always given top billing, but the hostage? Not so much. The kidnapped become an after-thought once the day has been saved, though I certainly do not feel like some cast extra right now. But if that was the plan here, they missed the mark.

"But I'm not with Joy," I say, as if that matters now. I'm still here, kidnapped, regardless of my relationship status.

"Huh. Weird. Well, I'm sure they had a reason for abduct-ing you. A lot of these villains may be reckless, but they're not dumb."

I don't understand, though. Why me? Why was I a target?

I've only been part of Warrior Nation for a few days, and I have the lowest level of security clearance. I can't possibly have any information someone would want. Barely anyone in the organization knows I exist! Oh god . . . would anyone even know to rescue me? Would Joy?

Bridgette sighs, interrupting my silent string of rapid-fire questions. "Well, when the Warriors do get here, just try not to freak out and scream. They know you're here, so yelling will only distract them and attract attention. Okay?" Her vexation is palpable. I don't know her deal, but it's clear this is not her first rodeo. And she seems way less than thrilled about it.

I nod, but then realize she can't see me and add, "Okay." I want to be brave; I really do. Even if every inch of my insides is still shaking. Bridgette's detached reassurance has soothed me some, though another wave of adrenaline is coursing through. *I'm actually going to see the Warriors in action*, I think. Some combination of heroes will be here, fighting for *me*, and I'll get to witness every last wham, bam, and pow. Just like that day Blue Streak saved me. My heart races, but this time in anticipation.

I hear voices coming from some corner of the warehouse and crane my neck to find the source. A band of goons walks toward us as if in slow motion, confident in their villainy, but despite my extensive mental catalog of Warrior Nation foes, I don't recognize a single one. There are three in total, each of them wearing suits covered in spikes, skulls, and other bad-guy clichés. Their getups look cheap, thrown together at the last minute, but that doesn't make me any less terrified. Flexing their skills by shooting bolts of lightning in the air and punching a giant crack in a concrete wall, it's clear this trio have superpowers, though they choose to use them for evil. You know, like villains do.

They laugh, circling us like vultures, making a river of sweat drip down my back. But I remember Bridgette's instructions: Try not to scream. My fellow captive leans her head back against mine and makes the most exasperated sound I've ever heard from a human being.

"If they start monologuing, I swear to god . . ." She trails off.

That is the least of my concerns. As they approach, the one who assaulted me on the street looks me up and down like I'm a tasty treat, stopping just short of licking his lips. I try to hold my chin up and act cool, but I'm so terrified and have to squeeze every muscle to keep from peeing myself.

"Well, well, well, what do we have here?" says one of the masked men, a little too playfully for my taste. He leans in with rotten-egg breath, running a jagged fingernail along my jawline. I close my eyes and try to think of puppies and rainbows. "Boys, these new recruits are much better-looking than the last batch."

Huh? New recruits? Is he talking about us? The cronies chuckle, nodding in agreement. Two of them disgustingly high-five each other.

"You ready to leave that hero bullcrap behind and team up with some real power?" another says in Bridgette's direction.

"Don't talk to me," Bridgette spits. She has the confidence I wish I could muster up right now. Must come with experience.

But my captor ignores her, crouching down before me, touching my knees with his gross, gropey hands. "What's your name, sweetheart?" he asks me.

"Don't tell them!" Bridgette quickly instructs.

I swallow hard. "I . . . I wasn't going to."

The creep looks past me. "C'mon, Bridgette, it's no fun if your friend doesn't play along."

"Yes, because our life's purpose is to bring you joy," she replies.

"That's the spirit!" he booms, missing her blatant sarcasm. He moves in closer to me, burying his nose in my hair, taking a deep inhale of conditioner. My bottom lip trembles as my eyes fill with tears; his hot breath on my neck is somehow more invasive than his paws on my thighs. I want to scream, to run, but my nerves freeze me in place, enacting the whole "play dead" survival tactic you're supposed to use during a bear attack. Somehow I would prefer being eaten by a grizzly than prowled by this monster of a man.

"Don't be afraid, girly," he whispers, but thankfully the sound of a door opening distracts him from moving in much closer. My heart, which is already at maximum stress level, takes it up another notch, beating violently against my rib cage. Are my Warriors here?

No. In fact, the opposite. A massive figure enters, dressed head to toe in black, a giant helmet covering the face. Another stranger, another unknown, but from the way his body moves, it's clear he's beyond strong. Like a mountain towering over us, this person commands the room, and now it's the trio of lackeys who tremble.

"We got what you asked for, boss!" one of them shrieks, gesturing to us like we're game-show prizes.

"Yup, top-quality recruits!" another chimes in. They chatter excitedly, proud of their work, but the dark figure holds up an enormous hand, silencing them.

This person—their boss—takes another step closer to Bridgette and me, looking down on our sorry state. At least I think he's looking down—I can't see his eyes or face at all, covered as they are by the blacked-out motorcycle-type helmet. His head turns toward Bridgette, and after several seconds of quiet contemplation, fists clench, grabbing one of the henchmen by the throat.

"Why did you bring me these two?" he asks calmly, his voice distorted through some kind of robot mechanism.

"You told us to find Warrior Nation defectors, right?" one of them asks. "Well, I read online that Bridgette and that Vaporizer punk broke up."

The guy next to him snorts. "You read WarNat blogs? Dude, I'm embarrassed for you."

"It was research!" He shoves his partner. "I figured a pissed-off ex-girlfriend would be ready for vengeance."

"You thought wrong," Bridgette says behind me. How she's staying so calm through this is a mystery to me, but she's easily my new idol. "Mostly because we're still together."

"But the blogs—"

"Someone is always writing something like that. They just want Matt to be single."

"Ah, man!"

The boss stares at Bridgette for a long time before turning my way. "And her?" the crackling voice asks.

The man who chased me speaks up. "I don't know much about her but saw her brawling with a hero a while back. Girl Power was holding her over the edge of a boat. Figured they must be enemies."

What?! *That's* why I'm here? They think I'm against Warrior Nation and want to join forces? Wait . . . are they part of this siege against the city? Is that what this is? Are they building an army of haters?

For all my love toward Warrior Nation, there are plenty who hate them. It's hard for me to fully understand why, but I know a lot of people who are born with powers hope to join the hero ranks but never make it. Thousands of people who can turn sound waves into light, manipulate the weather, or freeze time never get the chance to join a chapter. There are only so many slots, after all. But would getting rejected be enough to turn would-be heroes against Warrior Nation—against the whole city? I can't imagine that mind-set, but if I get out of here alive, I'm going to search every last corner of the internet for information on this.

"Neither of them will do," the boss says. His three henchmen hang their heads.

"So what do we do with them? Kill 'em?"

I grit my teeth so hard they could break. Boss man steps closer, deep breaths rattling through his voice modulator. What is he thinking behind that helmet? All the ways he can torture us? The most painful way to silence two young girls? Every minute he delays his decision I dread it more, praying that whatever he chooses will at the very least be quick. But shockingly, all he says is "Leave them be."

Huh? We get to live? Seconds later, the back door breaks down, and the most beautiful sight I've ever seen rushes in.

Warrior Nation, in the flesh. Light streaming in from behind them as if they are literally heaven-sent. Earthquake, Aqua Maiden, Vaporizer, and . . . Joy. I gasp at the appearance of this amazing group, but my heart swells at Girl Power, dressed in her super-suit prototype that's so new, I can still see sewing pins clipped in the sides. Fashioned from slim-fitting baby-blue spandex, this new silhouette covers yet accentuates her toned arms and legs, with a rose-gold utility belt strapped across her waist. White combat boots give her a strong stance, with matching gloves ready to go. A cat-eyed mask hides part of her face, but the fear in her eyes is palpable.

The heroes spring into action, with Earthquake stomping his foot into the ground, shaking the foundation and making everyone stumble. The baddies pull out their power moves, throwing out lightning sparks and sonic waves in response, and Bridgette and I become an afterthought as the battle begins. Vaporizer poofs in and out of visibility, deftly weaving around the commotion, throwing powerful punches before disappearing and relocating. Aqua Maiden moves like a samurai ballerina, elegantly evading her attackers and setting them up for a blow from Earthquake. They work as a team, playing off each other's strengths, moving so fast the villains can't keep up, no matter how many fireballs they direct at the heroes. If I wasn't so scared, it would be freaking awesome.

But through all of this, Joy hasn't moved. She lingers in the doorway, clinging to the frame for protection. She ducks as Vaporizer lands a punch not far from her; she cowers as Earthquake tosses a crate at a villain's head. Aqua Maiden cartwheels past her, confusing the criminal on her tail, but Joy remains frozen, refusing to engage.

C'mon, I think. *You were trained for this! You can do this!* The other Warriors have nearly finished the fight, having trapped two of the three baddies in a shipping container, and yet their boss is getting away, a dark outline slinking out the back of the room.

"Girl Power!" I scream, and she flinches upon hearing her name. I call again, and she finds me in the scuffle, jaw dropping upon seeing me as the hostage. "He's getting away!" I look to the back corner, and she follows my sight line.

For a second, she hesitates, shaking her head in doubt, but I force my face into a smile, nodding in encouragement to hopefully give her the jolt she needs.

With one sharp nod she joins the fray, weaving through fistfights and roundhouse kicks. But she's awkward, clumsy: afraid to engage with anything around her, hands shielding her eyes. It nearly gets her kicked in the face multiple times, but her only blow occurs after Earthquake pummels the ground with his mighty fists, causing everyone to fall over, including the chair I'm tied to. Bridgette and I topple onto our sides, and she screams out in pain, neither of us able to shift position. I struggle to see the rest of the scene, my vantage point flipped mostly to scuffling feet.

"Are you okay?" I call out to Bridgette, but the grunts and groans of battle drown out my question.

I try to squirm to get a better view, but before I know it, the commotion has died down and Joy is at my side, gently running a gloved hand across my cheek.

"Claire?" She pants, out of breath. "Are you hurt?" Big blue eyes dance around my face. Even though she was just in the middle of the worst kind of mosh pit, her concern is all about me . . . and I kind of love it.

She quickly unties me, and though I can see Vaporizer tending to Bridgette, my focus is entirely on Joy—blond hair cascading down her neck, gentle hands sliding under my body. She pulls me to stand with hardly any effort, not letting go even after I've found my footing. We should run, get out of this warehouse to real safety, and yet I can't move, transfixed by the proximity of this girl. A hero. *My* hero.

We stare at each other, still in shock that we made it through. We could've been hurt—we could've died—and yet we're here. Together. All the fear and uncertainty churning inside me congeals into one supercharged force: want. I want to feel safe, feel protected. Feel loved. Her body, her breath, her brave heart warm me, and every part of me hums, electrons begging to pull her closer.

And so I do.

I kiss her, without thought or reservation. She returns my kiss with equal intensity, hands pulling at my hips, and the pressure of her full lips causes my skin to break out in goose bumps, igniting something deep within. I ball up fistfuls of her super suit, trying to pull her as close to me as humanly possible. It feels so good, her body against mine, melting away the anxiety of being kidnapped and replacing it with the highest high of a perfect, passionate first kiss. I never thought facing death would make me feel so alive.

When we finally come up for air, Bridgette and Vaporizer are gone. Earthquake and Aqua Maiden are calling for Joy, asking her to come help carry away the crooks.

They didn't see us. She has to go, but I hold her tight.

"You saved me," I whisper, my forehead leaning into the silky fabric of her cowl. She smiles beneath her mask, a soft giggle escaping her lips. "I mean, how hot is that?"

Who are the Anti-Heroes? LET ME TELL YOU
WarriorHunt.usa

You may have heard drama across the interwebs about a new batch of super LOSERS in Chicago who are straight up WASTING their powers committing a bunch of super-basic crimes. Well, I've decided to call them the Anti-Heroes because I am already OVER their dumb games. They seem to be part of this crazy siege that's going down that I hope flames out IMMEDIATELY on account of being total bs.

Thanks to WarNat intel, I've determined there are at least 3 of these Anti-Hero idiots:

- Fungi
- BlazeBoy
- Lazerous

Gross. So far they've been spotted lurking off the beaten paths, not even brave enough to fully assert their stupid faces in the public eye, WHICH IS LAME. If you're gonna be bad, COMMIT. God. Why would anyone use their superpowers for crime? It's pathetic.

JUST STAY AWAY FROM MY VAPORIZER! HE'S MINE!

BRIDGETTE

BROKEN. MY RIGHT HAND IS BROKEN.

Sitting in the emergency room in Warrior Nation HQ, Matt
and I stare at the X-ray of my hand, the bluish-white glow of
my fractured bones casting a haunted haze over us both. I've
been in the medical unit countless times with Matt, as both of
us have needed the kind of quick, discreet care only Warrior
doctors can provide. I've endured black eyes and bruises, gashes
and scars, but nothing compares to this. We sit in silence as
a team comes to set my cast, wrapping my fingers, wrist,
and forearm in plaster. It finally happened: This relationship
broke me.

When the chair got kicked over, I'd been trying to reposi-
tion where the rope was touching my skin. The girl I was tied
to kept squirming, causing too much friction. Now a wrist burn
is the least of my problems.

The hand I make art with is broken.

Matt sits in a corner, his white Vaporizer costume taking on
a gray hue in the dimmed room. He keeps balling up his mask

in a tight fist, then letting it dangle toward the floor, his dark, messy hair following a similar cascade over his drooped head. The nurses and doctors pay him no attention. They don't ask what happened, and they don't need to. This scene has played out many times.

"Six weeks," the doctor says, regarding my recovery. Six weeks. Nearly two months of figuring out how to be left-handed, of taking double the amount of time to do daily ordinary tasks. Six weeks of not being able to work on my portfolio, which I'm supposed to present to Dean Hucksley at the end of the summer. I promised myself I would spend these months cutting and shaping the most intricate paper art CAC has ever seen, making an elaborate pop-up book with each page plunging to depths so detailed and captivating, they'd have no choice but to include me in the Spring Showcase.

What am I supposed to do now?

The doctor hands me a prescription for painkillers, should I need them, and leaves Matt and me alone in the curtained-off space. Matt continues staring down at the linoleum; I don't think he's looked me in the eyes once. In the hallway, a team rushes by with another patient—looks like Earthquake took a pretty bad hit—calling for various treatments. Usually Matt can't help but watch a big commotion like this, wanting to be part of the action somehow, but he still doesn't budge.

"I want to go home," I say quietly from my perch on the table. He glances up, and the pain on his face is palpable. From my slightly elevated position, he looks so small, definitely not the powerful man plastered on posters all over the city. All of his bravado and confidence are gone, leaving him with nothing but tight-fitting insecurity. Yet I'm sure it's nothing compared to the emptiness I feel right now.

"Okay," he says, equally timid. "I'll get your stuff and we can—"

"No. I don't want you to come."

His face twists in confusion. "What?"

"I'm going home by myself."

"But you're hurt—"

"I need to take care of myself."

He takes a beat before shaking his head. "Bridge, this night got way out of control, but I got to you as soon as I could, and I'm not leaving you now."

"My hand is broken."

"I realize that."

"Do you?" I ask, trying to stay calm, although I'm pretty sure my eyes will betray me any second now. "I can't create, I can't do anything for almost two months. Do you know what a loss that is for me?"

"Yes, I—"

"I know you *think* you know, but you don't. This is the absolute worst thing that could've happened."

"Well, I'm pretty sure *dying* would've been the worst possible thing," he says, trying to lighten the mood but failing tragically. Normally, this kind of snarky comment would set me off, but I can't even yell. I'm too tired.

I look down at my cast, this hard, foreign glove forcing me to put my dreams on pause. I can't have any more delays; I can't let anything else keep me from staying on track. If I stay with Matt, who knows what might happen next? Maybe I *will* end up dead. It's not like villains give a damn if I'm already injured. "It's never gonna stop. They'll just come after me, again and again, until there's nothing left to hold as bait. Right now it's a broken hand, but tomorrow it could be a leg, an arm, a spinal cord."

Matt scoots his chair over to my table, resting his white gloves on my knees. "I would never let that happen," he says.

"Like you let this happen?" I hold up my cast, and he hangs his head. Suddenly I feel like I'm drowning, the weight of the plaster pulling me down deeper and deeper, until the only chance for air is to release what's in my heart. "Matt . . ." I say softly, tears instantly forming. "It's over."

He doesn't move.

"I can't do this anymore," I add.

His forehead rests against my legs, hands wrapping around my calves. I feel the grippers in his gloves press into my skin. "Bridgette, I'm so sorry."

I nod, even though he's not looking at my face. "I know you are."

"Please, don't do this. We've been through so much. . . . I can fix this. I can save us."

I shake my head, a few wet streaks rolling down my cheeks. "I . . . don't want to be saved."

He looks up, eyes shining with disbelief. For a second, he fades away, his invisibility taking over, and when he reappears, he's standing in front of me, taking my face in his hands. His thumbs wipe away tears as he says, "You don't mean that."

"I do. You can't protect me like you want to, and I can't keep being the victim of your life choices." Salty sobs break my speech. "I have a life too. And I have to live it."

He wraps his arms around me, but my limbs hang limp, tired and unable to reciprocate his affection. Lips meet my neck as he breathes, "Please don't do this. Please. I love you."

I squirm in his embrace, awkwardly pushing him away with my clumsy new cast. "I love you too," I choke. "That's not what this is about."

He kisses me, long and hard, lips desperately trying to find what's been lost, and I press into him, feeling his fingers in my hair, wishing it were that easy. Wishing that his body against mine was enough, but knowing the spark between us has been the only thing holding us together. I am done playing with fire. I'm the only one who ever gets burned.

I pull back, leaving one last soft kiss on his cheek. Matt turns away, dark, distant eyes accepting he's lost the fight, and I slide off the table, the gentle clicks and beeps of medical equipment providing a soundtrack to our breakup. I do my best to collect myself, and head out into the hallway, barely able to stand, as if my legs were broken too.

It's over. It's really over. I lean against a glass wall, staring up at the blue lights overhead, not really sure where to go next.

I know Becca will be worried about me, but she'll also demand I spill every detail about this night, right down to the last tear. I don't think I can share the story yet; I could barely say the words the first time. But it's not like I can stay here, especially if I'm no longer a superhero's girlfriend.

Seconds later, fingers wrap around my left hand, although there's no one in sight. Matt stands next to me, the faintest of sobs wafting from his invisible body.

"You have to let go," I whisper to him, not wanting to cause a scene as various Warrior Nation personnel pass by. We stay there for a long time, neither of us saying a word as he holds my non-broken hand, until finally he disappears completely.

"So You're Dating a Superhero! What to Expect"
(video transcript)

Hello! And welcome to Warrior Nation! We're excited to have you as a tertiary member of our organization. It is our goal to keep both you and your hero safe, which is why we set a high level of precautions for you to follow.

Due to the pressure your hero will be under on a daily basis, it is likely he or she may share confidential information about missions and internal processes with you. For the security of the public, it is vital that you never share this information with anyone, not even trusted sources such as family members and friends. Divulging secret details can put everyone at risk and, per your nondisclosure agreement, may result in legal action being taken against you. If you ever feel the need to talk to someone, Warrior Nation employs an experienced staff of mental health professionals to offer guidance.

You will be given a security card that grants you access to headquarters. Please use discretion when accessing any of our nineteen top secret entrances. You are now permitted to use any of our state-of-the-art facilities, including our world-class gym, recreation area, and multiple cafeterias and kitchens. Be aware that hero training takes first priority in any of these spaces, so check the calendar for availability.

On the back of your security card, you will find a secure 800 number to call if you suspect that you or your hero is in danger. Because of your close relationship with your hero, it is likely you will know if they are in danger before we do. If your hero does not return your calls or texts within a reasonable amount of time, it's better to assume something has happened, and alert our team right away. You are their first line of defense!

In the unlikely event you become caught in the crosshairs of a battle, the top-notch Warrior Nation medical team will tend to your needs, ensuring you are always cared for.

CLAIRE

"AND HOW ARE YOU FEELING?"

A Warrior Nation clinical psychologist sits across from me, stoically taking notes on her tablet. Apparently post-battle psych evaluations are required for employees to resume work, but I'm nervous my answers may not clear me for duty. Because while I guess I should be feeling some kind of residual fear from being kidnapped, all I feel is AMAZING.

I mean, holy crap! Not only am I alive, which is obviously a plus, but I was rescued by a hot girl who kissed me in a heart-pounding, life-altering mouth-to-mouth moment of awesome. I keep replaying it in my mind, over and over until the scene becomes not just a memory but a sensation of pure bliss that runs in my veins. I break into a stupid grin and cover my face so the therapist doesn't think I've snapped.

"Claire?" she questions, eyebrows scrunching over the screen. "Are you all right?"

"Yes, sorry." *Pull it together, girl.* I summon my best debate-team face: serious but not severe, focused yet not stiff. "It was scary being kidnapped; I never expected to be in that kind of situation. But I'm relieved—and thankful—to be here."

"Mmm-hmm." My evaluator nods. "And do you still feel you'll be able to perform on the job after being thrust into sudden danger?"

"Yeah!" I exclaim too enthusiastically, startling her. "I mean, if anything, it just makes me want to work harder. Watching the Warriors in action . . . I want to be on their level."

This pleases the therapist, and I'm released to Teddy, whose slightly rumpled shirt makes me think he never got the chance to go home last night.

"Claire!" he says, running his fingers through his day-old gelled hair. "My god! How did you find yourself mixed up with this siege?"

"I don't know, I was leaving HQ and—"

"I told you not to go poking around in all this," he huffs as we head down the hall.

"Uh, this was not my fault. It's not like I kidnapped myself!"

"You're lucky you weren't killed! I read this report late last night that . . ." He trails off, second-guessing whether he should finish his sentence.

"What? Tell me!"

He grimaces, lowering his voice. "The police pulled some bodies out of the Chicago River. Four of them, innocent fans who were leaving a costume party. Each of them wearing a different Warrior Nation costume."

"Oh my god." I haven't been home now in twenty-four

hours, unable to check my forums. I can only imagine what my fellow WarNats must be speculating about this, though. "Was there one dressed like Girl Power?"

He gives me a weird look. "Why?"

"No reason, just curious."

"You need to be a little less curious."

I roll my eyes, but we're walking so fast, he doesn't notice. "Thanks for the advice. I'll try my best not to mistakenly step into any more unforeseeable traps." Teddy sighs, and up ahead I spot a familiar face: Bridgette, leaning against a wall, looking lost in her own little world. I never actually saw her during the fight and am relieved she made it out okay, except . . . is that a cast on her right hand?

"Bridgette?" I cautiously approach, forcing Teddy to stop for a second. She blinks several times, like she's waking up from a weird, intense dream, then looks to her left, searching for something that's not there.

"Um, yeah?" She turns my way, confused.

"Hey, I'm Claire. The girl you were tied to a chair with?"

"Oh . . . hey." I shift in my sneakers, unsure of what to say. I'm so used to seeing her picture with drawn-on devil's horns, I'm surprised to see her eyes are green, not red.

"Claire, we need to go," Teddy nags. "You too, Bridgette. The debriefing is about to begin."

Bridgette begrudgingly pushes herself off the wall.

"Do you know what's going on?" I whisper to her as we make our way to a small conference room. It feels like being sent to the principal's office, although truth be told I've never actually been there.

"It's just a recap of what went down," Bridgette sighs, wiping smudged mascara from under her eyes. Even though she seemed tough during the kidnapping, she clearly broke down afterward, her face puffy and red. "They want to make sure you don't say anything dumb to the press."

"It's more than that," Teddy clucks, eavesdropping. "It's important to get everyone from the scene in the same room to make sure we have the full story. It's about solving crimes."

"Mmm-hmm," Bridgette grumbles.

Everything is happening so fast. "Do I have time to call my mom?"

"No."

"Will Joy be there?" I ask. The second we got back to HQ, we were whisked away to separate spaces, and I haven't seen her since.

"Yes. . . ." Teddy eyes me. "Why do you keep asking about her?"

Luckily, we arrive at the meeting before I have to answer, and it looks like everyone's waiting on us. Sitting at a long rectangular table are Earthquake, Aqua Maiden, Vaporizer, a bunch of corporate suits I don't recognize, and Joy, still wearing her new Girl Power suit. She sits up straight upon seeing me, and I happily choose a chair directly across from her, though I can't help but notice how Bridgette takes a seat on the opposite side of the table, as far away from Vaporizer as possible. Dark, swollen eyes follow her, and for a second, he turns invisible, reappearing slouched down in his chair.

We sit for a beat, an empty podium waiting for someone to take the lead. Millie huffs in her seat, repeatedly swinging her head toward the door, until finally popping up in frustration and taking a place at the front of the room, a step stool at the podium giving her three extra inches in height. Teddy rushes to be at her side, taking notes on his tablet.

"Let's talk about what happened today, yes?" Millie doesn't wait for us to respond. Clearly this is not a time for questions.

"Last night between six p.m. and eleven p.m., Miss Rice and Miss Rey were kidnapped by a group of men as part of the recent crime wave known as the siege. While we originally assumed the siege was against the city as a whole, we now have reason to believe these villains are aiming attacks specifically at Warrior Nation."

"What else is new?" Earthquake asks, rubbing a bandage on his head. "Bad guys always have it out for us."

"What's new is all of the criminals we've identified as part of the siege so far all have superpowers, several having been dismissed from previous chapter auditions," Millie says. "They are being called the Anti-Heroes."

Aqua Maiden laughs, tossing back her long red hair. "Jealous much?" Earthquake gives her an annoyed look. "What? Some lame-ass wannabes are mad they don't have what it takes, and now they're taking it out on us? They sound like total losers."

"That doesn't mean they're not dangerous," Earthquake

spits back. "That resentment makes them reckless. Thank goodness we got to Claire and Bridgette in time. What if they had taken Anna, or Houston?"

"Whatever." Aqua Maiden purses her red lips, and her attitude reminds me why I've never been a big fan of hers. She's been trying to get reassigned from the Chicago chapter for years, saying her ability to breathe underwater would be much better served in NYC or LA. Personally, I think she just wants to go somewhere with more paparazzi, because it's not like Chicago doesn't have water. In fact, if what Teddy said is true, her powers could've helped save those people pulled out of the river; instead, she was helping the Warriors rescue Bridgette and me. If this Anti-Hero siege continues attacking in multiple places at the same time, it will be harder for the heroes to be effective, forcing them to split up, which ultimately makes them weaker. "We always save the day; I'm not worried."

Millie continues. "Our team found some want ads plastered in various youth-oriented establishments, looking to assemble those desperate to use their abilities. A lot of these hopefuls don't have a great grasp on how to control their powers, and rather than having their night vision or telepathy go to waste, they are joining the siege."

I look over at Joy, who's stayed silent throughout. She's pale as a ghost, and her big blue eyes barely blink, hands balled into fists on the table.

"How many do you think there are?" Earthquake asks.

"Unclear at this time. But we're bringing in backup security surveillance to start monitoring for patterns and clues." Millie takes a beat, looking down at the podium. Her normally perfect gray bob is slightly disheveled, her pantsuit in need of a good ironing. "The press is already having a field day with these bodies in the river. We are getting slammed for not having any hero presence at the scene." She grits her teeth, white knuckles clenching the edge of the podium. "If you are approached by the media, the official Warrior Nation position is that we are aware of the siege and have already successfully thwarted at least one attack. In fact, Claire, Bridgette: I'd be happy to schedule a press conference so the two of you can share any personal positive anecdotes about the strength and determination of our heroes."

"Pass," Bridgette says under her breath.

"Um, no thanks," I add, not particularly interested in sharing my trauma on television. "But there was something I wanted to note, since we're all here. Did anyone get a good look at that guy wearing the black helmet? He seemed like maybe he was in charge of the other villains."

Millie's face hardens, as Teddy bristles at her side. This whole time he's been furiously taking notes, but now he's frozen, glaring at me with his beady little eyes.

"We have no reason to believe the Anti-Heroes have a leader at this point," she says. "All their crimes have been completely random without any connecting factors."

"Oh, okay," I say, shifting uncomfortably under Teddy's stare. Ugh, what is his problem? I feel like anytime I say anything to Millie he takes it as a personal offense, like we're competing to be the favorite child. It's so stupid. "He just seemed different from the others. He specifically said not to hurt us."

Teddy pulls at his shirt collar and clears his throat, excusing himself from the room. I've never—ever—seen him leave a meeting early; he's usually the first one in and last one out. Millie watches him with a close eye before continuing. "Noted. Anyone else have anything to add? Mr. Rodriguez, you've been uncharacteristically quiet."

All eyes turn to Vaporizer, who has been fixated on Bridgette the entire time. "Huh? Oh, nothing."

"Fine. Good work today. You're excused."

As everyone stands and starts to leave, Roy Masterson suddenly bursts into the room, looking completely bewildered, like he's been lost in a hedge maze for hours. "Oh, apologies, all!" he blusters, smoothing down the front of his rumpled tie. "What did I miss? Is everyone okay?"

I catch a glimpse of Millie, working hard to keep her facial features in check, although she's clearly a step away from steam coming out of her ears. "It's fine, Mr. Masterson. I handled the debriefing. I'll get you caught up."

"Wonderful, Millie; you're a real peach!" Roy beams, hands on his hips. "And thanks to you all for another rousing success at keeping this beautiful city safe!" While he clearly missed the memo on what went down last night, his positivity is helpful, even if slightly misplaced. Mr. Know-It-All eagerly shakes hands with everyone leaving the room, and I try to get to Bridgette, hoping to thank her for keeping me calm while we were tied to that chair, and to make sure she's okay. Clearly she's been through this before, and I can't tell if that debriefing was truly unsettling or just another run-of-the-mill rundown. I personally am not psyched to hear that an infestation of pissed-off power-having goons are plotting against Warrior Nation, but maybe that's because I usually just read about this stuff and don't experience it in real life. Maybe to everyone else, this is just a typical day. But she runs off before I can get to her, with Vaporizer hot on her trail.

A soft hand touches my elbow, and all my arm hairs stand at attention. "Hey, can I talk to you?" Joy asks, and I wonder how one simple touch can send a jolt of electricity through me. I nod, not wanting her fingers to leave my skin. "Not here, though," she adds, worry creasing her forehead. Blond hair swishes back and forth across her baby-blue suit as she looks for a safe space. Finally, she ducks into a nearby supply closet, shutting the door behind us. It's a tight space, and we're so close, I can feel her panicked breath. "Are you okay?" she asks me.

She's shaking, and not in a "we're so close we could start making out" kind of way. Even in the near dark, I see worry swirling in her eyes. "Yeah . . . are you?"

Her head hangs heavy, moving rapidly back and forth. "No, no I'm not. Sorry if this is, like, not a heroic thing to say, but I was freaking terrified during that fight, and I cannot. Calm. Down." She holds her vibrating hand out to me. "See? What is that? It won't stop!"

I lower her palm, lacing my fingers with hers to give her

something to hold on to. "Hey, it's okay. You're just riled up. I was scared too—"

"But you were the hostage! You're supposed to be scared. I'm the freaking hero! I can't be more afraid than the people I'm trying to save!"

I think of her face when she entered the warehouse; even from behind a mask, it was clear she was frightened. While the others rushed into battle, instincts taking over, Joy held back, paralyzed in the doorway. "It was your first real fight," I remind her. "I'm sure it will get easier."

Her lips tremble. "But that's the thing—I have to do it again! And again and again . . . like every day. How? How am I going to do this?" Her voice quivers as she turns away from me, hiding her tears. I scroll through my mental index of past Warrior Nation interviews, trying to think of a reassuring quote about how the heroes deal with this lifestyle. But they're all so media-trained, all they ever say is boring stuff about honor and duty, so I come up short.

"I don't know," I say, feeling completely unhelpful.

"It all happened so fast. One minute I was eating a grilled cheese, and then boom! Danger. I'm pulling on my suit, not knowing where I'm going or what's gonna happen when I get there. And then when I saw you tied to the chair . . ." She looks at me, eyes shining. "I went numb. Couldn't move, couldn't fight—all I could think was *Claire could die.* And it would be all my fault."

My heart squeezes as fat tears roll down her cheeks, shoulders shaking with guilt. "But I'm fine," I say. "Because of you, I'm safe. You are the one who rescued me. You did what you were supposed to do." She keeps shaking her head, mouth frozen in a frown, unwilling to accept my words. "Did you know . . . I added you to my grail diary?"

Sunshine peeks through the clouds. "You did?"

"Yup, you have your own page and everything."

She sniffles, wiping her nose on her sleeve. "I'm in that big dorky book of yours?"

I smile, nodding.

"But why?"

I hold back a laugh. "Because you're a hero, Joy!"

She almost flinches when I say "hero," pressing a palm into her cheek. "I have no idea what I'm doing. I keep telling myself, *Suck it up, Joy. Stop being such a damn baby. You've been given this chance; people are counting on you.* But who am I to be saving the world?! I'm just some girl who randomly discovered she has super strength, and now I'm standing next to these other three icons who are larger than life, part of this huge show, and . . . I'll never measure up! I'll never be able to do the things they do! But I can't make it stop, not now. I . . . I'm trapped."

I recognize this kind of rambling, this weight of the world coming out in verbal form. Because I do the same thing, getting caught in these mental tangles where I feel like nothing I do will ever be enough. It doesn't matter if I have a perfect GPA or off-the-charts test scores; I always feel like I need to be better, to work harder, because I'll never compare. Whether I'm adding one more extracurricular to my already-exhausting schedule or battling Demi for that valedictorian spot, there's no victory that ever makes me feel like I've arrived. That I'm done, that I've achieved what I set out to do. We all fight our own battles, even if we're not wearing capes.

"Listen, I know you probably won't believe this, but you are strong," I tell her, giving her hand a squeeze. "Anyone who willingly puts their life on the line for someone else is a straight-up badass. You think the other Warriors weren't scared last night? Bull. Vaporizer's girlfriend was tied to that chair too; you don't think he peed himself a little? But he fought anyway, and so did you. You are part of this now. And you saved my life, so you're part of . . . me." My face bursts into flames the second the words leave my lips, nervous that maybe I've said too much, delirious over being trapped in a tight space with a beautiful girl. But she smiles for the first time, her storm finally breaking, reaching for my other hand as all the air leaves my lungs.

"Wow. Claire, thank you," she breathes, stepping so close, there's barely an inch between us. The slick spandex of her suit brushes against me, covering me in goose bumps from head to toe. Her mouth opens ever so slightly as she carefully chooses her next words, and now I'm the one who's trembling. "I still don't know if I belong here, but I do know I like being . . . here."

She kisses me, soft and gentle, and this time, I get to slowly melt into her lips, her curves against mine. At the warehouse, everything was so heightened, I could barely catch my breath. But now, in the quiet, we can just be, enjoying each other without interruption. She feels so good, so right, I never want to go home . . . HOME. I pull back, grasping onto Joy's shoulders.

"Oh my god! I have to go!" I yelp, much to Joy's confusion. Her cheeks turn red as she tucks her hair behind her ears.

"Oh, I . . . Was it something I did?" She frowns.

"No! Oh god, no." I take her face in my hands, placing one more kiss on her lips. "It's just, my mom is probably losing her mind. And Demi! I called her right before I got kidnapped. I need to let them know I'm okay."

★

Joy insists on seeing me home, and a block away from my apartment, it's clear that the best night of my life was my mom's worst. The sun starts to rise as blue and red police lights flash, neighbors waking up and peeking out their windows to investigate the commotion. Mom is huddled on our front steps, head collapsed into her knees. Demi sits next to her, staring at nothing. I jump out of the Warrior Nation ride-service SUV and race toward Mom, pushing past a burly cop to be at her side.

"Mom!" I call, my voice instantly whipping her into high alert. Upon seeing me, her face contorts in relief, cheeks already wet with tears as I wrap my arms around her shaking shoulders. "It's okay. I'm here."

"Where have you been?" she sobs, clinging on to me for dear life. "Where have you been? What happened?" Bloodshot eyes search my face for answers, but the best I can give her is the hero behind me.

I look over my shoulder where Girl Power stands tall, giving my mom a warm, comforting smile as her blond hair billows behind her in the morning breeze like a hero's cape.

"Ms. Rice, officers—my name is Girl Power. I'm the newest recruit of Warrior Nation." Mouths fall open in tandem as I grin; I can tell they already love her. Demi shoots me an "Are you freaking kidding me?" look, unable to say a word. "Claire was kidnapped late yesterday afternoon. Warrior Nation has become aware of a new criminal element, but we have already successfully thwarted one attack." She sounds exactly like the spiel Millie gave, not missing a beat. "Luckily, we were able to retrieve Claire and another victim, safe and sound."

The nearest police officer turns toward her, pulling a notepad from his pocket. "Can you describe the villains for me, please?"

"Of course!" Girl Power beams, an easy request considering what this night put her through.

"Claire!" Mom grabs my wrist. "You were kidnapped? Oh my god . . . my baby!" She forces my head into her chest, stroking my hair. Kissing Joy somehow erased the trauma of being a damsel in distress, but I know Mom's probably reliving the terror of that day on the train when Blue Streak came to our rescue.

"I'm fine, Mom, I promise. See?" I show off my lack of open wounds. "Not broken, not bloody."

She exhales deeply, wiping her face with her palms as Joy kneels down next to us. "Don't worry, Ms. Rice. Warrior Nation will be keeping a close eye on Claire from now on. This won't happen again."

Mom takes both of Joy's hands. "Thank you."

A series of beeps pulses from Girl Power's wrist; I recognize the Warrior Nation theme song, which I have had as a ringtone since the second I got a phone. Joy looks around for the source but finally finds a homing signal woven into the fabric of the suit.

"Guess that means I gotta go," she says. "Sorry. Are you going to be okay?"

"Don't worry about me." I smile. "Go save the world, Girl Power." She returns a knowing grin before jumping back into the SUV.

"Is that . . . her?" Demi asks once Joy has pulled away.

"What do you mean?" I ask.

But she's not in the mood for games. "The new hero? Did she save your life?"

"Yeah, she did."

Demi raises an eyebrow. "Well, well." She stands up, giving me a quick hug. "Glad you're alive and stuff. But I'm exhausted and have to start walking dogs in an hour, so . . . bye."

Mom wraps me back up in her arms. "Are you sure you're okay? The police have been here for hours."

"I'm fine, I promise. I'll tell you everything upstairs."

Once inside, I start making Mom some calming tea, but

she passes out before the water boils. I, on the other hand, will never be able to fall asleep after the night I've had, not with the memories of Joy's mouth on mine still racing through me like a wildfire.

Marshall and Mindy in the Morning

Mindy: Today's top story is packed with power—Girl Power, that is! Stepping in to replace beloved icon Blue Streak is a new young female Warrior who calls herself Girl Power. This blond bombshell just hit the scene and already has Warrior fans in a flurry.

Marshall: Well, it's been a while since we've gotten a new woman in the lineup. And everyone knows Aqua Maiden has been vying for a trade to the Los Angeles chapter, wanting to stretch her fins and all that.

Mindy: You know she doesn't have fins!

Marshall: Do I? Honestly I can barely remember her. Seems like she's never around.

Mindy: You'd forget your own name if it wasn't part of this show's theme song.

Marshall: That's true.

Mindy: Do you miss Blue Streak?

Marshall: You know what? I do. I know you'll roll your eyes at this, Mindy, but he was a man's man. Tough as nails, solid and strong, I always thought he'd be fun to get a beer with.

Mindy: As if that's important.

Marshall: It's important to me!

Mindy: Sheesh. I liked him too, but I'm excited for Girl Power. Any time a woman can stand up and smash the patriarchy, I'm here for it.

Marshall: Oh boy, here we go again!

BRIDGETTE

WALKING INTO BECCA'S APARTMENT at six a.m. feels strangely anticlimactic. Her ratty couch, threadbare rug, and massive record collection stare back at me, annoying in their normalcy. How are they all still sitting here exactly as I left them? Didn't they feel the seismic shift, the earth crashing down on its axis? How can everything look exactly the same when everything inside me feels different, my world turned upside down? Yet in the light of morning, I guess I'm the only one who experienced cataclysmic change last night.

We broke up. It's over. Matt and I . . . are done.

I should sleep, but I still have the aftermath of adrenaline lingering in my veins, buzzing just enough to keep me alert to possible continuing danger. In all these years, I've never found a great way to come down after a Warrior endeavor, my fight-or-flight senses ready for battle hours after it's ended. The only thing to do is channel that energy into something else, and I have made some pretty killer art pieces while being hyped up on post-action anxiety. My hands want to move, create, and even if I'm physically tired, my brain rarely stops, floating through colorful dreamscapes. I get that others recharge through Netflix binges and lazy mornings, but I am most at peace when I make something new.

Kicking a few empty pizza boxes out of the way, I pull out a portfolio from under the couch, where I keep one of my stashes of art papers and supplies. Since moving into Becca's one-bedroom apartment, I don't have a designated studio space, but luckily, everything I need stores flat, and I can work on pretty much any solid surface. I lay my rubbery cutting board on the rug, leafing through my collection of artisan papers, seeing if inspiration will strike. I pull out a red sheet of handmade paper speckled with tiny gold-leaf flecks. I love the soft, uneven texture of these papers, their intricate patterns and details part of a larger story. But the nice feeling drifts away when I reach for my X-Acto knife.

Holding the razor blade in my left hand feels all kinds of wrong. Awkwardly gripping the handle, I try positioning my fingers as I normally would on my right, with my left pointer finger pressed onto the top side of the tool. My hand feels like a weird, flaccid claw, clumsily wrapped around some foreign torture device. *Sigh.* I look at my right hand, talent trapped under layers of plaster, and curse those bastards for kidnapping me, leaving me in this broken state. But I won't let them win, so I gracelessly press the knife into the paper, seeing if anything will come.

It's comical, really, seeing how ridiculous my lines are with my left hand, but I don't give up, cutting ugly shapes out of pretty paper. Even as I struggle to use the materials, it feels good to try, twists of paper shavings piling up on the floor as I go. My thoughts wander to my portfolio, due to Dean Hucksley at the end of the summer. I will not give up on this, not after I worked so hard to transfer to CAC. I do have a couple pieces I could show, but I had plans for so many more. I may need to experiment with other paper techniques, like quilling, or origami, or even hand-ripping strips of paper into something interesting. Sometimes I make scenes by adding layers of paper, creating depth as I pile on shapes. Other times, I take away, making a statement with what's left. This is definitely a "work with what's left" kind of scenario.

An hour or two later, I haven't produced anything of note, but I've written down a couple of ideas in my terrible, left-handed scrawl. Becca comes stumbling into the living room, eyes barely open, brown hair matted to her cheek. In just a tank top and boy-short undies, she flops onto her oversize beanbag that moonlights as an armchair, reaching for a can of Cheez Whiz lying by her feet. She sprays a wad of artificial orange into her mouth.

"Um, gross much?" I say, moving my makeshift floor desk away from any possible flecks of cheez goo.

"Good morning to you too," she gargles, swallowing down her disgusting breakfast. From the way she's casually slumped, I don't think she noticed I never came home last night, but to be fair, I do stay over at Matt's a lot. Or, at least, I did. But once her

159

eyes fully come into focus, she springs up, leaping to my side. "Hey! What happened to your hand?"

"It's broken. I . . . was kidnapped again last night," I say softly, hoping to avoid a freak-out.

"WHAT?" she yelps. "Again?" She reaches for my cast, running her fingers over the plaster. Fiery eyes look up at me as she curses, "Damn it! He broke you! That stupid boy broke you!" With last night's mascara smudged under her eyes, she looks ready to straight-up murder my ex.

"Becca . . ." I start to tell her the news, but she doesn't want to hear what I'm sure she thinks will be one of my many excuses.

"No! I'm so tired of this! Aren't you? Jesus, B, he's a *hero*; he's supposed to freaking protect you—"

"Becca—"

"If I were this terrible at my job, I'd get fired—"

"BECCA!"

"What?"

"We broke up."

She freezes, her rant on pause, mouth twisted open on her last rage-fueled thought. Her fury then dissolves into something softer, brown eyes cooling in sympathy. "Oh," she says, rubbing her hands over her bare knees. Embarrassed, she lets her long, tangled waves cover her face, and it's so quiet, I can hear her stomach rumbling. "Okay, well, get up."

"Why?"

"We're not going to sit here all day."

"What if I want to?" I ask, perfectly fine to continue cutting mangled shapes forever.

"You don't. And even if you do, too bad." She stands up, offering me her hand.

I groan. "Becca, I've been up for over twenty-four hours, and—"

"Ugh, just let me help you!" She scoops her hands under my arms, pulling me to my feet. After wrapping my cast in Saran wrap, I take a very unrelaxing shower, bumbling with the shampoo lid and razor. Not having use of my right hand is going to get really old, really fast. Wiping the steam off the mirror, I take a good look at my face, assessing the damage from my late-night cry session. There's the expected under-eye circles, but not as much puffiness as I would've thought. Nothing a little concealer can't fix. What bothers me most is my hair: short, choppy strands dripping with sadness. I hate having my hair this short, especially since it wasn't my choice.

Two months ago, Matt and I were actually on a date, enjoying a walk by the lakefront, when a random guy coming from the other way recognized Matt and suddenly spun around and grabbed me, holding a lighter up to my neck. It happened so fast, terror spiked through me, fire threatening to lick my skin. I screamed bloody murder as Matt went into Vaporizer mode immediately, disarming the guy, but not before he triggered the lighter and caught my hair on fire. My hair was crazy long then, all the way down my back, and even though Matt used his jacket to extinguish the flame and prevent me from getting burned, it melted a considerable chunk of hair, forcing me to chop off the other side to match. Now my length barely passes my ears, a daily reminder of what's been lost.

Becca helps me get dressed, the two of us performing a weird dance to pull on a pair of black skinny jeans and simple tank. An hour later, we're standing outside the Art Institute, giant stone steps beckoning us to come inside.

"Oh!" I exclaim, looking at the banners hanging near the entrance. "There's that new textiles exhibit I wanted to see! I almost forgot about it."

"I know! It's like I'm a really good sister or something." She smirks.

Arm in arm, we wander through the halls, taking in rooms filled with paintings, sculpture, photography, and more. I lose myself in it, my heart taking a sabbatical from its pain and soaking in all the beauty around me. The art takes me away, pausing the incessant thoughts of heroes and heartbreak, allowing me to just be in the moment.

I'm leaning over a glass case full of early Chinese hemp paper when Becca says, "You'll be here someday."

I look at her, confused. "In the ancient papermaking section?"

"Yes, that's definitely what I meant." She rolls her eyes. "No, in a museum."

"You have to say that because I'm sad."

Her face pinches in offense. "Excuse you, no I don't. I'm saying it because it's true. I have a lot of artsy friends who drag me to a lot of strange shows, and nobody is putting together the kind of weird, beautiful stuff you do with paper. Trust me."

"Thanks." I blush.

She immediately darts toward a nearby coffee cart, my appreciation clearly making her uncomfortable. "You need some caffeine? I'll get you one." She comes back with two giant iced mochas, and we find a bench for a coffee break.

She takes a big sip, eyeing me over the edge of her cup. "So . . ."

"So . . . ?"

"Are you . . . ? I mean, how do you . . . ?"

"Feel?" I finish her thought, and she nods in relief. Becca is always there for me, letting me stay at her place and taking my mind off my problems, but she's never been great at talking about emotions. "I'm fine."

She snorts in disbelief. "Right." I frown at her reaction. "It's just . . . you dumped your boyfriend of four years yesterday. Plus, your hand is freaking broken. There's no way you're fine. You can tell me the truth."

"I appreciate that, really, but I can't talk about it in public."

"Huh? Why not?"

"The WarNats," I groan. "I never know if they're lurking, and if I say the wrong thing, or have the wrong emotional reaction, they'll probably do a slideshow on 'Top Ten Reasons Why Bridgette Will Be a Spinster Forever.'"

"Ugh, screw those trolls!" Becca kicks a foot up into the air. "I will karate-chop all their dumb faces."

I picture my sister taking on an army of heartsick hero lovers. "I don't know. That could become a full-time job."

"Worth it." She winks. We watch a family of tourists go by, all wearing matching "I ♥ Chicago" shirts. "Also . . . I'm sorry about Matt."

I almost spit out my mocha, laughing. "No you're not!"

"Yes I am!" she shouts indignantly, her messy bun wobbling on the top of her head.

"I'm pretty sure you called him stupid this morning."

She grimaces. "Well . . . he is stupid sometimes. All boys are. Do you know what Sam did last night?" I shake my head. "He tried to jump over a fire hydrant and ended up falling right on his face. He could've broken something! And for what? Just to make me laugh?"

"He loves making you laugh."

She tries to hold back a smile, but it breaks through anyway. "My point is, it doesn't matter how I felt about Matt. You loved him. And . . . he had his qualities."

My eyebrows shoot up. That is probably the nicest thing she's ever said about him, and it's not even a very specific sentiment. "Like what?" I press.

She taps her chin dramatically, as if it's a real struggle to think of something. "He made a mean mac and cheese. He could reach stuff from the high shelves. And . . . he always looked at you like you were made of starlight or something."

Her phrasing calls me back to the first time Matt came to one of my art shows, before he was the Vaporizer, and we were just two dumb high school kids enamored with each other. It was the first time he'd seen my art on display, not just over my shoulder while we hung out at my apartment, and I was nervous. I'd spent five weeks cutting a five-foot-wide butterfly out of a roll of craft paper, all the swirls and patterns of the wings cut in intricate detail. I wanted him to like it, or to at least think it was worth the effort, and I was shaking as we walked through the show.

When Matt saw my piece, he stopped dead in his tracks, dropping his program like he'd been shot by a freeze ray. He moved in closer, jaw hanging open in wonder, examining the natural shapes with lines so thin you could almost tear them with a sneeze. It felt like he was gaping at it for ages, though it was probably only a few seconds; still, when he turned back to look at me, he was different from moments before. There was a sparkle in his eye, a curiosity, that made my heart swell almost beyond my rib cage. He took my hands gently, slowly running his fingers over mine like he'd just unearthed a rare, newly discovered treasure, and asked, *"You made this?"*

And I'd never felt more whole, more seen, more connected to another human being.

Matt wasn't always there, but when he was, he made me feel like I was the only person in the world.

A burst of yelling from the museum entrance rips me from my memory, and Becca and I jump up to see what's going on. Stepping outside, onto Michigan Avenue, we see that crowds of people have gathered around the intersection in front of the Art

Institute, where a man is standing in the middle of the street. Unbothered by the cabs and cars honking all around him, he removes his jacket, revealing what looks to be a bomb strapped to his chest.

Everyone in the area starts screaming, and we're suddenly trapped in a stampede of people who have no idea where to go. Shoulders and backpacks slam into us as the museum doors become barricaded by bodies, leaving us no option but to climb up the bronze lion statues on the staircase, saving us from being trampled. Becca pulls me up, my cast making it difficult to climb, and we hide behind the lion's giant mane, hoping it will protect us from whatever is about to happen.

Instead of detonating a bomb, though, the man starts furiously flapping his arms, generating a red-and-orange fireball around his body. "The siege will prevail!" he yells, just before his pyrotechnics engulf him. The flames grow bigger and bigger, melting the asphalt below, until the street's structure can no longer hold, and a giant sinkhole crumbles, sending pedestrians, streetlights, cars, and a CTA bus over the edge, plummeting beyond sight. Screams echo down the street as Becca buries her face into my back, quivering in fear. But I can't look away.

Moments later, my heart leaps when I spot Vaporizer running toward the scene, a flash of white heading into danger while everyone else claws to get away. Behind him is that new girl—Joy, I think—awkwardly bumping into scared bystanders and trying to stay on Matt's trail. Once they reach the sinkhole,

Girl Power jumps in, lifting people up out of the hole and back to safety, while Vaporizer disappears in and out, working his way through the crowd to try to find the flame bomber villain. People cling to him, pulling at his hero suit, so he keeps turning invisible, staying in pursuit.

I've seen Matt in action plenty of times, not only in person but on recorded rescues he'd watch for training purposes. But this feels different somehow. Usually when I'm watching him work, it's because he's rescuing me, fighting tooth and nail to save his love. He'd be focused on his purpose, doing everything it took to get to his girlfriend in time. Here, on the corner of Michigan and Adams, he's lost, frazzled, frantically searching for a bad guy he can't find. He moves sloppily through the crowd, invisibility blinking in and out. He's off his game, and it's the kind of careless behavior that could get him hurt.

I want to yell to him, words of encouragement to snap him back into form, but there's no way he'd hear me over the calamity. He stands on the edge of the sinkhole, looking out into the panicked mayhem, and for a split second, I think he sees me, clinging to this lion. But then Girl Power is pushing the bus up out of the concrete crater, and he's back to helping victims as ambulances arrive on the scene.

Sirens wailing, Becca finally looks up, peering over my shoulder. After taking in the mess before us, she says, "Don't worry, B. He knows what he's doing."

And I hope she's right, because while Matt may no longer be in my world, I still need to know he's here.

Vaporizer Is Single!
HeroHearts.usa

The day we've all been waiting for has come: Vaporizer is a free man! Reputable sources claim Matt Rodriguez has finally detached from his longtime girlfriend, Bridgette Rey. While Warrior Nation does not comment on the heroes' romantic lives, both Matt and Bridgette have been spotted separately crying in public, and Matt's social media has gone dark. Vaporizer has been off the market since the day he entered our hearts, much to the dismay of his countless fans, but now that he's single, we expect Vaporizer fever to flame into a total frenzy.

182,000 Comments

@VaporLover29
OMG Matt's so hot this is the best news of my liiiiiiiiiiiiiiiiife

@hot4heroes
Yes yes yes all my dreams are coming true!

@invisiblegirlfriend
Can't believe he ever dated that B in the first place

@TruWarriorGrrl
MATT I'LL COMFORT YOU

CLAIRE

"AND WHERE DO YOU THINK YOU ARE GOING?"

My hand freezes on the doorknob, my mom somehow materializing out of thin air. I wanted to do something nice for her, to make up for the drama of last night's kidnapping, but it won't be as good if she gets mad at me first.

"Um, to get donuts?" I admit, caught in my good deed. "I figured we could both use the extra sugar rush after being up so late."

But despite her raging sweet tooth and weak spot for morning pastries, she's not having it. Arms crossed over the front of her fuzzy pink robe, dirty-blond bob sticking up on one side, she taps a fluffy bunny slipper and somehow makes it menacing. "You're not leaving. We can have oatmeal."

I turn my nose up. "Blech, am I being punished?"

"No . . . Yes . . . I'm not sure yet." She slumps down onto the couch, rubbing her hands over her tired face. Puffy half-moons hang under her bloodshot eyes, and she curls herself into a ball as I sit at her feet. "We need to talk about this internship."

I pause, mid-blanket-cocooning. "What do you mean?"

She clears her throat, propping her head up on a throw pillow. "I know how hard you've worked for this"—I don't like where this is going—"but working at Warrior Nation doesn't seem like a good idea anymore."

I feel like I'm stuck in some kind of gelatinous goo, like in *Blue Streak*, issue #134, where my favorite hero battled Sludge, trapped in his swamp of oozing muck. Fictionalized but based on real events, the comic depicts how Blue Streak became temporarily paralyzed by the glop, unable to move until Sludge finished his monologue about how easy it was to spread his treachery across the city. But eventually the Warrior found his strength, unwilling to listen to such nonsense. I have to do the same here, even if the opponent I'm facing is my own mother.

"Mom, I'm not quitting," I say firmly, confident in my resolve.

Her face hardens. "Claire . . ."

"I know last night sucked—"

"Last night was unbearable!" She sits up abruptly, robe falling open to reveal her teddy-bear pajamas. "Do you have any idea what it was like for me to not have my daughter come home? To receive a panicked call from Demi, crying that you had been attacked? I had no idea where you were, whether you were injured, or if I'd ever see you again." The more she talks, the closer she leans toward me, and I can feel the stress radiating off her skin. Hands balled up in the blanket, she squeezes the fabric like it's her only lifeline. "When I called the police, they connected me to Warrior Nation, but all they would tell me was that the heroes were 'on it,' whatever that means. They wouldn't give me any details, no indication as to whether or not you'd come home safe. All I could do was wait, checking the door and my phone on an endless loop, hoping to hear from you."

I pause before responding, collecting my thoughts. When you're in a debate, it's important to choose your words wisely and not counter out of pure passion. You don't win by losing your cool. "Mom, I hate that you went through all that. I'm so, so sorry." I reach for her trembling hand. "I never expected to be kidnapped, and it was terrifying. But . . . it doesn't change my commitment to Warrior Nation."

She squints, looking at me like I've lost my mind. "These people—these *villains*—they know who you are. They tracked you down, they attacked you! How can you not run from this screaming?"

I think about my abductor, hungrily running his hand over my thighs. How my skin felt ready to disintegrate in my panic. But then I think about Joy's hands on me afterward, how her touch made me feel so safe, so alive. Sure, there is risk being tied to this hero organization, but it's not without some pretty amazing perks.

"Those guys made a mistake; they thought I was someone else, that I would be willing to turn against the Warriors," I tell her. "It's not like that would ever happen again."

"You can't know that!" she scoffs. "And I can't be in a state of worry every time you're not with me!"

I've never seen her act like this before. As a single mother with only one child, Mom's always been protective but not to the point of keeping me from experiencing life. She's the kind of parent who threw me into a pool before I was ready to swim, who let me ride the CTA by myself when I was ten. My whole life she's encouraged me to be independent and not let anything stand in the way of my dreams. But now she looks one thought away from binding me in Bubble Wrap before I leave the apartment.

"You don't have to be scared," I reassure her.

"Of course I do!" She throws her hands up. "Claire, you are my whole life. And I can't knowingly send you into danger. Have you seen what's going on in this city?" She grabs for yesterday's *Chicago Tribune* sitting on the coffee table. "Just yesterday, they pulled four bodies out of the Chicago River. . . ."

"I know," I say sadly.

"You know?"

"Yeah, we . . . talked about it at our debriefing. That attack, my kidnapping, and some other stuff are all connected somehow. . . . It's like a siege against the Warriors."

Mom stands up, pushing her bangs up off her face. After pacing back and forth a few times, she makes her decision. "You are quitting."

"No!" I yelp, jumping up to meet her height. "You can't make that choice!"

"I am your mother! Protecting you is my job, and nothing is worth your life."

"But this is!" I fight back, completely losing my debate team composure. "Warrior Nation IS my life!"

She takes a breath, trying to keep this from exploding into a full-blown screaming match. "I know how much being a WarNat means to you."

"No, Mom, this is more than just fandom. This is it for me. Being part of this team, working for the Warriors . . . that's what I want to do. Forever."

"You're seventeen." She shakes her head. "You don't know where you'll end up after college, let alone forever."

The word "college" pierces a hole in my heart. I've been putting off this conversation for as long as humanly possible, but I guess the time has come. "Mom, I'm not going to college," I reveal, my voice shaky.

She stares at me, unable to process. Once the weight of my words finally settles, she almost shrinks an inch, like my plan has somehow increased the gravity pushing down on her body. "What are you . . . What are you talking about?"

"I don't want to keep going with school after I graduate."

"But . . . your grades, your extracurriculars! God, Claire, you're almost valedictorian!"

"I know." I rub my bare arm, feeling exposed after baring my secret. "I did all that for this. To get where I am, to get a foot in the door. Mom, I'm actually making a difference there! I've been helping with a new hero—Girl Power, the one who saved me. She listens to me, and other people do too!"

"But you have to get an education!"

"Why? Why do I have to? School is all about figuring out what you want to do with your life, but I already know! I've been in like a hundred clubs, and gotten As in every possible subject. But nothing has ever made me feel like this. Like all my time and talent could be put toward something that matters."

Mom eases herself into an armchair, spacing out. I kneel beside her, placing a hand on her teddy-bear pj pants. She turns, slowly, to face me, blue eyes welling with tears. "I just want what's best for you," she chokes out. "I'm trying to protect you."

"Mom, I love you, more than anything. But I'm almost an adult. I don't need your protection; I need your support."

A tear runs down her cheek, and I do my best to curl my lanky arms and legs up into her lap, holding her as she cries. I never meant for any of this to happen; I never meant to cause my mom pain. All I can do is try to be more careful, to make sure I never get in any dangerous situations again.

"I'm gonna make this okay, you'll see," I say as her tears begin to slow. "I'll do anything it takes to make you feel better about Warrior Nation. I'll live-tweet my commute to and from. . . . I'll check in every hour, on the hour. . . . I'll wear a GPS tracker!"

She gives a little laugh, wiping her face. "I trust you, you know that, right?" I nod. "I just don't trust anyone else."

"That's fair. The world is full of terrible people. But that's why I have to do this . . . to help fight them!"

Mom sniffles. "I'll take those donuts now."

"Really? Okay, I'll go to Kuppie's around the corner. You

want a bear claw and a chocolate sprinkle?" She smiles. "I'll be right back."

Stepping onto the sidewalk, I feel a wave of relief. Maybe Mom isn't 100 percent Team Warrior right now, but I talked her off the ledge of outright forbidding my future involvement. And that's all I need right now.

Kuppie's, our favorite bakery within walking distance, is a tiny, hole-in-the-wall spot that just happens to be filled with the most intoxicating vanilla-bean aroma I've ever encountered. Standing at the glass display case stocked with a tempting rainbow of pastries and treats, I almost get a sugar high just from breathing. It's a tough decision, but I eventually choose a lemon pistachio for myself, along with Mom's picks. Then I realize there's no one there to take my order.

"Hello?" I call out. I hear something coming from the back, like a muffled television, and after a few minutes of no one answering my calls, I tiptoe back to see what's delaying service. I need these donuts to cement Mom's belief in me!

"Hello?" I repeat, announcing my entry to the kitchen, only to find the staff crowded around a small TV tuned to the news. With everyone glued to the screen, no one even notices as I peer over.

Whoa. It looks like there was an incident by the art museum downtown . . . some kind of suicide bomber or something? Clearly I missed the beginning, but there's a giant sinkhole where Michigan Ave should be. My WarNat brain starts firing off possible villains who could have done this. . . . Crumbler?

Dr. Destroy? Aerial cameras swirl around the scene, capturing the absolute chaos of crying victims clinging to paramedics as officials try to ensure everyone is getting the care they need.

And then . . . Girl Power is on the screen! OMG, there she is! Giving a statement to the reporter. My heartbeat quickens as I search Joy's image for signs of injury or distress, but while her baby-blue suit is covered in dirt and debris, she looks okay. Better than okay: unscathed, and even maybe a little pumped up coming off her mission.

"What happened here today?" the reporter asks, shoving a microphone in Joy's face.

"It appears a villain known as Fuego set off a firebomb in the middle of the street," Girl Power states, voice calm and collected. "He's been known to use this power in previous crimes, escaping during the chaos that always ensues." The screen cuts away to earlier footage, showing Girl Power lifting an entire CTA bus up over her head and out of the sinkhole. Holy shit!

"Girl Power, this is one of your first official rescues as part of Warrior Nation," the reporter states. "How are you feeling?"

Joy smiles, her pearly whites beaming below her mask. "While I am disturbed by what took place here today, I'm proud to be part of this team, and I'm confident we'll be able to stop this siege."

Yes! She nailed it! None of that fear that plagued her last night. I knew she could do it, I knew it! I feel so proud, I instantly want to call her, to make sure she's okay, but before I can, a calendar reminder goes off in my phone.

Warrior Nation charity event, 7:00 p.m.

Oh, right, while Teddy wasn't looking, I uploaded the official Warrior Nation social calendar to my own personal account so I could invite myself to any cool events that I knew he'd fail to mention. This is perfect! I'll show up tonight, giving myself the chance to check on Joy and congratulate her on her victory today.

And by congratulate, I mean make out with her furiously.

Girl Power Sweeping Chicago

Get it, Girl! With a recent crime surge in Chicago, Girl Power has become a regular figure in the community, swooping in to save the day time and time again. Her recent rescue during a Michigan Ave attack has shot her star to meteoric status, with a receptive audience clamoring to know more about the woman behind the mask.

"I just love her!" exclaimed feminist blogger Katy Bloom. "She's showcasing the kind of power and strength that really packs a punch. That image of her lifting a bus over her head? ICONIC!"

While she's only been part of the Chicago chapter for a short time, Girl Power is already in high demand, as several prominent designers are itching to have her rep their brands. Images of her with the bus are being plastered on everything from T-shirts to stickers, and cosplay companies have already been selling out of her signature hero suit, a blue bodysuit with rose-gold triangle accents and accessories that allow any wearer to feel empowered.

"I just want to do a good job and help people," said Girl Power in a recent interview. "I wasn't looking to be a role model, but I'm honored to be bringing people joy."

With so much attention on this hot young star, it would not be surprising if she begins to outshine Warrior Nation's current poster child, Vaporizer.

@TruWarriorGrrl
uh excuse you but no one will ever top Vaporizer.
I'm all for girl power but like let's calm down

@NeverCeaseNeverSour
you are, like, a disgrace to feminism

@TruWarriorGrrl
eye roll all I'm saying is that Vaporizer is ESTABLISHED and Girl Power has been on the scene for like 5 seconds. Let's see what she can really do before we call her an icon

@GirlPowerSparksJoy
love all of this! Girl Power is my new all-time fave! She is everything!

BRIDGETTE

IT'S BEEN A LONG TIME SINCE I'VE BEEN OUT by myself. Or even gone out, period. There's not a huge paparazzi scene in Chicago, but Matt's smile never met a smartphone he didn't like. Showing up for a movie and having girls claw at your boyfriend while you're standing in line for popcorn gets old fast, so by the end, our limited time together consisted of exclusive showings and backdoor entrances. Even going out to grab a coffee on my own was often met with someone secretly recording me, and trying to act nonchalant about it was totally exhausting. Staying home became easier, and while I'm all for snuggling up on the couch, sometimes you have to force yourself to experience the world.

But you don't have to do THIS, nags the voice in my head. Warrior Nation charity events have never exactly been my favorite outings, since they usually unravel into war stories and shop talk as the night goes on. Still, I feel personally connected to tonight's gala, an auction benefiting arts education in Chicago public schools. It's an idea I floated to Millie months ago at the last event I attended, suggesting that Warrior Nation take a break from donating to firefighters and police precincts and experiment with being heroic in other ways. In the four years I've known her, Millie has been an impossible nut to crack, but somehow my idea slipped through, and she summoned me to HQ a couple times for brainstorming sessions. No matter how awkward it will be for me to show up single, I at least have to make an appearance. And, okay, secretly, I want to check on Matt. We don't have to talk; I just want to see him, to make sure he's okay after today's sinkhole trauma. Then I can go home and feel like I did something.

Standing on the sidewalk outside, I smooth out my black A-line skirt in the glow of the gallery window. "All That Shines" is the name of tonight's event, and the entrance is strung with an intricate web of fairy lights, hundreds of strands crisscrossing in a pattern that looks impossible to untangle. I take a deep breath, fluffing out my short waves with my good hand to give them any ounce of extra volume. *Just a quick appearance. See the exhibit, check on Matt, and get out.*

The place is packed, people laughing and clinking champagne flutes to the sound of tinkling chimes playing over the gallery speakers. The exhibit is all about artists experimenting with light, and there's a wide variety of mediums showcasing the theme. A sculpture made of shattered mirrors casts twinkling sparkles all over the room, while a large installation of flickering Edison bulbs blinks phrases in Morse code. There are also several blinking LCD screens, playing a looped video showing extra-close-ups of shiny objects like tinsel and diamonds. I weave through the crowd, though not undetected, as familiar faces and strangers alike recognize me, each looking past me for a certain superhero, confused when they realize I'm alone. But I keep moving, doing my best to avoid small talk so I can complete my mission as quickly as possible.

"Bridgette!" calls a female voice from the crowd, and I cringe, not wanting to engage in any kind of post-breakup interrogation. I turn to see Anna waving furiously at me. I give her a friendly nod, which she takes as an invitation to bop over like a tiny woodland mouse, larger-than-large eyes taking me in with absolute curiosity. "Oh my gosh, are you okay? I heard that you and Matt broke up! And your hand, it's broken? Oh no, that's terrible! What about your art? How are you handling all this? Do you need something? A drink? A goat-cheese-stuffed mushroom cap? They're really good, I can get you one. But, oh, are you allergic to dairy? I—"

"Anna, it's okay, I'm fine," I interrupt her, knowing she could continue this one-sided conversation for a very long time. Every time I see her, she rambles on and on until she's completely sure that every person in her vicinity is cared for. Matt and I joked that it must be her coping mechanism, since having a boyfriend who throws himself into danger is a situation she cannot control. Offering people beverages or a shoulder to cry on is her own little way of saving the world.

"But you and Matt! Oh my god, I'm devastated!" she continues, clutching the front of her dress. "You've always been my inspiration. The way you've stayed together through all this craziness? Wow, it's just . . . Wow! Like sometimes I feel like I'm going to explode when I know Ryan is fighting, you know? What am I saying, of course you know! It's so hard! He's so strong but it's so much, and now there's this siege and—"

"Geez, Anna, give the girl some room," says Houston, swooping in to save me from Anna's ramble. He puts some space between us, though Anna quickly darts back around him to ensure she's not left out. "Nice to see you, Bridgette."

"You too," I say with a warm smile. "You both look really nice."

"Aw, thanks, but I'm nothing compared to my girl," Houston says, nodding at Aqua Maiden across the room. She's way over-dressed in a floor-length green-sequined gown, long red hair falling down her back. Of all the heroes, she's always been my least favorite, exceedingly fake and only in it for the fame. But Houston is crazy for her, and never misses a chance to compliment his lady. "You know, even if you and Matt are . . . separated . . . it doesn't mean you can't reach out. We can still have our regular Super Adjacent Club brunches."

"Oh, yes! I love those brunches!" Anna beams, pulling on the arm of Houston's suit. "Especially when there's an omelet station. Or a buffet! Because then you can eat as much as you want. And breakfast food is so good! Definitely the best of all types of food."

I laugh, thinking about what a strange trio we make for those monthly gatherings. Neither Houston nor Anna have been in the Warrior Nation world as long as I have, and when we were all getting acquainted, we joked about how weird it is to date a superhero. To be so close to so much power, but to have none of our own. And since we all signed airtight NDAs, it makes it hard to share our experiences with our actual friends, so we started venting to each other over eggs and coffee, talking about how annoying it is to be stood up for dates just because some villain is having a tantrum, or how being kidnapped always happens at the least convenient time.

"Sure, that'd be fun. I can tell you about how I got this." I raise my cast, but before Anna can spill into another soliloquy, Aqua Maiden strides over, tossing her hair in my face as if I'm not even here.

"I'm bored," she says to Houston, pressing her chest up against him. His face turns all kinds of red as he breaks into a goofy smile. "Art is lame. Let's go somewhere more interesting."

"Yeah, okay, that's fine," he agrees as she runs red fingernails over his chest.

"Go get my purse and call a cab." She saunters off, the crowd parting at her whim. He gives us a little wave before heading after her like an obedient lapdog.

"Ugh, art is *lame*?" I scoff once they're gone. "Houston could do so much better."

Anna nods, giant eyes blinking in agreement. "Yeah, but you know boys! They get so flustered by hot girls, they stop thinking. I'm glad Ryan's not like that. Or maybe he is. . . . Do you think he is? No, no way. I should go find him! Make sure he's not getting distracted! There are a lot of pretty girls here. I'll find you later, okay?" She disappears without getting an answer, and I decide I better find Matt before getting sidelined again.

The gallery is packed, making it exceedingly hard to track him down. Maybe he didn't show? Or maybe he is here, choosing to stay invisible. After two full laps, I've yet to find him, so I stop at an appetizer table, lingering over the impressive selection of cheeses. After several helpings of Brie, I feel a pair of eyes on me—my least favorite sensation—and when I turn, it's that girl who was tied to a chair with me. What was her name again? Blair?

"Oh, hey," she says, swallowing down a chunk of gouda. "Sorry, I didn't mean to stare at you."

"Don't worry about it, it happens more than you'd think."

She frowns. "I bet. It must be weird. Having total strangers recognize you? I mean, I'm a WarNat through and through, but some of us are . . . a lot. I remember reading about what happened at your high school graduation. . . ."

I nod. "Well, you're not wrong. I once had a girl run up to me on the street and throw half a milk shake in my face, saying that I was a witch who put a spell on Matt and forced him to love me instead of her."

"What? That's awful! And what a waste of perfectly good ice cream."

"I know. It was a tragedy on many levels." Purple hair smoothed back into a low bun, wearing a simple but sweet polka-dotted dress, the girl beams at me, friendly and eager. I cringe at my forgetfulness and say, "I'm sorry, I feel like the biggest jerk, but what is your name again?"

"Oh! It's Claire. Claire Rice." She extends her hand but then lowers it, instantly realizing I can't exactly complete a handshake with this cast.

"Nice to meet you again," I say. "That day we met . . . it was a lot, and my brain is kind of a mess right now, so I'm sorry."

"Don't worry, I get it. I heard about . . . your whole thing." She grimaces, but kindly doesn't press, quickly changing the subject. "I've never been to something like this before. It's pretty cool."

"Well, Warrior Nation loves a good party," I say, looking around at all the half-tipsy guests. "Donating to charity makes people forget how much they make a profit off of saving people's lives, and with everything that's going on right now, they need some good press." Claire's eyebrows furrow, taking in my comment. Crap, I have to remember that not everyone has been put through the wringer by this organization, and some people want to believe in all the glitz and glamour. I pinch my lips, making a silent vow not to say anything else even remotely negative. "But, you know, it's also fun and very cool that they're supporting the arts tonight."

Before she can comment on my Warrior bashing, Girl Power comes up to Claire from behind, playfully tapping her shoulder. "Hey, killer! I found you!" she says, and Claire whips around, instantly lighting up, breaking into a starstruck smile.

"Hey! Hi!" she says awkwardly, and the two of them hug, lingering longer than your average embrace. "Joy, have you met Bridgette?"

"No. Hey, what's up?" The blonde gives me a quick nod, clearly uninterested in conversing with anyone else but Claire. Joy's blond waves swirl around her shoulders, and she's wearing a tight pair of tuxedo pants and a low-cut top. She steps closer to Claire, the two of them sharing a quick, knowing look. Claire must be Joy's date. They certainly look ready for something romantic to happen, and they make a cute couple for sure.

"Nice to meet you, Joy," I say, though she couldn't care less. "I, um, I was outside the Art Institute this morning; I saw what you did, raising that bus out of the sinkhole. It was really impressive."

This gets her attention. "Oh yeah? Thanks! It was super intense! I'd never lifted anything that big before."

Claire jumps in. "Seriously, Joy! A whole bus! Damn! I saw it on the news. You looked . . . amazing." She blushes, twisting her hands behind her back.

"Well, I couldn't have done it without your pep talk," Joy says, gazing at Claire's mouth.

"I'm pretty sure you could have. You're the one with the super strength." Claire's ears turn red.

Suddenly feeling like a major third wheel, I turn my attention back toward the cheese, topping a cracker with a cheddar spread. Joy and Claire start talking more softly; then Joy darts off into the crowd, leaving Claire to stare after her with cartoon hearts practically floating out of her eyes. I crunch my snack in amusement.

"Hey, um, I gotta go," she manages to say. "But would it be okay if I text you sometime? Just cause . . . I have some questions? About Warrior stuff. Stuff that I don't really know anything about. And I figure you must be the expert."

I bite my lip. "I don't know if you want advice from me."

"No, I really, really do. There's literally no one else I can talk to, and stuff is . . . happening. Please?" she begs.

"You may not like what I have to say."

"It's okay, I want the truth." She hands me her phone, and I save my number in her contacts. "Thanks. I gotta go find . . . someone." I watch her get swallowed up by the room, wondering where the two of them are sneaking off to. Good for them. Someone should be able to find love here, even if I failed so spectacularly.

Feeling tired, I give up on finding Matt, unwilling to do more laps in these heels, which is how I immediately bump right into Matt's chest, spilling his pop all over the both of us.

"Ack, sorry!" he yelps, wiping his tie with a napkin. His dark eyes widen when he realizes the soda spiller is me. "Oh. Hey, Bridge," he says softly, suddenly disinterested in the wet splotch on his shirt. "I didn't know you would be here."

"Small world," I say, my voice shaking in surprise. I reach for a napkin of my own to blot the top of my dress. We stand there for a second, taking each other in. I do a quick inspection— no new bandages, stiches, or wounds that I can see—assuming that means he made it out of today's incident unscathed. I sigh in relief, happy he's okay. But now I'm left with the awkwardness of standing with my ex-boyfriend.

"Man, have these events always been so weird?" he asks, thankfully breaking the tension. "I mean, everyone here is just talking about work. Like, take a break, guys! It's a party! No one's even mentioning all the cool stuff in this place."

"You never noticed?" I ask, suppressing a smile. "That's always how these nights go."

"Really? That must have been so boring for you. Why didn't you ever mention it?"

"I did."

"Oh." He frowns, swallowing this information like a lump of coal. We walk a few steps, stopping in front of a tower of teetering mirrored balls, stacked precariously in a corner. I catch pieces of us in their warped, convex shapes—his shoulder, my knee—turning us into fun-house versions of ourselves. We look just as wrong as I feel, standing next to him, my now-ex-boyfriend, in this new reality where our love story came to an end. I never wanted it to be like this, to create the chasm between us, yet here we are, two halves of a former whole, trying to exist in the same space. "I was a shitty boyfriend," I hear him whisper.

"Matt . . ." I sigh deeply, not ready to talk about this. Especially not here.

"No, I'm serious. I've been thinking about everything you said. I can't stop thinking about it, actually." In the mirrored balls, I catch him repeatedly tightening and releasing a fist, a nervous habit he's had since high school. The WarNats think it's some kind of intimidation move, making villains think he's about to throw a punch, but it's actually just Matt trying to psych himself up. "You are right, about everything. Of course you're right. I let all the hero stuff take over. I was doing what I thought I was supposed to—saving the world and all that—but I didn't take care of you."

I meet his eyes, sad but earnest. Dark brown pools of regret stare down at me, and it's hard to keep my composure. How long have I wanted to hear those words, for him to acknowledge his behavior and its effect on our relationship? Getting an apology now, after we've already said goodbye, is completely bittersweet.

"I . . . appreciate you saying that," I say, forcing myself to remember why we're done in the first place. "But it doesn't change anything right now."

He stands tall, breathing deeply through his nose, and I prepare myself for some kind of retort or quip at my response. But surprisingly, it doesn't come.

"Okay, I can respect that." He walks to the next piece—a canvas covered in stripes of iridescent paint—and his acceptance of my wishes is so unexpected, so selfless, so not Matt, that I have to follow him, if only to be sure his body hasn't been snatched by some personality-swapping evil genius.

"I'm sorry, what's going on with you right now?" I ask, tugging at his suit jacket. It fits him like a glove. "Where's the Matt

Rodriguez who wants to sweep everything under the rug and just pretend everything is okay?"

"Oh, that guy? Yeah. Turns out he's a terrible person, so I took care of him." He slices a finger across his throat, tongue hanging from the corner of his mouth.

I stifle a laugh. "Just like that?"

"Just like that. I am a hero, after all. It's my job to rid the world of assholes, so I did." He smiles, not the toothy cheeseball smirk splattered on T-shirts and posters, but a sweet, authentic grin. It's like seeing a ghost, but not a spandex one, more like a ghost of my past: the face of the boy I fell in love with. No winking, no posing, just a real human look that's so unexpected, it throws me for a total loop. *Where have you been hiding? Why did you disappear for so long?*

"Well, rest in peace," I say, working hard to keep a straight face. I don't want him sensing how fast my heart is beating.

"I miss you, Bridge," he says throatily.

My voice catches at his honesty. "We just broke up."

"I know, but it already feels like a lifetime. I hate it. You've been by my side for four years, and now . . . do you think we could still be friends?"

Friends? We were never really friends. Our attraction was instantaneous, and things took off from there. "Matt . . ."

"I just . . . I don't know how to exist without you. We've been together so long, and . . . do you know how hard it is not to call or text you? I've basically written you an entire novel of texts that I've deleted. I don't want to lose that connection. I don't want to miss all the good stuff." I raise an eyebrow. "Not *that* stuff—I mean, yes, I miss that too—but like . . ." He looks around, trying to find the words. "Look at this." He points to a prism suspended in the middle of a fishbowl. "Like, what is this? Your art is way better than half the stuff here, and someday you're going to be this successful artist. I don't want some random dude at your side; it should be me, the one who's seen all your drafts, your experimentation, your evolution. I'm the one who understands, and I want to be in it. Part of the action, supporting you however you need. I want to stay in your orbit."

It's so much, so sudden, and I don't know what to do. My heart wants to trust what he's saying, but my head says no. "I need time, Matt, to figure this out. We just broke up, and I'm trying to understand how I feel. Because, to be honest, I'm not sure I can be just friends with you. I like the idea, but it's too soon. I need to do stuff on my own for a while, you know?" I feel breathless, light-headed, letting it all out before I change my mind.

He frowns but then pinches his mouth in acceptance. "I don't, but I want you to be happy." He leans in, kissing my forehead lightly, heat spreading from his lips. "I'll disappear if you want—" But before he can finish his sentence, the lights flicker, and the entire room descends into darkness. A few screams ring out, and Matt steps closer to me, our arms touching. It's pitch-black, my eyes yet to adjust, but I look up to where he is just the same, knowing his hero senses are probably on hyper alert.

The TV screens throughout the gallery flick back on, only

this time they're not showing pretty images of glitter and sparkly jewelry. A man wearing a black helmet that hides his entire head flashes onto the screens. An uneasy murmur ripples through the crowd. He doesn't move, staring at us all from many vantage points, and after a few seconds that feel like years, he speaks, though his voice is distorted.

"Warrior Nation, your time has come to an end," he threatens, in a strange, robotic voice. "Your powers shall no longer reign supreme. Surrender your capes, or the siege will continue." The longer I stare at his image, the more I realize it's not the first time I've seen this villain in black. That weird voice, the huge helmet . . . he was at my kidnapping!

"Matt!" I whisper-screech, reaching for him in the dark. "I know that guy! He was there, at the warehouse where I was kidnapped! He had some other lackeys with him, and Claire thought maybe he was their leader!"

My eyes finally adjusting to the dark, I see him nod in recognition. "We don't know who he is, though," he says, worried. "I, um . . . haven't been able to sleep, so I've been digging around HQ for more information on all of this. There's no record of him. He's the only guy in this siege we haven't been able to identify. I'm going to keep looking—"

The screens cut to black, but the show isn't over, because spraying from the vents above is a white vapor that descends over us with terrifying efficiency.

"It's poisonous gas!" someone screams, and the room erupts, everyone pushing and shoving to get to the front door. Matt picks me up and throws me over his shoulder, quickly darting in the other direction to find a less congested exit. I hold on to him as he moves through the panicked throng, glasses breaking as tables flip over and artwork is forever ruined.

"Hold your breath!" he demands as the vapor reaches the middle of the room. I fill my lungs and pinch my mouth shut, eyes starting to sting from whatever is trying to kill us. Using his shoulder, Matt opens a back door, setting me down on the concrete in the alley. "Are you okay?" he exhales, out of breath, running a hand through my hair.

I nod, taking some deep breaths, and then he removes his suit jacket and covers his face, diving back into the poisoned room to help others get to safety. With his help, several more people join me on the ground, each of us awkwardly sitting in our cocktail attire. Finally, when the gallery is cleared, Matt flops down beside me, hair sweaty and eyes red.

"Breathe," I tell him, placing a hand on his chest, feeling it rise and fall. He saved me—again—but I can tell these back-to-back rescues are wearing on him. Normally, he'd be working the crowd, posing for pictures and making dumb puns like "Well, that was a gas!" or something, but instead he just lies there, slowly letting his body relax.

This siege is relentless, pushing the heroes to their limits.

I'm terrified Matt will reach his.

Anyone crack this siege yet?

WarriorHunt.usa

Ever since the siege began, WarNats everywhere have been trying to track the attacks and nail down the plan. But this is like nothing we've ever seen. Villains usually follow a set of patterns, committing the same kinds of crimes over and over, but everything that's been done in name of the siege so far is completely random, from kidnapping, to robbery, to vandalism. I've been trying to connect the dots, but I've reached my limit. Anyone figure this out yet?

> **@WNlyfer**
> no. It's a mystery. Which is weird. At this point you would've thought these Anti Heroes or whatever would've made some kind of specific demand.

> **@GirlPowerSparksJoy**
> it's freaking me out because anything could happen at any time. I don't leave the house much anyway but now I really don't want to

> **@VaporLover29**
> I recently reread the Rise of Warrior Nation series and it kinda makes me think of that time NYC was under a blackout after the Squids attacked? Except that they were radioactive sea monsters, but still.

> **@SillyMouseTrap**
> lol that's a deep cut. That series is bonkers

> **@TruWarriorGrrl**
> the Warriors look WRECKED so they better figure this out soon

CLAIRE

I'M WORRIED. JOY IS AN HOUR and three minutes late for our date. Our first real date that doesn't involve impromptu make-out sessions in a supply closet. Or maybe it will, I don't know, but it has to start first. I've been sitting in this booth the whole time, ears perking up like an anxious rabbit every time someone walks through the door, only to slump back down in disappointment. After three minutes, I double-checked my phone to make sure I was in the right place: yup, Portillo's on Ontario. Five minutes later, after showing tremendous restraint, I sent her a quick "hey r u on ur way" message, heavily edited from the original "do you still want to grab hot dogs and shakes because I'm here but if you've changed your mind I understand." A full thirty minutes sans response later, the scent of french fries became too strong, and I started munching on a fresh batch with cheese sauce. At forty-five minutes past, a wave of angry questions crashed over me. *Where is she? Why hasn't she responded to my texts?* Even if she's out saving the world, a simple emoji would do. Or have Siri reply with a quick "Sorry! Kicking ass and taking names! Be there soon!"

And now I've come full circle, worry flooding my veins. Things have been too good for her to randomly ghost me. She's always finding ways to visit me at work, taking me off coffee duty or whatever random busywork Teddy throws my way, pulling rank to say she needs my help, when really she just wants to hang out. Not to mention she kisses me like no one else ever has before. That has to count for something, I know it.

Something must be wrong. I trash my fry container and head outside, looking up and down the sidewalk to make sure I don't see her coming, and when I don't, I start picturing Joy in various states of distress: dangling off the Hancock building, tied to the L tracks, buried under Wrigley Field. *God, brain, how is this helpful?!* Breaking into a light jog, piles of potatoes sitting heavy in my stomach, I hope a run will burn off some anxious energy. But the scary Joy-in-danger scenes keep coming, causing the liquefied cheese product in my gut to make a sudden and urgent reappearance. Orange-colored vomit hits the sidewalk as I hear Millie's monotone voice cutting through my Girl Power death montage.

"Significant others are often a Warrior's first line of defense," Millie told me a few days ago, after a very panicked Anna called in to say Earthquake wasn't returning her calls. "It is very likely they will know their hero is missing before anyone else." I pull out my security card, flipping it over to find the emergency 800 number on the back. While Joy isn't technically my girlfriend—yet—we have been spending a lot of time together, and I don't think she'd ditch me if she wasn't in danger. Do I dial? What if it's a false alarm? What if I'm getting all worked up over nothing, and Joy is just blowing me off? I will be crazy embarrassed if she ends up being fine and this is the most extreme way of being dumped. On the other hand, I won't be able to live with myself if not calling means she actually gets hurt.

I call the number, entering my Warrior Nation pin number when prompted. As the line rings, I look around for an inconspicuous place to talk, since I guess I shouldn't really be blabbing sensitive information in public, but the groaning buses and screeching train tracks rolling past Chicago Ave make it hard to hear much of anything, so hopefully I'm okay.

"Warrior Nation emergency response. Am I speaking to Claire Rice?" a chipper female voice answers.

Whoa. I didn't expect the operator to call me by name, though I guess the Warriors have way more sophisticated technology beyond caller ID. The emotion of the moment scrambles my memory, mixing up the prompt I'm supposed to deliver in times of crisis. "Hi, um, yes. I'd like to report a"—Broken? Endangered? Stolen?—"missing hero."

"And which Warrior is this in reference to?" the operator asks, a keyboard clacking in the background.

"Girl Power," I choke out, again tortured by the thought of Joy in peril.

"One moment, please, while I retrieve her most current status." She puts me on hold as the Warrior Nation theme music plays, a blaring set of triumphant horns that would normally bring me comfort, but today, the loud brass rattles rather than inspires. What I could really use is some gentle harp strings or whale sounds. Either would be more soothing right now.

The music cuts out abruptly. "Claire? Thank you for holding," the operator resumes. "Joy checked in at her home address about ten minutes ago. According to her report, she and Vaporizer intervened in a bank robbery that turned violent. She sustained a head injury but is in stable condition with Warrior Nation medical personnel stationed at her home."

"Injured, injured, injured" is all I hear as the woman goes into autopilot, reading me a brief guide on stress-relief techniques and how to deal with trauma. But no deep breathing or visualization exercises will get me through this. I need to get to Joy, NOW, and see how I can help.

*

In the cab ride over, my head swelled with grand gestures of healing and support: me, kneeling at Joy's bedside, gently dabbing her forehead with a warm wash cloth while whispering words of encouragement. But now, standing outside her South Side apartment, I feel ridiculous, completely unequipped to handle whatever is waiting on the other side of her front door. Who am I kidding? I'm not a healer. I once fainted while trying to get my first aid badge in Girl Scouts, the only patch I never earned. The operator said Joy was stable, but how severe was her injury? Did she get punched in the face, or is her brain leaking out of her ears? Neither option is acceptable, but the truth is, she's hurt. How can I help her get through this when I'm not even sure I can stomach it?

I swallow hard as I ring the buzzer. The operator gave me the address, though I'd hoped my first visit to Joy's place would be under better circumstances, like a Netflix-and-chill session. But there are no smiles when her mom answers the door, eyeing me like she was afraid the grim reaper would be on the other side.

"Yes?" she says, voice sounding like it's been through a rock tumbler. Despite the worry lines crisscrossing her face, it's clear Joy gets her good looks from her mom. They share the same thick golden hair and voluptuous shape, though her mom's blue eyes lack the sparkle I'm so used to seeing in Joy's.

"Hi. Um, I'm Claire, I . . . work with Joy."

Her face hardens. "Did Warrior Nation send you?"

My heart sinks a little when she doesn't recognize my name. Part of me hoped Joy would've mentioned me at home. "No, not officially, but, um . . . can I see her? We're friends."

I recognize the dead-tired look on her face, like she's been on a red-eye to hell and back. It's the same way my mom looked at me when I got home from my kidnapping, a mix of desperation and despair spiked with horror. Whatever happened to Joy must have shaken her family to the core, and my mounting terror threatens to churn up whatever's left in my stomach.

Her mom nods, cautiously opening the door farther to let me through, and I'm surprised by what I see. Joy's apartment is smaller than small, technically a one-bedroom but with a small kitchenette in the living room. A messy Murphy bed hangs open, almost touching the stove, with cardboard boxes packed with stuff taking up almost every inch of available floor space. Looking at the cramped living quarters, it occurs to me that in between kisses Joy and I have never really talked about her home life, although she's alluded to how being a hero will "make things better." I just thought she meant better for the world, not her personal circumstances.

Her mom starts leading the way through the piles of stuff, and all the mess is giving me severe claustrophobia. Just before we reach the bedroom door, she pauses, turning around to address me. "Claire, can I ask you something?"

"Of course," I say.

"What do you think of Warrior Nation?"

Words catch in my throat. "Awesome," "inspiring," and "best thing that ever existed" don't feel appropriate right now, my heart unable to conjure up its usual excitement. It's weird for me not to burst into a long diatribe on how this organization is basically the most important group of people in the entire world, but I can't muster up any other feeling but fear. Mrs. Goodwin stares at me, eyes begging for some kind of reassurance, but I struggle to think of what would appease her right now.

"Well. Heroes help people. They save lives," I offer, flashing back to my childhood rescue with Blue Streak. I've never thought about him outside of his professional duties. . . . What did he do after he saved the day? When he flew out of the train and pulled bullets from his body, did he go home and nurse his wounds? Did he cry in relief that he made it out alive yet again? Or did that event barely register, just another day at the office? Blue Streak saving me was one of the most formative experiences of my life, but for him, it's probably just a blip on his long career of wins. Maybe that's how it will be for Joy someday. "A Warrior saved my life when I was little. I don't know if I'd be here today if it weren't for him."

Nodding but not quite accepting the sentiment, she replies, "It's just all so dangerous. Joy is so young. She's been out fighting almost every day. . . ."

"And she's doing amazing work! I mean, the bus thing? That was huge! I've already started seeing WarNat fan art online of Girl Power carrying a bus on her shoulders." But this doesn't make her smile like I'd hoped. Maybe she needs to see how cool it looks? "Here, I'll show you." I pull out my phone to find the image, but her mom shakes her head.

"No, I . . . don't like seeing my daughter in danger."

"Oh, this is more like a hero pose. Very inspiring—"

"NO," she says with more force, then presses her fingers into her temples, ashamed. "I'm sorry, but I've had enough with heroes for today."

Okay, I tell myself, *when you see Joy, you have to be brave. Don't let her see how completely terrified you are. She needs you, just like you needed Blue Streak. You can do this, you can do this. Never cease, never cower.*

But the second I get a glimpse of Joy, head wrapped in a giant bandage, my resolves crumbles and my hands fly up to cover my mouth. Lying on a pile of bohemian-style pillows on the bottom bunk of a bunk bed, Joy reclines like a beaten Sleeping Beauty, bandaged hands in her lap and a damp fishtail braid snaking down her neck. A shadow of blood seeps through the head wrap, a small waste bin filled with used medical supplies by her bed, the scent of antiseptic in the air. Joy's dad stands in the back corner, whispering to a Warrior Nation doctor in scrubs.

"Greg," Joy's mom says, talking to her husband. "Greg. Joy's friend is here." He turns our way, tired eyes taking me in. "This is Claire," she adds.

He raises his eyebrows in acknowledgment, gesturing for me to come in. "Thank you for coming, Claire," he says, his voice sounding far away. Upon hearing my name, Joy opens her eyes. She's pale, void of her usual magnetism, but smiles when she sees me. Two fat tears stream down my face, betraying my goal for courage. So much for heroism.

"Hey, killer," Joy slurs, blurry from pain meds. She tries to push herself up despite her wrapped hands, and her determination to be strong even when she's battered floors me. Some people are born to be heroes. Joy is one of them. "I'm ssssorry I missed our date."

Our date? OUR DATE? "God, Joy, who even cares about that?!" I kneel at her side, stroking her forearm in concern where a series of tubes feed her medicine. "I'm just glad you're okay!"

Her parents excuse themselves to the living room, the

Warrior Nation doctor following. I lean in closer, wanting to kiss her but worried I'd hurt her somehow. "Joy, what happened?"

Her eyes flutter as her heavy head flops my way. "The police called us to a scene as backup—those guys that kidnapped you? They were robbing a bank. Hostages, guns: the whole thing. Matt and I snuck in the back, and after we took out those goons . . ." She pauses. "The guy with that weird black helmet thing? He picked up a safe and threw it at my head."

I cringe, the mere suggestion of metal scraping scalp making me squirm. She continues. "It just grazed me, but . . . I must have blacked out. Mom said they brought me home from the HQ hospital this morning, but I don't even remember being there."

I squeeze her hand, and she winces, quickly pulling it away. I squeal, "Oh god, I'm sorry!"

Joy frowns but then shakes her head. "My hands hurt more than anything. Those guys were wearing some kind of rock-hard protective armor, and no one tells you how much it hurts to throw a punch. Matt says I'll get used to it."

This is different from her other incidents. Her first real injury. And I know she says she's okay, but she sure doesn't look it, hooked up to an IV with a full bolt of bandage around her head. I get that she's on massive drugs right now, but she's making her attack seem like no big deal, while I am completely freaking out inside. "How is it that you're handling this so much better than I am?"

"Maybe all your Warrior teachings are finally rubbing off on me." I'm glad she's in good spirits, but I'm having a hard time with all of this, especially since her parents are fighting outside the door. In between Joy's words, I catch snippets of theirs through the thin walls.

"It's not worth it, Greg!" her mom shouts. "I don't care if we signed that new lease. She's getting hurt!"

"We agreed—Joy agreed—to be a Warrior for a year," her dad says, pained. "One year to make some money for the family and then quit. I know today's been hard, but try to see the positives. She's getting endorsement offers—"

"Are you kidding me right now? We can't put our daughter through this just to make some money. . . ."

"I don't feel good about it either, Marsha, but what are we supposed to do? She signed a contract! We need her to get through this!"

Wait a minute . . . what? Girl Power's only planning on being a hero for a year? She has never—ever—mentioned that before.

Joy reaches with her wounded hand for mine. "I'm really glad you're here."

I know this probably isn't the right time to ask, but I'm having a hard time understanding what I just heard. "Joy . . . is that all true?"

Her head slumps deeper into the pillow as she exhales deeply. "I mean . . . yeah? It was at first. It wasn't my lifelong dream to save the world, you know that. But the Warrior recruiter shoved a lot of dollar signs in my face. And my family needed the money. . . ."

I blink rapidly, trying to process. "Did your parents force you into this?"

"No, god, nothing like that. I wanted to do it, for all of us. Being a Warrior for one year will make more money than either of them could in a lifetime."

My chin crumples into my neck in disgust. I don't like what she's saying; Warrior Nation is not some get-rich-quick scam. "Being a hero is an honor, not a paycheck," I say, disappointed.

"C'mon, don't look at me like that," she objects, trying to sit up in her bed but struggling to find the strength.

"Like what?"

"Like I just kicked a sack full of puppies."

I cross my arms. "That's not what I'm thinking."

"No, you're thinking Warrior Nation is some sacred birthright and how dare I belittle this position by thinking of trivial things like money when people's lives are on the line. Am I close?"

Shit. Did she recently pick up telepathy as a superpower? "Well . . . yeah. I don't think you realize what you've started here. You took a spot in this chapter when there were probably hundreds of other hopefuls. People are already invested in you, your story. What would it do to them—your fellow Warriors—if you just picked up and left?" I don't understand how she could even consider that option. After all her training and all this buildup. This isn't some random part-time job;

becoming a Warrior is the beginning of a legacy. How do you walk away from being a hero, the most incredible gift there is?

"So Warriors never quit?" she asks. "Isn't Blue Streak's retirement the whole reason I'm here?"

The knife digs deeper. "Yeah, and he left a giant-size hole in the hearts of WarNats everywhere. A hole that you're starting to fill. What you do now means something, Joy. You can't just make people fall in love with you and then disappear." My teeth clench, realizing I've hit my own nerve. If she can easily drop the affection of an entire city, will she do the same to me?

"Hey." With much effort, she rolls onto her side, getting her face as close to mine as possible. "Listen to me. I'm not going anywhere."

"Not now, anyway," I grumble, looking away.

"No. Not ever."

I turn back, hopeful. Despite her fragile state, her expression is fiercely resolute. "Did I start this gig for money? Yes. But these past couple days, fighting against the siege, something clicked. I've saved people's lives and it's . . . changed me." A grin spreads across her bruised face. "People are thanking me in the streets. I'm making a real difference. I didn't expect to feel this way, but I don't think being a hero is something I could give up. Not now, now that I know how it feels. Now that I know you."

"Really? What about your parents?"

She rolls her eyes. "I'm not gonna tell them now, not when my head is all wrapped up scary. By the time this year is over,

I'll be eighteen, so I can make my own choices. And I know what I want."

Joy touches my cheek, cotton bandage grazing my skin. I should feel relieved, but I'm still unsure. My heart is in this for the long haul, and she's a little all over the place. The night she rescued me, Joy didn't think she could ever jump into another battle; now suddenly she loves it? What if she changes her mind again? What if one bad fight or bad guy takes her down and she decides she's over it?

What would the Warriors do? What would I do?

This world means everything to me, and I don't like the idea of it being toyed with. But for now, I rest my head on her mattress, letting her run her fingers through my hair, and feeling thankful she's okay.

Hey Bridgette this is Claire :)

Hey what's up

Can we meet up sometime? I need some help

R u okay? R u in danger?

No nothing like that. More of a personal thing
Related to heroes
I don't want to write it down but I know you'd understand

Oh okay. But like I said I'm not sure if you really want
advice from me

Trust me I do
Meet me at HQ tomorrow?

Is there anywhere else we can meet?

I'm working all day, and my mom is being real strict
about me coming home immediately after

Okay I'll make it work
See u then

BRIDGETTE

DESCENDING INTO HQ VIA THE LYRIC OPERA HOUSE, I can feel my blood pressure rising. There was a time when I loved coming here, when using a top secret entrance into a hero lair was the coolest thing in the world. I'd hang out just for fun, exploring all the different training rooms while I waited for Matt to be done with his official business. The zero-gravity chamber was my favorite; Matt and I would sneak in there, wrap our arms and legs around each other as we spun around a simulated night sky. We'd do the waltz or country line dance, neither of us knowing the steps but taking every chance we could to find the other's ticklish spot or sneak a midair kiss. Every visit to HQ was full of adventure, and I'd leave ready for my next visit.

But that feels like a really long time ago.

The elevator opens, and I'm met by a burly security guard blocking the next door. He stares at me, or at least I think he does, since he's wearing blackout sunglasses even though we're several feet underground. I know most of the Warrior Nation staff at least by name, but I don't recognize him. After a very awkward staring contest during which neither of us moves, I finally ask, "Um, is there a problem?"

"Name," he says, not a question.

"Bridgette Rey."

He taps his tablet with a meaty finger. "There's a problem with your clearance. Wait here." He disappears through the sliding door, leaving me alone in the five-by-five-foot room. I thought this might happen. Now that Matt and I are no longer together, I can't imagine Warrior Nation will continue letting me come and go as I please. Not that I'd really have any reason to, besides Claire asking me here today.

The guard returns, only now he's joined by Teddy, Millie's conniving assistant. Great. Black hair slicked back like a helmet with a stiff pomade, white button-down starched to within an inch of its life, he gives me a slimy smile, reaching for me like we're long-lost best friends.

"Bridgette," he oozes, and I do my best to contort my face into a friendly expression. "So sorry about the inconvenience here, but with this whole siege going on, we've had to tighten security down to essential personnel only. And since technically you're no longer associated with a Warrior . . ." He shrugs, wrinkling up his nose in fake sympathy.

I've never liked this guy. Ever since he got hired, he's been like a pesky fly, buzzing around where he doesn't belong. He used to drive Matt crazy, hanging on his every word, acting like they were lifelong pals. It got so bad, Millie had to enact an employee-wide "don't disturb the heroes" rule, but really it was just for Teddy. I don't want to deal with him right now, especially when Claire needs me, so I try to play on his weaknesses. "I get it, but how long have you known me, Teddy? We're like Warrior Nation OGs! I'm not a threat. I'm just here to see your intern, Claire? She works for you, right?" I say, knowing he'll enjoy the power trip of having his own intern, even if it's not true.

And I'm right, because his snooty little mouth purses into a smile. "Well, I guess I could make an exception for you. Just this once."

The guard lets us pass, and Teddy instantly starts going off about how crazy everything has been lately, emphasizing what I'm sure is his inflated importance in the daily HQ activities. "It has been an absolute zoo here, Bridgette; you would not even believe. I have been losing my mind trying to keep this place under control!"

"I bet," I say, suppressing an eye roll.

"My already long list of responsibilities has quadrupled, and navigating Millie's calendar is like a minefield."

"Mmm-hmm."

"I've even had to start processing criminals!" he gasps, though I can tell he's secretly delighted. "They never trained me for that, but of course I'm handling it fine. These villains aren't talking to anyone, but I have my own theories." He looks over at me, waiting for me to ask what they are. "No one cares what I think, though."

Sigh. I think about the time Teddy interrupted a debriefing to announce his hypothesis that the mayor is secretly funding criminal activity for publicity. His argument was completely unfounded and drove all the heroes nuts. It's clear Teddy wants to be a bigger part of the action, but he doesn't have the right skill set. He's good at booking conferences and setting appointments. But decoding villain masterminds? Not so much.

"Everyone's got a lot on their plates right now, Teddy," I say as a young woman runs past us clutching her tablet to her chest. "There's probably just not enough time to hear out every single person's theory about the siege."

He frowns. "But you know better than anyone that a lot of people here are idiots. Like Aqua Maiden: Do you think she has any clue what's going on? Just yesterday she had some Kate Spade reps in here talking about setting up a photo shoot. As if there's time for that right now! She's probably doing a live video tutorial on waterproof eye makeup as we speak." Well, he's not wrong there. Matt may have a serious social media presence, but when he's in the field or there's a crisis going on, that's his focus. Aqua Maiden has been known to pause mid-battle for selfies. "And then there's my intern, Claire—for some reason, everyone wants to hear what she has to say."

"Oh, really?" I ask, proud of her. With so many people trying to grab the spotlight in this organization, it's not easy making an impression.

"It's obnoxious," he sneers, then corrects himself quickly. "Sorry, I know she's your friend. But just because she's young, she gets picked to basically be Girl Power's adviser? I think there's something else going on there. And it's not fair."

Just as the words leave his lips, Claire and Joy stumble out of a closet, all disheveled and splotchy, grinning from ear to ear. Claire works to smooth down her purple hair, while Joy quickly turns and heads off, disappearing down the hall. It was a quick, blink-and-you-missed-it moment but definitely not the most covert move I've ever seen. There are lots of places in HQ to sneak away for privacy (Matt and I frequented the service elevator in the west wing), but that doesn't mean there's not somebody always watching.

Teddy rolls his eyes. "See what I mean?" He turns to Claire. "We missed you in this morning's committee meeting," he sneers, delighting in the fact that she apparently forgot to attend.

"Wait . . . what?" She panics, pulling out her tablet. "I didn't see any meeting on my schedule."

"Well, check again, because it happened. Without you. Did you finish steaming Millie's pantsuit for the press conference this afternoon?"

"Yes, it's hanging in her office," she replies, still scanning her screen, face turning red. "Um, I'm going to take my lunch break now."

"Only thirty minutes today," he says, trying to assert some authority. "I need your help transcribing the anonymous tip hotline."

"I'll be there," Claire assures, less than enthused. Teddy gives me a parting nod, then dashes off to insert himself into a situation that probably doesn't require his help. "Uuggghhhh," Claire groans once he's out of earshot. "I swear my schedule was completely clear when I checked this morning. Teddy's always checking in on me like I'm a child."

"I'm not his biggest fan either," I admit. "Actually, I don't think he has a lot of fans around here."

"Shocker." She feigns surprise. "Anyway, thanks for coming! I am super excited to get some advice from *the* Bridgette Rey."

"Tip number one," I say as we start heading toward the cafeteria. "Find a less obvious make-out spot."

She freezes, hyperalert like a rabbit about to get snapped up by a fox. "Wha-what?"

"Even Teddy knew what you two were doing in there, and you don't want that guy in on your business. Try somewhere with less foot traffic, like the records department or decommissioned weapons storage area. I think there's an abandoned tank previously used by—"

"War Path! Yes! That G.I. Joe guy from the eighties? OMG, you are a genius." She opens up a giant notebook from under her arm, a leather-bound book so packed with scribbles and additional Post-it notes, I'm surprised the spine hasn't disintegrated from exhaustion. Somehow finding a blank page, Claire starts writing.

"Are you taking notes?" I laugh.

"Uh, yeah! This is good information." She leads us to a table in the back corner of the cafeteria, far enough away that no one else should be able to hear us talk. The space makes me catch my breath, because hanging on the wall is a giant paper mural I made three years ago.

"It's still here," I whisper, looking up at the colorful shapes depicting the Warrior Nation chapter at the time. It's an abstract representation, focusing more on the movement and strength of the heroes, with Blue Streak's massive navy arms punching toward the sky, and Vaporizer's swift invisibility represented with a semi-transparent vellum. All of my most recent visits to HQ have been to either the hospital or briefing room, and I almost forgot about all the hours I spent cutting and placing these paper pieces together for a community I was excited to join. It looks even better than I remember, except for one piece of misplaced purple paper in Blue Streak's cape. At the time, I was running low on supplies, using up every scrap of blue I owned. I tucked in an indigo square to fill in a patch of midnight blue, but never liked the way it looked, sticking out like a sore thumb. Matt said I was being ridiculous, yet there it is, taunting me just like before. Still, I snap a few pictures with my phone, thinking this could be a good entry for my portfolio, especially since my injury has made it hard to create anything new.

"Isn't this this coolest?" Claire asks, beaming up at the paper heroes. "I have a mural at home, but it's crap compared to this."

"It's mine," I admit, heart swelling. "I made this."

Claire's mouth drops. "You did?"

"Back when I was Team Warrior Nation for Life."

"Oh." Her face bends in embarrassment, teeth clenched like

she's made a huge mistake. "Crap, I'm sorry, Bridgette, I didn't even think what it would mean for you to come here today. I'm, like, so consumed by my own junk."

"It's okay. Don't worry about it," I reassure her.

"No! Demi's right—every time I start catching feelings for someone, I turn into a total zombie."

"Who's Demi?"

"My friend. Kind of. Actually . . . I haven't talked to her in a while."

"Yeah, that happens," I say. "Hero life is kind of consuming. It's hard to maintain friendships when your life is constantly hanging in the balance."

"See, that's what I'm struggling with." She sits down, holding her chin in her hands. "It's like, I like Joy—a lot—but I'm also afraid of what dating her will entail, you know? Like if she doesn't text me back, is she blowing me off or is she dead?"

I nod, having had that same existential crisis many times.

"And getting kidnapped?" Claire continues. "No thank you. I'm not ready for that to ever happen again. I mean, you've gone through that a couple times, right?"

"I've lost count, if I'm being honest."

"Oh god!" She buries her face in her hands, and I feel guilty. I'm not helping here. But I'm also not sure what she's wants me to say. Does she want me to talk her out of this life, or is she looking for a seal of approval? I don't feel good about either. And will my advice even matter? If some older hero ex-girlfriend had warned teenage me against dating Matt, there's no way I would've listened. I was so crazy about him, I was too naive to think—or care—about what his saving the world would mean for me. All I knew was that I loved being with him, and couldn't imagine anything keeping us apart.

"Listen," I start, "I can't tell you what to do. Is dating a superhero hard? Yeah, it's nuts. Your average couple doesn't have to think about ransom notes or villains crashing their movie nights. It's annoying and scary and deeply unnerving, but it's not without its perks."

Claire peeks out from between her fingers.

"Being rescued by someone you love is nothing short of incredible. To be safely wrapped in your hero's arms after fearing for your life—I'd be lying if I said that wasn't a high." She nods, a faint smile returning. "And Warrior Nation does do a lot of great things. I mean, they're not perfect, but they do help people in times of need."

"Yes, and that's what I love!" Claire says, aimlessly flipping through her journal. "I know I'll never have a superpower or be a hero, but I want to help people in my own way. Being here makes me want to be part of something bigger than myself, and being with Joy . . . she makes me feel like I can accomplish that."

I smile, knowing she's already found her answer. "Then hold on to that feeling. Keep reminding yourself of what you want and what's important to you."

She looks up at my paper Blue Streak in the mural, stars in her eyes. "These heroes mean more to me than anything else in this world. I do wish Blue Streak were still here, though. Although I'd probably faint every time I saw him."

"He's a great guy," I say. "I wonder how he's doing. I honestly never thought he'd be one to retire."

Claire grips the table, brown eyes suddenly flooding with that intense WarNat passion I've seen from so many fans. "Wait. WAIT. You know him? Like . . . YOU KNOW HIM?"

I lean back in my chair, slightly nervous she's going to pounce on me for information. "Yeah, I've even been to his house. Maybe I can introduce you sometime."

She reaches out for me, clutching my cast. "I think we're best friends now. Is that okay?"

I laugh. "I'll be waiting for your friendship bracelet."

Where Have All the Real Superheroes Gone?

In the weeks since Warrior Nation announced Blue Streak's retirement, a giant chasm has erupted in the once-great public service organization. Instead of true strength and bravery, the remaining heroes are nothing but showboating celebrities obsessed with fame and product endorsements.

Blue Streak was the last of an era, a hero from a time gone by. Never on social media, never concerned about branding or followers, Blue Streak kept his head down and got his work done, eliminating danger almost before it began. He was an icon, a legend, the ultimate picture of what a hero could do and what a man should be.

Now a new criminal element roams the streets of Chicago, and what has that chapter done? Nothing. A squad of villains are taunting and teasing the general public, committing increasingly dangerous crimes, and while individuals such as the clownish Vaporizer and the already-exhausting Girl Power may rush to the scenes, why aren't they doing more to get to the root of the problem? Chapters from days past would have been more strategic, staying two steps ahead of every misdeed, but these camera-ready so-called heroes just spin in circles, putting out fires without extinguishing the flame.

It's disappointing, and embarrassing. Bring back heroes like Blue Streak, who know how a villain's mind works. Experience and skill should be valued over youth and flash any day. Otherwise, we'll all end up dead.

CLAIRE

"SO, YOU'RE STILL ALIVE, THAT'S GOOD TO KNOW," Demi says as she flops down in the restaurant booth across from me. It's been weeks since I've seen her, and I feel awful for disappearing. But it's comforting to see she looks great, locs twisted up in a high bun, arms toned from wrangling probably thousands of dogs at this point. She glows with entrepreneurial success; I guess we're both having amazing summers.

"Yeah, sorry for being MIA," I say, passing her a menu. "Mom's had me on a strict curfew since the whole kidnapping thing, and—"

"And you're spending all your free time with that girl instead of me," Demi wisely guesses, not even looking up from the breakfast specials.

"It's not like that."

"Yeah, it is, but whatever. When I eventually get a boyfriend, I'm totally going to ignore the crap out of you too."

I throw a couple of grape jelly packets her way, which she deflects using her menu as a shield. We've spent a lot of time together at this twenty-four-hour breakfast diner in our neighborhood, cramming for finals and drafting debate team speeches. Our record for consecutive time spent in one booth was five hours, during which we consumed our weight in pancakes while creating our own student government plan for AP History. We got an A-plus for our five-thousand-word constitution, but what I really remember from that experience was Demi accidentally taking a swig of straight syrup instead of coffee and spitting it all over the table. When we're not at each other's throats to become valedictorian, we do have fun together.

"How's your business?" I ask once I've decided on my order.

"Exploding, in a good way. I developed a new leash belt system that lets me walk up to ten dogs at once. I walked a hundred dogs last Friday."

"Are you serious?"

Her face softens in a satisfied smile. "At this rate, I'll be able to pay for one year of vet school by the end of this summer."

"Dang!"

"I know." She grins. "I'm basically crushing it. But what about you? How crazy is it to be part of Warrior Nation with all this crime going on? One of my dog clients was in that bus that your girl rescued."

"Really? I—"

Just then, Joy comes swooping in, taking a seat next to me in a white tank top and jean shorts. Blond hair pulled up in ponytail, the spot on her forehead that was previously wrapped in gauze is now blemish-free, thanks to some kind of Warrior

Nation miracle drug. The second she sits, warmth rushes through me, and even though her bare arm simply brushes mine, it's enough to cover me in goose bumps.

"Glad I could help!" Joy chimes, pouring herself a cup of coffee from the carafe on the table. "You're Demi, right?"

Rather than responding, Demi shoots me a look of death, which actually isn't super far off from her regular expression, but it's still unsettling. I invited Joy here so the two of them could get to know each other, but Demi's fire eyes give me reason to believe I failed to mention this part to her. I cringe, mouthing an "I'm sorry" her way, but her annoyance level has gone from average to extreme in five seconds flat.

"Oh, would you look at that," she deadpans, not even pretending to look at her phone. "I'm needed for a dog emergency."

"Dog emergency?" I mock. "What even constitutes a dog emergency?"

"You know, when someone's acting like a bitch." She slams her palms on the table, propping herself up before storming out the door. *Crap.* I motion for Joy to let me out of the booth and then chase after Demi. All that walking has given Demi a significant advantage, though, and I'm practically out of breath once I catch up.

"What . . . the hell . . . was that?" I pant, jumping in front of her imperial march.

"You're asking me?" she shouts. "Why did you invite her?"

"I thought it would be fun!"

"Why? Why would that be fun?"

"Because! You're my best friend, and she's my . . . girlfriend, although not officially? I don't know. I don't know! I wanted you two to hang!"

She hangs her head, groaning. "Claire, I haven't seen you ALL SUMMER. And I know you're off saving the world or whatever, but I have a life too. And it's kind of sucked not having anyone but freaking dogs to talk to."

Bridgette's comments about how hard it is to maintain friendships float into my head, kicking up extra guilt as I stare at Demi's frustrated face. Arms crossed, eyes glossy, she stares off, blinking rapidly to ward off tears. In all the time I've known her, I've never seen her upset like this. Angry, definitely. Competitive to the point of insanity, always. But sad? She always wears such a tough shell, I didn't think anything I could do would hurt her.

"I'm so sorry, Demi, I really am," I say, regret tingeing my words. "I can tell Joy to leave. . . ."

"Don't bother," she spits. "I have to go pick up a Pekinese a few minutes away, so I guess I'll just see you in September."

One last dirty look pierces my heart before she heads off, ignoring me as I call out her name. I trudge back to the diner, collapsing back into the booth across from Joy.

"Is everything okay?" Joy asks, funneling a sugar packet directly into her mouth.

"No, she—" I pause, distracted by the sweet granules coating her lips. Brows furrowed in concern, blue eyes squinting in worry, Joy reaches out for me, completely oblivious that her concerned expression looks totally silly while she's covered in sugar. I laugh to myself, thinking about how this girl who now graces billboards and nightly news reports is not some larger-than-life, flawless icon, but simply a sweet person who does her best to do what she thinks is right. I don't know why, but something clicks in my heart, skipping past all the pros-and-cons lists I've been making, and ignoring all the worries about what super-hero romance will mean. I like this girl, and I'm ready to be all in, no matter what lies ahead. It's been fun flirting, but I'm ready to make this relationship official, to lock her down and make her my girlfriend. "Actually, can I talk to you about something?"

"Duh, I'm always word-vomiting about all my stuff to you." She smiles. "I'm here for you. What's up?"

I take a deep breath, my heart suddenly taking off like a rocket. "Well, um, I don't know about you, but I've never had an official girlfriend before. I mean, I've been out since middle school, and I've kissed girls and stuff, but with all my classes and extracurriculars, I've never really had time to lock down a relationship."

"I could see that about you," Joy says, but then immediately startles, eyes wide. "Not that I think you're undateable or some-thing! Quite the opposite, actually. I just get you prioritizing grades over your love life."

"Right, exactly. I've always been about keeping my eye on the prize, but I'm realizing I can make time for both." I swallow hard, gazing at her beautiful face for courage. "I have some-thing I want to ask you. Will you—"

A waitress steps up to the table, smacking a piece of pink bubble gum between her teeth. "Hello and welcome to the Hungry Waffle. How can I . . ." She freezes mid-chew, doing a wildly comical double take after looking at Joy. "Oh my god!" she squeals. "Are you Girl Power?" A few heads from neighboring tables perk up upon hearing her name, turning to see what's going on.

Joy's face turns bloodred, completely caught off guard by being recognized without her super suit. She looks at me, panicked, and I choke down my question, nodding at her to respond.

"Uh, yes . . . I am." She forces a smile, and the waitress squeals in delight, plopping down her ordering pad, an empty sheet just begging for an autograph.

"Would you sign this for me? Make it out to Linda," she asks, leaning over the table.

"Excuse me?" I ask. "May I place my order, please?"

Linda the waitress shoots daggers at me, bewildered that I'm interrupting her celebrity moment. "Hon, can't you see I'm talking to Girl Power, here? Give me a minute!"

Oh, like how you totally gave me the space I needed to ask a very important question? Rude! But before I can speak my mind, a little girl approaches our table, wearing a pink Warrior Nation T-shirt and a replica of Girl Power's baby-blue eye mask as a headband. Joy finishes up her first autograph and then turns to give her tiny fan her full attention.

"Hello!" Joy says, leaning down to meet the girl's eyes.

"Hi, um, are you for really the real Girl Power?" the girl asks, bouncing on her tippy toes in excitement.

"I was going to ask you the same thing!" Joy replies, causing the little fan to giggle with pure happiness. The girl asks to take a picture, and once the selfie is snapped, the floodgates open, everyone in the restaurant coming over to get an autograph and photo, abandoning their plates of French toast and omelets to get a piece of a Warrior. The booth is swarmed by bodies, all pushing against each other, with some even getting so close, they're practically sitting on top of me. An oversize purse hits me in the face; our silverware and cups get knocked over from stray hands reaching out for her. Suddenly I know what it feels like to be in a trash compactor, as walls of people close in from every side. I call out Joy's name, but since I'm not the only one, my call for help is lost in the crowd. I slouch down in my seat, making myself as small as I can, panic-sweating from the lack of space around me. I've even lost sight of Joy, who must be making progress because, eventually, the swarm begins to subside, fans slowly returning to their tables, taking my sanity with them.

But whereas all this surrounding activity has me drained, Joy looks recharged, somehow even more radiant than before.

"Wow! That was . . . Holy crap!" she exclaims, fanning her glowing face with the menu we never ordered from. "Did you see all those people?"

"Uh, it was kind of hard not to. Some dude had his elbow in my cheek." My tone is less than enthused.

"What? That's gross." She cringes. "Why didn't you say anything?"

"I tried to!"

"Really? Sorry. I've never had anything like that happen to me before." She pulls out her ponytail, golden waves falling down her back, before getting up and moving to my side of the booth. As she snuggles up to me, a sea of smartphones pop up all around us, technological telescopes aiming to record Joy's every move. A wave of self-consciousness runs through me, and I pull my hoodie up over my head. I know they aren't looking at me— no one seems to notice I'm even here—but I must be in every shot, panic sweat and all. Slideshows of Vaporizer with Bridgette pop into my head, WarNats drawing devil horns or witch warts onto her face. I used to laugh at them, reading though all the funny comments about how stupid and simple she seemed compared to him. I wonder if they'll do that to me too.

"So, what did you want to ask me?" Joy asks hopefully.

"Actually, I think I'm ready to go."

"What? Aren't you hungry?"

"Starved, actually. But everyone is . . . watching us."

She looks around, noticing the phones for the first time. "Try to ignore them; that's what I do when they start filming while I'm fighting." What? How can I ignore this? I think of the thousands of Warrior candids I've viewed over the years, WarNats overanalyzing every little thing. *Oh, she ordered eggs? Must be low on protein, or gearing up for a fight.* Rambling, overreaching conversations about the most inane details. I freely admit I used to be right there with them, building these imaginary stories around every shot of Blue Streak. But being here now, seeing how . . . *ordinary* these moments are . . . how did Bridgette deal with this? How did she hold on for four years while having zero privacy and total strangers unfairly ripping her apart?

"Yeah, I can't. Okay? Can we go? Please?" I beg, already standing.

She frowns, worried. "Of course, yeah, let's go. Are there any other good places around here?"

Outside, I take a deep breath, trading claustrophobic diner air for hot summer humidity. But it still feels better than having people breathing down my neck, clawing for my girl and prying at me.

"Are you okay?" Joy asks, rubbing my back gently. We're not even ten steps outside the door when her phone rings, playing the familiar tones of the Warrior Nation theme song.

"Yes?" she answers, and her face immediately falls. She paces up and down the sidewalk, covering her other ear with her hand so as not to miss any details. I stare at her, trying to glean what's going on, but she keeps her face locked in a permanent state of distress. "I'll be right there." She hangs up.

"What's wrong?" I ask, stepping toward her. She's visibly shaking, running her fingers across her scalp.

"It's Matt. He's gone."

"Gone?"

"Kidnapped, they think. Or, actually, they don't know for sure. He hasn't checked in over twenty-four hours, which is against protocol. But . . ." She shakes her head, breath quickening. "They think it's connected to the siege."

A Warrior, kidnapped? No. No! My heart shoots off in its own private hundred-yard dash. "WHAT! How?"

"I don't know. . . . They've been increasing their threats against the Warriors. . . . I just didn't think . . ." She wipes her face. "Sorry. I just . . . Earthquake and Aqua Maiden are already out there. I have to help. Shit. Shit! I need to change." She rummages through her purse, pulling out a corner of her light blue spandex suit. "Can you help me?"

"Here?"

She rolls her eyes, clearly unable to filter herself in her panic. "No, like . . . in a restroom. Please, I need you. C'mon." We run back into the restaurant, much to the delight of the clientele. Locking the bathroom door behind us, Joy quickly strips down to her underwear, a lacy bra and a pair of boy shorts. My face flushes at seeing her undressed for the first time, but we don't have a second to spare.

She steps into the formfitting bodysuit, and I do my best to pull the high-tech fabric up over her curves. It's not easy, especially in a cramped bathroom stall, and together we perform a strange, interpretive dance of squats, bends, and twisting limbs. Her foot lands in the toilet once; I almost tangle her hair in the back zipper. It's like the world's most complicated wetsuit, full of secret weapons, communications systems, and technology, requiring her to ensure every seam and zipper hits her shape in the exact right spot. A state-of-the-art health sensor must line up correctly against her spine; her wrist comm must lie on top of her radial artery. We always see heroes come bursting onto the scene, colors and capes blazing, but holy hell, their wardrobe is so complicated. It takes the two of us to twist and secure every last inch, both of us breathing heavy under pressure.

Once her suit is secure, she pulls on her boots and face mask, fully transforming herself into Girl Power. My heart can barely take it. Where is she running off to? Will she come back safe? I reach for her as she touches my cheeks with her extreme-grip gloves. Webbed fabric brushes my skin as she whispers, "Thank you. I gotta go."

I nod, fighting back tears. She's about to disappear into danger. What should I tell her? What do I say?

"Good luck" is all I can manage. She kisses me, soft and quick, before running out the door, leaving her bag and clothes behind. I hear a roar of applause in the restaurant as she blazes through, but I stay behind, giving myself a few minutes to collect my emotions. I pick up her things, stuffing her top and jeans into her bag. Her phone lights up with a stream of urgent messages, illuminating her wallpaper: a picture of the two of us from the charity night, just before that toxic gas was released. We're all dressed up, smiling and cute, pressed cheek to cheek.

A tear rolls down my face. I should have asked her to be my girlfriend then, or a million times since. My head was fighting it, trying to tell me to do the smart, logical thing when I should have just followed my heart and asked.

Will I ever get the chance?

BREAKING NEWS!

In a Channel 5 exclusive, we have learned that all four Warrior Nation heroes are currently missing, reportedly captured by the villains responsible for countless attacks during the recent siege. Never before in our city's history has an entire chapter been out of commission, and Warrior Nation is refusing to comment at this time.

Stay tuned for the most up-to-date Warrior coverage.

BRIDGETTE

"BRIDGETTE. BRIDGETTE. BRIDGETTE!"

I hide my head under the covers, trying to hold on to a few more precious moments of sleep despite my sister shaking me. She hardly ever gets up before nine a.m., so I don't understand where this burst of energy is coming from.

Undeterred, Becca jumps onto the couch where I'm sleeping and starts bouncing up and down, shaking all the cushions. "WAKE! UP!"

"Argh, what?" I groan, wiping the sleep from my eyes. "Leave me alone! I'm too tired to run lines with you right now."

She hops off, kneeling beside me. "B, something happened."

It's the somber tone that gets me. I pull the blanket down, meeting her eyes. Becca is never serious except for when a scene calls for it. "What's wrong?"

She shows me her phone, screen flashing with the words "WARRIOR NATION UNDER SIEGE," accompanied by the most recent group shot of the entire chapter, all shiny and smiling. *What?* I spring up, scrolling through the article but only taking in bits and pieces.

Unprecedented . . .

Chicago law enforcement baffled . . .

Entire chapter missing . . .

"Wait . . ." My voice trembles, sleepy brain struggling to catch up. "All four heroes are gone?"

"Yeah, I guess so," she says. "Apparently Matt was captured first, and as the rest of the heroes went in to save him, they each fell into a trap or something like that. No one knows where they are. It's all over the news."

I give her back the phone, taking deep breaths as reality sets in. Kidnapped? *ALL* of them? But . . . how? Usually when Matt gets in a bad spot, there's another Warrior who can swoop in and save the day. It's the whole reason each chapter has four members—so they can have a superhero buddy system.

Warrior Nation will have to call in the other chapters for help.

My body starts to tremble, fear's muscle memory setting back in. *But you don't have to worry,* my head reasons. *Matt's not your boyfriend anymore.* Yet my heart knows better, beating with the same passion that's propelled me all these years. I still love him; obviously I do. I can't just turn off these emotions, especially in a time like this. Even if we're not together, I don't want him to get hurt . . . or worse. . . . I swallow hard, my mind playing a slideshow of all the injuries he's incurred over the years, all the times he slid in through my window, needing to feel me,

235

needing to feel safe himself. I think of him now, wherever he is, beaten and bruised amongst the other Warriors. . . . Oh god . . .

"B, are you okay?" Becca asks, waving a hand in front of my face. "You look like you're visiting some kind of scary mental place. Do you need some water, or whiskey?"

I shake my head, even though my throat is dry from panic. "How . . . How long have they been gone?" I croak.

"Um . . ." She taps on her phone, looking for an answer. "I'm not sure. But couldn't you still call up that Warrior Nation hotline you've used before? Ring up that Millie chick or Mr. Know-It-All, get the news directly from the source?"

"That's a good idea." I reach under the couch for my phone, pulling it off its charger. A stream of notifications waits for me, most of them from Claire, in an increasing state of panic.

Hey Joy's been out on a mission for like 10 hours with no word . . . how long until I should be officially freaked?

Still nothing

I called HQ but they straight up gave me a no comment

Something must be wrong

The WarNat forums are going off! Help!

Oh no, oh, Claire. She must be losing her mind right now. I can't let her go through this alone.

My only other text is from Millie, as part of the contact

thread she created a while back for all those closely connected to the heroes.

> Due to the current state of events, we strongly encourage all Warrior friends and family to report to HQ immediately

Maybe I'm not Matt's girlfriend anymore; maybe they sent me this message by mistake. But there's no way I'm not heading down there to find out what's going on and what I can do to help. Without another thought, I quickly get dressed, grabbing my bag to head out the door.

"Wait, where are you going?" Becca calls after me, yanking me by the elbow.

"Where do you think?"

Her eyebrows knit in confusion, ponytail flopping to one side. "But . . . why? You broke up with Matt so you wouldn't have to deal with this anymore."

She's right; I wanted to be rid of all this drama, free from constantly looking over my shoulder and wondering what kind of mayhem would happen next. I wanted to live my life in peace, but I can't breathe easy knowing people I care about are in trouble. As it turns out, this world is a bigger part of me than I thought. "I may not be a hero, but I can't watch the world fall apart."

★

HQ is a total disaster. People running left and right, every screen flashing bright red warning signs. High-pitched alarms blare from each cavernous hall, and random paperwork scatters across the glossy floors. I've never seen it like this, not even that time two years ago when a hacker broke into the system and gave all the heroes false missions. Warrior Nation employees have always felt like corporate drones to me, gliding from room to room without emotion or thought, simply following whatever it is those tablets they carry say to do. But today, real fear flashes across their faces, the strain of panic pushing them to race back and forth. I knew having the entire chapter gone would be bad, but this is much worse than I expected.

After getting through security, I make my way to what I've nicknamed the "Bad News" room, a pseudo Zen garden complete with bubbling fountains and bonsai trees where Millie and Co. most frequently deliver difficult news. Maybe they think this setting will soothe away distress, but in my experience, no amount of looped harp sounds can wipe away the feeling that someone you love may die.

Currently, the room is filled with Warrior family members, most of whom I recognize. Houston and Anna huddle near their partners' parents; a lot of them are crying or pacing in tight circles. I search for Claire, finding her in the back corner, sitting on the ground with her arms wrapped around her legs. Her eyes are red and puffy, with a pile of Kleenex at her feet. Her hoodie is soaked with tears.

"Claire!" I exclaim, dropping my stuff as I drop down next to her.

She looks up, bloodshot eyes widening. "Oh my god, I'm

so glad you're here!" she sobs, reaching out for me. I hold her close, the sound of her tears inspiring some of my own. "I . . . I didn't know what to do! My mom wouldn't let me leave so I snuck out. . . . She's gonna be so mad . . . but I had to be here, you know? Just in case."

"I totally understand." I nod, giving her a warm smile. I know she's only three years younger than me, but where she stands—experiencing a missing hero for the first time—feels like a lifetime ago, the beginning of a journey I would not wish on my worst enemy. I only hope I can help her make sense of it.

"Have you heard from Joy at all?" I ask her gently, already knowing the answer.

She sniffles. "No. I mean, yeah, I saw her yesterday. I was gonna officially ask her to be my girlfriend. . . ." Her lip trembles. "What if I never see her again?"

"Don't talk like that, okay? Joy is super strong, inside and out. Warrior Nation will figure a way out of this. They always do." But even as I'm saying the words, I don't know if what I'm saying is true. No chapter has even been through something like this, and I can't imagine how they'll come out the other side.

"But how?" Claire cries, reading my thoughts. "They're ALL trapped—all of them—and that's never happened before." She pulls out that giant journal of hers, frantically flipping through the pages. "See? Nothing, nothing like this on record." She looks at me with great urgency, begging me to have the answers. How many times have I sat in panic, crying myself to sleep, unsure if Matt would be alive when I woke up? That uncertainty—the unknown—is the worst part.

Just then, Roy Masterson walks in, hushing the crowd. It's been ages since I've seen him in a situation like this: a real hero moment, not just a flashy parade or celebration. Mr. Know-It-All has always excelled at signing autographs and posing for pictures, but leading a team? Not so much. Unfortunately for Warrior Nation, they operate under an archaic rule that only former heroes can assume the top leadership positions in the organization, and very few superheroes are willing to give up their capes to go corporate. Matt once told me he'd rather die a slow, gruesome death than have to work every day at HQ, which is how Roy, the most ineffective hero in history, got to be the chapter president. He stands before us all, haircut and bow tie both flopped to one side, nervously swinging his scarecrow arms, trying to figure out where to begin.

Beside him is Millie, dark circles hanging under her eyes, her normally perky bob drained of all its luster. Teddy lurks in a corner, frantically typing on his tablet. I can't imagine they've had much, or any, sleep in the last twenty-four hours. Millie adjusts her black-framed glasses and impatiently nudges Roy, who mumbles, "Oh, um, please, everyone find a seat."

No one feels like getting cozy, as emotions are running high. "Where's my daughter?" calls Aqua Maiden's mother from the crowd, followed by several similar cries. "What is going on?"

Roy looks down at the floor, rubbing the back of his neck in worry. The mood lighting in the room is not to be trusted, but I swear he's turning green. "Um . . ."

Millie, a seasoned pro from a lifetime of Warrior press conferences, jumps in, remaining cool despite the growing heat. "We have no new updates at this time, I'm afraid."

"What about the other chapters?" Houston asks. "When are they arriving as backup?"

Millie holds her chin high, continuing to take the lead since Roy looks a second away from vomiting. "We've been in contact with Los Angeles, New York, Boston: We are not calling for outside chapter backup until we can further assess the situation with the siege."

What? That makes absolutely zero sense. Why wouldn't you bring in your greatest allies during a time of extreme crisis? This does not sit right at all.

"You're telling me my son's life is in danger, and you won't call for backup?" asks one of Earthquake's dads, balling his hands into fists in frustration.

"We cannot have other cities without active heroes, in case the siege spreads," Millie continues. "This is an unprecedented situation, and as a national organization, we need to be strategic."

"So leaving my son to die is your strategy?!" Outrage fills the room as Claire tightens her grip on my arm. The surrounding panic starts to seep through my skin, and I breathe deep to keep it at bay. I won't let the undertow sweep me away. Not yet.

"We . . . um . . ." Roy attempts, swallowing hard. His eyes are watering from the pressure, knowing he should say something—anything—but can't find the words of comfort everyone needs. "We are . . ."

"We are doing everything we can," Millie says, saving him. "I understand how distressing this is. You are welcome to stay at HQ if that helps you feel safe. We have plenty of accommodations. I do advise you stay as close as possible, as we are unsure of who or what will come under target now that the city is unprotected." This is the last straw, and family members start clawing their way up to Millie and Roy, in need of something else, something more reassuring. Teddy, ever the martyr, throws himself in front of his boss, and she scurries away before they can get to her, although several follow her anyway, their angry shouts echoing through the halls. I stay behind with Claire, who's back to poring over the pages of her book, searching for something. Two adults I don't recognize, possibly Joy's parents, approach her, the mother looking absolutely beside herself.

I look around and spot Matt's dad standing alone, biting at his thumb, eyes unfocused. Mr. Rodriguez is a nice man who's always been kind to me, but struggled with the superhero stuff. He didn't like Matt putting his life on the line, but as a single father, all those product endorsements and appearance fees did help pay the bills.

"Hey, Bridgette, I didn't expect to see you here," he says, stepping into a familiar setting for us both. I've probably spent more time with this man in hospital waiting rooms than any other setting, each of us lost in our own worry as we sat side by side in silence, waiting for news. He wears a worn Cubs hat over his dark mocha hair, the same shade and wave as his son's. Matt gets his good looks and charm from his dad, though neither takes center stage in these situations.

"I couldn't stay away," I admit.

"Matt's been a real mess since the two of you split," he says, running a hand over his stubbled cheek. "You were always good for him, gave him something to fight for. . . ." He pauses, staring off in the distance.

"You okay, Mr. Rodriguez?"

He doesn't fake a smile or put on a front; he doesn't need to with me. "Matty's a smart kid, I keep telling myself that. I just wish I'd never let him get mixed up in all this in the first place."

"Well, knowing Matt, he probably would've done it anyway," I say.

He manages a laugh. "That's true. Stubborn little shit." He squeezes my shoulder, lingering for a second as his eyes start to water. "I can't stay here; I'll drive myself crazy. Keep me posted if you hear anything, okay? You can always count on me if you need anything."

"Thank you."

"You hang in there." He walks off, just as Claire throws her hands up in the air, cursing under her breath.

"What's going on?" I ask.

"I just . . . I don't understand why Millie is not calling the other chapters for help," she steams. "That's what they do; it's what they've always done." She opens her journal to what looks like a list of comic book titles and synopses. "See? Look. In *Blue Streak* #52, the Chicago and Boston chapters work together to defeat Madame Mayhem. And again in #103—Blue Streak assembles heroes from both coasts for a mission against an underground army of assassins."

"Do you always carry this with you?" I ask, flipping through a few pages myself. Even after just a few seconds, I can already tell it's the most detailed account of Warrior Nation I've ever seen.

"Oh, my grail diary?" She blushes, tucking a stray hair behind her ear. "Yes."

"It's amazing." I find a section on Matt, listing all his professional victories over the course of his hero career. I've never seen them all spelled out like this. . . . There are so many of them, it's overwhelming. I touch my fingers to her handwritten "Vaporizer" headline, wishing I could connect with more than his name right now.

"Thanks."

"And I agree, I don't get why they're holding back," I say. "Matt's worked with heroes like Kitty Vicious and Webby on way less dangerous problems than this."

"Yes! I remember that!" she exclaims, getting all red in the face. "The whole point of a national organization is that they're supposed to work together. The individual heroes work on a buddy system, and the chapters do too. Chicago's buddy is Boston. Never cease, never cower—hello? This feels a lot like cowering to me."

She's right, and I don't understand what's going on. Millie says they have a strategy, but why do I get the sense she's just stalling?

And when someone you love is in danger, every single second counts.

Warrior Nation Boston Chapter @OfficialBostonWarriors
Stay strong, Chicago heroes! Never cease, never
cower!
#WeStandWithChicago

Storm Chaser @MakeItRainStormChaser
We believe in you! This siege will end!
#WeStandWithChicago

Webby @theRealWebbyHero
You are in our hearts! Don't disappear on us,
Vaporizer! #WeStandWithChicago

Warrior Nation NYC Chapter @NYCHeroesOfficial
Ready to fight by your side, Chicago!
#WeStandWithChicago

CLAIRE

WHAT IF JOY CAN'T BE SAVED? *What if she dies? What if I never see her again?*

A combo of worry and anger churns inside me, bubbling up over and over before I can stop it. I'm going to lose it if I let these thoughts rule my head. I need to do something. *We* need to do something. If belonging to every single club at school has taught me anything, it's that standing idly by is the best way to get eaten alive, so we need to keep ourselves busy. Proactive.

Because this thing between me and Joy has only just begun; she can't be taken away from me yet. Not before I get to kiss her under the stars or take her to the prom. I don't even know her favorite color or go-to karaoke song. I can't let anything happen to her.

I *can't.*

"Claire, I'd like you to meet Houston and Anna," Bridgette says, kindly trying to redirect some of my frantic energy. "Houston is dating Aqua Maiden, and Anna—"

"Yes, I recognize you both," I admit, having seen their faces splashed on countless WarNat sites. "Hi."

"OMG, Claire?" Anna latches onto me, tightly wrapping her hands around my wrists. "Are you dating Joy? How have I not met you yet? Did you just get together? You must be so scared! I know I am. I mean, when Ryan didn't come home I just worried and worried and worried and—"

Bridgette lightly taps her shoulder, breaking her rampant thoughts. "Take a breath," she reminds her, and Anna quickly breathes in through her nose, blowing it out with a high-pitched "Ooooo."

"I didn't know Joy was paired up either," Houston says, giving me a tight-lipped smile. Looking at him now, I realize I've never actually seen his whole face, thanks to his girlfriend usually hogging all the camera angles. It's disorienting seeing Houston and Anna in person. While neither has garnered the kind of attention or trolling that Bridgette receives, their names do pop up from time to time, usually by WarNats complaining about how significant others get "in the way" of real hero work by getting themselves kidnapped and sticking their noses where they don't belong. I myself was once part of an epic thread of fans ragging on poor Anna for being the pawn in a shoot-out in Grant Park, where Earthquake got severely injured trying to rescue her.

If only these heroes could stay single, I wrote, *their dumb girlfriends wouldn't cause so many distractions.*

Well, hello there, irony.

"It's new," I tell him, still mentally slapping myself for letting her go. "We've, um, been trying to stay under the radar."

He laughs. "Yeah? And how's that going?"

"Great, really great," I deadpan.

"Did either of you hear from Ryan or Ashleigh before they disappeared?" Bridgette asks. "Any clue as to where they were going, who they were fighting?"

"No, well, I mean, maybe?" Anna nervously claws at her chin. "He's been so tired, you know, completely run ragged by all this. In and out, in and out—he's barely been able to stop. Usually I make him a nice meal when he's done with a fight—calorie loading and all that—but there hasn't been time! He gets home, I start baking a chicken, and he's gone before it's done! Madness! The man needs his protein!"

Houston nods. "Yeah, I knew Ashleigh got called after Ryan went missing, but I wasn't too concerned. She had a photo shoot scheduled for later that afternoon, so I knew she'd be gone a while. I didn't know then that Matt was already captured too." He hangs his head, wiping tired eyes with his palm. "Dammit, I hate this."

"So what do we do?" I ask as three pairs of puzzled eyes turn my way.

"What do you mean?" Anna asks. "What do we do? Are we supposed to do something? Did I miss instructions?"

This woman's nervous chatter is going to drive me up a wall. "I mean, we can't just stand around while the people we care about are in danger, right?"

"Well . . . what do you have in mind, Claire?" Houston questions, eyebrow curved in confusion. "I mean, if they aren't even calling in the other Warrior chapters, what are a bunch of non-supers supposed to accomplish?"

I look to Bridgette for support. She nods in encouragement. "I mean, I don't know exactly, not yet. . . ." I guess before I suggested action I should've had a makeshift plan in mind.

He pats my shoulder like I'm some pathetic dog. "I like where your head's at, and believe me, I'd love to help Ashleigh. But the people here have access to technology and tools we can't even dream of. If anyone's going to get our heroes back, it's them."

I know this; of course I do. I've read every behind-the-scenes interview and expose ever published: Warrior Nation keeps their official specs on lock, but I've gobbled down every rescue mission log made public. They never talk about their weapons arsenal, since they don't want villains replicating their tech, but every now and then they release peeks into how things get done. I'm not dumb: I obviously don't have night-vision goggles or invisible drones, but having power isn't the only way to help. Heart counts for something.

"I think, um, what we're trying to say is, Warrior Nation knows what's best," Anna mumbles, wringing her hands. "Not that *you* don't know stuff! I'm sure you're totally smart and capable and strong! It's just . . . none of us have any real powers? And Ryan always feels better when he knows I'm safe at home. Or here! Being safe is what matters."

Bridgette looks down at her cast, turning her broken hand back and forth as if something heavy has just occurred to her. She and Matt are broken up; she doesn't have to join this fight. Yet I really hope she does. I can't do this alone. "I don't think any of us should consciously throw ourselves into danger or anything, but let's stay in touch, okay? If Ryan, Ashleigh, Joy, or Matt finds a way to get ahold of us, we need to let the others know right away."

"Agreed," Houston says.

"Yes! I can do that!" Anna echoes.

My heart sinks. Stay in touch? That's *it*? We're not going to help the Warriors with a stupid group text! How could you be part of this amazing organization, even tangentially, and not get involved? My whole life I've wanted to help others, to do something of worth, and now . . . here's my chance. We need to take action! Do *something*! I'm about to argue that very point when Bridgette loops an arm through mine, pulling me out of the weird little Zen room.

"I can't just do nothing!" I whine as she quickly ushers me down the hall.

"I know," she says, green eyes hard. "Me neither."

"But wait . . . you just said . . . Where are you taking me?" I ask her.

"Somewhere I can think." We twist through several corridors, taking a path I've yet to explore on my own, until we reach what looks like a storage facility, full of dirty boxes and yellowed old papers. Based on the way my sneakers leave dusty footprints on the floor, no one's been in this room for a long time. "There has to be a reason why they're not calling in backup," she says once we're alone.

"Agreed. But how do we find out why?"

She paces around the abandoned space, hands on her hips. "We need access to someone or something that can get us behind the scenes." She stops, face brightening. "Your tablet! You work here; can you get into internal Warrior files? Poke around a bit?"

I sigh, feeling worthless. "No, not really. I have next to zero clearance. All I can really do is schedule appointments and read training manuals."

"Oh. I thought maybe you'd be one of those brainy types who could hack into security systems or something."

"Yeah . . . I'm more of a book-smart nerd, which only counts on placement tests." Note to self: Sign up for more computer science classes next year! "Ooh! What about . . . Do you know any heroes from the other chapters?" I ask hopefully. "Maybe they'll have some intel?"

Bridgette shakes her head. "I've met a few of them but only in passing. I don't have their numbers or anything." Crap, this is going to be harder than I thought. You'd think pairing up a superhero's ex-girlfriend who's been in the game longer than anyone and a WarNat with an encyclopedia's worth of Warrior history in her head would be enough to get started, but somehow we're stuck at square one.

But then her eyes light up with an idea. "Although . . ."

"What?"

"I could call Charles."

My heart stops. Call . . . Charles? BLUE STREAK HIM-SELF?! I lunge forward in excitement, grabbing on to her shoulders. "You have Blue Streak's number?!"

She grins. "Yes."

"Holy— Talk about burying the lede! Yes! Let's call him! RIGHT NOW!" I shake her, excitement taking over my worry.

"Okay," she laughs, carefully freeing herself from my claws. "We'll have to get aboveground, though. I don't get any cell service down here."

"Great! Let's go. Let's— Wait, let me just check my schedule real quick." I've somehow missed several meetings lately, which is very not me. Meetings keep randomly disappearing and then reappearing seconds before I'm supposed to be somewhere; I'm starting to believe my calendar is cursed. "My afternoon looks clear, so let's gooooooo!" I take Bridgette's non-broken hand, running back through the HQ halls. Maybe all hope isn't lost after all. If we can talk to Blue Streak (god, just the thought of it!), maybe he can give us a clue as to what Warrior Nation is doing, and how they'll put an end to all this siege madness. Dang, meeting my idol, saving Warrior Nation: If Joy's life weren't at stake, I'd be the happiest girl alive right now.

But I'm definitely not, because before we can make our exit, Teddy stops us in our tracks, staring down at us from his upturned nose.

"Where are you going?" he asks, specifically to me. "Where

have you been? Haven't you noticed we're in a bit of an emergency?"

Why does he always talk to me like I'm a complete idiot? "Obviously! I'm trying to help," I spit back, not wanting to waste time dealing with him.

"By doing what? Making yourself completely unavailable and avoiding responsibility?"

I roll my eyes. "Right, because getting people coffee is such a priority right now."

He doubles down in his anger. "It is to the team doing vital recon work! Millie has been working around the clock, and she needs our help. In fact, she's issuing a series of staff meetings to—"

"But I'm not invited to any of them; I just checked," I say matter-of-factly. "Besides, I won't have anything interesting to add until I get back from what I'm about to do."

Teddy pinches the bridge of his nose in frustration. "When will you get it in your stubborn little head that you are here for support, not organizational intelligence! You're not a hero, Claire; you're not even out of high school. You young upstarts think you know everything, when you should be showing respect for those who came before you!"

Bridgette wisely inserts herself between us before we throw down. "Teddy, it's my fault. I asked Claire to help me with something."

Teddy looks at her, incredulous. "You're not serious."

"I know you must be stressed and incredibly overworked

right now," Bridgette says softly, as if she's attempting to appease a toddler on the verge of a tantrum. "But we really are trying to do our part."

"By doing what?" he sneers.

"Ugh, there's no point in telling you unless it turns out to be useful!" I groan, so tired of him needing to micromanage everything I do.

His nostrils flare as he straightens, clutching his tablet to his chest as if he too is holding a secret. "Fine, don't tell me. Go hurl yourselves into an unprotected city and see if I care. But know this—nothing gets past me at HQ, and you'll be sorry you messed with me."

His words stay with me as we ascend to Michigan Ave, ready to call someone with actual power. Ugh, Teddy. Always so melodramatic. For someone who says he loves Warrior Nation, he sure acts like it's the worst.

Why aren't other heroes doing anything?
WarriorHunt.usa

Okay, so the Chicago chapter is MIA, but wtf is up with the rest of Warrior Nation? Besides a few pathetic tweets, NO ONE is saying anything! What are we WarNats supposed to think? Is this the beginning of the end or what?! Get off your asses, Boston! NYC! LA! Where you at? Has Warrior Nation locked you all away?

> **@TruWarriorGrrl**
> yeah. Like I really like all the chapters but this silence is ??? Also, I know Blue Streak just retired but the least he could do is issue a statement or something. Ease our worries and stuff. C'mon, man. Grow a pair.

> **@NeverCeaseNeverSour**
> that dude is so media shy. He never says shit! Millie practically has to force him to open his mouth.

> **@SillyMouseTrap**
> honestly forgotten what his voice even sounds like

> **@GirlPowerSparksJoy**
> I live in Chicago and some local WarNats are organizing a demonstration outside Blue Streak's house tomorrow. Let him know we still love him and need him! Any and all are welcome.

> **@WindyCityWarrior**
> nice! Details?

@VaporLover29
sign me up!

@TrueBlueStreak
love this, I'll be there.

BRIDGETTE

I'VE ONLY BEEN TO CHARLES'S HOUSE ONCE. A cocktail party, thrown by his late wife. Matt and I had just started dating, and I felt very grown up going to an event like that. The two of us spent most of the time trying to see how many maraschino cherries we could fit in our mouths, which was not very mature, but we were having fun being dressed up, holding crystal tumblers, and eating appetizers we could barely pronounce. I only remember seeing Charles once that night, sipping bourbon alone in his library, stealing a moment away from hosting. Despite being one of the most recognizable faces on the planet, he's a very quiet guy. He came up at a time when Warriors were more focused on work than building a brand. While his face may have graced a cereal box or two, he certainly never worried about his image. No website, no social media: He did his job without needing attention, only answering the call of danger, not fame.

After taking the Purple Line up to Evanston, an affluent suburb just north of Chicago, we start the walk to his home, a legit

mansion on the shores of Lake Michigan. As we pass by artisan shops and farm-to-table restaurants, I can't help but notice
the increased presence of law enforcement, with armed officers
patrolling the sidewalks and police cars slowly cruising by every
few minutes. The city is on high alert, waiting for the aftermath of
the Warriors' capture. Will the villains who kidnapped our heroes
make themselves known? Ask for ransom or make other demands?
The chapter has been missing for almost twenty-four hours now,
and the longer they're gone, the higher the stakes.

I'm obsessively checking my phone for updates, while
Claire grows increasingly distant, slowly imploding the closer
we get to Charles's home. A subtle sort of mania has crept over
her, eyes wild and hands constantly rubbing against her shorts.

"Hey, are you okay?" I ask her—a stupid question, really,
considering the emotional roller coaster she's on. But even with
her girlfriend being in danger and the two of us going solo on
this side mission, there's an extra element of panic rising in her
since we got off the train.

"Uhhh . . ." She tucks stray pieces from her French braid
back behind her ears, nervously smiling like a guilty party who
just got caught. "Not really."

When she doesn't elaborate, I prod. "Because . . . ?"

She stops, nervous energy forcing her feet to jog in place. "I
don't think I can do this."

"Do what? Help the Warriors? This was your idea—"

"No. I mean meet Blue Streak." She grimaces with embarrassment.

I smile in sympathy. Chatting with a retired hero seems like a silly thing to get hung up about, considering the circumstances, but I know this means something different to her than it does to me. "Charles is chill, don't worry. He's not all over-the-top like the rest of the Warrior Nation bam-pow machine." I do some air punches on the "bam-pow" with my good hand for emphasis.

She looks up at the sky, blinking like she's forcing herself not to cry. "But that's the thing. He's not *Charles* to me. He's Blue Streak. Longest-running Warrior Nation member. Chicago all-star, defender of all that is good and true." She anxiously hums a few bars of his theme song. "He is my absolute idol, my greatest hero in every sense of the word. How can I just . . . *meet* him? Talk to him? He *saved my life*, Bridgette. . . . What can I ever say that won't sound completely lame?"

Oh. I had no idea he saved her life. This visit really is on a different level for her. "Be honest. Tell him how much his actions that day meant to you," I suggest. "Or say nothing, if that's easier. I can handle this; we're old friends." Claire nods, but frantically. I can almost feel her vibrating. "It'll be okay. What does Blue Streak always say?"

She manages a whisper of a smile. "Weakness is strength that's yet to be tested."

"That's right. C'mon. Let's put you to the test!" We link arms, and I guide the way several more blocks to his estate. Once we get close, we spot a group of WarNats assembled on his sidewalk, some dressed in full super suits, holding signs that say things like "We need you, Blue Streak!" and "Save our city!"

They don't seem angry, just scared, and we have to squeeze past their posters and pleas to get to the front gate. A tall, pointed iron fence surrounds the perimeter of his property, but it's really just for show. Once the technology emerged, Charles had a force-field dome installed over his property, after countless fans kept trying to hop the gate.

A security guard stands on the other side, ignoring the hubbub. I wave to get his attention, but he's apparently grown numb to the calls surrounding him.

"Excuse me!" I call, getting directly in his sight line. "We need to talk to Charles."

Without turning his head, he snorts, "Yeah, you and everyone else."

"Tell him Bridgette Rey is here to see him," I demand. "Tell him . . ." I drop my voice. ". . . *blue is the color of my heart.*" This is a code phrase that Warrior Nation uses in emergencies, a secret slogan that's supposed to specify when shit is going down. I've never had to use it before, but the guard immediately takes notice, turning away to make a phone call. Claire stares at me like I'm a wizard once the guard decides to let us through, much to the frustration of the crowd behind us.

"That . . . was . . . awesome!" She freaks as we walk up the cobblestone path to his house. "God, I am so nervous, I can't stop sweating. I think I'm gonna pee myself!"

"Don't do that," I say, looking around his estate. The house itself is grand and gothic, dark stonework spiraling toward the sky. Perfectly trimmed hedges dot the front, with hundred-year-old trees stretching toward the force field that hums above. Claire is like a baby deer walking on ice, about to dissolve into a puddle of herself, so I remind her, "He's only a person, okay? Just like Matt and Joy, you and me. He puts his spandex on one leg at a time, just like the rest of us."

I can't read her reaction, as her face is frozen in excitement.

When we reach the front door, the security guard says, "Mr. Williams is out back; I'll take you there."

Stepping inside, I feel the air instantly change, cool and quiet compared to the hot, sweaty crowds outside. Despite all the towering windows, a sense of gloom surrounds us as our footsteps echo in the halls. Every room we pass is filled with dark wooden furniture and heavy drapery, yet the place feels empty—almost haunted—like no one actually lives here. I wonder how Charles spends his time now; his retirement came as such a shock to me. Out of all the heroes I've met, he was the most impassioned, the most dedicated to the cause, and I honestly thought the only way he'd leave Warrior Nation was if he died in action. What made him change his mind and leave decades of service behind him? Will he be willing to help us?

Claire's phone chimes, and her face falls upon reading the text. "Oh, of course. Teddy just scheduled me for a meeting that starts in two minutes," she grumbles. "He's messing with me on purpose. Can't he just let me have this?"

"Ignore him," I say. "There's nothing you can do about it from here."

Before we get to the backyard, we pass through a hallway that is absolutely exploding with Warrior Nation paraphernalia. Claire's jaw drops in wonder as we take in all the newspaper clippings, chapter posters, and shadow boxes filled with past Blue Streak suits hanging from the walls like commemorative flags, grouped by different decades. Trophies, plaques, ribbons: It's like a mausoleum of heroism in here. I can't help but notice that there's not much merchandise displayed, at least not a lot of the tacky crap Matt has in his likeness. There's no lip glosses or cheaply made jewelry, no life-size body pillows fans can snuggle with. Rather than framing his own action figures, Charles has chosen to hang letters from his fans; there's an entire wall dedicated to the thank-yous he's received throughout his career.

Claire scans the letters. Suddenly she grabs my arm and screeches, "OMG!" pointing to a note written in blue crayon. I lean in, noticing the paper is signed *Love, Claire* and features a child's drawing of a girl and Blue Streak together.

"I can't . . . I just . . ." Hands cover her mouth, eyes watering. "He kept this? I didn't even know he would *read* it, let alone frame it!"

I rub her back, taking in the patchwork of collected thanks. It is truly something, a compilation of what an impact this man has made. "Saving the world meant as much to him as it does for you, Claire." I always knew he was a good man, but this blows me away. "You are part of his story."

She gasps. "You mean it?"

"Yes!" I laugh, pointing at the evidence. "You're right there!"

Claire wipes her face. "Well, I definitely can't face him now!"

"It'll be fine. In fact, he'll probably enjoy hearing from you again." My heart catches as I spot a framed photo of Charles with Matt, both of them in their hero suits, arms thrown over each other's shoulders in comradery. Matt looked up to him—the whole world did—and just seeing his boyish grin beaming out from behind his white mask guts me with a wave of worry.

Where are you? Are you hurt? Are you okay? Please, please be okay.

We're guided out to the expansive backyard, facing the lake. There's a guesthouse that's probably the size of most normal houses tucked into a wildflower garden. Charles exits the guesthouse, running a hand through his salt-and-pepper hair. Even from a distance, he seems flustered and almost doesn't notice us until we're right upon him.

"Charles?" I ease in, not wanting to startle him and have him go all hero on me.

He blinks, taking in my familiar face in an unlikely setting. "Bridgette? What are you doing here?" Standing at least six feet tall, his distinguished features still look like they were chiseled from stone, even if they are graying around the edges. Under his summer-weight sweater, I can see his strong arms that have carried many to safety. Just being in his presence makes me feel more at ease. "My staff said you used the code? Did Warrior Nation send you here?"

"No, not officially. But everything is kind of a mess, and we need your help," I say.

Steel-gray eyes stare down at my cast, crinkling at the corners with concern. "What happened to your hand?"

"Oh, it's okay, or at least it will be. Just another side effect of dating a hero."

He nods, turning toward Claire. "Who's your friend?"

Claire emits a high-pitched squeak, then immediately berates herself under her breath. I step in to save her. "This is Claire. She's new to the Warrior Nation game, an intern. And she just started dating your replacement, Joy."

His jaw clenches before warming into a smile. Maybe I shouldn't have used the word "replacement." I wonder if he's as conflicted about retiring as I am about breaking up with Matt. "Nice to meet you, Claire." He extends a weathered hand, and she melts at his touch. "Welcome."

"I . . ." She swallows hard. "I love you!" Blushing the brightest shade of red I've ever seen on a human being, she can't stop herself from blubbering. "I mean, I love what you do. For the city! For the world. Oh my god." I hope she doesn't start crying, but I'm honestly surprised she was able to speak at all.

"Well, thank you, I appreciate it," he says kindly, radiating gentlemanly charm. "It's been my honor to protect this city." He bows his head, but there's a twinge of sadness in his eyes. "Here, let's take a seat, shall we?" He guides us away from the guest-house, toward a seating area with white Adirondack chairs.

Once we're settled, I get down to it. "So, let's talk about this siege. Judging by the crowd of people outside your gate, I don't think we'll be the first ones to come to you for help." He says nothing, a blank canvas. I know he's generally a man of few words, but I kind of expected at least some sort of response. "Has Warrior Nation contacted you?"

After a beat, he finally says, "We've been in touch."

"Really? That's great!" Claire and I exchange a hopeful glance.

But he picks up his palm to stop our excitement. "Not in the way you're thinking, I'm afraid."

"Why not? They don't want your help?" Claire asks.

He frowns, gripping the arms of the chair. "That's not procedure. Bringing in a retiree . . . it would make them look weak." He pauses before adding: "Their words."

That makes no sense at all. "It seems like they'd be bringing in experience and wisdom, but what do I know?"

He brightens, giving me a sad smile. "I always liked you, Bridgette. Why are you getting yourself wrapped up in this anyway? Aren't you and Matt . . . ?"

"Even if we're not together, I don't want anything to happen to him." My heart pinches as I say the words, feeling their truth in my bones.

"That is admirable," he offers, "but you should stay out of this. Keep yourself safe."

"We're not going to charge into a secret lair or anything. Claire and I just want to get a rescue mission going."

Charles leans forward, bushy brows furrowed. "Why? Isn't Warrior Nation doing anything?"

"I don't know *what* they're doing, but they're not calling

in the other chapters for help, and we don't understand why."

He sits back, staring off at the lake, gaze hard. This is a man of action—a warrior—and to see him so still, so contemplative, is bizarre. Sunlight kissing his chiseled profile, he is the picture of heroism yet stuck in some kind of strange stupor. I can't tell if he's formulating his own secret plan, or if he's just exhausted by it all, giving up before he even begins.

"Will you help us?" Claire asks, hands twisting in her lap.

He turns back to us, expression as still as stone. "I'm not sure what I can do."

"Help us understand," I say, my urgency building. "You know the inner workings of this organization better than anyone. We—the whole city—need your expertise."

"This world doesn't need me anymore," he admits, not out of want for pity, but as statement of fact. Sad words hang among us, chilling the air, but Claire is not having this resolution.

"That is just not true!" His biggest fan is all fired up, and she won't go down without a fight. "You can still do great things! You're . . . my hero!" I give her an encouraging grin; if I had a cheerleader like Claire, I think even I could save the world. The way she's looking at him, it's like he's the sun and she's just lucky to be in his orbit. "You probably don't remember, but you saved my life when I was ten. My mom and I wouldn't be here if it wasn't for you. You inspired me to do something with my life, to help make the world a better place. That's why I joined Warrior Nation, and that's why I'm here now."

Her honest admission breaks him out of his sorrow. "Claire,

thank you for sharing that with me," Charles says quietly. He reaches for her hand, cupping it gently like he's holding a baby bird. "All I ever wanted to do was help people."

"And you still can," I say, leaning forward. "Chicago needs you."

"I'm . . . having trouble believing that," he answers. "I've been following all the story updates, trying to piece together what's going on. But no one will answer my calls; the other heroes don't want me around. My age makes me a liability, apparently."

"That's ridiculous!" Claire shrieks, offended on his behalf. "You're still just as strong if not stronger than all of them combined!"

"Be that as it may, I can't force myself into a situation where I'm not wanted. My contract states that me leaving the organization means I can no longer get involved—"

"Since when do you bow down to pieces of paper?" Claire counters.

"Since going off on a mission by myself, without the intel or support of my chapter, could get me killed," he says somberly. Claire and I share a pained look; she shudders at the thought. "Look, I think you both know I would get involved if I could, but my hands are tied. You two, on the other hand . . ." Charles pauses, deciding whether or not he should share his thoughts.

"Please," I encourage him, "if there's anything you can think of that will help us . . ."

He frowns, unsure. "Only if you promise you will stay out of harm's way."

"Of course, we promise," I say, awkwardly crossing my heart with my cast. Claire nods enthusiastically.

"If it were me, I would focus on the other chapters," he begins, tone laced with conspiracy. "Not sending in backup is against protocol, so what's going on there? What are they afraid of?"

"Losing more heroes?" Claire asks.

"Possibly. But what if it's something more?"

Something more? I don't know what this could be. I'd be the first to admit that Warrior Nation is not a perfect organization, but Charles is implying they're hiding some kind of serious skeletons in their closet. Like what? My biggest red flags have always been around the rigorous requirements of a hero's job, but could there be something I'm missing? I can already see Claire's brain working to decipher his potential clue.

"But what do I know?" Charles stands, towering above us. It's almost impossible not to imagine his blue cape fluttering behind him. "I'm just an old man."

"Not true—" Claire tries, but he stops her with a forced smile. Charles is not great at accepting praise, despite his years of practice. He motions for us to exit, but as we make our way back to his mansion, he holds me back, putting a strong arm over my shoulder.

"I want you to get yourself out of this, Bridgette," he instructs, face stern. "You are too young, too bright, to have your light extinguished."

This isn't a friendly request; it's a desperate demand. I've never seen him look like this, with such fear written on his face. "Charles . . ."

"I will do what I can to help," he offers, tightening his grip on my arm. "But this . . . siege may be more than I can handle." Could it be the reason he doesn't want to help us is dread? I didn't think Blue Streak was frightened by anything, but if the bravest hero of all time doesn't want to get in this fight, what are Claire and I doing?

"Thank you." My voice quivers. "People I care about are in danger."

He releases me, giving one last grim stare. "I know. I fear what will happen next."

Blue Streak Theme Song

Who saves the day when the world is weak?
Blue Streak!

Who's brave and strong when the rest are meek?
Blue Streak!

Who fights with honor, courageous and true?
Willing to risk it all for you?

Blue Streak!

CLAIRE

I TOUCHED HIS HAND. I WAS *IN* HIS *HOUSE*. Blue Streak has
MY childhood thank-you letter framed on his wall. I'm float-
ing, I'm dying—am I even still in my body? Oh, yes, because
Bridgette just threw a crumpled train pass at my forehead.

"Hello? Claire? Are you coming?" she calls from the other
side of the L turnstile.

"Sorry!" I fumble for my Ventra card, nestled safely in my
phone case, and join her on the platform. I don't even remember walking back to the Purple Line. I must have been orbiting
planet Starstruck.

"That was weird, don't you think?" Bridgette asks, staring
down the train tracks.

"What do you mean? Chatting with Blue—er, Charles?"
I recoil after saying his civilian name. It feels wrong in my
mouth. I don't think I'll ever get used to being on a first-name
basis with my idol.

"Yeah." Her forehead crumples above her sunglasses,
mouth puckered in thought.

"I don't know, that was pretty much one of the most amazing experiences of my entire life, so I can't really say." She nods, but the way her features are all tight and serious, it's making me think I need to get my head out of the clouds. "Why?" I add.

She looks around, as if checking for eavesdroppers, then pulls me over to a covered vestibule. "It's just . . . it doesn't make sense," she whispers, casually pulling at the ends of her hair to cover her lips. "Why wouldn't Warrior Nation bring him in to help? He's literally their only hope, even if he is retired, since they aren't calling on the other chapters. And he's right. . . . Why aren't they? Did the other chapters refuse to come?"

"I can't imagine that happening," I say, thinking about all the social media and press the other chapters have been giving. Nearly every hero across the country has issued some kind of statement about Warrior solidarity and support. "Heroes aren't really ones to see danger and go, *Nah, I'm good.*"

"Right. So then what? What's the holdup? Because right now it feels like Chicago is intentionally keeping other heroes out, even Blue Streak."

I will admit it was slightly disappointing not to have him immediately spring into a fully formulated plan to save the day, but that letdown was greatly overshadowed by just being in his presence. "It seemed like he kinda tried to offer help, even if he is retired . . ." I offer lamely.

I can almost feel her eyes rolling behind her shades. "No." She shakes her head. "Heroes don't just quit their day jobs. This life, this quest, to help others—it doesn't go away. For Matt, it's a compulsion. He can't *not* help. The thought of standing idly by fills his lungs with sea water. I'm sure you've seen it in Joy too—that look in her eye that says, *This is what I was born to do.*"

I bite my lip, thinking about the real reasons Joy got into the hero game. Bridgette doesn't need to know that, though, not right now, especially since that's been starting to change, with Joy embracing her heroic lifestyle more and more every day. "You don't spend every second of every day making the world a better place and then randomly stop caring. You know when you give this up? When you're six feet under."

Whoa. I shudder at the thought, the reality of why we were even talking to Blue Streak in the first place settling back in. A city in peril, Joy in danger. My head jerks at the mental image.

"Sorry," Bridgette says. "What I'm trying to get at is there must be a reason Warrior Nation doesn't want his help nor the other chapters'. Because I'm not buying the 'it will make them look weak' BS."

She's right that it doesn't make sense. How could anyone not want Blue Streak to come to the rescue? He's the guy you want on your team, and even if for some inconceivable reason you don't, there's a whole roster of heroes getting sidelined. My head swirls with the entire Warrior Nation lineup from coast to coast, specific superpowers popping up that may be helpful for Chicago's current predicament. Like Heat Wave, who could go all X-ray-vision-style and scan buildings to see if the heroes are being held against their will. Or Storm Chaser, who could put the city under a deep freeze and catch villains on their way to their next crime. These powers plus so many more are talents we desperately need, and saying that they're just hanging out until they can better assess the situation is faulty logic that would never hold up in a debate.

No, keeping the heroes away is no accident. This is a calculated choice. "They're hiding something," I say softly.

Bridgette instantly accepts this, nodding sadly. "I agree."

"But I don't understand what that could be."

The Purple Line pulls up to the Evanston station, screeching to a stop. We get on the train, and I pull out my grail diary as we take a seat, flipping through the pages to see if anything will spark an idea. A clue. Anything.

"Claire, you're a WarNat, right?" Bridgette asks as the L pushes ahead. I hold up my diary in response, and she snorts. "Right. Well, what do the fans go on about in the forums? Are there any major conspiracy theories?"

"Oh god," I sigh. "Now that's some *Alice in Wonderland*, never-ending-rabbit-hole stuff."

"I'm serious. When they aren't talking about how much they hate me or want to marry Matt, what are the big hot-topic issues?"

I pause. I'm not much of a conspiracy theorist, though I still browse those threads just to be in the know. People like to look for clues in places they don't exist, like pulling inane details from comic book panels and trying to tie the fictionalized accounts of the heroes' lives back to reality. It feels like a waste of time to me, though it can be amusing occasionally.

"I don't know. . . . There's the classic debate as to why each chapter only gets four heroes and whether or not there is symbolism in the number four. There's way-out-there stuff like Room E33 and how there's a phantom chapter in the Bermuda triangle. But lately the boards have been filled with the siege, people wondering what's going on, where these anti-hero villains are coming from, why Millie seems to be telling us less and less every day—"

"That!" Bridgette interrupts, pointing a finger my way. "Tell me more about that."

"Oh." I pause, surprised that's the detail that caught her attention. "Well, Millie has always been super thorough in her press conferences, going above and beyond to detail what happened and who was involved. But that's kind of fallen off in the past couple weeks, and sometimes she's skipped public press altogether, which is understandable, I guess, since there have been so many back-to-back crimes." I picture Millie scurrying around HQ, always on top of every single movement within the organization. She personally crafts how every battle and victory is perceived in the press, both writing and delivering the media messaging. Teddy always complains about how she never delegates press releases, and how he could easily take those off her plate, but I think she likes being the one to shape the story. Publicizing the heroes and showing off their strengths is what she does best; the only time she squashes a story is when it highlights a mistake, a less-than-heroic fumble. Like that time when the police pulled bodies out of the river without the Warriors being there. She didn't seem that upset about the actual victims; she was more annoyed at being called out for messing up.

Wait a minute.

A terrible idea strikes, instantly doing a number on my central nervous system. "But maybe she's not skipping press because of her schedule. Maybe . . . she's scared."

"I mean, how could she not be scared?" Bridgette asks. "Everyone is."

The thought snowballs, tumbling down a cliff so steep, I don't want to picture its cavernous end. "No, I mean, maybe she knows the truth about the siege—what's really happening—and she's scared because it's something bad about Warrior Nation, something that would ruin the organization."

Bridgette sits up in her plastic seat, turning toward me. "Claire! That makes total sense! If something damning has happened in Chicago, something that would cause all of this, bringing in backup from other chapters would only shine a spotlight on the issue. Which means . . . the problem is coming from HQ."

"Like . . . a mole?"

"Yeah! Think about it!" She slides her sunglasses up on her head, eyes blinking as fast as her thoughts. "In the seventy-something years Warrior Nation has been around, no villain has ever defeated an entire chapter. And then, suddenly, wave after wave of crimes completely wears them out, to the point where they're so tired, they all fall into a trap? Someone would have to intimately know these heroes—what they're going through, their stamina, their weaknesses. They'd have to truly understand when and how to strike against them."

I know I suggested it, but now that it's outside my head, it's sounding even worse. "So what you're saying is . . . the siege isn't just some general term for what's been going on in the city, but a person? A mastermind with an agenda? Like . . . *capital-S* Siege?"

"I hate to say it, but yeah. Someone has to be pulling all the strings, coordinating all these attacks." She stops, before shuddering with a thought. "Like that guy who was at our kidnapping! And on the video at the charity event! Even though a lot of these attacks have been random, he's been the most consistent presence, wouldn't you agree? He could be leading this whole thing, and maybe he's using insider information to do it."

It's a lot to take in. "And you think Millie knows who it is?"

"Maybe? But maybe not. She could be doing something behind the scenes, trying to smoke out the culprit before the other chapters swoop in. Trying to save face for Chicago."

I think of all my coworkers, our innocent conversations and casual interactions not setting off any red flags. Everyone I've met this summer loves the Warriors. Maybe not as obsessively as me, but the appreciation is there just the same. "But who? Who could do this?"

She slouches down in her seat, face creased in thought. "A rogue hero? Maybe one of them has faked their kidnapping to cover their tracks?"

"What?!" I yell, causing a few passengers to look my way.

"No, no way!" I shake my head so hard that pieces of my braid shake loose, unwilling to accept that possibility. "Absolutely not! Can you picture Ryan actively trying to hurt Matt? Or Joy? No. No! They're a team!"

"Yeah, you're right," she agrees. "And Ashleigh only seems interested in herself." We sit in silence, watching neighborhoods fly by as our train heads southward. "Well, what about a disgruntled employee?" she suggests after a minute. "Someone fed up with their job?"

The second she says it, a face flashes before me. Dark, beady eyes and a sharp, upturned nose, with hair so slicked back and shiny, it may as well be a helmet.

"Teddy!" we shout in unison, turning to each other in alarm.

"He knows everything about the Warriors and their schedules!" Bridgette shouts.

"And he's always complaining about how no one appreciates him, how someday he'll make his mark!" I add, his last words—"You'll be sorry you messed with me"—ringing in my ear. "Remember when we had our debriefing after our kidnapping? Teddy straight-up left the room when I mentioned how there seemed to be a leader. I thought at the time he was just jealous of me pointing out details of the crime, but maybe he couldn't be in there any longer because he was guilty and didn't want to give himself away."

"Yeah, he's never been great at hiding his true feelings. And he's vindictive as hell: He once sent Matt on some wild-goose

279

chase to rescue a shelter dog that was allegedly running back and forth across Lake Shore Drive, but as it turned out, there was no dog—Teddy was just mad at Matt for not inviting him to his birthday party."

I shake my head, embarrassed for Teddy. "Also, he's been messing with my schedule for weeks! Never in my life have I ever missed a meeting, but thanks to him, I've been pulled out of important talks so that I wouldn't be able to press the idea further!"

We stare at each other, frozen by this realization. Could Teddy really do this? Plan a citywide panic and hurt the very people he's been sworn to protect? He's never been my favorite, yet it doesn't feel out of the realm of possibility. Even though the villain who organized our kidnapping seemed to have a bigger build than Teddy, it wouldn't be the first time a baddie padded their suit to seem more intimidating. And honestly? Crafting fake muscles totally seems like something he would do. I was sitting the whole time, so it's hard to tell if Teddy and Siege would be the same height, but lord knows he loves hovering over me, staring down with gross self-righteousness. Blind ambition is something I understand all too well, but maybe Teddy was finally pushed over the edge.

"We have to do something," I say as Bridgette nods. "We have to warn HQ!" But before I can pull out my phone, a set of screams from our adjoining train car demands our attention. All the Purple Line passengers flock to the windows as we speed by a neighborhood on fire, flames licking the buildings and trees, black smoke filling the sky. Bridgette gasps, holding on to a handrail for support, and I nearly fall out of my seat from the startling sight. The train only lets us see a sliver of the mayhem before safely carrying us by, but it's enough to shake me, riling up my worries for Joy, the Warriors, and Chicago at large.

Without the heroes, villains are free to do whatever they please, Siege clearing the way for total chaos.

Without the heroes, no one is safe.

I zone out, all the scariest scenes from Warrior comics and movies colliding into one epically chilling montage in my head, until Bridgette gently squeezes my arm. "Claire? Your phone is ringing."

I look down, fire still dancing in my eyes, and answer my phone. On the other end, Mom screams, "GET HOME NOW!"

To: All Staff <chicagoHQ@warriornation.com>

From: Millicent Montouse <mmontouse@warriornation.com>

Subject: All Staff Interrogation

All employees must report to headquarters immediately for mandatory interrogation and polygraph tests. No one is to leave the premises until granted permission, and all staff must be prepared to answer questions regarding exact whereabouts during the heroes' kidnapping.

Any employee who fails to comply will be turned over to the authorities immediately.

Millie Montouse
Chief spokesperson, Chicago Chapter

BRIDGETTE

IT'S WEIRD TO BE IN SOMEONE'S HOUSE for the first time when the inhabitants are screaming at each other. Sitting alone in Claire's room, I try not to eavesdrop, but keep overhearing scraps of their argument.

I don't know what to do with you. . . .

Mom, I am making a difference! I am helping to stop this!

I don't want you caught in the crosshairs!

That last thought, especially, is copied straight from the Rey-family-drama capsule. Neither of my parents ever supported my relationship with Matt, and it's no shock as to why. I'm sure it's not fun to wonder where your child is when the world is literally on fire. I know for a fact my love life impacted my parents', as fights about my safety turned into failed parenting accusations, which spiraled into dark marital rabbit holes of blame. I even tried to lie and say Matt and I broke up early on to help make peace at home, but his star shone too bright to keep our dating a secret. I eventually stopped looping them in altogether, tired of being in the middle of their blame game, and moved in with Becca. She was protective of me too but trusted me to make my own choices and didn't make me feel like shit when I chose wrong.

Voices settle in the room, screaming melting into sobs. I breathe deep, hoping they've found some common ground. In the relative quiet, I get up to examine an enormous Warrior Nation mural on Claire's wall, a massive floor-to-ceiling installation crammed with seemingly every scrap of hero ephemera that exists. Magazine covers, stickers, fan art: all lovingly curated and arranged with care. It's a little . . . much, and yet, knowing Claire, I understand it comes from a place of admiration and not stalker obsession.

A glossy picture of Matt catches my eye: his *Time* magazine cover from about a year ago. He was so proud to be featured, and even though he'd been on other covers before, for some reason this one was special to him. Standing tall with his dark features looking amazing against his shiny white suit, he looks proud. Confident. Like he's exactly where he's supposed to be. There's a printed quote next to his face—*Heroes put others first*—and I remember feeling frustrated about it at the time. It's funny to read these same words through Claire's eyes; she probably saw this as inspirational, a token of hope worthy of her collection, whereas I took it as a symbol of what was wrong with my relationship.

I touch the photo, tracing my finger over Matt's jawline. If I were really touching him like that, he'd start squirming, since he's extremely ticklish. I think about the scar that runs from under his right earlobe to midway down his jaw; most people think he got it from some heroic endeavor, but it's actually a childhood injury from stealing cookies late at night. Just when he thought he was in the clear with his handful of Oreos, his family's cat darted out from a shadowy corner, causing him to trip and hit his face on the corner of a coffee table. There are so many things that only I know about him, secrets never shared in blogs or broadcasts.

I miss you, I think, and the unexpected feeling catches in my throat, eyes glazing over with sudden tears. I could blame it on exhaustion or the worry shaking me to my core, but no, I really do miss being part of our couple. The intimacy and the quiet moments. I miss Matt.

Claire walks in, splotchy and angry, with her mom close behind. I quickly sit and stare intently at a random book on her desk, as if I wasn't just stroking a picture of my ex-boyfriend's face. Luckily, neither of them seems to notice, still calming down from their argument. I've never met Claire's mom before, but I can already tell they have a much different relationship than me and mine. Just the fact that they're sharing the same space post-fight instead of creating as much distance as possible proves a tighter bond. I haven't been back to my house in months, and while my mom checks in with a text every now and then, she really doesn't know much about my life at this point.

"Bridgette, hello," her mom says, extending a welcoming hand my way. Since I can't complete a normal handshake with my cast, I give a small wave back instead.

"Nice to meet you, Ms. Rice."

"You can call me Mary." She smiles, blue eyes still watery. "I'm sorry about all that."

"Hey, I get it. Believe me."

Claire plops down on her bed, arms crossed in defiance, back facing her mom. Based on the closed-off look on her face, I guess I'll need to be the moderator here.

"Tell me, Bridgette," Mary continues, wringing her hands. "Have you ever been in this situation before?"

"Not exactly. I mean, Matt's been in danger plenty of times, but the other Warriors usually come to his rescue."

"Sure, but I guess what I mean is, what does Warrior Nation do to keep you safe?"

I scratch at the back of my neck. "Um . . . there isn't like a security detail or anything, unfortunately. There's a help hotline, and we can always stay at HQ if we feel more secure there." Though I've always felt like staying underground is no way to live, regardless of the circumstances.

Mary sits down next to Claire, trying to reach for her daughter, but Claire jerks away, whipping her braid over her shoulder. Her mom takes a sharp breath, swallowing down whatever it is she really wants to say. "Claire said you thought staying together would be best. . . . You're welcome to stay here, if you like. It would make me feel better to know Claire is home safe."

"Mom, no! I said we need to get back to HQ!" Claire spits. "We have stuff to do!"

"Claire," Mary says through her teeth, clearly reaching

286

her frustration limit. "There are professionals who can handle this."

Claire jerks around, fire in her eyes. "Yes! ME. *I'm* the professional!"

"You are only seventeen! You are not a hero!" her mom shouts, the mural of Warriors from decades past staring down from above. "Do you think this is why Blue Streak saved you all these years ago, so that you could throw your life away? This is not your fight!"

"Yes it is! Why won't you listen to me?" Claire begs, struggling to hold back tears. "Bridgette and I just stumbled onto something big, something that could put an end to all this. Right?" She looks to me for support as Mary silently begs me to back her up too.

In all my years of watching the Warriors fight, I never wanted to jump in. There's nothing in me that feels the need to chase danger and beat it to a pulp. The only part of battle I enjoy is the end, when the villain is defeated and everyone can go home to the person they love. I crave those quiet moments, the afterglow of safety and peace. But I know all too well there is no calm unless you face the storm.

"Claire's right," I start as Mary shakes her head in frustration. "And trust me, I'm not looking to put us at risk." I hold up my cast for dramatic effect. "But we can't just stay here and hope it all works out." Claire wipes her face, beaming at me.

"You're both too young to be dealing with this," Mary croaks.

"Well, so is Joy! And Matt!" Claire explains. "They're the same age as we are."

"But they have powers, they have . . . training!" her mom exclaims, not backing down from this fight.

They continue to argue as my phone buzzes with a text message from Becca:

ARE YOU WATCHING?!?!?

Huh? Watching what? I send back a "?" and she immediately sends a link to *ABC 7 News*, which is live-streaming a Warrior Nation update. But this is not some official organization-produced segment: There's no branding, no upbeat theme song. The screen is black, with a line of white text that reads:

Stand by for the Fate of Your Heroes

"Oh god," I whisper, silencing the room. Claire and Mary instantly stop bickering, jumping up to watch over my shoulder.

I can't look away, fingers gripping the phone for dear life. What is about to happen? What are we going to see? My mind races with dark possibilities: Matt, broken and bloody, hollow eyes giving in to the fear that no one is coming to his rescue. All the Warriors gagged and tied together, an entire chapter worthless and defeated. This Siege has yet to make any demands, and literally anything could be waiting on the other side of this warning.

Suddenly the screen changes, with a close-up on a dark, familiar helmet. The camera holds on a person draped in black, instantly striking fear in my heart.

"Claire!" I yelp. "That's him! The guy from our kidnapping!"

"That's the person who took you?" Mary gasps, covering her mouth in horror. Then the camera pans down to a shot of Matt's face.

I almost drop my phone.

He's only been gone for two days, but he looks like he's been to hell and back. Most of his mask is pulled up into his dark, sweaty hair. An eggplant-colored bruise covers his right eye, so swollen it can't even open, as only his left stares hopelessly at the camera. The top of his white suit is tattered, jagged pieces hanging at the neckline, and a black leather glove grips his shoulder, holding him down.

Matt. Oh, Matt.

Claire holds on to me as Mary cries, uttering a breathless "Dear god" as Matt struggles to move his mouth to speak.

"Citizens of Chicago," Matt starts, lips chapped and bloody. "Your heroes have failed you. But truly, you have failed yourselves. Why do you place your faith in only the supers, ignoring the strength within you? You place your lives in the care of those who fly and fight, but why? Why does some organization get to decide who is super and who is not? Why do some powers get treated with respect, while others are cast aside?" Matt coughs, struggling to continue reading the message he's being forced to deliver. The gloved hand squeezes him tighter, pushing him to continue. "Siege has assembled a team of cast-offs to prove that Warriors are not the only ones who can make a difference. He is freeing this city from the social constructs that bind us, that make us believe that only certain people can save the day."

"We were right," Claire mumbles, without a hint of satisfaction. "Siege is one person."

"A person who's torturing the people we love," I choke. A tear runs down my cheek as my fingertips graze the screen; I desperately wish I could give Matt even an ounce of comfort right now.

"Siege has done the impossible, proving that heroes are nothing but worthless idols unworthy of fame or adoration. This is only the beginning. Warriors across the country will fall, and from the ashes a new era will rise." Matt pauses again, catching his breath, but this time, something changes in his face, like he's mustering up every last bit of strength to finish what he's started. His drooping head snaps up straight, eyebrows lifted toward the sky as he says, "But the purple paper makes it whole!" just as the hand that held him smacks across his face, screen cutting to black.

The three of us scream in Claire's bedroom, mom and daughter grabbing on to each other, sandwiching me in between. I keep staring at my phone, willing it to bring back Matt's face, but it remains dark.

"Oh my god!" Claire shouts in my ear, burying her forehead into my shoulder.

"Those poor kids," Mary says on my left. "I . . . need some wine." She wiggles free to give us both a kiss on the head, fighting back tears as she leaves the room.

"Matt's face . . ." Claire breathes into me. "What is Siege doing to them?"

"I don't know," I answer honestly. "I don't know."

"They have to do something now, right?" Claire asks, releasing me from her tight squeeze. "Millie and Roy and everyone? If they know it's Teddy, now would be the time to release that information, consequences of having it be one of their own be damned. There's no way they don't go in guns blazing after this."

"Yeah . . ." I trail off, taking a seat on Claire's bed. I feel dizzy, light-headed, with the image of Matt's beaten face taking over my vision, his words swirling on a constant loop. How awful it must have been for him to speak those lies, to go against everything he believes in and fights for. Every sentence in direct opposition to his work, his heart . . . except . . .

"Wait a minute," I say. "It was a clue!"

"What?"

"Matt said *the purple paper makes it whole.* Remember my mural, and how I ran out of blue paper?" I start, a small drop of excitement diluting the panic in my veins. "I wanted to swap out that purple piece that didn't match, but Matt told me to leave it there, that it made the mural whole. He said that someday when we're all gone, that paper will still be there, contributing in its own small way." I'm on my feet, bouncing with hope. "Matt was trying to tell me something. . . . There must be something on that piece of paper . . . a clue, a note he left behind. Something!" I exhale deeply, looking back at Matt's smiling face on Claire's wall. Even though we're not together, Matt still trusted I wouldn't give up on him. He left me some kind of information. Hoping I'd be watching. Knowing I'd be watching.

Claire is right there with me. "Because he knows it's Teddy! Maybe he's leading us to some kind of literal paper trail, like a file that indicates a history of violence or something incriminating!"

Teddy. No one at HQ is safe if he's lurking about unchecked. I quickly text Anna, asking if she's still there and if she's seen him.

> Yes I'm here but no I haven't seen him why? Everyone is freaking out over that video! God I hope Ryan is okay. Are you? Matt's face! I can't! What's going to happen

A gunshot fires outside, distracting me from reading the rest of her lengthy response. A series of car alarms awaken, and Claire and I rush to the window. The neighborhood takes to the streets, screaming and shouting in response to Matt's video. Two men get in a fistfight; a trash can goes flying through a car window. With no heroes on patrol to stop nor save them, there's no telling where this will lead.

"We gotta go; it's not safe here," I say as Claire nods in

agreement, swallowing hard. "If Teddy's inflicting violence on the heroes, there's no telling what he'd do to the people at HQ. We need to get there, find out where the paper leads us, and tell Millie what we know."

"But what about my mom? I feel like she's going to barricade the door with her body before letting me out there."

"We'll bring her too—keep everyone together and safe. I'll text Becca. We can't stop now."

Matt is counting on me.

MSNBC report

After a disturbing video of Chicago Warrior Nation hero Vaporizer was sent to the press, local residents have taken to the streets, erupting in a series of riots and demonstrations. While some of the gatherings have proved to be peaceful meetings of neighborly concern, many have dissolved into violence, especially in larger areas such as Grant Park, where thousands of Chicagoans have assembled.

Local police are urging residents to stay in their homes if possible until the situation can be contained, issuing a citywide curfew of 9:00 p.m.

At this time, Warrior Nation has not released any statement about the video or their next course of action. This silence is causing extreme unrest throughout the city.

We will continue our coverage as the story unfolds.

CLAIRE

SIRENS WAIL OUTSIDE, EMERGENCY RESPONDERS trying to extinguish yet another fire. *What are you doing, Warrior Nation?* Why are you letting this happen? Despite my passionate pleas about needing to save the day, there's a tiny, nagging part of me that agrees with Mom. Why do *I* have to be the one stepping in? How the hell did it come to this? As the weakest link in the Warrior food chain, there is absolutely zero reason why an intern should have to help, and yet here I am, getting ready to put it all on the line when Millie and friends are actively choosing not to get backup. Staying silent, when they should be keeping everyone in the loop, at least internally. I want to believe that something else is going on, that there's a valid explanation as to why the organization I've spent my life worshipping is in a holding pattern, but doubt sinks its teeth in, gnawing away at my resolve.

I wish Blue Streak hadn't retired. I wish he would do something, no matter the consequences.

Heading into the kitchen, I spot Mom standing over the sink, quietly sipping a pinot grigio while staring off into space.

Her usually perky blond bob lies flat against dull skin, and her tired eyes are void of sparkle. I hate that we fought, I hate scaring her like this. We've been a two-person super duo for most of my life, and now I feel like I'm sinking our own ship. Tiptoeing up behind her, I wrap my arms around her waist, resting my cheek on her shoulder as she sighs deeply.

"Claire," she exhales, setting down her wineglass. "I'm sorry I yelled. I want you to know: I don't doubt your abilities. I know you're strong, smart, and capable of anything you put your mind to. But . . ." She turns around, facing me. "I'm so scared for you. I don't want anything bad to happen to you."

"I don't want anything bad to happen to me either," I admit as she strokes my cheek with her thumb. "I always thought that given the chance I'd be brave, you know? Stand up for what I believe in. And while I'm not backing down, it's not without doubt."

"Because you saw what they did to Vaporizer?"

"Yeah, I mean, it's one thing to think about torture, but then to see it . . ." A vision of Matt's oozing purple injuries is overlaid on Joy's face, and I'm instantly sick, my stomach churning at the mere thought of her in pain. Blond hair stained with blood, blue eyes swollen shut . . . Her mom must be losing her mind, especially since she didn't want Joy to become a hero in the first place. It's too much, too much, and I'm completely scared out of my mind—scared for Joy, scared to sneak around HQ, scared that Warrior Nation is not the organization I idolized my whole life.

"Claire?"

I snap out of my nightmare, remembering that Joy will stay that way if I don't do something to help. "We have to go to HQ, okay?" I tell Mom, who starts to resist, but I add, "We'll be safe there, and we'll be able to help."

She swallows down the rest of her wine in one giant gulp, setting down the glass with renewed force. I know I haven't convinced her; I know that torture video only made things worse. She looks at me like I'm far away, like I've put her in a position way beyond her parental reach, a place where there is no clear right thing to do. "Okay," she eventually relents. "As long as we're together. Never cease, never cower?"

I nod, yet the words don't give me that usual sense of pride.

Bridgette suggests we bring everyone we care about, so I text Demi, whom I haven't heard from since our fight.

> Hey, are you okay? Are you safe?

Yeah there were a bunch of idiots rioting down the street but we're okay

> I'm taking my mom to warrior hq for safety—want to come?

Uh not really sure how I'd leave the house with this curfew and all. But thanks anyway. Hope your gf isn't dead

I try not to roll my eyes, giving her the benefit of the

doubt that her tone is getting lost via text. But she has a good point. How can we save the day when the city is on lockdown?

"Hey, Bridgette?"

I find her at my desk, folding pieces of ripped scrap paper into small flowers. The surface is covered in tiny white blossoms, yet she keeps going, silently bending and creasing away. She works slowly, creating little botanical masterpieces with one hand. It must calm her, keeping her hands busy. I wish I could find some calm right now, but my favorite obsession is causing me more harm than good at the moment.

"Um, how are we gonna get to HQ?"

"I called Matt's personal driver, Walter, to come pick us up. He's on the Warrior payroll, drives an armored car. He owes me a favor, so . . ." She folds another paper flower, like a form of meditation.

"Is your sister coming?"

"No, but she's with her boyfriend, Sam, so at least she's not alone."

"You're not alone either," I offer, and she looks up, giving me a shadow of a smile. Bridgette's seen so much more than I have, dived deep, beyond the glossy magazine covers and slow-motion action shots. All that stuff I've fixated on—the wins, the successes—that's only part of the story. Everything leading up to the victory is hard, dark, a world I never even considered. A world I don't like.

"Thanks," she says softly, pausing her flower making. "Are

you sure you want to go through with this? I know how much you love the Warriors. . . . If we're right . . . If Warrior Nation knows what's going on but is doing nothing to stop it . . . it may change the way you feel about all this."

My nerves shake with this truth, and I look up at my mural for strength. Friendly, comforting faces smile down at me: Blue Streak's stoic, tight-lipped grin; Vaporizer's charming, playboy smirk; Girl Power's bright, glowing beam. These will always be my heroes—the people who have shaped my life's mission and helped me become the woman I am today. My heroes haven't done anything wrong, and even if the organization supporting them has gone a little rotten, will it change my commitment to the cause? Would I turn my back on their mission, their motto? I try to puzzle this out, forecasting how I will feel after unveiling the truth, but I'm stuck. We don't know for sure what we're going to find; maybe we're completely off base. Even though I want to get down to the bottom of this, part of me hopes we're wrong.

My veins run blue with Warrior blood. Maybe I'm naive or just plain stubborn, but I still want to believe everyone tied to Warrior Nation is good, that my love and devotion was not in vain. But I can't know what's waiting for me on the other side.

"I don't know, but I'm not stopping now."

*

Things have shifted at HQ. Whereas before everyone was running about, quickly trying to figure out what to do next against Siege, the compound is now eerily silent, distrust hardening every face. The hallways are filled with whispers and stolen glances, people walking alone with heads hung low in suspicion and doubt. The panic is palpable, wafting from every teary eye and hunched shoulder.

Everyone smells a rat, but no one knows where it's coming from.

It takes us forever to get Mom through security; even though Millie encouraged us to bring family members underground, the blind terror of that video has everyone on alert, and she has to undergo a strict vetting process just to walk through the door. And not only her: Apparently while we were away, Millie issued staff-wide polygraph tests, so I find myself strapped to multiple sensors before I can even think about finding Teddy or that purple paper.

"Is your name Claire Rice?" asks my interrogator, a man I've never seen before.

"Yes." The polygraph needle remains calm, though I am not. I have no reason to be nervous—I have nothing to hide—but all the sensors strapped to my body, plus the high-pressure situation of knowing the only reason this is happening is that something has gone terribly wrong, have me feeling light-headed.

"Are you an intern for Warrior Nation?"

"Yes."

He asks a few more baseline questions before launching into "Are you in any way connected to Siege?"

"No," I say with more anger than I mean. This is a waste

of my time! The real culprit is out there right now, roaming these halls!

"Where were you when Joy Goodwin, also known as Girl Power, was kidnapped?"

For this, I don't have an answer. I don't know the exact moment she was taken, or what exactly transpired. My imagination has certainly dreamed up the worst, though, flashing images of her being held down against her will, her super strength overpowered by chains, cages, and other terrible torture devices. Thinking of these possibilities, the needle starts to sway a bit, but I recount the last time I saw her, right down to me helping her change into her suit in that bathroom stall, and how I went home and cried, praying for her safety.

I pass the test and meet up with Mom and Bridgette, who looks as frustrated as I feel.

"That was ridiculous," Bridgette says, gritting her teeth. "Nothing like creating internal hysteria to keep people on edge and away from finding the truth."

"It's not good," I admit, my heart sinking. Either Warrior Nation has no clue what's going on with Siege, or they do and are working overtime to cover up their mistakes. No matter what, it's discouraging.

Under different circumstances, getting to show off HQ to Mom would be a really cool moment, since she's lived the WarNat life just as long as I have. But with all the blue lighting switched to red for the state of emergency, and people walking around like the world is coming to an end, it isn't exactly the chill family tour I would have preferred.

"This is . . . this is . . . wow." Mom's jaw hangs open as she takes it all in, flashing screens and weary faces passing us by.

"It's usually, um, less grim," I admit. Everywhere we turn, there's someone either crying alone in a corner or tiredly typing on their tablet, trying to find a shred of hope on their screen. This is not the place I've come to know and love; this is not the Warrior Nation spirit. With every step, it feels more and more possible that Millie, Roy, Teddy—someone—is guilty, and they are doing whatever it takes to keep themselves out of trouble. Mom keeps a death grip on my arm as Bridgette stays laser-focused, leading us toward the cafeteria.

In our hurry, we pass by the Bad News room, where Anna sits alone, mesmerized by the flat screen. A loop of Matt's hostage video plays, over and over, yet she doesn't move, his battered face reflected in her giant glasses.

"Anna? What are you doing?" I ask, straying off course. I sit next to her, but she barely moves, keeping her eyes glued to the screen. "How many times have you watched this?"

"Not sure," she whispers. "I've lost count."

I could barely make it through the first time; how can she keep going? "Why don't you look away for a sec, okay?" The screen cuts to black, but a second later, it starts again, Matt's bruised mouth beginning his message.

"I can't," she says, pushing up her frames. "I keep thinking maybe the camera will pan left, just a bit, so I can get a glimpse of Ryan. If I look away . . . I might miss it. And I don't want to miss it. He's hurt, somewhere he's hurt, and no one is trying to help him. I won't know what to do with myself if he dies."

I wrap my arm around her, sharing her wish. If only the camera would move an inch, just to let me know that Joy is there. Breathing. Alive.

Matt delivers his "purple paper" line, and it dredges up the last bit of courage I have left. We are here to take action. I need to move.

"Anna, have you seen Teddy?"

She shakes her head, frustrated. "No! Why do you two keep asking me that? Who cares about stupid Teddy when my boyfriend is out there being tortured, held against his will?" She cries so hard she starts to choke, lungs gasping for air. Mom immediately goes into caretaker mode, kneeling beside her and gently stroking her back.

"Slow it down, nice and easy," she coos as Anna gargles the word "asthma," clutching her chest. Mom looks through Anna's bag and pulls out an inhaler, pressing the device against her lips. A few deep breaths later, she's back on track, but still incredibly shaken.

"We need to keep moving," Bridgette whispers to me. "Can your mom stay here with Anna, make sure she's okay?"

"Go," Mom says, eavesdropping. "But just promise to check back soon."

I kiss the top of her head, and we head off. The fact that Teddy hasn't found us yet, that he isn't breathing down my neck about something pointless, feels very incriminating.

"How do you think he pulled it off?" I ask Bridgette as we race down the halls. "I mean, sure, Teddy's smart and all, but he's not exactly strong."

"He knew all the heroes' weaknesses," she says matter-of-factly. "Like how Matt can turn invisible, but he can't walk through walls. Most villains don't even realize that and assume he's just disappearing through drywall. But if you trap him, he can't get anywhere."

Wow, I don't even think I knew that. I make a mental note to add it to my grail diary later.

"When we get to the cafeteria," Bridgette continues, "you keep an eye out and I'll stand on a table to yank out that purple paper."

"Yes, can do," I reply. "Do you think anyone will get suspicious? I mean, it's a pretty random thing to do, start tearing down a mural."

"I don't know. All of HQ has turned into demoralized zombies. Either they will care a lot and go straight for our brains, or barely notice at all."

God. I hate that what she's saying is true. "I cannot wait to take Siege down."

We turn a corner and crash right into Teddy, who greets us with a slimy grin.

"Oh, so you think you know who Siege is now?"

For a second, I freeze, too many thoughts and emotions fighting for my attention at once. Teddy, always thinking he's above everyone else. Teddy, who used his insider knowledge to game the very system he was sworn to support. Teddy, who's been deliberately messing with my schedule to keep me off his scent and away from face time with Millie, just so he could execute his plans to torture my would-be girlfriend for his own personal gain!

"YOU!" I lunge for him, knocking his tablet out of his arms. I sink my nails into his shirt as the device shatters, glass crunching under our feet. Wild, rabid with rage, I claw at him as he stumbles back in surprise.

"Claire! What is the matter with you?" he yells, desperately swatting at me. But I don't stop my assault—I can't—ripping away at his buttoned sleeve until he finally overpowers me, squeezing my hands with his long, bony fingers.

"Let her go!" Bridgette screams, pounding both her fists—cast be damned—into his arm.

"What has gotten into you two?" he cries, beady eyes growing three sizes in shock.

"We know! We know you're Siege!" I shout, hoping someone will overhear. "We're here to put an end to your villainy once and for all!"

Slowly, ever so slowly, Teddy's expression twists from dismay to delight, his horrified gape bending into a satisfied smile. "You think I'm Siege?" Bridgette and I share a quick glance. Teddy releases me, tapping his chin in amusement. "Well, well, I must say I'm flattered."

Okay . . . definitely not the response I was expecting. "Flattered? You're happy we're accusing you?"

"Do you have any idea how many employees have been accused of being Siege since that video aired? It's like a witch hunt up in here! Of course, you would know that if you cared to stick around and help."

"But we know it's you," Bridgette insists, eyebrows tight. "You have the motive, the access to information."

"And you've been messing with my schedule! Keeping me away from any new developments because you know I'm a Warrior expert!" I add.

Teddy fans himself in mock embarrassment. "Again, flattered. But no. Claire, you think you're the only one who's had a crazy schedule lately? We are in an emergency state here, which means things have been changing minute to minute. Everyone's been running around trying to chase every new lead, every new development, meaning that, yeah, meetings get canceled and rescheduled with hardly any notice." He picks up his shattered tablet, which continues to flash with notifications despite the destroyed screen. I watch as a non-stop stream of texts from different department heads pop up, asking him to book conference rooms, cancel press conferences, and clear afternoons in a mind-bending dance of calendar tango.

I guess it wasn't just me getting yanked around.

He drops his tablet back on the floor as if it no longer holds any use for him, kicking it under a nearby empty desk. "This has been fun, but I have actual business to attend to. Like capturing the real Siege."

"But we already did! It's you!" I say, even though certainty is seeping out of me like a deflating balloon.

He sighs. "Listen, while everyone here has been burying their heads in the sand, I discovered what's really going on. And since our ridiculous chapter president refused to acknowledge my work, I've been running my own side mission. You're welcome to join the cause, since you're so enthusiastic."

"Right, like we'd ever trust you!" I snort, and Bridgette nods in agreement.

Teddy bends down so that we're level, dark eyes peering into mine. "You don't have to trust me. The evidence speaks for itself." And with that he spins around, disappearing down a red-lit hallway while whistling an unsettlingly cheery tune.

Curious, we have no choice but to follow.

NBC 5 special report

With Warrior Nation on a media blackout, reporters have been desperate for commentary, turning to anyone with even the remotest of hero connections to sit down for an interview.

NBC 5 recently visited a Cook County prison to speak with Chomper, an inmate convicted of five counts of kidnapping and grand theft auto. Chomper was brought to justice three years ago by Blue Streak during a high-speed chase on I-88 in which Blue Streak flew behind the villain's stolen Lamborghini, lifting it up off the expressway and carrying him directly to local authorities.

When asked for his thoughts on Siege and his superpowered Anti-Heroes, Chomper said:

"It's smart, you know? I don't know why nobody has thought of it before. Organizing a bunch of crooks to use their talents together? Yeah. Most of us work alone, but that makes no sense. Even though I like being the boss, I wouldn't mind working under a guy who gives me free range and protection to do what I want. Those Warriors . . . forget 'em. The days for heroes are numbered."

BRIDGETTE

"I DON'T LIKE THIS," CLAIRE WHISPERS TO ME as we follow a disturbingly cheerful Teddy through HQ. "Why is he so freaking happy?"

"He has a secret," I murmur back to the sound of him humming "Whistle While You Work." "If I know anything about Teddy, it's that he loves being an insider." While Teddy is the king of acting chipper for his superiors, brownnosing pleasantries are different than genuine smiles. Without the weight of his constantly flashing tablet, he's looser, shoulders down and stride relaxed. I don't think I've ever seen him in such high spirits, so this pep in his step must mean he's got something good, something liberating. Something you'd have to see to believe.

"But, like, he's not taking us to some hidden murder den, is he? Shouldn't we be going to get the purple paper instead?"

I shake my head. "We will. Let's just see what he knows first." We're headed toward the east wing, the first HQ hub from the 1950s. As technology advanced and Warrior Nation grew in popularity, the need for more offices and space exploded, causing the Chicago chapter to build out into the underground labyrinth it is today. But for some reason, the original space never got a face-lift and was basically abandoned. Now it's used primarily for storage. There are no glass walls or floor-to-ceiling screens: just concrete rooms painted white in an attempt to make it not the most depressing environment of all time. I've wandered around here once or twice, but the deserted vibe always creeped me out.

"Why are we all the way over here?" I ask Teddy, who pulls a brass key from his pocket.

"Well, it's kind of hard to do secret investigations when your office is see-through, don't you think?" he answers with sass. Unlocking a large metal door, he gestures for us to go inside, but Claire is not having it.

"Yeah, right!" She crosses her arms in resolve. "I'm not going in there just so you can trap us inside!"

Teddy rolls his eyes. "Oh, Claire, if I really wanted to lock you up, I would have done it a long time ago." This doesn't exactly boost our confidence. Neither of us moves, causing him to sigh dramatically, handing me the key. "There. Now will you come in?"

Claire shakes her head in warning, brown eyes blinking in doubt. But we've come this far, and while I'd never consider Teddy an ally, I desperately want to learn what is causing his self-righteous glee. Placing my non-broken hand on Claire's shoulder, I say, "C'mon, we need to see this through. For Matt, for Joy." Claire nods, face pinched in determination.

The concrete office is like a jail cell, only outfitted with stolen technology. He's created his own mini control room, with outdated screens fighting for space on an old wooden table, yellow legal pads filled with pages and pages of hand-scrawled notes. This isn't a last-minute, thrown-together project; Teddy's been at this for a while. We squeeze inside, both of us marveling at his hidden detective bunker.

"How long have you had this office?" I ask, shocked at how he could assemble something like this without anyone noticing.

"Hmm, probably over a year now. My hours under Millie kept getting longer and longer, and sometimes it was just easier to sleep here." He nods at a sleeping bag rolled up under the desk. "It's probably why I'm so pale."

Claire flips through his legal pads, eyes wide in disbelief. "But all these notes! They go back . . . wow, years?"

"Well, I am a WarNat at heart, after all," he says, thin lips twisted in vindication.

Claire's jaw drops, unsure how to process this information.

He gives her a fake pout, ruffling her hair like she's a lost puppy. "Aww, I know, you thought you were the only one. But no. I've been tracking Warrior crime stats since I was a teenager, and that didn't change when I got hired. I just got access to better information. And when Siege came onto the scene, I knew something was wrong."

For someone who claims not to be a villain, he sure is going into monologue mode with ease. "Teddy, this is all very . . . impressive," I say, stoking his ego, "but just tell us what you know. The heroes are hurt—they need us."

He smiles at the word "us," chest swelling with pride. "I agree. Now, what I'm about to say may come as a shock, but I think the real Siege is . . ." He pauses for dramatic effect. "Roy Masterson."

What? Claire frowns as I cautiously ask, "Okay . . . why?"

He laughs in surprise, shocked that we didn't immediately see things his way. "Don't you think it's obvious? The man is chapter president, yet he's never around. He hardly ever shows up to important meetings, and even when he does, he's clueless. Millie usually has to cover for him, stepping up to speak on his behalf because he's been gone doing god knows what!"

All of that is true, though none of it feels like a smoking gun. While Roy is definitely an absentee leader, I always felt that came from a lack of talent, not malicious intent. Matt used to joke that Roy literally fell into this job, crashing and burning in the field but then suddenly finding himself in the highest command. I mean, he was the most inept hero in Warrior history, and for a guy known as Mr. Know-It-All, it's pretty clear he's usually in the dark on most things. "I don't know, Teddy. Just because he's incompetent doesn't mean he's guilty. Do you have any evidence against him?"

Teddy shuffles through his papers as Claire looks at me, utterly confused. "I would've never thought of Roy, honestly," she says. "WarNats call him President Doofus, mostly for all his failures in battle, but also because of that dopey smile of his. But now that you mention it, it *could* make sense. His power is detecting other people's superpowers, which would definitely help him build up a crew of anti-heroes. . . ."

"Yes!" Teddy agrees. "I was going to say that! Also, he does not have alibis during the heroes' kidnappings. I cannot find a time stamp for him on any HQ security cameras, and no one I've spoken to can definitively place his whereabouts during our estimated times of abduction."

Okay, well, that is suspicious.

"He's been driving me crazy since the day I started here," Teddy continues, shaking his head as he flips through his notepad. "All smiles and no work ethic. While some of us bust our butts to make this chapter the greatest one in the entire organization!"

"What does Millie say about your theory?" I ask.

"Oh . . . Millie?" He grimaces. "I haven't told her yet."

"Why not?"

"You have to understand—Millie is very busy. She has a lot of pressure on her right now. I don't want to bring this to her attention until I'm absolutely sure."

"But you seem pretty sure about this," Claire says. "You brought us to this little bunker of yours to drop your big discovery."

Teddy glowers at her. "I AM sure, but I want to have undeniable proof before I go accusing the chapter president of villainy. Something neither of you had when you pointed a finger at me." Claire starts to spit something back, but I hold her off, resting my cast on her shoulder. He continues. "Everyone has been undergoing polygraph tests, per Millie's decree. I've been trying to access his session, but so far the reports haven't been uploaded into our system."

"Dang, how high is your security clearance?" Claire asks, jealous.

"The highest." He grins. He spins around to the ancient desktop computer on his table, quickly typing a password into the keyboard that opens up a Warrior Nation screen I recognize from peeking over Matt's shoulder from time to time. When Matt first joined Warrior Nation, he was locked to his laptop for weeks, ready to learn anything and everything about the hero life. I'd sometimes look up from my sketchbook and see him reading Warrior lore. He'd get all nerdy about it, gushing about all the great men and women who'd come before him, and how he wanted to make a difference too. I remember the look on his face, how he'd glow with excitement like a little kid on Christmas morning. When he first discovered he could disappear, it scared him, made him feel like he'd never make his mark on this world. But becoming a hero changed that forever.

My heart pangs at the thought; I hope I can make a difference for him now.

Dozens of icons fill the desktop, labeled "Training," "Rescue Protocols," "Advanced Weaponry," and so on. Claire marvels at the rows and rows of folders that would likely make any WarNat's head explode, tentatively reaching out, fingers itching to dive in.

Teddy smirks with superiority, reveling in Claire's jealousy. "Yes, it's all right—" Suddenly he looks off, his Bluetooth device chirping in his ear. "Right away," he answers his caller, tapping the earpiece to end his call. "I have to go."

"What? No! Let's get into these files!" Claire pleads.

"I have to keep up appearances—some of us can't just disappear." He groans, and I don't know if that's a dig at Matt, or Claire, or what. He leans over his desk and quickly logs out, much to Claire's dismay. "I'll check back with you two later. Try not to do anything stupid while I'm gone."

Once the door's closed behind him, Claire turns to me. "God, for someone who clearly wants us on his side, he has a weird way of showing it."

"He needs to go outside sometimes. Sunshine might help jump-start his personality."

She snickers. "Okay, but what do we do now? Do you think Roy could be Siege?"

"I'm really not sure," I admit, feeling pulled in too many directions. Solving a Warrior Nation crisis has never been on my bucket list, and yet here I am, caught in a web of confusing clues and red herrings. Besides Claire, it's impossible to know who to trust as the organization slowly collapses in on itself, but I don't want the whole ship to sink before I discover what's really going on.

The purple paper makes it whole. Matt. He will have to be the voice of reason here; whatever he left behind will have to be our guiding light to the truth.

"C'mon, let's go to the mural," I say. "We'll finish what we started and bring our heroes home."

FOR IMMEDIATE RELEASE

Chicago, IL - The Chicago Police Department has set up a dedicated Siege crisis hotline. Residents who experience an act of violence, witness a crime, or have any pertinent information regarding Siege or the Anti-Heroes are encouraged to call the 800 number or tweet at @ChicagoPDSiegeHotline. At this time, it is not recommended to contact Warrior Nation if you are in immediate danger.

Due to a large volume of calls, a law enforcement professional will get back to each message within 24 hours. A list of safe houses can be found online.

CLAIRE

TEDDY'S THE BAD GUY. . . . NOW ROY'S THE BAD GUY? I just want to know . . . who is hurting the heroes?

I didn't think saving the day would be so hard. And okay, maybe that's stupid to admit: Obviously I understand that the heroes do a lot of work. But all my years of studying Warrior Nation have come with the blessing of hindsight. I've never had to piece together what really happened during a crime; all I had to do was read the recaps, and yeah, everything seems obvious when you have the final result. Even on debate team, it's pretty rare that opponents throw me for a loop, since I work to anticipate every angle on every topic. But this—*this*—is almost more than my admittedly sizable brain can handle. I was SURE Teddy was Siege, but now? I wouldn't be able to confidently argue that stance.

"I wish they would give it a rest with this red lighting," Bridgette says as we walk toward the cafeteria, looking up at the scarlet bulbs overhead. "I feel like I'm being drenched in pig's blood."

"Yeah, it's definitely adding to the 'you're all guilty' vibe,"

I add, looking down at my ruby-lit palms. "I mean, I get that they want to catch someone red-handed, but this is overkill." Bridgette says nothing, marching forward with total determination. "Hey, um, Bridgette? I'm sorry I wasted our time accusing Teddy. I really thought he could be Siege."

She stops, startled by my apology. "You don't need to be sorry. He still could be guilty. We can only trust each other at this point, okay? And Matt. Whatever he left behind on that paper will guide us to the truth."

Right, she's right. Blue Streak would never apologize. I shouldn't either.

While most of HQ has turned into a desolate wasteland of empty corridors and people hiding in their offices, the cafeteria is apparently the place to be, with employees scattered at every table, staring sadly at their cherry-red plates. Great, how are we supposed to deface a piece of art when everyone in the organization has gathered for the saddest mealtime ever?

"Well, this is . . . unexpected," Bridgette sighs, looking around the room. Even though there are lots of people in here, the space is silent, distrust making everyone wary. A few somber eyes look up at her, recognition bending their lips in sympathy. Some shift in their seats, wanting to get up and offer condolences over Matt's video, but their worry over making a wrong move keeps them glued to their chairs. "Okay, how about this: I'll distract everyone by making some remarks about Matt while you climb up and grab the purple paper."

Seems easy enough. "Sure. It's in Blue Streak's cape, right?"

"Yeah, you can't miss it."

I break from her side as she clears her throat, instantly draw-ing everyone's attention. "Hello, my friends," she starts as I tiptoe toward the back wall. "I just wanted to thank you for everything you've done to try and fight Siege and bring the heroes home."

With all eyes glued on Bridgette, I slide a chair underneath Blue Streak's section of the massive mural, taking my first close-up view of this impressive installation. Wow, I never real-ized how involved this piece truly is, with thousands of tiny paper scraps expertly layered together to create the illusion of motion while standing still. I run my fingers over the shapes, surprised by their delicate texture. I can't even imagine starting a project like this, let alone executing it to this level of perfec-tion. How in the world did Bridgette do this?

"I'm sure you all were as disturbed by Matt's video as I was," she continues, keeping her silent audience captivated. "None of us have ever been in a situation like this before."

I scan Blue Streak's paper cape, but the reality of this hunt strikes fear in my heart: All these colors look practically the same! Dark blue, navy blue, royal blue—I'm not seeing purple at all! Am I color-blind? I keep searching, looking at each piece indi-vidually, hoping one will stand out. But the more I look, the more they all blend together, forming a giant blob of certifiably non-purpleness.

Panicked, I look back at Bridgette, throwing my arms out in defeat. She keeps talking but nods her head slightly to the left, so I focus on that section of the cape, hoping to find a grape in a sea of blueberries. But I can't, all the colors are too close, so instead, I start flipping up the individual pieces, hoping the winner will have a written clue on the back. As quietly as possible, I run my hand against the grain of the mural, causing an audible ripple of paper. A man sitting not far from my chair perks his head up at the sound, but before he can turn, Bridgette starts fake crying, keeping his gaze ahead.

WHERE IS THIS PURPLE PAPER? I can almost hear Joy teasing me for taking so long—*What are you doing up there, killer? C'mon, hurry up!* I'm sure she would have found it already. I'm sure Joy wouldn't be up here floundering like a total dork. I keep turning them over, standing on my tiptoes to reach the top of the cape, when finally—finally!—I see pen scribbles, and I rip the paper so fast I lose my balance, toppling to the floor. Several people turn my way, but I pop up quickly, pocketing the paper and pressing my hands together in prayer. "Sorry I . . . was just so moved by what you said. Bridgette, you are so brave. Thank you for your kind words today, they mean so much."

A few people quietly clap in agreement as my friend wipes the surprise of my fall off her face. "Oh, you're welcome," she says, voice shaking.

I dash out of the cafeteria, catching my breath as I wait for my accomplice to join me.

"Oh my god, are you okay?" she says once she's by my side.

"Yeah, yeah, I'm fine," I reassure her, taking the paper scrap out. "Um, for the record, this is NOT purple."

"What are you talking about? It's indigo!"

"You said I couldn't miss it! I thought it would be, like, lavender or something!"

"Okay, well, sorry! It stands out to me. But anyway, who cares?!" she exclaims. "Flip it over! What does it say?"

I do as she says and read the awkwardly scrawled letters and numbers:

$$E33$$

What. What. WHAT. "Room E33! It's real?!" I shout, sounding extra loud in the haunted halls.

Bridgette's green eyes open wide, surprised at my surprise. "Yeah? Why wouldn't it be real?"

Too many questions. TOO MANY QUESTIONS! "E33—the room where Warrior Nation hides all its deepest, darkest secrets? Where lost missions and failed weaponry get locked away forever? E33—where the bones of the fabled first Warrior lie?" Without realizing, I've grabbed on to her shoulders, our noses inches from touching. There may or may not be tiny specks of my spit on her cheek.

"Um." Bridgette gently pries my fingernails out of her skin. "Okay. Let's get on the same page here. Room E33 is a real location in HQ, but I don't know anything about what you just said. Is that a WarNat thing?"

"Yeah! I mean . . . I guess? I thought it was a Warrior Nation thing." I take a step back, embarrassed by my sudden fangirl outburst. "I mentioned it before when we were talking about conspiracies. . . ."

She scrunches up her face. "I know, but I didn't realize why. Room E33 is basically a glorified trash dump."

Huh? That does not compute at all. This is a fan theory that goes back decades; why would WarNats spend years endlessly dissecting the possibilities of a glorified garbage heap? "But . . . but . . ." I stutter, clinging to the last shreds of my dignity. "But it's not on the HQ map! Believe me, I've looked. Isn't that suspicious? Why purposely leave a garbage room off your map?"

She shrugs yet doesn't tease me; the nice thing about Bridgette is that she never makes me feel like an idiot. For someone who's been dragged through the mud, she never stoops to that level. "I don't know, maybe I'm wrong. But regardless, Matt found something there, so we have to trust his judgment. C'mon."

Trash heap or not, I may be the first WarNat to ever set foot in Room E33, and something tells me this secret space is going to prove us both wrong.

All the known items in Room E33:

- Magnetic force field able to render a hero's power worthless
- The Sword of Infinity (featured prominently in Warrior Nation: Nonstop)

- 2 million counterfeit US dollars
- bones of the First Warrior
- a serum that delivers 24 hours of unbeatable powers
- brutal training plans rumored to have killed many recruits from exhaustion
- battery pack that hyper-charges any bomb to nuclear levels

BRIDGETTE

HOLDING THE SCRAP OF DEFINITIVELY PURPLE PAPER in my palm, I stare down at Matt's childlike scrawl, the clue he left behind for only me to find. What was he feeling when he scribbled this down? Frightened? Angry? Was someone hunting him, forcing him to drop a quick bread crumb rather than leaving a traceable trail?

He's never been one to question authority or stray outside the Warrior Nation buddy system. When he told me at the charity event he'd started digging for information on Siege, I didn't think much of it at the time, too overwhelmed by the swell of conflicting emotions twisting my heart. But for him to go off on his own, and to hide his findings, is serious. Maybe Claire is right: Maybe Room E33 isn't just a dump, but a place where things get buried.

"According to my notes," Claire narrates as I navigate, determined to reach this room as fast as possible, "Room E33 was created in the mid-1950s, about ten years after Warrior Nation was established. After the disastrous attack of the first supervillain—Quandary—during which three-quarters of the Chicago chapter was wiped out, the organization decided to bury the mission, hiding away the malfunctioning weaponry and defective super suits that ultimately caused the Warriors' demise." She keeps flipping through her diary, frantically searching for the most pertinent information. "Since then, the room has become a graveyard of Warrior ghosts, locking away objectionable truths that would shake public trust. It's rumored to hold a long list of forbidden items that have been completely erased from the official record, such as dangerous training regimens, the Sword of Infinity, and more."

"The Sword of Infinity?" I balk. Man, these WarNats . . . It's hard to believe some of these things she's saying. They sound slightly ridiculous, though I guess the rumors must have sprouted from some kind of truth. "I thought that was a movie prop? From one of the first Warrior films?"

"Art imitates life!" she exclaims. "Well, allegedly . . . I guess we'll find out."

Room E33 is not far from Teddy's little self-made bunker, tucked away where hardly anyone visits. The only reason I know it's here is because of my early days exploring HQ with Matt; we were always looking for new places to hide and be alone in between his training sessions. Once we stumbled into E33, a room that was only labeled from the inside, but it was so full of dust, it proved to be a pretty unappealing make-out spot.

"We're here," I announce, standing outside a plain metal

door with no handle. Claire takes it in, underwhelmed by its appearance.

"This . . . is it?" She frowns. "I thought there'd be, like, lasers or poisonous darts protecting the entrance."

"I guess they're going for the whole 'hidden in plain sight' thing. Can you help me pry this open?" I hold up my cast, annoyed at how much this keeps holding me back.

"Of course." Claire curls her fingertips under the metal edge, pulling it open enough for us to squeeze through. Closing the door behind us, we find ourselves in neither a trash heap nor a sparkly treasure trove of lore, but a dark room filled with rows and rows of storage shelves, each packed with identical brown cardboard boxes labeled with unhelpful combinations of letters and numbers. "Yikes, this is . . . Where do we even begin?"

"I don't know," I admit, running my finger over a dusty ledge. "It doesn't seem like people come in here much. . . . Maybe look for a spot that's been recently disturbed? If Matt was in here, he may have left something out of place."

"Good call. Split up to cover more ground?"

I nod, and we head off in different directions, wandering through the maze of storage systems. With every box looking the same, it's hard to even know where to dig in. Any box could hold a damning document, a hidden file . . . a sword . . . but from the outside, each container looks innocent, effectively tucking away whatever Warrior Nation doesn't want the world to find. My only reassurance is that everything is coated in a fine layer of dust, something not even Matt's invisibility could keep intact.

After a few minutes, I find myself in a back corner, where an ancient TV and outdated technology sit on a table. Yet the space is remarkably dust-free, as if someone had been working here recently. "Claire!" I shout, thinking Matt must have been here. She jogs over, clutching a study labeled "Mental and Physical Illnesses Common Among Heroes" in her arms.

"Did you find something?"

"Did you?" I ask, nodding to her file.

"Oh, uh, I don't know. I've kind of been grabbing random things. There's just so much to see!"

"This table—it looks like someone was recently here." I gesture to the dust-free spot. "Maybe there's something—"

"Whoa, is this a VCR?" Claire sets down her file, leaning in for a closer look at the out-of-date device. "I don't think I've ever seen one of these."

"I think we had one, when I was little," I say. I fumble with the buttons, pushing a variety of commands before hitting eject. Out pops a video tape, a clunky black box with inner coils of ribbon. Claire and I look at each other, simultaneously saying, "We have to watch!"

After rewinding to the beginning, the TV screen opens with a title card that reads:

Radiator—Exit Interview

The name sounds familiar, but I can't place it.

"Oh yeah, that guy!" Claire instantly chirps, mind like a

steel trap. "He was a Chicago hero about, hmm, eight years ago? But only for like two years. I think he could jump-start machinery with his fingers or something? Yeah. He didn't like being in the spotlight, though, so he left."

The video fades to Radiator himself, sitting alone at a table with a light overhead, not unlike an interrogation scene. He smiles warmly, clean-shaven honey skin beaming, answering a series of questions from an off-screen speaker.

"Why are you leaving Warrior Nation?" the male interrogator asks.

"I am appreciative of all the time and effort put forth by this worthy team." He grins. "But I'm afraid this life is not for me."

"And why is that?"

Radiator shrugs, kind eyes offering their apology. "I like helping people, but being in the spotlight is a type of pressure I didn't anticipate. I don't feel comfortable with people knowing me, recognizing me on the streets."

I laugh to myself. "This guy is so different from Matt."

Radiator continues. "Also—and I mean no disrespect—but there have been times when I feel Warrior Nation doesn't take my opinions into consideration. The things I want get pushed aside. I understand it takes a lot to run an organization as large as this, and I'm sure there are many moving parts I'm not even aware of, but I don't want my voice getting lost. I don't see myself being happy in this life, so I feel it's in everyone's best interest if we part ways sooner rather than later."

We watch the whole interview, before it cycles to a

different exit interview, this time with PsychTyke, a hero I definitely remember. She experienced severe mental and physical trauma in the 1980s after a failed mission that involved electricity frying her internal systems. We start her video, set in the same room as Radiator's, but after a few seconds of watching her sob uncontrollably, I hit stop.

"She passed away a year ago," Claire says sadly. "Such a terrible loss."

I nod, but the content of these videos isn't the only thing confusing me. "Why do you think these interviews are on VHS? I mean, who even uses VCRs anymore?"

"It is weird, especially since almost everything at HQ is digital. Besides your mural, there's barely any paper here, with everything else accessible from the main server. I mean, I can't access everything with my low clearance, but theoretically everything's there for the taking."

"Except for this, I guess," I add. "You can't hack a video tape."

We fast-forward to the next title screen, only to find Blue Streak's name flashing before us. Claire perks up, eyes wide in interest, though her brows quickly curl in confusion. Instead of being greeted by the stoic, iron-willed man the world has come to expect, Charles is disheveled. Gray stubble prickles his jaw, and rage runs rampant on his face. He's seething, teeth clenched tight, staring at the camera like he wants to rip out the spine of the person controlling it. The hair on my arms stands at attention. Something isn't right.

The off-camera interviewer, a woman this time, starts with the same questions as with Radiator and PsychTyke, but Charles ignores them completely, ready to spew whatever has him so riled up.

"A total charade right until the end, huh?" he growls, cracking his knuckles. "Think you can throw me through this last hoop even after forcing me out?"

"Wait, what?" Claire gasps. "*Forcing* him out? But that's not . . . Did he not retire?"

"I don't know." I gulp, stomach churning at the sight of Charles, my friend, seething with an animosity I didn't think possible.

"Now, Charles . . ." the woman objects, trying to pacify him. Her voice sounds familiar, but I can't place it.

"Now nothing!" Blue Streak slams his fist, nearly breaking the table. "You are forcing me to turn my back on the only life I've ever known, not to mention all the other would-be heroes you've tossed aside. With all the superpowers in this world, you could have a hero on every street corner, protecting citizens at every step. But no, only a few meet your impossible standards, turning heroism into a marketing scheme to get people to buy cereal and soft drinks. We do the work, and you get the profit! It's a travesty, something I've never understood and never will. Especially now, now that I've fallen out of your precious demographic, turning me into a relic when I'm still in my prime. You just don't want to market an old man."

I feel like I'm going to throw up. A part of me suspected

something was odd with Blue Streak's retirement, knowing the man behind the cape would struggle if he couldn't be out there, saving the day. But knowing is different than questioning, and hearing his angry story turns my insides upside down. While I've always struggled with my relationship with Warrior Nation, I just thought I was biased, frustrated by the organization that stole my boyfriend from me. I never thought they would sink so slow, to cast aside their most powerful member just because of a few gray hairs. The public never cared about how old he was when he came to their aid; they only cared that he was there, risking his life for theirs. They loved him. They still do.

Claire. I turn to my friend, her face already wet with tears. "How could they do this to him?" she asks, barely audible. "They *fired* him? After all he's done, all the lives he's saved . . . ?"

"Charles," the interviewer continues, mildly annoyed with her subject's intense reactions. "We understand you're upset—"

"Do you, now? Do you really? And tell me: Why are *you* the one doing this, anyway?" Charles asks with venom to the woman off camera. "Is Roy such a coward that he can't fire me to my face?"

There's a pause, the sound of shuffling papers off screen. "Roy agrees this chapter is long overdue for a much-needed face-lift, and you said it yourself: It's incredibly difficult to market a past-his-prime hero to the eighteen-to-forty-five demo."

Charles chuckles to himself, shaking his head. "And Roy—a fellow Warrior—said that? Those exact words?"

"Not exactly," the woman responds, calm against his storm. "But it's for the best. I'm the only one who thinks about the future of this organization."

"Is that so?" Charles snarls, slowly coming to a stand, nearly cutting his face out of frame. "So this is *your* decision, then? You're making a big mistake here. You think dropping me is the answer? You'll only give me power. Having fought beside this chapter, it would be easy for me to bring them to their knees. An afterthought really, considering I've watched them fumble with my own two eyes."

There's a hesitation on the other side. "You wouldn't."

"Wouldn't I? I'm not afraid of you, or any of the others. Matt's only strength is the power to evade, but one punch to the gut and he's down for the count. Ryan's earth-shaking abilities are rendered useless once he's standing on man-made materials, and Ashleigh is a joke on dry land. While I don't know Joy, isolating a rookie should be enough to bring her to her knees."

Claire gasps, clasping her hands over her mouth. These words—these threats—are coming from such a hateful place. They burn inside me, cutting off my air supply. I can only imagine what she's feeling.

"You're bluffing," the woman says dryly. "You wouldn't risk your legacy."

Charles places his knuckles on the table, strong shoulders looming to intimidate his interrogator. "Try me. This can all be avoided, of course, if you reinstitute my hero status. The choice is yours, Millie."

Millie! I knew I recognized that voice! She fired Charles? She set off this entire string of events? Oh my god, oh my god . . .

"Goodbye, Charles," Millie says, and though I cannot see her face, the smile in her tone is clear. "I'll inform Roy of your retirement plans immediately."

He grits his teeth, fuming, rising to his full height before flipping the table, knocking the camera to the floor. The feed goes dead.

Claire sobs, short, rapid-fire breaths bouncing in her chest. Her head rattles from side to side, unable to sit with the information we've discovered. "No," she moans, voice trembling. "No."

This is what Matt wanted me to find, the secret Warrior Nation doesn't want exposed. That one of its own was forced out and in turn sought revenge against the system that wronged him. From the very beginning, Millie knew what was happening, and still she did nothing to stop it, choosing to hide her mistakes rather than solve them.

"Claire," I start, voice soft like I'm talking to an injured animal. "Claire, I think—"

"No!" she shrieks, lips quivering. "Please, please don't say it. I don't want to hear it." I bite my lip, watching her implode right before my eyes. Years and years of love and admiration oozing from her heart, charring into an unrecognizable sludge. It's too much, too much, and my soul hurts just looking at her. She knows the man who's been terrorizing her girlfriend, who kidnapped both of us and had us tied to a chair. It's the same man whose face has been hanging in her bedroom, the man who launched her devotion to Warrior Nation in the first place.

I don't want it to be true, but there's no denying it.

"Blue Streak is Siege."

Case study: The Challenges Heroes Face Upon Reentry to Civilian Life

This study will look to examine the success and challenges Warrior Nation members experience after leaving their chapter and assuming a civilian lifestyle. We will look to understand:

- how heroes acclimate to their former lives after years of being a public figure in a high-stress work environment
- what, if anything, continues to trigger their sense of duty
- how organizational liabilities can be minimized
- whether or not Warrior Nation is at risk for releasing these individuals back into society

We have chosen three possible heroes for evaluation, who will be watched without their explicit consent.

CLAIRE

MY STOMACH HEAVES, AND I TURN AWAY from my friend, throwing up next to the table. The vomit looks exactly like I feel: diluted, weak, thin. I wipe my lip, curling into the tightest of balls as the world crumbles beneath my body.

Blue Streak is Siege.

Blue Streak . . . is a villain? It feels wrong to even think the words. The man I have worshipped, followed with blind devotion . . . How could he do this? How? How could the same man save my life and then turn around to put it in danger? I went to his house, I shook his hand: His home was a shrine to all that is good and true. Even if Warrior Nation wronged him, even if his anger is just, how could *this* be his response?

It cannot be real. And yet, I can't ignore what I just saw. Blue Streak, ranting and raving about the same exact points Siege has stressed from the beginning. Superpowers being treated unfairly, Warriors failing those they promise to protect.

I remember Siege standing over me, frame covered in darkness. I was so scared, I could barely look at him, but his powerful form demanded attention, commanding the room. Just like Blue Streak.

My fallen hero.

"Claire, we gotta go." Bridgette ejects the tape, tucking it under her arm. She nudges me, gently pushing my hair back off my face. Her eyes are so sad, so apologetic, it makes me want to cry even more. "Come on." Standing feels like a Herculean effort, but she one-handedly pulls me to my feet, dragging my wobbling legs down the hall.

The first time I walked through HQ, it felt like magic. A place manifested from my daydreams. Everything was shining with hope, every corner glistening with the promise of a better world. Now, as Bridgette guides me on a zigzagging path through the underground labyrinth, it feels like a cave, a twisted place that spawns secrets and lies, darkness and shadows.

A place that breeds villains.

I've lost track of where Bridgette is taking us, her determination my only compass right now. We weave past my shared desk with Teddy, who springs to his feet after seeing us rush by.

"Where are you going?" he asks, taking in my breakdown with a curious glance.

"To talk to Roy," Bridgette says matter-of-factly.

"What?! No!" He recoils. "You can't just barge into the chapter president's office and accuse him of being Siege! We need a plan, we need evidence—"

"We have evidence, and he's not Siege. Blue Streak is."

Teddy stops in his tracks, her words paralyzing him. Jaw hanging open, beady eyes pinched tight, he tries to process this but shakes his head in denial, unwilling to accept this revelation.

"He never retired: Millie fired him, and he used his insider knowledge to exact his revenge."

"But . . . no . . ." he whimpers, and for the first time ever, I feel connected to Teddy. We may be completely different people, but he's still a WarNat at heart. Learning that one of the most iconic heroes of all time has switched sides is not an easy pill to swallow.

"I'm sorry, this isn't easy for any of us," Bridgette says softly, giving me another concerned look. I want to be brave for her—for Joy—but my insides feel full of lead, rooting me to the ground. "But now that we know, we have to do something. Will you help us, Teddy?"

He looks as lost as I feel, like suddenly he doesn't recognize his surroundings and has no idea where to go next. But he nods slowly, taking a place on the other side of Bridgette as we head toward the executive section of HQ, Bridgette nearly dragging us both.

I push back another round of tears as she swings open the door to Mr. Know-It-All's office. He's nowhere to be seen, though there is a faint rustling coming from underneath his massive veneer desk.

"Hello?" Bridgette calls out, and we hear a *thump*, followed by a quiet "Oww."

A pair of eyes peek out from under the desk, Roy cautiously

venturing from his little protective hole. "Oh, hey there, kids," he says sheepishly, pulling himself to a stand. Each hand holds a different kind of fidget device, one spinning uncontrollably, the other rapidly twisting between his long fingers. "I was just, uh . . . getting a little meditation in, you know? In a quiet space." But with the way he's shaking, it's clear he wasn't able to find any sense of calm. "What can I help you with?"

Bridgette steps forward. "Mr. Masterson, we've discovered the identity of Siege."

Roy brightens. "Really? You have? That's wonderful!" he exclaims, picking up his phone receiver. "Let me call Millie in here and—"

"No," Bridgette interrupts, authority in her command. "You need to see something first." She holds up the incriminating VHS tape, at which Roy tilts his head.

"I don't . . . I don't have any way to play that," he admits.

Teddy sighs quietly. "Yes, you do, sir." He walks over to a keypad on the office's back wall, typing in a passcode. Suddenly two floor-to-ceiling panels open up, revealing an overwhelming set of technology that looks like it could easily program a space launch. Roy looks on with complete shock, dropping his fidget spinners in surprise.

"I had no idea that was there!" he yelps, running a hand over one of the many screens that's been sitting behind him all this time. "Did this just get installed?"

"No, sir," Teddy says, eyes clouded with disappointment.

Bridgette inserts the tape, and once again I have to watch

my idol transform into an alternate version of himself, hissing and snarling unthinking threats against the heroes I love.

"Oh my god, Millie," Teddy says, one hand over his mouth. "What have you done?"

"Wait . . . wait . . . wait," Roy repeats, rubbing his temples. His eyes are so wide, I worry they could pop from their sockets. "Charles didn't retire?"

"Millie fired him. . . . That wasn't your direction?" Bridgette asks.

"No! I mean, why would I fire Charles?! He's a legend! When Millie told me he retired, I was surprised, sure, but I had no reason not to believe her," Roy blubbers. "Millie handles everything around here; most of the time she takes care of things without even needing me. . . ." He trails off, likely realizing how ineffectual he's been all along. "I never wanted this job, you know? I wanted to help people, but I was just . . . not powerful enough. It was so much easier to let Millie take the reins. I had no idea. . . ."

"Millie screwed this up from the very beginning," Teddy admits, words laced with regret. "Had she alerted the other Warrior chapters about a possible rogue hero right away, this all could have been avoided." He frowns, looking up at the ceiling in annoyance. "But Millie doesn't like to shine a light on problems, and she got herself in too deep. She couldn't ask for help because it would reveal her actions. I worked by her side every day. . . . I should have known, somehow."

"We're not gonna get anywhere by beating ourselves up,"

Bridgette says, the only one who's staying level-headed here. "We need a plan."

"But what?" Roy asks, forever clueless. For being Mr. Know-It-All, I can't believe how completely in the dark he is about literally everything.

"No one here is physically strong enough to face Blue Streak—er, *Siege*—and his band of anti-hero wannabes," Bridgette starts, wheels turning. "But there has to be a way to get to him. Something that doesn't involve weapons or a massive bodily attack. He has to have a weakness." She turns to me, biting her lip. "Claire? What do you think?"

"Me?" I full-body flinch.

"You know him better than anyone," she says. "You're the Blue Streak expert. I know this is a terrible ask, but you have to think of Joy. She needs you—they all do." I shake my head, burying my face in my hands. "What are his weak spots, Claire? How can we get to him?"

I did not sign up for this. To play an active role in bringing down my hero, my savior. I wanted to change the world for the better, not see my existing world fall apart. It's not right; it's not fair—I shouldn't have to bear this burden. Tears continue to build as I try, and fail, to recall all the terrible events of the past few weeks, but they all smudge together in one messy nightmare. Blue Streak saved my life, changing my trajectory forever, and now I have to be the one to destroy him? It's too much, too much, but Bridgette is right: The heroes need us. Need me.

The last remaining shreds of my heart begin to unravel as

I pull out my grail diary, trembling hands flipping to the Blue Streak section. Glittery blue ink taunts me with its happy, swirling letters, as I start from the beginning:

> Blue Streak
> Powers: super strength, flight, bulletproof
> Weaknesses: his fans

"That's it," I breathe, my voice so broken I barely recognize it. "He's always had a soft spot for his fans. Real, innocent people, the kind of people he was sworn to protect."

Eyes wet, Bridgette nods with acceptance before Teddy interjects. "Except that he's been terrorizing them all summer."

"But not really," I say, reading through my meticulous notes. "During every episode where a civilian got hurt, Siege wasn't there. His Anti-Heroes did most of the damage." I turn to Bridgette. "Remember at our kidnapping? He ordered the other villains *not* to hurt you. Because he knows you, he cares about you." *He cares about you.* . . . The thought squeezes the air from my lungs, but I push on. "Blue Streak has never liked the spotlight; we can't draw him out with a spectacle. It has to be quiet, real. If we want to lure him out, *we'll* have to be the bait. Ourselves."

"I'm sorry, who are you baiting?" Out of nowhere, Millie stands in the doorway, eyes hard behind her glasses. She has no right to question us, considering what she's done, yet she stands defiant, a bull ready to charge.

"Millie, it's over," Teddy says in a condescending tone.

"What are you talking about?" she snorts.

"We all know Blue Streak is Siege."

Her eyebrows shoot to the sky, yet she admits nothing. *I trusted you*, I think, the years of watching her conferences and reading her recaps cascading down on me. *You were a voice of reason.* Roy approaches her, mouth bent in disgust. "How could you do this?"

"Me? It's not my fault Charles couldn't handle his own retirement."

Roy shakes his head, ashamed. "We all saw the tape. You betrayed me; you betrayed this organization. What do you have to say for yourself?"

Millie's glance flits between us, a mouse caught in a trap. Yet she doesn't flee, pointing her chin up to give her extra height before the firing squad. "I didn't expect this to happen; how could I have?"

"Charles threatened the Warriors!" Bridgette yelps. "He did it to your face!"

"I thought he would go after you, Roy," Millie admits defiantly. Roy's jaw drops, placing a hand over his shocked heart. "Do you know what it's like, being so perfect for a position only to have an underqualified man take it from you? Rules be damned, I thought this organization would recognize my years of service and appoint me as chapter president, but no, they deemed it more important to have a Warrior in charge, rather than a competent professional. I've spent years cleaning

343

up after you, Roy, and I hoped a citywide disaster would finally prove your incompetence, forcing you out of office."

Bridgette grits her teeth in anger. "This was about a job title?"

I wait to see Millie's response, but she doesn't even flinch; a lifetime of on-air questioning conditioned her into stone. This is the woman I've put my faith in all these years? The face of reason and truth? "Again, I didn't expect Charles to go so far off the rails. Even when he did, I tried to reach out, to offer him his job back, but he was too far gone."

Roy towers over her, rage boiling deep within. "This is what's going to happen," he says coolly, a sudden surge of confidence taking over. "We are going to draw out Siege and put an end to all of this. Immediately afterward, you will schedule a press conference, announcing your resignation."

"I will do no such thing," she spits. From the back of the room, Teddy starts replaying the tape, her recorded voice offering all the evidence needed to lock her away. Her lip trembles; she's trapped, she knows she's trapped, and after several seconds of increasingly uncomfortable tension, she finally whispers, "Fine, then."

It's as close to an admission of guilt as we'll get. From day one, Siege was not a mystery. While the city was in panic and my whole world was falling apart, Millie did nothing, choosing to stay quiet instead of launching into action. She shut out other chapters, cut off the public in an attempt to cover her own ass—and secure a promotion—even as others suffered.

Has it always been this way? Has every rescue, every life saved, just been some calculated power play? No . . . no . . . My heart seizes, ventricles collapsing against each other, making every movement, every thought impossible. How could I have wasted so much time and effort on this? Am I stupid? Am I blind? There must be something wrong with me that I loved something so wretched so passionately.

Roy makes a few calls, and moments later, Millie is in handcuffs, her tiny body dragged away. My eyes squeeze tight, trying to hold back the tears that won't stop coming. I'm not sure how there's any left, yet my soul keeps wringing them free. I feel a pair of arms wrap around me: Bridgette, whispering in my ear. *It's gonna be okay. It's time to save the day.* But I shake my heavy head, chin touching my chest.

"I can't do this," I weep. I can barely stand. I can't save anyone. And I certainly can't face my hero in his villainous role.

"Yes, you can," Bridgette insists, her face a blur before me. "They need you. I need you."

No one needs me. What good am I?

I can't even tell a hero from a villain.

To: All Staff <chicagoHQ@warriornation.com>

From: Roy Masterson <mrknowitall@warriornation.com>

Subject: Urgent Update

For reasons that will later be disclosed, all current internal and external communications will be handled by either myself or junior communications officer Teddy Sizemore. No one is to interact with Millie Montouse, and anyone who has had recent involvement with her should report to me immediately.

We are still on lockdown, but do not panic. I know the past couple days have been extremely stressful, but as your chapter president, let me relieve your tension by saying we know none of you had anything to do with Siege, and we are currently formulating a rescue plan to bring the heroes home. Details to come.

Please be on alert for any instructions regarding the upcoming rescue mission.

It is an honor to work with you.

—Roy

BRIDGETTE

I DIAL THE NUMBER, EACH RING SENDING a shiver down my spine.

"Hello?" Charles answers, audibly confused about seeing my name on his cell phone screen. "Bridgette, what's going on?"

"Charles!" I scream. "I need your help!"

"What? What is it?"

"It's Claire! She's been kidnapped!" I warble, digging deep from my worries over Matt as Claire sits safely by my side. Teddy and Roy stand by, solemnly watching my performance.

"By whom?" Charles asks on the other side.

"Someone named . . . Frenzy?"

He pauses. "I don't recognize that name."

Of course you don't; I made it up. "I don't know. I got a text from an unknown number; that's the name they gave."

"Bridgette." His voice drops, patience waning. "How did this happen? I told you to stay away from this."

"I know you did, and we tried to be smart. But we couldn't stop, especially since Warrior Nation isn't doing anything to take down Siege." I look up at Roy, who bows his head sheepishly. "Claire and I were tracking some clues and got separated. . . . The next thing I know, this Frenzy guy is asking for ransom!"

"What does he want?"

"Some kind of weird decoder ring of Matt's. I went by his place and got it; Frenzy wants me to meet him in two hours at the Lakefront Trail to do the exchange. Will you come with me, Charles? I'm too scared to go alone."

He exhales slowly. "I don't know if I can."

"Charles, please. I have no one else to turn to. Claire . . . she's your biggest fan." My friend flinches beside me and I squeeze her hand in solidarity. I know she hates this, and I do too, but the only way we'll get through it is together. "We can't let anything happen to her, but I don't want to get kidnapped too. Please."

There's a long delay as Charles contemplates his options. I can almost hear him struggling, caught between his two larger-than-life personas. There's still a part of me that can't believe this is happening, like any minute I'm going to wake up from the worst, most twisted dream. *C'mon, Blue Streak*, I think, hoping he still has a shred of humanity intact. *Do what's right.*

Finally, he replies. "All right, I'll meet you. Send me the coordinates."

"Oh, thank you, you have no idea how relieved I am," I say, telling the truth for the first time on this call.

"But, Bridgette?" he adds. "This is the last favor I can do for you."

"Understood. I know you're putting yourself at risk."

He hesitates before signing off with "See you soon."

"Great job, Bridgette," Roy says once I hang up the phone. He gives me a pat on the shoulder, and one for Claire too. "Now, does everyone understand what's happening next?"

"I'm going to the meeting spot, pretending to be alone," I begin, recounting the plan Claire helped us formulate only moments ago. "The Warrior Nation backup unit will be circling the area in full disguise. Once Charles arrives at the scene, they'll apprehend him."

"And you're sure you can handle this?" Roy asks nervously. "I don't want to put either of you in danger."

Can I handle this? I'm honestly not sure. I've unwillingly been bait in many a villain's scheme, but I've never had any control over those situations, helplessly flailing until Vaporizer swooped in to save the day. Now that I'm an active participant in the plan, can I pull it off? I'm terrified, to be sure, but the thought of bringing Matt and the others home safely propels me, pushing me past any rumbling doubt.

I'm not sure Claire can say the same. Her complexion is completely green.

"This plan is the best shot we've had so far to bring Siege down," Roy says to her. "Your insight has been invaluable to this mission. As the mastermind of this operation, it's up to you whether you want to join in person or monitor our progress from HQ. Either way, I'll ensure you are protected."

She looks up at me, eyes wide, like a toddler waiting for guidance. I'm not going to tell her what to do, especially since neither option sounds appealing. We've been by each other's side since the heroes were lost, and while selfishly I want us together until the end, I'm not going to force my friend through a traumatic experience.

"I'll go," Claire says quietly. "I'm not letting Bridgette go through this alone." I smile, mouthing a silent "thank you" her way.

*

The summer sun beats down on me, causing tidal waves of back sweat that I'm sure would be there regardless of the temperature. Lake Michigan's shores are usually teeming with runners, cyclists, and carefree families all enjoying the outdoors, but with the city under high alert, there are few people stepping foot outside their homes. Claire thought picking a public meeting place, rather than some darkened alley, would be best, as Charles hopefully wouldn't choose to inflict pain on innocent bystanders.

But who knows what he's thinking at this point.

The few people around are actually the Warrior Nation backup unit, undercover hiding high-tech weaponry, to which not even Blue Streak is immune, beneath the casual athletic wear. They completely surround me, pretending to picnic, bike ride, and fly kites while keeping a watchful eye out for Siege. Claire is fully out of sight, yards away behind a restroom. Even though my team is everywhere, I stand alone by the water, a tasty worm wiggling on a hook.

I really hope I can pull this off.

Every second feels like a decade, my heart pounding with

such intensity it's a wonder it doesn't explode. I keep searching the crowd for Charles's familiar face, hoping an incognito Warrior spots him before I do. I look out at the gently lapping lake, wishing I could exude the same kind of constant calm, when I hear a voice whisper, "Bridgette."

I turn to see Charles, standing right next to me. Almost completely unrecognizable in a large, floppy sunhat and a cooling bandana wrapped around most of his face and neck. I gasp, but my surprise instantly melts into something new, all my terror and worry from the past few days merging into one powerful supernova of rage. Talking to him on the phone was one thing, but right here, breathing the same air, I can no longer put up a front. I ball up my one good hand, hot, angry breaths streaming from my nose. I know I need to stay calm, to keep my true feelings to myself until Charles is safely locked away, but being in his presence after knowing what he did, I'm exploding with fury, wanting to hurt him as much as he's hurt me.

Over his shoulder, the nearest Warrior operative sneaks up, gun at the ready, but Siege stills, reading my body language and the possible trap he's stepped into. Before any shot is fired, Siege grabs fistfuls of my shirt, dangling me off the ground and positioning my body against him like a human shield. "Don't shoot!" he yells, roaring in my ear. "Or I will snap her neck!"

The few non-Warrior passersby scream, people suddenly running in all directions as the disguised unit members come forward, a wide array of guns and weaponry pointed in Siege's direction. He holds me like I weigh nothing.

"Put me down!" I scream, kicking my legs violently. But he doesn't budge. An operative tries to make his way toward him, but Charles swats him away as if he were a fly, causing the rest of the squad to freeze in place.

"How could you do this?" he growls at me, spit flying from his lips. "Set me up like this? I was going to help you!"

His massive fingers begin to wrap around my neck, making it hard to breathe, let alone answer his insane question. "It doesn't . . . have to . . . be like this!" I manage to choke out. But my comment has the wrong effect, as his grasp tightens.

"Yes, it does," he says, jaw clenched. "They gave me no choice. I have to show them they are weak! That Warrior Nation is not all-powerful."

I gasp, using every last bit of strength to pry his fingers off my throat, hitting my cast against his hand. But he's too strong, and I'm running out of air. "Please . . . don't hurt me," I beg.

"I don't want to," he admits, revealing the remnants of his moral compass. "But sometimes there have to be sacrifices for the greater good."

The world starts to go dark as I hear a scream in the distance.

CLAIRE

"STOP!"

Something inside me shakes loose, breaking me from my mental prison. Seeing Bridgette's life dangle in the balance, I burst out from my hiding spot, racing toward her. Out of surprise, Charles loosens his grip, helping my friend gasp for the air she so desperately needs, though he continues to wrap her body around his for protection.

"Stop," I repeat as two Warrior operatives instantly flank my sides. One of them tries to pull me back out of reach, but I brush him away.

I need to be here. He needs to hear what I have to say.

Wild gray eyes narrow on me as I stand, splaying my hands to show I'm not a threat. "This isn't you," I say sadly. "Blue Streak . . . how could you?"

He shakes his head, still clutching Bridgette. "Don't call me that."

"What . . . Blue Streak?" I repeat, the words frighteningly unfamiliar on my tongue.

"I warned you once: Don't."

"Blue Streak is your NAME," I emphasize, in case he forgot. "You are a WARRIOR. Not a villain."

His jaw clenches, savagely squinting at the Warrior Nation squad behind me. "They took that from me. Those people— your people. Because of them, I'm no longer a hero."

"You're *always* a hero!" I cry, once again in tears. "For half my life, I've worshipped you, following your example of strength and truth. You made me believe there was goodness in the world, that people could make a difference. You saved my life; you gave me something to strive for." My lip quivers, snot running down, but I don't stop. The sight of him hurting Bridgette is wreaking havoc on my heart. "You always said that people needed to stay strong against adversity, to take the higher road. You told us to lead by example, to stay true when times get rough." I step closer, pointing an accusatory finger at his chest. "What about now, huh? This is your answer, to hurt people? Just to prove a point?" I shake my head, wiping my face. "It's wrong, and you know it."

For just a second, his resolve cracks, arms lowering as Bridgette's toes touch the ground. He blinks, as if he were just waking up from a nightmare, face softening ever so slightly. Sadness swirls behind his eyes as he says, "I had to do something. I had to take a stand."

"But not like this," I reply.

He closes the gap between us, two-hundred-plus pounds of solid wrath hovering over me, a giant vein pulsing in his neck.

"And what would you have done, huh?" he screams, hot breath burning my cheeks. "If one day everything you loved was suddenly gone, pulled from under your feet with no warning?"

"You mean like today?" I yell back with equal force. Bridgette's desperate eyes plead with me to back away, to let this go, but I can't. It's too late. "Like when I found out that one of the only people on this planet I trust with my entire life is rotten? Life as I knew it is over! FOREVER!" And the moment I say it, I know it's true. This isn't just about ending Siege; it's the end of this chapter in my life. How could I go on with Warrior Nation after experiencing this? After this loss? I can't just pretend it never happened; I would think of this moment every time I walked through HQ's doors, every time I looked into Joy's beautiful blue eyes. And that's not fair to anyone, least of all me.

No, it's over. I'll have to find a different way, a different purpose. There's no coming back from this.

"You destroyed everything I believe in." Salty tears lace my words as I add, "I can no longer call you my hero."

I know I'm just a blip on his radar, one of the thousands he saved. But this is the arrow that pierces his heart. Everything suddenly moves in slow motion and he stumbles back, finally releasing his grip on Bridgette as his strong, proud body seemingly folds in on itself in shame. I drop to her side as the Warrior crew charges, taking him on ten to one. For a second, it's like he's forgotten who he is, refusing to defend himself, but a blow to the head snaps him back into action, and he begins throwing jabs left and right, effortlessly picking off the defense unit.

But this is not his best fight. I know his style, the way his body moves, and it's clear his heart is not in this one. There's no pow behind his punches, no passion in his attack. His raw strength still manages to keep the team from easily defeating him, but it's only a matter of time.

I help Bridgette crawl off to safety, her bruised throat still gasping. The Warrior team starts to thin, their guns useless against Siege's bulletproof body. He launches himself into the sky, his power of flight halting the battle below, until one of the only Warriors left shoots a bolas at Siege's ankle, the weighted weapon pulling him back to the ground. The remaining unit pushes Charles down, and there's lots of shouting and yelling as bodies crowd the space to apprehend their criminal. Frightened onlookers either cover their faces or take pictures from the sidelines.

I don't even realize I've been holding my breath until I see Siege apprehended, hands cuffed behind his back with super-power-neutralizing cuffs. "It's over," I tell Bridgette, who is lying on the grass with her eyes closed. "They're going to make him tell us where he's keeping Matt and Joy."

"Good," she rasps, wincing in pain.

The team drags Siege toward our van, but before he's gone forever, our eyes lock, his steely gaze glazing over as his head hangs low.

It's a look that haunts me, chills me to the core. A look that says *I'm sorry.*

I failed you.

Even heroes make mistakes.

But I won't show him any sympathy; I have none to give. Even though we stopped him, this is not a victory. Seeing my hero dragged away in disgrace has left me hollow, scooped empty and questioning everything I've ever known.

As we pack up to leave, I look south down the lakeshore, spotting the North Avenue boathouse, where my summer began. Was it only a few short weeks ago that I first met Joy, that I slid down a tunnel that was supposed to make my dreams come true? Everything felt so magical then, the world full of nothing but possibility.

I should feel proud of how far I've come. Triumphant in ending this disaster.

But I feel nothing.

*

Siege confesses to keeping the heroes locked in his guesthouse, neutralizing their powers with the same kind of cuffs he was dragged away in, stolen from Room E33 before being fired. Standing on his property now, I see the circle of white Adirondack chairs where we met before. I had sat across from him, in total awe, while Joy was locked up just a few feet away. Could she hear me, gushing over him? Asking him—her kidnapper— for help? I hang my head, ashamed.

I've reached a level of exhaustion I didn't think possible, and I bury my face in Bridgette's back. I want to see Joy, but I'm terrified. What kind of scene are we about to walk into? Matt's broken and bruised face flashes before me, and I wonder if she has similar injuries. Or worse? I could barely deal when she had a minor head wound, so how can I possibly handle this?

The Warrior team leads us through, searching for traps. Bridgette pulls ahead, anxious to get to wherever the heroes are.

"We're coming for you!" she croaks into the guesthouse. I wish I shared that enthusiasm, that this ending filled me with hope rather than dread. I keep imagining the worst, picturing them dead in pools of their own blood. But there's no more time to worry about it, because the search party has found our missing heroes.

Tucked away in the back bedroom, Joy, Matt, Ryan, and Ashleigh are on the ground, all four tied and bound together. Rope burns on their skin, bloodstains on the floor. Super suits ripped, hair matted, slumped against each other in defeat. The smell is awful, open sores festering. I swallow the urge to vomit.

There's a lot of confusion at first, as the heroes are sleep deprived and extremely dehydrated. But when Joy's eyes meet mine, unbelievable grief floods my system, making it impossible to breathe, to move, to think.

I did not expect to feel this way.

I should be happy—relieved—to see Joy in one piece. But all I can think about is how a hero did this: *My hero* did this. Disgust riles up my insides, bile rising in my throat. I stand frozen, paralyzed by shame and guilt, as Bridgette drops to her knees, gently caressing Matt's battered face.

The Warrior medical unit comes rushing in, quickly attending to the heroes' needs. But while Bridgette refuses to leave Matt's side, I clear a path, hanging out in a corner until the professionals have brought in a gurney for each, the heroes' weakened powers making it difficult for them to move. Only after Joy is safely strapped to a bed being wheeled out of her prison do I go to her, staring down at this incredible creature who was needlessly tortured by a monster.

A monster whose face still graces my bedroom walls.

"I'm so, so sorry," I sob, instantly blubbering over her condition. While not as battered as Matt, she still looks like she's been to hell and back, a giant gash oozing across her cheek.

Joy reaches for me, a pained, slow movement, and I wrap her dirty, bloody fingers in mine. "What do you have to be sorry for?" she croaks.

Everything. Nothing. Logically I know I'm not responsible for any of this, but my heart has clearly abandoned all logic. "I hate that this happened to you."

"It's okay, killer." I lay my head on her chest, wanting to hear the strong, reassuring beat of her heart. The rhythmic pulses soothe me, helping me find a small sense of solid ground I haven't felt in days. "It's over now," she whispers, touching her other hand to my hair.

She's right. It's over. I am not built for this world, not capable of watching people I love get thrown into danger they do not deserve. I thought I could handle it, that forums and grail diaries would prepare me, but I was wrong.

I have to say goodbye to Warrior Nation.

Dear Blue Streak,

Thank you for saving my life. My mom and I were so scared on the train. You were so brave and strong—I will never forget what you did for us.

Never cease, never cower! Warrior Nation forever!

Love, your biggest fan,

Claire Rice

BRIDGETTE

WE DID IT. IT'S OVER. WE WON.

Matt hugs me like it's his final wish, like my embrace is giving him life. Burying his broken face into the crook of my neck, battered hands digging into my back, he can't stop himself from kissing me, and I don't stop him. It's intoxicating, being so close to him again. Even though he's only been missing for a few days, it feels like a lifetime since he's held me with this intensity. This need.

He pulls back, glassy eyes gazing into mine. Half his face is swollen in dark purple bruises, and his nose is clearly broken, bent to the wrong side. Yet he reminds me of the first time I met him—not as a hero, but a boy, full of imperfections and quirks. A boy who put himself last, who would do anything for just five more minutes together. The memory of our first kiss floods me, and maybe it's adrenaline or maybe it's nostalgia, but I melt into him with a kiss that's slow, thankful, making us both shudder with relief that we found our way not just back to safety, but to each other.

"Oww." He pulls back after a minute.

"Oh, I'm sorry! Did I hurt you?"

He winces. "Dang, Bridge, I mean, I did just get my face pummeled to a bloody pulp."

"I got swept up in the moment, I'm so sorry, I—"

He smiles, pressing a dirty finger to my lips. "Don't ever be sorry. And don't ever stop kissing me."

A Warrior Nation medical unit rushes in, gently but quickly attending to the heroes, untying their binds and lifting them onto carts. I stay by his side until the very last moment, not letting anything come between his hand and mine. He needs to go: for medical treatments, for press conferences. The city needs to know he's safe; I understand. Just before he's finally pulled away to an ambulance, I kiss his filthy, sweaty forehead, and he looks back to send me a smile that warms me more than I thought possible.

I did not expect to feel this way.

Claire stands off to the side alone, dead eyes detached from the commotion. Joy gets carried away to safety, but Claire doesn't move, somehow more broken than the heroes who were tortured for days.

"Claire, are you okay?" She doesn't force a smile as I approach, instantly sobbing the second I wrap her in a hug. She clings to me, entire body quivering. I don't placate her with false hope, but let her cry, wringing out whatever is left. But I do tell her one thing, something true that I hope will help her build solid ground. Not today, but someday.

"You are so brave, Claire," I whisper, not letting her go as she trembles in protest.

"No," she sobs. "I can't do this." Her body shakes harder with the truth. "This world . . . it was all I ever wanted. But now . . . I can't. I can't live every day with the fate of the people I love always hanging in the balance, never knowing what will happen next. I can't be brave and strong all the time. I just . . . can't."

"First of all," I correct her, "you are incredibly brave. Do you know how hard it is to even admit something like that? To acknowledge that something in your life isn't working and take actions to change it? So many people just go with the flow, accepting whatever fate comes their way. But you're fighting for what you want. And that's important."

She pulls back, face red and splotchy. "But this was my dream! Since I was a little kid. I wanted to meet heroes, to be in their world. . . . How could it be wrong?"

I give her a sad smile. "Sometimes dreams change."

"I feel like I let Joy down . . . let myself down."

"You just helped save her life. You talked down a man on the edge. You fought for them. It's okay to fight for yourself."

She wipes her cheeks even as the tears continue to flow. A Warrior Nation guard is motioning for us to leave, everyone hustling to get back to HQ for debriefings, care, and bringing Siege to justice.

"I'll tell you one thing, though," I continue. "You can't get rid of me. Whether you're in this world or not, you and I will remain super friends."

"Super friends?" she chokes on a laugh.

"Yes, it's my new spin-off. We're the stars. Why should the heroes always hog the spotlight?"

ABC 7 Chicago News Update

It's been three weeks since the Chicago chapter of Warrior Nation returned to duty, and the city has finally settled into its former rhythm. After Millie Montouse's surprise resignation, new procedures are being put into place to prevent a similar situation from ever occurring, as the organization works to find her replacement.

While citizens are still mourning the sudden retirement of Vaporizer, many fans were delighted to learn his replacement would be not one new hero but many, in an effort to expand chapters nationwide and provide greater safety across the country. This effort has been championed by Girl Power, who stepped into a leadership role after her return, encouraging those with powers to suit up and join the chapter.

An open audition is being held this Saturday at Grant Park. Applicants should be ready to display their unique superpower and be willing to take a series of health and aptitude tests. For more information, visit Warrior Nation's official website.

CLAIRE

"OMG, YOU'RE DOING IT WRONG!"

"Wrong? How does one walk dogs wrong?"

Demi walks over to me, deftly untangling the ten-pronged dog leash around my waist. "I don't know, but somehow you're achieving it." I didn't realize how much skill it takes to walk nearly a dozen dogs at once, but after a lot of groveling, Demi agreed to show me the ropes.

"There," she says, helping the trio of beagles at my feet get back on course. "Just remember: You're the alpha."

"Right." I nod. "It's all about confidence."

"And treats. These suckers will do anything for a bacon bite."

"Okay," I laugh as a Pomeranian licks my leg.

"You can handle this, right?" Demi eyes me with concern, having already run through her dog-walking checklist multiple times. As the first official employee of Demi's Dogs, I know it's a lot for her to relinquish control. But at some point, she needs to let go. "I don't want any bad reviews from my customers."

"Don't worry! I'm going to be the best dog walker Chicago has ever seen," I reassure her.

"Well, after me, of course," she snarks.

I roll my eyes. Our race for number one has reignited.

"Call me THE SECOND your route is done, okay?" she asks, checking her phone. "I need to go pick up a husky three blocks away."

"Aye, aye, Captain," I say with a mini salute, and she heads off, leaving me alone with ten tiny pups ready to strut their stuff. "Okay, everybody . . . let's go!"

The air outside has finally cooled, summer humidity replaced by brisk autumn breezes. School started a couple weeks ago, and I've dived into my senior-year routine, front-loading my schedule with debate team, model UN, and some intro coding classes, just to mix it up. But I kept a few weekly slots open to work for Demi. It's a nice, aboveground job with plenty of sunshine and minimal risk, unless you consider stepping in poop particularly hazardous. Plus, I need the money. College isn't going to pay for itself, especially since I'm pretty late to the game on planning.

A few blocks into our walk, a girl is heading toward us, and I do my best to corral the canines over to the side. The leashes wrap around my legs, and I'm instantly stuck, trapped in a tangle of fur and fabric.

"Gah! C'mon, dogs, don't do this to me!" I beg as they stare up at me innocently.

"Need some help?"

I turn away from the dogs to see Joy, hidden behind huge aviator sunglasses and a woven infinity scarf, her hair tucked into a baseball cap. She smiles, that big goofy grin that first captured my heart.

My face immediately flushes. I can't believe she's here. "Hey. What are you . . . ?"

"I wanted to say hi, catch up." Even in disguise, she looks incredible, tight jeans challenging my ability to remain cool. It's been at least a month since I've seen her; after everything with Siege, I told her I needed to break up with the superhero world and figure out my next steps. But that's really hard to do when your crush is still flinging herself into danger on the daily. We haven't been talking, but I've still been following her every move, thinking of her constantly. Some passions never let you go.

"Hi," I choke out, bewildered at seeing her beautiful face outside of my daydreams. Joy's star is really taking off in Warrior Nation, as she's decided to be very public about who she is and what she's about. The fandom is obsessed with her authenticity, and now that Matt stepped down, she's become the star of the Chicago chapter. It's a big change for someone who only planned to save the world for a year, but if she survived Siege and wants to keep going, I doubt anything will stop her.

It's good—I want that for her. I just can't have that for me.

Not in the way that I thought, anyway.

"Um . . ." I'm fumbling and not just because I have a pack of dogs winding around my feet. "How's it going at HQ?"

"Surprisingly not terrible." She smirks. "Roy has actually stepped up to be a real leader, and now that Teddy feels like he helped save the city, he's become way less insufferable."

"That's good." I've seen Roy on TV, standing up during all the Warrior Nation press conferences. He's already made some waves as far as how the organization will operate moving forward, emphasizing more inclusivity and support systems for those who struggle with handling their powers. The WarNats are still freaking out over all these changes, but I feel he's making the right moves.

Joy nervously inches closer, careful not to step on any paws. "I do miss seeing you around HQ, though," she admits, voice soft. "Supply closets have mysteriously lost all appeal."

I blush, imagining her hands grabbing my waist, her lips on mine. I still think about her—all the heroes—all the time. Warrior Nation has left a gaping hole in my heart, one I'm not sure how to fill. But I did take down my mural. While I couldn't bring myself to throw away all my Blue Streak stuff (not yet, anyway), I also couldn't have it staring at me while I sleep. In its place, I've started a new collage of stuff that's really important: pictures of Bridgette and Demi, me and Mom, brochures from college visits. And a picture of me and Joy, because . . . I'm not ready to let go of her yet. "I miss you too," I say honestly.

"Are you sure you won't take Roy's job offer?"

"What, and leave all this?" I laugh, gesturing to the dog pile.

"Yeah, I guess that'd be pretty hard to walk away from."

"I'm glad you came." I reach for her hand, and she gives a

quick squeeze, big blue eyes wanting more. Sometimes I wonder if I made the right decision turning my back on Warrior Nation. If I'd tried to stick it out a little longer, to make the stress and drama of hero life work, would it have become the new normal? Would I have gotten used to the constant fluttering in my chest and knot in my stomach? I still struggle to take a relaxed breath, though it's getting easier every day. Even if being without Joy has stirred up a new kind of pain.

"Can I call you sometime?" she asks, hopeful, and I nod, intertwining her fingers in mine. My skin prickles with goose bumps, relieved to feel her touch again. I'd hoped the next time I saw her I'd feel this way: feelings soaring without the weight of Siege causing doubt. Maybe now I can step forward instead of retreating. Maybe now I've been granted the power to heal.

"Maybe we can finally go on our first real date," I suggest.

Joy smiles. "Okay, talk soon," she says, before turning to walk away. Part of me wants to call her back, to wrap her in my arms and kiss her right now. But I don't want to rush it.

I once thought my days had to be larger than life for me to amount to something.

But as it turns out, following your heart can be an equally epic adventure.

BRIDGETTE

MY COLLECTION OF ART PAPER IS SPREAD over the floor like a rainbow magic carpet. It's been a while since I've had time to lay them all out like this, taking stock of all the colors, patterns, and textures. I have an assignment due soon, to create something that projects *strength*. I finally got my cast off, and it feels so good to have my X-Acto knife back in my right hand. Working with my left actually created some interesting results, but I'll never admit it to Matt.

"How many cookies do you want?" he calls from Becca's kitchen. We've slowly started hanging out again, focusing on our friendship first. I know he wants our time together to blossom into something more, but I'm not sure if I'm there yet. While our wounds have healed, I can still see Matt's bruises and feel Charles's fingers around my neck. I refuse to let either of us cause the other any more pain. Still, he asked if he could come over and bake me some "creativity fuel" while I work, and I couldn't very well say no to cookies. The scent of cinnamon and sugar has been wafting through the tiny apartment for too long, and I'm dying to try them.

"What is the maximum number?" I call back.

"The limit does not exist!"

"Okay, then, I'll take them all."

"All?" He walks into the living room with sugar-dusted fingers and lips. "You wouldn't leave any for me?"

I consider this. "Well, maybe one. If you're good."

He smiles. "Whatever you say, boss." He takes a seat on the floor, a plate piled with cookies between us. We're both essentially dressed in our pajamas: oversized T-shirts and cozy flannel pants. After all the excitement, neither of us are really psyched to go out into the world unless we have to. Besides, we have a lot of work to do here.

"So, what's the plan?" he asks, chocolate eyes surveying the strips of paper strewn across the hardwood.

"Well, I'm going to take all these long pieces and weave them together into a heart," I reveal. "Not, like, a valentine shape, but a human heart. Because what's stronger than that?"

Matt laughs to himself, shaking his head in disbelief. "That's awesome. How do you think of this stuff?"

"I don't know. How do you turn invisible? You just do it."

"I guess." He shrugs. "But your thing seems cooler. You're putting stuff into the world. All I can do is disappear, and . . . I don't want to do that anymore." When Matt told me he was quitting Warrior Nation, I didn't believe him at first. Even after everything that happened, I figured he'd bounce back and snap into action like he always does. Never cease, never cower, and all that. But something about seeing one of his own turn evil changed him, and as soon as he was done reassuring the public that he was safe, he turned in his cape for good.

I supported this, of course, but told him not to do it because of me. Resentment hardens deep in the bones, and I don't want that for him—for either of us. As the weeks have passed, he's talked about going to college and planning for life after he's no longer super. He says he wants me to be in it.

My phone lights up with a text from Claire:

Hey what u up to?

Art stuff. Matt is here.

WHAT ♥ ♥ ♥

Calm yourself, fangirl

can't help it. I ship it!

I'm really glad that everyone walked away safely from Siege, but the best thing to come out of this adventure has been my friendship with Claire. It's been a long time since I had a real friend; I don't know what I'd do without her.

"Claire says hi and that she wants us to make out," I tease Matt, who is immediately on board.

"You know, I really like that girl." He leans in at the suggestion, the scent of honey drawing me closer. "But not as much as I like this girl." Our lips lightly touch, just enough for me to taste him. To see if this is what I really want. I'm not going to blindly jump into his world again, letting my needs play second string. If Matt and I find our way back to each other, it will have to be on an even playing field. Both our stars deserve to shine; never again will I be a damsel in distress.

After all, if I'm not the hero of my own story, who is?

ACKNOWLEDGMENTS

When I first got the idea for *Super Adjacent*, I had no idea where this journey would take me, but being in the headspace of heroes for the past several years has shown me all the different sides of heroism and what it means to exude bravery.

Heroism is pulling a stranger from a burning building, and it's also finding the strength to get out of bed. It is sharing your voice to change the world, and it's living a quiet yet fiercely truthful existence. You don't have to have muscles or powers to be a hero; leading a life that reflects what's in your heart is the boldest, most powerful act of heroism there is.

I dedicated this book to my mom because she was the most incredible person I've ever known. A single mom who ran a small business, battled cancer, and raised two girls all on her own, she fought wars without ever making my sister or me feel like the world was about to cave in. My mom taught us to fight for what we want and never give up, even when things get hard. Her bravery shaped me into the person I've become, and I carry her spirit with me every single day.

My life is filled with heroes. Heroes like my editor, Kieran, who pushed me through the complexities of this story to make it the best that it could be. Your insight and support never fails to astound me, and your advice to embrace my inner Xander to help the non-supers save the day made all the difference.

The entire Hyperion team is packed full of heroes who go above and beyond to keep everything on track. Thank you to Jamie and Jasmijn for your incredible book designs, and to everyone who has touched this book and continued to believe in me.

Jess, you never gave up on this story, and for that, you will always be my hero. I will never stop being thankful for having you by my side.

I live with several heroes, like Todd, who keeps me supplied with love and Tater Tots; Molly, who warms my heart with bouncing and drawings; and Autumn, one of the very first readers of this book, who constantly inspires me to be brave and try new things.

Thank you to all my friends and family who keep me going even when I start feeling lost. Whether I'm slurping milk shakes with Cheryl, eating biscuits and pie with Stephanie, fangirling with Meghan, singing with Natalie, having a sister date with Tiffany, or sharing a laugh with any of the incredibly special, talented people in my life, all of these moments fill my heart with love, and I am so grateful.

And you, dear reader, are quite an amazing hero yourself. Thanks for following me on these journeys of make-believe and magic. May you embrace all your unique superpowers and share them with the world in remarkable ways.